RULES FOR A ROGUE

Also by Christy Carlyle

The Accidental Heirs Series
One Dangerous Desire
One Tempting Proposal
One Scandalous Kiss

Coming Soon
A Study in Scoundrels

RULES FOR A ROGUE

A Romancing the Rules Novel

CHRISTY CARLYLE

AVONIMPULSE
An Imprint of HarperCollinsPublishers

Excerpt from *Along Came Love* copyright © 2016 by Tracey Livesay. Excerpt from *When a Marquess Loves a Woman* copyright © 2016 by Vivienne Lorret.

EPub Edition NOVEMBER 2016 ISBN: 9780062572356
Print Edition ISBN: 9780062572363

Avon, Avon Impulse, and the Avon Impulse logo are trademarks of HarperCollins Publishers.

AM 10 9 8 7 6 5 4 3

For John. I couldn't do it without you.

And to Grandma S, for teaching me how to "behave like a lady" and loving me even when I didn't.

ACKNOWLEDGMENTS

Many thanks to my fabulous editor, Elle Keck, for your insight, encouragement, and kindness and to the Avon publicity team and art department for your help making each book shine.

CHAPTER ONE

> "Duty foremost. A true gentleman puts no
> appetite, ambition, or enterprise above duty."
> —THE RUTHVEN RULES FOR YOUNG MEN

London, September 1894

He always searched for her.

Call it perversity or a reckless brand of tenacity. Heaven knew he'd been accused of both.

Pacing the scuffed wooden floorboards at the edge of the stage, Christopher Ruthven shoved a hand through his black hair and skimmed his dark gaze across each seat in the main theater stalls of Merrick Theater for the woman he needed to forget.

Damn the mad impulse to look for her.

He was a fool to imagine he'd ever find her staring back. The anticipation roiling in his belly should be for the play, not the past.

Finding her would be folly. Considering how they'd parted, the lady would be as likely to lash out as to embrace him with open arms.

But searching for her had become his habit. His ritual.

Other thespians had rituals too. Some refused to eat before a performance. Others feasted like a king. A few repeated incantations, mumbling to themselves when the curtains rose. As the son of a publishing magnate, Kit should have devised his own maxim to repeat, but the time for words was past. He'd written the play, and the first act was about to begin.

Now he only craved a glimpse of Ophelia Marsden.

The four years since he'd last seen her mattered not. Her bright blue eyes, heart-shaped face, and striking red hair had always distinguished her from other women, but Kit knew they were the least of the qualities that set her apart. Clever, stubborn to the core, and overflowing with more spirit than anyone he'd ever known—that's how he remembered Phee.

But looking for her wasn't mere folly; it was futile. She wouldn't come. He, after all, was the man who'd broken her heart.

As stagehands lit the limelights, Kit shaded his eyes from their glare and stepped behind the curtain. The thrumming in his veins was about the play now, the same giddiness he felt before every performance.

Hunching his shoulders, he braced his arms across his chest and listened intently, half his attention on the lines being delivered on stage, half on the pandemonium backstage. He adored the energy of the theater, the frenetic chaos of actors and stagehands rushing about madly behind the

curtains to produce rehearsed magic for the audience. Econo-
mies at Merrick's meant he might write a play, perform in it,
assist with scene changes from the catwalk, and direct other
actors—all in one evening.

Tonight though, beyond writing the words spoken on
stage, the production was out of his hands, and that heightened his nerves. Idleness made him brood.

Behind him a husky female voice cried out, and Kit
turned to intercept the woman as she rushed forward, filling
his arms with soft curves.

"There's a mouse!" Tess, the playhouse's leading lady, bat-
ted thick lashes and stuck out a vermillion-stained lower lip.
"Vile creatures. Every one of them."

"Tell me where." Kit gently dislodged the petite blonde
from his embrace.

"Scurried underneath, so it did." She indicated a battered
chest of drawers, sometimes used for storage, more often as
a set piece.

Kit approached the bulky wooden chest, crouched down,
and saw nothing but darkness and dust. Bracing his palms on
the floor, he lowered until his chest pressed against wood and
he spied the little creature huddling in the farthest corner.
The tiny mouse looked far more frightened of him than Tess
was of it.

"Can you catch the beast? We can find a cage or give it to
the stray cats hanging about the stage doors."

"Too far out of reach." He could move the chest, but the
mouse would no doubt scurry away. Seemed kinder to allow
the animal to find its own way to freedom. Kit knew what
it was to be trapped and frightened. To cower in darkness

covered in dust. His father hadn't shut him up in a cage, just a closet now and then, but Kit would be damned if he'd confine any creature.

Tess made an odd sound. Of protest, Kit assumed. But when he cast a glance over his shoulder, her gaze raked hungrily over his legs and backside as he got to his feet.

"The little thing will no doubt find its way out of doors, Tess. Not much food to be had here."

Tess took his attempt at reassurance as an invitation and launched herself into his arms.

She was an appealing woman, with tousled golden curls, catlike green eyes, and an exceedingly ample—*Ah, yes, there they are*—bosom that she shifted enticingly against his chest, as if she knew precisely how good her lush body felt against his. Without a hint of shame or restraint, she moved her hands down his arms, slid them under his unbuttoned sack coat, and stroked her fingers up his back.

"Goodness, you're deliciously tall."

Kit grinned. He found female praise for his awkward height amusing, since he'd been mercilessly teased for his long frame as a child. In a theater world full of handsome, charming actors, his stature and whatever skill he possessed with the written word were all that set him apart.

"You're like a tree I long to climb," she purred. "Feels so right in your arms. Perhaps the gods are telling us that's where I belong."

Tess wasn't merely generously built. From the day she arrived, she'd been generous with her affections too. Half the men at Merrick's were smitten, but Kit kept to his rule about avoiding intrigues with ladies in the troupe. Since coming to

London, he'd never sought more than a short-lived entanglement with any woman. He relished his liberty too much to allow himself more.

"Perhaps the gods are unaware you're due on stage for the next act," he teased, making light of her flirtation as he'd done since their introduction.

"Always concerned about your play, aren't you, lovie?" She slid a hand up his body, snaking a finger between the buttons of his waistcoat. "I know my part. Don't worry, Kitten."

The pet name she'd chosen for him grated on his nerves.

"The music's risen, Tess." Kit gripped the actress's hand when she reached toward his waistband. "That's your cue."

"I'll make you proud." She winked and lifted onto her toes, placing a damp kiss on his cheek. "You're a difficult man to seduce," she whispered, "but I do so love a challenge." After sauntering to the curtain's edge, she offered him a final come-hither glance before sashaying on stage.

"Already breaking hearts, *Kitten*? The evening's only just begun." Jasper Grey, Merrick Theater's lead actor and Kit's closest friend, exited stage left and sidled up beside him. With a few swipes across his head, Grey disheveled his coppery brown hair and loosened the faux silk cravat at his throat. The changes were subtle, but sufficient to signal to the audience that his character would begin a descent into madness and debauchery during the second act. Having explored many of London's diversions at the man's side, Kit could attest to Grey's knack for debauchery, on and off the stage.

"I'm sure you'll be more than happy to offer solace. Or have you already?" Choosing a new lover each night of the week was more Grey's style than Kit's, though both had attracted their share of stage-door admirers and earned their reputations as rogues.

Grey's smirk gave everything away. "Whatever the nature of my private moments with our lovely leading lady, the minx is determined to offer you her heart."

"Bollocks to that. I've no interest in claiming anyone's heart." The very thought chased a chill up Kit's spine. Marriage. Commitment. Those were for other men. If his parents were any lesson, marriage was a miserable prison, and he had no wish to be shackled.

Kit turned his attention back to the audience.

"Still looking for your phantom lady?" Grey often tweaked Kit about his habit of searching the crowd. Rather than reveal parts of his past he wished to forget, Kit allowed his friend to assume he sought a feminine ideal, not a very specific woman of flesh and freckles and fetching red hair. "What will you do if she finally appears?"

"She won't." And if he were less of a fool, he'd stop looking for her.

"Come, man. We've packed the house again tonight. This evening we celebrate." Grey swiped at the perspiration on his brow. "You've been downright monkish of late. There must be a woman in London who can turn your head. What about the buxom widow who threw herself at you backstage after last week's performance?"

"The lady stumbled. I simply caught her fall."

"Mmm, and quite artfully too. I particularly admired the way her lush backside landed squarely in your lap."

The curvaceous widow had been all too willing to further their acquaintance, but she'd collided with Kit on opening night. Having written the play and performed in a minor role for an indisposed actor, he'd been too distracted fretting over success to bother with a dalliance.

Of late, something in him had altered. Perhaps he'd had his fill of the city's amusements. Grey's appetite never seemed to wane, but shallow seductions no longer brought Kit satisfaction. He worried less about pleasure and more about success. Four years in London and what had he accomplished? Coming to the city had never been about indulging in vice but about making his mark as a playwright. He'd allowed himself to be distracted. *Far too impulsive* should have been his nickname, for as often as his father had shouted the words at him in his youth.

"How about the angel in the second balcony?" Grey gestured to a gaudily painted box, high in the theater's eastern wall. "I've never been able to resist a woman with titian red hair."

Kit snapped his gaze to the spot Grey indicated, heartbeat ratcheting until it thundered in his ears. Spotting the woman, he expelled a trapped breath. The lady's hair shone in appealing russet waves in the gaslight, but she wasn't Ophelia. Phee's hair was a rich auburn, and her jaw narrower. At least until it sharpened into an adorably squared chin that punctuated her usual air of stubborn defiance.

"No?" Grey continued his perusal of ladies among the sea of faces. "How about the giggling vision in the third row?"

The strawberry blonde laughed with such raucous abandon her bosom bounced as she turned to speak to her companion. Kit admired her profile a moment, letting his gaze dip lower before glancing at the man beside her.

"That's Dominic Fleet." Kit's pulse jumped at the base of his throat. Opportunity sat just a few feet away.

He'd never met the theater impresario, but he knew the man by reputation. Unlike Merrick's shabby playhouse, known for its comedies and melodramas, Fleet Theater featured long-running plays by the best dramatists in London. Lit entirely with electric lights, the modern theater seated up to three thousand.

"What's he doing slumming at Merrick's?" Grey turned to face Kit. "Did you invite him?"

"Months ago." Kit had sent a letter of introduction to Fleet, enclosing a portion of a play he'd written but been unable to sell. "He never replied." Yet here he was, attending the performance of a piece that revealed none of Kit's true skill as a playwright. Merrick had demanded a bawdy farce. In order to pay his rent, Kit had provided it.

"You bloody traitor." Grey smiled, his sarcastic tone belying his words. "You wouldn't dare abandon Merrick and set out for greener fields."

"Why? Because he compensates us so generously?"

Though they shared a love of theater, Grey and Kit had different cares. Grey possessed family money and worried little about meeting the expenses of a lavish London lifestyle. Kit could never take a penny from his father, even if it was on offer. Any aid from Leopold Ruthven would come with demands and expectations—precisely the sort of control he'd left Hertfordshire to escape.

"You belong here, my friend." Grey clapped him on the shoulder. "With our band of misfits and miscreants. Orphans from lives better left behind."

Belonging. The theater had given him that in a way his father's home never had. Flouting rules, tenacity, making decisions intuitively—every characteristic his father loathed were assets in the theater. Kit had no desire to abandon the life he'd made for himself, just improve upon it.

"We came to London to make something of ourselves. Do you truly believe we'll find success at Merrick's?" Kit lifted his elbow and nudged the dingy curtain tucked at the edge of the stage. "Among tattered furnishings?"

"That's only the backside of the curtain. Merrick puts the best side out front. We all have our flaws. The art is in how well we hide them." Grey had such a way with words Kit often thought *he* should be a playwright. "Would you truly jump ship?"

"I bloody well would." Kit slanted a glance at his friend. "And so would you."

Merrick paid them both a dribble, producing plays with minimal expense in a building that leaked when it rained. Cultivating favor with the wealthiest theater manager in London had been Kit's goal for months. With a long-running Fleet-produced play, he could repay his debts and move out of his cramped lodgings. Hunger had turned him into a hack writer for Merrick, but he craved more. Success, wealth, a chance to prove his skill as a writer. To prove that his decision to come to London had been the right one. To prove to his father that he could succeed on his own merits.

"Never!" Tess, performing the role of virginal damsel, shrieked from center stage. "Never shall I marry Lord Mallet. He is the worst sort of scoundrel."

"That's my cue." Grey grinned as he tugged once more at his cravat and dashed back into the glow of the limelights. Just before stepping on stage, he skidded to stop and turned to Kit. "You'd better write me a part in whatever play you sell to Fleet."

With a mock salute, Kit offered his friend a grin. He had every intention of creating a role for Grey. The man's acting skills deserved a grander stage too.

Kit fixed his gaze on Fleet. He seemed to be enjoying the play, a trifling modernized *Hamlet* parody Kit called *The King's Ghost and the Mad Damsel*. He'd changed the heroine's name to Mordelia, unable to endure the sound of Ophelia's name bouncing off theater walls for weeks. Months, if the play did well.

After his eyes adjusted to the stage-light glow, he pointlessly, compulsively scanned the crowd one last time for a woman whose inner beauty glowed as fiercely as her outer charms. He wouldn't find her. As far as he knew, Phee was home in the village where they'd grown up. When he'd come to London to escape his father, she'd insisted on loyalty to hers and remained in Hertfordshire to care for him. All but one of his letters had gone unanswered, including a note the previous year expressing sorrow over her father's passing.

He didn't need to reach into his pocket and unfold the scrap of paper he carried with him everywhere. The five words of Ophelia's only reply remained seared in his mind. *"Follow your heart and flourish."* They were her mother's words, stitched in a sampler that hung in the family's drawing room. Kit kept the fragment, but he still wondered whether Ophelia had written the words in sincerity or sarcasm.

A flash of gems caught his eye, and Kit spied Fleet's pretty companion rising from her seat. The theater impresario stood too, following her into the aisle. Both made their way toward the doors at the rear of the house.

He couldn't let the man leave without an introduction. Kit lurched toward a door leading to a back hall and sprinted down the dimly lit corridor. He caught up to Fleet near the ladies' retiring room.

"Mr. Fleet, I am—"

"Christopher Ruthven, the scribe of this evening's entertainment." The man extended a gloved hand. "Forgive me, Ruthven. It's taken far too long for me to take in one of your plays."

Attempting not to crush the slighter man in his grip, Kit offered an enthusiastic handshake.

"I want to have a look at your next play." Fleet withdrew an engraved calling card from his waistcoat pocket. "Bring it in person to my office at the theater. Not the one you sent. Something new. More like this one."

"You'll have it." Kit schooled his features, forcing his furrowed brow to smooth. So what if the man wanted a farce rather than serious drama? He craved an opportunity to succeed, and Fleet could provide it. "Thank you."

"If we can come to terms and you manage to fill my playhouse every night as you have Merrick's, I shall be thanking you."

Kit started backstage, his head spinning with ideas for a bigger, grander play than Merrick's could produce. Never mind that it had taken years to grasp the chance Fleet offered. Good fortune had come, and he intended to make the most of it.

As he reached the inconspicuous door that led to the back corridor, a man called his name.

"Mr. Ruthven? Christopher Leopold Ruthven?"

Two gentlemen approached, both tall, black-suited, and dour. Debt collectors? The instinct to bolt dissipated when the two made it impossible, crowding him on either side of the narrow passageway.

"I'm Ruthven." Taller than both men and broader by half, Kit still braced himself for whatever might come. "What do you want?"

The one who'd yet to say anything took a step closer, and Kit recognized his wrinkled face.

"Mr. Sheridan? What brings you to Merrick's?" Kit never imagined the Ruthven family solicitor would venture to a London theater under any circumstances.

"Ill tidings, I regret to say." Sheridan reached into his coat and withdrew an envelope blacked with ink around the edges. "Your father is dead, Mr. Ruthven. I'm sorry. Our letter to you was returned. My messenger visited your address twice and could not locate you. I thought we might find you here."

"Moved lodgings." Kit took the letter, willing his hand not to tremble. "Weeks ago."

"Your sister has made arrangements for a ceremony in Briar Heath." Sheridan lifted a card from his pocket and handed it to Kit. "Visit my office before you depart, and I can provide you with details of your father's will."

The men watched him a moment, waiting for a reaction. When none came, Sheridan muttered condolences before they departed.

Kit lost track of time. He shoved Sheridan's card into his coat pocket to join Fleet's, crushed the unread solicitor's letter in his hand, and stood rooted to the spot where they'd left him. Father. Dead. The two words refused to congeal in his mind. So many of the choices Kit made in his twenty-eight years had been driven by his father's wrath, attempts to escape his stifling control.

Now Kit could think only of what he should do. Must do. Look after his sisters. Return to Briar Heath.

He'd leave after speaking to Merrick. Any work on a play to impress Fleet would have to be undertaken while he was back home.

Home. The countryside, the village, the oversized house his father built with profits from his publishing enterprise—none of it had been home for such a very long time. It was a place he'd felt shunned and loathed most of his life. He'd never visited in four years. Never dared set foot in his father's house after his flamboyant departure.

As he headed toward Merrick's office to tell the man his news, worry for his sisters tightened Kit's jaw until it ached. Then another thought struck.

After all these years, night after night of futile searching, he would finally see Ophelia Marsden again.

CHAPTER TWO

---

*"A true lady confines herself to all that is
decorative in society and especially at home,
for this is her rightful domain."*
—THE RUTHVEN RULES FOR YOUNG LADIES

*"Ladies, put down your feathers, ribbons, and
rouge, and leave outward decoration aside!
Let all thoughtful young ladies attend first
to their inner enrichment and festooning the
chambers of their mind."*
—MISS GILROY'S GUIDELINES FOR YOUNG LADIES

London unsettled Ophelia Marsden.

Buzzing energy bubbled up as the train puffed to a stop at Paddington Station. She arrived full of purpose, armed with lists and schedules and appointments, but the metropolis swept away her best intentions the second her foot touched pavement outside the station. Brimming with people and color and noise, London moved too fast for her to take it all in, but that didn't stop her from trying. A country girl at heart, who'd only visited the capital a handful of times, Ophelia cast a wide-eyed gaze about like a child in a sweet shop.

"A wee lil' penny for hours of fright!" Across from the train station a young boy stood hawking magazines and penny dreadfuls.

Unable to resist the prospect of fresh reading material, she approached to buy a copy, then dodged back. An overflowing omnibus careened across her path, reminding her that London could be dangerous too, especially for young women susceptible to distraction.

A few startled pigeons rose from the cobblestones into flight, and their fluttering gray drew her gaze to a coffeehouse. The aroma of fresh-baked bread set her stomach rumbling. She'd been too nervous before her journey to manage more than a scant breakfast.

No. Concentrate. There was no time for gaping or filling her belly. London's attractions drew her away from her purpose, and that was something she couldn't afford. She had an appointment and couldn't be late.

Ophelia lifted the fob watch pinned to her bodice to check the hour.

Time wasn't on her side when she visited the city. London minutes rushed by as quick as omnibuses, and she struggled to tick every item off her list.

Retrieving a rectangle of paper from her pocket, she double-checked to make sure she'd remembered to include a stop at the stationers.

Papa had often called her a worrier. Phee preferred to think of herself as a planner.

Still, all she planned to accomplish in the city vied with what required her attention back home. Now that their parents were gone, leaving her sister Juliet in the care of their elderly aunt weighed on Ophelia's mind whenever she left Briar Heath. Aunt Rose was too sweet to complain, insisting her nieces were consolation for never marrying and having children of her own, but Phee still felt responsible for Juliet. She'd been caring for her sister since their mother's death shortly after Juliet's birth.

But family worries and London's bustle weren't her only distractions when visiting the city.

Kit Ruthven lived here, and she had good cause to hate the metropolis for that reason alone. He'd chosen a life in London over a future with her. There was no denying the city's seductive power, but Ophelia hadn't quite forgiven Kit for breaking all the youthful promises they'd made to each other. She hadn't forgiven herself for believing those promises either. If the four years since their parting had taught her anything, it was to choose more often with her head than with her heart.

She avoided Kit during her visits, taking care to steer clear of the part of town where he'd taken residence. But keeping out of the man's path was far easier than banishing him from her thoughts. He was stamped on every site that caught her eye. Had he walked down this patch of pavement? Visited that bookshop? What if she turned a corner and found herself face-to-face with the only man she'd ever kissed?

He'd tower above her, blocking out the sun with those broad shoulders of his. Tip his head until his dark-as-treacle hair slid across his brow. She'd imagined such an encounter countless times. On past visits she'd even sensed him, as if they were knotted together on the same filament of thread. At times she felt a strange prickling sensation and convinced herself that wherever he was, his movements rippled across her skin.

Fanciful nonsense. As whimsical as the idea that he'd come back to her. It was long past time to put whimsy and fancies aside.

Practicality and prudence. Those were her watchwords now.

Wellbeck Publishing's office was on the other side of Hyde Park, on a row off the Brompton Road. Phee chose a quiet path through the green, hoping to avoid the crush on the main thoroughfares. But she found it difficult to enter the park without wishing to linger. Sunlight warmed her skin, a cool breeze rustled the leaves above her head, and she cast one longing gaze toward the sparkling surface of the Serpentine before picking up her pace.

Her editor's letter had been vague as to the purpose of his summons, and Phee pressed a hand to her middle and drew in a few deep breaths, trying to calm her nerves. She still couldn't quite believe he'd agreed to publish her book. Over the course of the previous year, four editors had rejected her manuscript, denouncing the very notion of an etiquette book that dared to challenge others in the genre. But Mr. Talbot saw merit in *Miss Gilroy's Guidelines for Young Ladies*. His belief in her work had given Ophelia a taste of success, confidence in what she could accomplish when she set her mind to a task. Most of all, she hoped publication might provide her with a bit of income. With their family home in need of repairs and no other funds than what she could earn, income was what she needed most.

Wellbeck's wasn't the only publishing office situated along Somerset Row. As she approached, Ophelia allowed herself a single gaze at a sign down the lane—*Ruthven Publishers*. A vivid image of the long, stern face of Kit's father arose in her mind. If she wished to avoid the son, she wouldn't find a safer spot in London than outside the father's offices. As far as she knew, Kit hadn't spoken to his father since the day he'd left.

"Do come in, Miss Marsden." Mr. Talbot ushered her into his cluttered office the minute she crossed the building's threshold. "Take a seat wherever you can find one. Here, let me move those."

The bespectacled older gentleman reached behind her to settle a box of books on the floor next to a chair, and Ophelia navigated around another tower of crates to take the seat he offered.

"Forgive the mess," he said as he settled behind his desk. "We're expanding into a larger space in a few weeks." For a man whose letters always exuded calm, Mr. Talbot seemed frazzled in person. A sheen of perspiration on his forehead received a quick mop from his handkerchief, disheveling his fringe of thinning gray hair. "Now, where were we?"

"We had not yet begun, sir. I've just arrived."

"Ah, yes!" After pointing an index finger in the air, he ducked his head to scratch around for something in his top drawer. He pulled out a slip of paper and covered it with his palms flat on the desk's blotter. "I have good news, and some you may deem less so. Which would you prefer first?"

"Bad news first, if you please." Phee didn't consider herself a pessimist, but experience had taught her to prepare for the worst.

"Your book has exceeded our expectations. As you know, Mr. Wellbeck approved a modest initial printing, but booksellers are reporting steady sales."

Ophelia let out the breath she'd been holding and arched an eyebrow. "That sounds suspiciously like excellent news."

"Yes, I suppose it is." Talbot's eyes crinkled at the edges, and she spied a grin under the man's neatly trimmed mustache. "One comes with the other, doesn't it? Your book is selling well enough to attract attention from critics."

Oh no. Her stomach began to rumble, and this time it had nothing to do with the scent of roasted coffee or freshly baked bread. Maybe she wasn't keen for bad news after all.

"Critics' judgements are decidedly mixed, Miss Marsden. Some have embraced *Miss Gilroy's Guidelines.*" His buoyant tone ebbed down, along with the edges of his mouth. "Of course, those who reject your book's forward-thinking tenets are the loudest of the bunch. Some have written directly to Mr. Wellbeck, insisting that he halt publication."

"Is he breaking our agreement?" Ophelia's little taste of success began to sour.

"Not at all, Miss Marsden." Mr. Talbot leaned forward and cast her a sympathetic gaze. "Your book is quite modern, your ideas provocative. We always knew it would stir a reaction." He ducked his head. "But in addition to those decrying its tenets, *Guidelines* has drawn the notice of Ruthven Publishing. We did anticipate this possibility too."

They had. In her first letter to Wellbeck's, she'd cited the renowned *Ruthven Rules* series of etiquette guides as her inspiration. While she'd made no direct mention of Kit's father's famous rule books in her manuscript, she couldn't deny that the small-minded strictures outlined in *The Ruthven Rules* had incensed her. In particular, the recently published edition for young ladies had made her seethe. She'd hoped too much, expected something new, or at least sensible. Instead, she'd found outdated ideas that ignited her so thoroughly she'd found herself driven to write in stolen moments between pupils, or late at night after Juliet had gone to sleep.

"We've had a request to meet with a representative from Ruthven's next week." Mr. Wellbeck lifted a letter from a pile of correspondence on his desk and laid it at the front edge for her perusal. "As you can see, they are concerned about similarities between your etiquette book and theirs. But worry not, Miss Marsden. There can be no question of literary theft. I know you took great care to avoid reference to Ruthven or his books."

Heart in her throat, Ophelia bent forward as far as her corset would allow. Beat by slowing beat, her pulse thumped a steadier rhythm. The note on Ruthven letterhead made reference to Miss Gilroy. She hadn't chosen her former governess's maiden name as a nom de plume in order to hide from Leopold Ruthven or his son specifically. She'd intended to conceal her identity from any who might read the book.

All that she'd written came from the heart, and she was prepared to stand by every word. But she couldn't do so as Ophelia Marsden.

After her father's death, she'd taken on students, teaching the decorum she'd learned from her mother and art and music skills she'd been taught by her father to young ladies from some of the wealthier families in Briar Heath. A few readers might embrace her guidebook, but her pupils' upstanding parents would not, and she desperately needed their patronage. Royalties from her book would never provide enough to keep Longacre, the country house she and Juliet had inherited from their father, afloat.

Why deceive myself? Longacre is already crumbling.

It was why Ophelia was giving serious consideration to the only offer of marriage she'd ever received. A local baron's proposal a few months after her father's death had come without affection or any prospect of passion. Lord Dunstan agreed to await an answer until the end of her mourning period, but Phee hadn't yet convinced herself to be quite practical enough to accept.

"Mr. Ruthven has known me since I was a child, Mr. Wellbeck. His family resides near my village." She didn't bother adding how much Ruthven loathed her. "The anonymity my pen name affords would be shattered if I met with him."

Her editor steepled his hands under his chin and stared at her. "I take it news travels rather slowly in your village."

"Not particularly, sir." Between the gossipy Mrs. Hollingsworth and the talkative gent who ran the public house, word passed as quick as a wink in Briar Heath. "Why? Is there more bad news?"

"Leopold Ruthven got a mention in the newspaper this morning." Mr. Wellbeck rifled through another pile on his desk and handed her a folded newspaper, the pages opened to the obituary section. "The worst sort of news, I'm afraid."

A chill chased up her spine as she read the block letters. *THE LATE LEOPOLD RUTHVEN.*

Pain came, tiny pinpricks of pressure at the corners of her eyes, and she sucked in a breath to keep her composure. She hadn't shed a tear since her father's death. Why cry for Ruthven? The man had dismissed her as an unworthy prospect for his son and heir. He'd done everything in his power to turn Kit against her.

"So you see," Talbot continued as she read the accolades for a man who'd banned her from his home and denounced her father as a heretic. "You needn't worry about encountering Mr. Ruthven. I believe it will be his office manager, Mr. Adamson, who attends the meeting next week."

Ophelia struggled to comprehend that the steely publishing magnate was dead. He'd always been an opposing force in her life, making Kit miserable and exerting his imperious influence over Briar Heath. One determined tear escaped, but as she swiped the streak of dampness from her cheek, she knew it wasn't for Leopold Ruthven. Her sorrow was for his daughters. She knew the grief of enduring a father's death, discovering that the man a girl looked to for guidance was gone. If Ruthven had shown kindness to anyone, it had been to Sophia and Clarissa. Perhaps there'd been too many expectations and disappointments between Kit and his father for any tenderness to thrive.

"Were you very close to the Ruthvens, Miss Marsden? Forgive me. If I'd known, I would have presented the news more gently."

Was there a gentle way to discuss a man's end? No amount of civility could to stop the Ruthvens' settled world from tumbling.

And what of Kit? Would he finally bow to the obligations he'd been avoiding for years? In death, would his father finally achieve the conformity he'd forever demanded of his son?

"I shall not break, Mr. Talbot, I assure you. I'm acquainted with his daughters and feel sympathy for what they'll face in the coming days."

"And the son? Are you acquainted with him? I understand he went astray and cares nothing for the family business." Though he spoke in a measured tone, there was an avaricious gleam in her editor's eyes. Of course he would take an interest in the fate of Wellbeck's fiercest competitor.

"I knew the younger Mr. Ruthven many years ago." The stark truth rang hollow, even when her voice broke on the admission.

Kit had been her closest childhood friend, a confidant as she grew older, and then…more. At a country dance, she'd watched him from across the room and seen him differently. His long, muscular body, sensual mouth, and heartbreaking dark amber eyes hadn't been those of the boy she'd known but the features of a man she craved. Now she doubted if he'd ever felt the same.

"I understand he's an actor."

"A playwright. He always wished to write rather than perform."

"Then perhaps he will sell." Talbot tipped forward in his chair, eager, almost breathless. "The end of *The Ruthven Rules* would bode well for you, Miss Marsden, and every other etiquette-book writer in London."

Ophelia nodded, though she loathed being called an etiquette-book writer. She'd never thought of herself as such. Wouldn't that make her as pompous as Ruthven, who spent his life dictating the actions of others? She referred to her book as one of guidelines, a voice of reason for young ladies who found themselves restricted by Leopold Ruthven's outdated rules. She advocated education, that women think for themselves.

A clock on the wall emitted a metallic ping as it struck the hour. Goodness, how long had she sat pondering the fate of the Ruthvens?

"I'm content to meet with Mr. Adamson if you wish me to accompany you, Mr. Talbot. Is there anything else, sir?" She'd need to be quick about it if she meant to accomplish all the other tasks on her list before catching a three o'clock train back to Hertfordshire. She'd promised Aunt Rose a new book and Juliet a bag of boiled sweets from Stimson's, the best confectioner in the city. A visit to the bank and milliner were on her list too.

"Just this." He finally lifted the piece of paper he'd laid atop his desk and held it out toward her. "Your first payment of royalties, Miss Marsden."

A sum greater than what she'd expected from initial sales of her book was written in precise, elegant script.

"You look pleased, and well you should be. The discussion can wait until we meet again, but I would like to hear your notions regarding future publications."

"Future publications?" She hadn't considered any others. *Guidelines* had been born in a heated rush of indignation, half instinct, half reason. A patchwork stitched through with strands from Wollstonecraft and John Stuart Mill, works her parents had encouraged her to read.

"Give it some consideration. I'll send word if our meeting with Adamson must be postponed for the funeral."

Considering Ruthven's standing and influence—it was said even Queen Victoria kept a copy of *The Ruthven Rules*—the ceremony would be an elaborate ritual.

"Will you attend, Miss Marsden, in light of your concern for his daughters?" Mr. Talbot had an expansive view of women's sphere. He'd championed her book, after all. But others considered funerals as too indelicate for feminine sensibility.

"No, sir." She'd been discouraged from attending her own father's burial ceremony. The Countess of Pembry, Briar Heath's wealthiest landowner, claimed ladies were too fragile for standing about by the graveside. In the end, Ophelia insisted. Nothing could have kept her away, but the prospect of attending Ruthven's funeral set off a roiling in her belly.

Ophelia could allow herself to imagine a fleeting encounter with Kit Ruthven on a crowded London street, but that was fanciful nonsense. The fact was she'd been avoiding the man for four years.

Exhaling a shuddering breath, she imagined hearing his voice again, glancing up to find those chocolate brown eyes of his looking back at her. He'd had the power to melt her once, but she could never allow the man to disrupt her life again.

Four years past she'd been frivolous, more interested in passion than practicalities. She'd given her heart too easily.

Now, at four and twenty, her life revolved around work and family. As Mr. Talbot suggested, she might even set herself the task of writing another book.

Kit had no place in her life. He would come to Briar Heath for his father's funeral and return to London.

Maybe then she could finally give Lord Dunstan an answer.

Chapter Three

"It is always proper for a lady to excuse herself
from visits of condolence and all ceremonies
attendant upon a funeral. Better she stay at
home, within her proper domain, and offer
comfort to her family."

—The Ruthven Rules for Young Ladies

She didn't come.

If his father's funeral proved anything to Kit, it was that he'd become the selfish, heartless man his father often accused him of being. While Leopold Ruthven's polished mahogany coffin was being lowered into hallowed ground behind the village church, Kit hadn't offered his patriarch a final farewell. Instead, he stood scanning the line of black-shrouded mourners, hoping for a glimpse of loose red curls at the edge of a veil.

Even after four years apart and yards of jet black bombazine covering every woman in sight, he told himself he'd recognize Ophelia Marsden's shape. She was taller than most, though he savored sweet memories of her lifting onto her toes to kiss him. She'd always been full of energy and forever on the cusp of movement, even when she stood still. Yet she wasn't slight. Phee possessed no hard edges, despite the way she could use that resonant voice of hers to cut as deep as a man's soul. Her softness and curves were what made his hands itch when he thought of her, all those vulnerable parts of herself she'd shared with no one else.

Who had touched her since he'd been gone? Who'd kissed her? Who'd made her laugh in that throaty way that warmed his blood? He shouldn't care. Years ago, he'd vowed to put his feelings for her aside. He had nothing to offer Phee.

As mourners proceeded toward the village green, he'd persisted in looking for her, hoping for just a single glimpse. She'd always walked with a confident stride, pretty head held high. Chin in the air, not out of arrogance but determination. She possessed the quality in bushels.

But she hadn't come, and as he started up the path toward the Ruthven estate, he gave up his search.

Now, sitting in the drawing room while he and his sisters waited for families from the village to come and offer personal condolences, he struggled to think of anything but Ophelia's face. He'd convinced himself that seeing her again, even if he didn't speak to her, would be his reward for returning to Briar Heath after such a long absence.

He was a fool.

Their parting had been agony. He'd left her in tears. Forced himself to walk away. Convinced himself that a clean break freed them both. Depart for London and never look back—that had been his plan.

And yet here he sat in the ostentatious house his father built.

"Do you think this is too much of a display? I could ask the servants to take some back to the kitchen." His sister Sophia stood before a long table weighed down with food-laden silver trays. Some of the blonde hair caught atop her head in a severe coiffure had come loose. She swiped a stray tress behind one ear before wringing her hands and frowning as their mother used to do when troubled. Thinking back, he could barely recall a time when their mother hadn't been troubled. He didn't want that fate for Sophia.

"Leave it and come sit down," he urged. "You've been on your feet all day."

"There's too much to do." When she finally stopped fussing over the food and turned to face him, she narrowed a single blue-green eye and crossed her arms. "You look far too comfortable, Christopher. Might you consider sprawling less languidly on that settee?"

Sophia's looks and gestures reminded him of their late mother, but she'd learned their father's belittling tone too well.

"Perhaps you do not care that Papa is dead," she continued, pitch rising with the color in her cheeks, "but the rest of us wish to mourn him properly. Not just the family but everyone. We've even had a letter of condolence from a colleague of Mr. Gladstone."

"Only a colleague? Not the prime minister himself, then. And what about the Queen? Have we heard from Her Majesty yet?"

Sophia's frown sharpened into a glare. Like their father, his sister seemed to think she could cow him with a steely gaze. But if the cruelty and guilt Father heaped on him over the years hadn't chastened him, nothing would.

In the tense silence between them, Clary's footsteps sounded in the hallway before she bounded into the room.

"Mercy, are you two quarreling already?"

"For goodness sakes, Clarissa, take care how you walk. A young lady does not skip about like a spring lamb on the day of her father's funeral." Sophia spouted admonitions as if she'd memorized the rubbish in one of their father's rule books.

"Let her be. She can walk however she pleases." He tried not to bark at Sophia, struggling to see in her the sister who'd once been his ally.

"Yes, of course, in your world everyone does just as they please. This isn't London, brother."

Clarissa glanced from him to Sophia and then stepped carefully toward the settee. It pained Kit to see her fighting to control her youthful energy and being chastised for how she chose to lift one foot and put it in front of the other.

"Do you think we're allowed to have any?" Clary eyed the sideboard of treats and whispered to him as she perched stiffly on a damask-covered cushion.

"No, you may not partake until all of the guests have gone." Sophia took after Father's infallible hearing too, it seemed.

Both he and Clary breathed a sigh of relief when their sister exited the room, apparently having forgotten some last piece of silver or decoration that would make the table complete.

Clarissa scooted against the back of the sofa gingerly, as if fearful Sophia was lurking around the corner, waiting to catch her in some misstep. He'd last seen Clary the previous autumn when she'd visited the city with their aunt and uncle. She'd grown so much in a few months and had crossed the bridge from childhood to young miss-hood.

"Tell me again when you turned sixteen?"

A grin plumped her cheeks. "You know precisely when my birthday is. Every year you send me a note on the day."

"And a gift." He usually sent her books. Fiction mostly. Anything but etiquette books.

"Sometimes…" She gnawed at her lower lip and slanted her violet eyes his way. "Papa didn't allow me to read them."

Kit swallowed hard and reached out to pat Clarissa's arm, as much to comfort her as to allay his guilt. He'd left her to this. Somehow he'd imagined his father would be more indulgent with the girls, especially Clary, who'd inherited their mother's gentler nature.

"I'll replace them. Any book you like, and I'll see that you get to read them." It felt odd to be certain of his ability to pay for anything. Odd and thoroughly liberating. Kit told himself he didn't wish for a penny of inheritance from his father, but he couldn't deny the good he might do with the money. He'd damn well indulge his little sister's love of books.

"Oh, he didn't get rid of them," she assured, turning to offer him a conspiratorial wink. "And I discovered where he instructed the servants to hide them. I sneaked one out just last week."

He smiled but feared the gesture didn't reach his eyes. He was all for defiance, but the thought of Clary sneaking about filled him with as much anger as sadness. Their father had provided his family with a home far grander than they required, paid to garb them in fashionable clothes, provided excellent educations, surrounded them with servants. Yet he'd failed to give acceptance, freedom, or any kind of real affection.

It was why Kit had left. Not only to escape his father's malice but for a bit of the liberty he'd never had at home.

He wouldn't allow his sisters to be forced into the same set of stark choices.

"I need to speak with Sophia. Should one of those pastries go missing while I'm gone, I won't tell a soul." He pecked a kiss against Clary's honey-blonde curls and stood. "On second thought, take two and save one for me."

Tension tightened his body as he strode into the hallway to find his sister. They'd clashed from the moment of his arrival, but it hadn't always been that way. Just two years apart in age, he and Sophia had once been close. Together, they'd endured Father's wrath and Mother's melancholy. Usually, Sophia had been the dutiful one, bowing to the rules Kit rebelled against, but she'd always defended him.

On a few occasions, his father had become so exasperated with Kit he'd locked him in a cupboard. Each time, Sophia had picked the lock with one of Mama's hairpins and set him free.

Turning toward the door that led to the kitchen below stairs, he stopped at the sight of her. Sophia sat on a low step of the main stairwell and bolted up as he approached. By the time he reached her, she'd turned her back.

"Are you unwell?"

"Of course not." Despite her strident tone, her voice quavered. "Fatigued, perhaps, but I am well." She squared her narrow shoulders before facing him.

Her eyes were still glassy, cheeks flushed. Kit knew she'd been crying. "Sophia…" He'd been prepared for a fight, eager to defend Clarissa's right to read the books he sent and flit about the house however she liked.

Now that Father was gone, their lives could be different.

But in that moment his flinty-eyed sister looked so fragile, thin and pale and worn down by grief. He drew near and wrapped her in his arms.

Sophia stiffened, and he feared she'd chastise him or reject whatever comfort he could offer, but then she leaned into him. Her body began trembling, and he heard the whimpers she tried to repress as she cried.

"Father is gone." She sounded young, more like the young woman she'd been when he left home. "What will we do without him?"

"We'll carry on." Kit could hold his sister, pat her shoulders, tell her all would be well, but he couldn't share her grief. She saw their father's death as a loss. He felt only relief, as if a weight that had been tugging at him, dragging him in a direction he did not wish to go, had finally been lifted.

"Kit?" Clary called from the drawing room doorway and then rushed toward them, wrapping her arms around his waist to join their embrace.

He could only remember one other moment of unity like this between the three of them. One Christmas, when Clarissa had still been in leading strings, Father took umbrage with a guest at their holiday celebration and flew into a rage. They'd huddled together in Sophia's room. She'd done her best to comfort Clary while he watched over his sisters, determined to protect them from Father's fury.

Suddenly, Sophia pulled back, twisting out of his embrace and taking two steps away. She crossed her arms and lifted her chin. "We should return to the drawing room and await any guests who wish to call."

"You needn't always be strong, Sophia." He gentled his tone, pleading with her, but his words only seemed to spark her ire.

"No? And on whom shall I lean? Now that Papa is gone, who will be strong when I'm not?" She lifted a hand to her chest, pressing her palm against her breastbone. Tears welled in her eyes.

"I am here." He pointed to himself, like a fool, to ensure she noticed him.

"Then you'll stay?" Clary released his waist and clasped his hand. "Say you'll stay with us, Kit."

He looked down into his youngest sister's eyes, a vivid brew of blue and lavender hues. So like their mother's. Her hopeful look tore at his resolve.

This visit to Briar Heath was just that. He'd come to console his sisters, but returning to London had never been in doubt. Lingering wasn't in his nature. He changed lodgings more often than he bought a new suit. But he hadn't counted on Clary pleading and Sophia furrowing her brow and wringing her hands like their mother.

"You won't even consider staying, will you?" Sophia sounded more triumphant than wounded. She even managed a smirk. "You embrace me, offer comfort, but I cannot rely upon any of it. You have every intention of abandoning your duties again. Just as you always have."

When he didn't contradict Sophia, Clary let out a disappointed moan and yanked her hand from his. Without a word, she hurried up the stairs and slammed her door a moment later.

"She's convinced herself you've returned for good and won't go back to London. I know better." Sophia brushed past him and headed toward the drawing room, giving him no time to defend himself. Not that he had a ready reply.

Perhaps she did know him too well.

"It's a great deal to expect of me, Sophia."

"Is it?" She returned to stand beside him. "You've shirked your responsibilities for years, and we've just lost our father. If Ruthven's fails, we will lose our home."

"Surely there are men to run the company. Father didn't do everything himself."

"Those men need to be managed, Kit." It was the first time she'd used his nickname in years, which seemed significant, since she was the one who'd given it to him. "Without strong leadership, I suspect many of them will abandon the business."

The prospect of Ruthven's failure might have once pleased Kit. He loathed the etiquette books upon which his father had made his fortune, but he knew the publishing house had expanded to include other titles, relationships with distributors, and a network of printers who produced their books. His father had even purchased several of his own presses and invested in companies that provided paper pulp and ink. He'd built a minor empire on the back of *The Ruthven Rules*.

"I would do it myself if I could." Sophia whispered the words, as if she feared their father might overhear. He and his etiquette books were very clear on what a woman should and must never do. Business, in Leopold Ruthven's opinion, was for men. "Gentlemen like Mr. Adamson would not wish to be dictated to by a woman."

"I know as little as you do about running father's company, Sophia."

She snapped her head up and stepped toward him. "I know a great deal about running the company. I've assisted father with his correspondence and maintained records regarding the business for years."

Kit cast her a surprised glance.

"I am a proficient typist," she added, as if that explained why their father had allowed his daughter to learn the inner workings of his business. "Together we could continue what he started. Perhaps even make improvements."

Father had never accomplished what Sophia was on the cusp of doing with a few sullen looks and a reasonable argument. She'd spun a web around him, with threads of guilt and logic, wound through with his desire to earn her forgiveness and make amends. He reached up to tug at his necktie. His chest felt pinched and empty, as if he couldn't get any air. "I need to go."

"Kit, please." Sophia reached for him as he passed, but his legs kept moving. He needed to get out of the house, to take a breath that didn't reek of his father's clothes and cigars.

On the front step he stopped only long enough to suck in a lungful of country air. Fresh-cut grass and the scent of autumn blooms flowering in the estate's manicured garden sweetened the breeze.

He started toward sunset's glow, striding to the western edge of the estate, past neatly clipped hedgerows and into a field where the tallest oak he'd ever seen still stood. Somewhere on its trunk, he'd carved his initials next to Ophelia's.

The graveyard didn't call to him. He felt no impulse to make peace with his father. He resisted the urge to flee to the station and catch the nearest train to London.

Ophelia. He was drawn to her like a lost man seeks the polestar.

Her face was the only one he longed to look upon again, her voice the only sound he needed to hear.

Even if she shouted at him. And she probably would.

CHAPTER FOUR

> "Much is expected of young ladies—perfect
> poise, modest behavior, agreeable smiles, spotless
> chastity. Fine aspirations, to be sure, but what of
> wisdom, strength, and confidence? Add these to
> your list, ladies. Put them at the top."
> —MISS GILROY'S GUIDELINES FOR YOUNG LADIES

Patience is a virtue. She'd heard the admonition countless times, but Phee was beginning to doubt she'd ever master that particular virtue.

"This book"—Mrs. Raybourn gripped a copy of *Miss Gilroy's Guidelines* between her thumb and forefinger as if it was a bit of rubbish she couldn't bear to touch—"is not suitable reading material for my daughters, or any young lady. If you see either of them with a copy again, you have my permission to burn it." To emphasize her point, she tossed the volume onto the grate.

Luckily the morning's fire had gone out, but the book's red cloth binding blackened where it touched the ashes.

Phee pressed her lips together and stifled the urge to scream. The muscles in her jaw ached and at some point she'd clenched her fists, allowing her nails to bite into the flesh of her palms.

"You've made your feelings perfectly clear, Mrs. Raybourn." Forcing a smile, she moved her students' mother toward the door. The quicker she got the irate woman out of her house, the sooner she could find Juliet and settle her sister down. Loud noises unnerved her, and she'd dashed off the moment their visitor began a boisterous tirade. "Now that the girls know you disapprove of the book, I'm sure they'll avoid it."

"I wish I shared your certainty, Miss Marsden." Mrs. Raybourn narrowed her eyes at her fourteen-year-old twins who sat side by side on the sofa, eyes downcast, no doubt biting their tongues as Ophelia had spent the last quarter of an hour doing. "Lady Millicent had the audacity to recommend that outrage last week during afternoon tea. Is that not shocking?"

"Exceedingly." Despite Mrs. Raybourn's ire, Ophelia stifled a grin. Having been friends with Lady Pembry's eldest daughter for years, Phee knew Milly took pride in her talent for shocking proclamations.

"My girls must marry well." The dark-haired lady leaned in, finally lowering her voice to its normal volume. "With your lessons and a good finishing school, they will do so. Surely you, of all people, understand the importance of making a fortuitous match." Pity rang in the lady's tone, and the sound was far harsher than her shouts. "I admire your determination to support yourself and your sister, Miss Marsden, but I do not wish for my girls to end as spinsters."

After lifting a hand to pat Ophelia's arm twice, she called to her daughters. "Come, girls. We mustn't be late for dinner."

As soon as the Raybourns departed, Ophelia retrieved her sooty book from the hearth and sank into a parlor chair. Letting out a ragged sigh, she soaked in the return of quiet and waited until her heartbeat steadied to the ticking rhythm of the wall clock. She couldn't comfort her sister while her own frazzled nerves were stretched thin. The familiar sounds of Longacre soothed her—a breeze fluttering against the shutters and the chatter of finches in the fruit trees outside—but Mrs. Raybourn's words echoed in her mind.

Phee never intended to become a spinster. After her father's death, she'd simply been too busy getting her tutoring business off the ground and caring for Juliet. Suitors were the least of her concerns. Other than Kit, no gentleman had shown her any particular notice.

Until Lord Douglas Dunstan. He'd persisted despite her disinterest, and shocked her with his proposal. She couldn't deny that his wealth and status could secure her future and provide the finest education for Juliet, but Phee had known the baron most of her life. As a boy, he'd been a bully. As a man, she found him insufferably arrogant and proud. He'd shown concern for her welfare after Father's death, but she'd never offered Lord Dunstan anything but gratitude in return.

Now she owed him an answer.

A *ping* sounded from a copper pot in the corner, strategically placed to catch drips from a soggy spot in the ceiling plaster. Phee stared at the watermarked splotch above the window, calculating how much tuition she'd need to earn before they could pay for repairs to the roof.

Was marrying Dunstan her answer? Accepting him would bring security but a cold, emotionless union. Could she endure a future without passion?

She chuckled at her own foolishness. She'd lived without passion for years. Why sacrifice her well-being and Juliet's future for what might never come?

She had to put practicality first and daydreams to rest.

"That's fifty percent." Juliet poked her head out from the family sitting room that also served as a library, the most cozily furnished space in the house. Other rooms had been shut up to save on the cost of heating. Though Phee sometimes mused about transforming Longacre into a boarding school for girls, it was an idea their finances would never support and Juliet consistently rejected. *A house full of children,* she'd say before shivering with disgust at the notion, apparently counting her twelve years as far beyond the bounds of childhood.

"Pardon?"

Juliet stepped into the parlor, her ever-present notebook clutched at her side. "Mrs. Raybourn has come to speak with you ten times, and she screeched or shouted during half of those visits. Excessive, don't you think?"

"Definitely." Ophelia grinned and lifted a hand toward her sister. Numbers dominated Juliet's world. Tallies, percentages, sums, and equations were her preferred language, though she'd proven an apt student in every subject. Aunt Rose expressed worry that she was "too much in her own head." From her youngest days she'd preferred books to friends and logic to sentimentalism. At twelve, her chief goal was to attend university rather than marry.

"Is she coming back?" Juliet approached warily, darting her gaze about as if fearing Mrs. Raybourn's imminent return.

"Not today, though I certainly hope she'll bring her daughters back tomorrow. They're my best pupils."

"In terms of income, yes. To be precise, they are your best and second-best pupils, but Elspeth Keene isn't far behind." Despite repeated admonitions, Juliet insisted on taking an interest in the household accounts. Phee considered the columns and balances too grim for her sister's perusal, but she had to admit the girl's aptitude for mathematics far exceeded her own. "The girls can come, but we should discourage future visits from Mrs. Raybourn."

"I'll do my best to ensure she doesn't shout next time." Ophelia had no idea where the girls obtained a copy of her book, but she'd abide by her employer's wishes and make sure they didn't study *Guidelines* during tutoring sessions. That should at least cut back on the lady's outbursts. "Shall we go and see if Aunt Rose needs any help preparing supper?"

Juliet shot her a dubious look. Though the family's long-time housekeeper remained, despite their meager budget, Aunt Rose insisted on doing all the cooking. She possessed a gift for food preparation as others did for art or music. With the simplest of ingredients, she made every meal memorable. In addition to caring for them and Longacre, she was keen on visiting, involved in several charitable endeavors, and was forever knitting or sewing some item to donate. Aunt Rose rarely needed anyone's help, but she always welcomed company.

Before Ophelia could gather her sister and head back to the kitchen, a knock sounded at the front door. Juliet clutched her notebook to her chest and bolted back into the library.

Slipping *Guidelines* behind her back with one hand, Ophelia grasped the doorknob with the other. She schooled her features into a pleasant expression in case it was Mrs. Raybourn or, heaven forbid, Mr. Raybourn, in need of more reassurance their girls weren't on the high road to ruin because of the book no one knew she'd written.

When she pulled the door open, all the breath whooshed from her body.

Their visitor wasn't any member of the Raybourn family.

"Kit Ruthven."

"You remember me, then?" He grinned as he loomed on the threshold, his shoulders nearly as wide as the frame. Eyes bright and intense, he took her in from head to toe, and then let his gaze settle on her mouth. When he finally looked into her eyes, the cocksure tilt of his grin had softened. She read a wariness in his gaze that matched her own.

She'd spent years trying to forget those dark, deep-set eyes.

"I remember you." Her book slipped, skidding across her backside and clattering to the floor as her throat tightened on sentiments she'd been waiting years to express. None of them would come. Not a single word. Instead, in outright rebellion, her whole body did its best to melt into a boneless puddle. Gritting her teeth, Phee fought the urge to swoon or, worse, rush into his long, muscled arms.

"I'm relieved to hear it." He had the audacity to kick his grin into a smile, a rakish slash that cut deep divots into his clean-shaven cheeks. Then he took a step through her door. "I worried that—"

"No." She lifted a hand to stop him. Looking at the man was difficult enough. Hearing his voice—deeper now but achingly familiar—was too much. If he came closer, she might give in to some rogue impulse. And that wouldn't do. That wouldn't do at all.

Ophelia swallowed hard. She needed a moment to gather her wits. To rebuild her walls.

"You dropped something." He moved toward her, so close his sleeve brushed hers.

She lowered her hand to avoid touching him and jerked back when he bent to retrieve her book, watching as he turned the volume to read its title.

"*Miss Gilroy's Guidelines for Young Ladies.* How intriguing. Looks as though Ruthven Publishing has some competition."

Seeing him again was worse than she'd imagined. And she had imagined this moment aplenty. Far too many times. Not just on her infrequent jaunts to London but most days since they'd parted. The man had lingered in her thoughts, despite every effort to expel him.

Taking a shaky breath, she braced herself and faced him.

He'd always been tall. When they were children, she'd looked up to him. Literally. But he'd never used his size to bully others. More often he'd born teasing about his physique. *Ungainly*, his father had called him, and Kit repeated the word when referring to himself.

Now he offered no apologetic hunch in his stance. He didn't cross his arms to narrow his body. More than embracing his size, he wielded his generous dimensions with a virile grace that made Phee's mouth water. He stood with his long legs planted wide, shoulders thrown back. His chest was so broad that she itched to touch it.

Stop being a ninny, she chided herself. The most essential observation was that he did not look like a man who'd pined for her. Not a hint of guilt shadowed his gaze.

He thrust his hands behind his back, and the buttons above his waistcoat strained against the fabric on either side, as if the muscles beneath were too sizable to contain. Phee's gaze riveted to the spot, waiting to see which would win—the pearly buttons or the dove gray fabric. When sense finally wound its way into her boggled mind, she glanced up into gilded brown eyes. *He* was the winner, judging by the satisfied smirk cresting his mouth.

Kit stood too near, close enough for her to smell his scent. A familiar green, like fresh-cut grass, but mingled now with an aromatic spice. Each breath held his spice scent heightened by the warmth of his body. The heat of him radiated against her chest.

His eyes were too intense, too hungry. He perused her brazenly, studying the hem of her outdated gown before his gaze roved up her legs, paused at her waist, lingered on her bosom, and caught for a moment on her lips. Finally, he met her eyes, and his mouth flicked up in a shameless grin.

She looked anywhere but at his eyes. On his neck, she noted the scar from a childhood adventure in the blackberry briar. Then she got stuck admiring his hair. Apparently his scandalous London lifestyle—if the rumors she'd heard were true—called for allowing his jet black hair to grow long and ripple in careless waves. Strands licked at his neck, curled up near his shoulders.

Time had been truly unfair. The years hadn't weathered Kit at all. If anything, his features were sharper and more

appealing. His Roman nose contrasted with the sensual fullness of his lips and those high Ruthven cheekbones. And his
eyes. Gold and amber and chocolate hues chased each other
around a pinwheel, all shadowed by enviably thick ebony
lashes. One theater reviewer had written of the "power of his
penetrating gaze."

Ophelia only knew he'd once been able to see straight to
her heart.

Retreating from his magnetic pull, she dipped her head
and stared at his polished black boots, the neatly tailored
cuffs of his trousers. Black as pitch, his clothing reminded
her why he was here. He'd come to the village to bury his
father. He was no doubt as eager to return to London as she
was to close her eyes and make the too tempting sight of him
disappear. But why had he come to her home?

"My condolences to you and your sisters," she offered, and
almost added *Mr. Ruthven*. That's what everyone in the village would call him now, and they would expect him to live
up to the name. Just as his father had.

"You didn't attend the funeral."

"Would your father have wished me to?" They both knew
Kit's father had never welcomed her presence in his life. She
didn't bother mentioning that Ruthven's rule book explicitly
instructed ladies to avoid funerals.

He shrugged. "I only know what I wished."

There it was. The heart of all that had passed between
them spelled out in six words. Kit had never doubted what
he wanted—freedom, fame as a playwright, financial success
on his own terms. Unfortunately, she'd never made it high
enough on his list.

"Forgive me for missing your father's funeral. I promise to call on your sisters soon." Ophelia slid the door toward him, forcing him to retreat as she eased it closed. "Thank you for your visit."

Pushing his sizable booted foot forward, he wedged it between the door and its frame. "I don't think we can count this as a visit until you invite me in."

For a moment Kit doubted she'd relent. Her eyes filled with blue thunder clouds, and her lush lips seamed together, quivering at the edges. Even when she scowled at him, he wanted to kiss her. Pressing his mouth to Ophelia's had been his first instinct the minute she opened the door.

Standing on her doorstep all evening seemed extreme, but now he stood close enough to trace the starburst indigo pattern in her eyes and see heat blooming in her cheeks. He wouldn't turn away. He'd waited too long for this moment. Just a glimpse of her and he already felt lighter.

"Come in, then. But only for a moment," she grumbled, issuing the chilliest invitation he'd had from a woman in years.

Every step he approached, Ophelia retreated, as if determined to put as much distance between them as possible.

Maybe he only felt lighter because his chest constricted the longer he looked at her, and her reticence tightened the vice. The pinching ache behind his ribs vied with the thrill of being near her, hearing her voice, reacquainting himself with the buzz of pleasure she'd always sparked in him.

This close, he couldn't help but note how she'd changed. The girl who'd let her rebellious curls hang in corkscrews down her back and wore wildflowers in the buttonholes of her gowns had been replaced with a woman who looked every inch an eager-to-chastise governess. Her drab dress imprisoned her figure behind a row of tiny, sentry-like buttons from belly to her chin. The coarse-looking fabric made Kit's skin itch.

Whatever caused her to hide her passionate nature away behind a guise of propriety, it didn't work. She still smelled like jasmine, though now the appealing scent was tinged with a bit of starch. Her red hair still glowed like a fiery halo in the afternoon light. Despite her changed appearance, Kit glimpsed the girl he'd once known as well as he knew himself. The young woman he'd missed every day for years.

"You're staring," she accused, clearly displeased with the fact. Lifting an arm stiffly, she gestured toward the room he recalled as the family's parlor for entertaining guests. "This way. I'll ask Mrs. Rafferty to make us some tea."

"Don't bother Mrs. Rafferty." He recalled the Marsdens' housekeeper fondly, but he wanted Phee to himself. "I've had my fill of tea today, thank you."

"As you wish." Pivoting with the precision of a soldier, she marched into the parlor.

Kit loathed her cool politeness, but he didn't mind studying the tight knot of curls and the pale flesh at the back of her neck. Mercy, she held herself ramrod straight. He dropped his gaze lower, and a patch of soot on the swell of her backside caught his eye. His hand twitched as he fought the urge to touch her curves and wipe the spot away.

"You have a mark on your dress."

"Where?" She stopped abruptly, and he nearly bumped into her. She turned.

He stepped back. "Just there." He reached to grip her waist and turn her.

She skidded away from him as if he'd set her gown on fire. "I can manage on my own."

"I have no doubts on that score."

After twirling in a circle, looking over her shoulder as she swiped at the spot on her gown, she pointed to a chair near the unlit fire. "Please, have a seat."

Kit waited until she'd taken her own chair, noting how she perched nervously at the edge. It was only then he allowed himself to shift his gaze from her and look around. Phee's appearance wasn't the only change since his absence from Longacre.

"I hardly recognize this room." The parlor had once been a place of color and music and artful chaos. He recalled impromptu poetry readings, her father's talent on the piano, and walls dotted with Phee's youthful watercolors and fine prints her father acquired in London. Now they were virtually empty, and wallpaper was peeling at the edges.

"We've had to economize." Her tone went raw and low, and Kit regretted pointing out anything that might remind her of losing her father. Had Marsden truly left his daughters so little in the way of funds?

"Nothing wrong with order. Nor tidiness." He sounded like his father or Sophia, and yet its cleanliness was the only aspect of the room he could praise. Every surface shone, but it was a barren spotlessness. The usual clutter of furniture and knickknacks had been replaced with practical pieces—a sofa, two chairs, and a table for tea. A single clock dominated the scrubbed shelf it sat on.

"What are those?" He pointed to rectangles of paper stuck to the walls with pins. They were arranged in scrupulously precise rows and covered with neat lines of script.

"Schedules. I tutor several young ladies in the village, and those list what they will study and when on each day they come."

"What do you teach?" So she *was* a governess, and a mercilessly exacting one, it seemed.

"Art, music, composition, and decorum."

"Decorum?" A flash of memory sparked a grin Kit wasn't quick enough to hide behind his hand. Ophelia as a long-legged sprite of a girl, tiptoeing across the rocks in Dunstan's pond, her skirt dirty and damp, her hair as tangled as the branches in a bird's nest.

He looked up to find her scowling at him.

"Despite what you may remember of me, I do know how to behave like a lady."

"Perhaps you should give Clarissa lessons." Sophia insisted their younger sister rebelled against all attempts to civilize her.

"I do."

"My father allowed it?" That shocked him. His father had never liked Ophelia's outspoken father and tended to paint her with the same judgmental brush.

"Only art lessons. Sophia arranged the tutoring sessions." She spoke as if hoarding her words, unwilling to spare him any more syllables than necessary.

It made him yearn to hear her laugh. To see her dimples and cause those turquoise eyes to light with pleasure.

"I'm glad you kept that up." He nudged his chin toward her mother's needlework, framed in gold above the mantel. *Follow your heart and flourish.*

Sitting a few inches from Phee, Kit sensed the past too keenly. Memories flooded his mind. A trove of moments they'd shared—raw and lovely and bittersweet. She couldn't have forgotten the words she scribbled so many years ago.

"Mama was an optimist." From the hollow timbre in her voice, he sensed she no longer shared her mother's sunny outlook.

Kit hated how much he wanted to know why.

London held his future, an opportunity he couldn't bear to lose. He would not allow himself to become entangled here—by Phee, his sisters' wishes, or his father's business.

He'd gotten what he came for—the glimpse of Ophelia he'd long craved.

"Surely you did not come to assess our decor or discuss my tutoring work. Is there something you wished to say to me?" She dipped her head as she posed the question, lifting the watch pinned to the bodice of her gown to stare at its face. Emphasizing how much of her time he'd already wasted.

What did he want to say to her? More than he could manage in the minutes she'd grant him. More than he might be able to manage in a lifetime.

He'd expected her anger. Could even admit he deserved every bit of it. He never blamed her for ignoring his letters. They were an insufficient offering when he'd promised to visit and never had.

Coming back to see Phee had always seemed a dangerous prospect, as if being near her might upend his London life. But her coolness now unnerved him. Let her rail at him, pound on his chest, call him the worst sort of scoundrel— anything but this attempt at unaffected calm.

She glanced at her damnable watch again and stood. "If you'll excuse me, our supper has already been delayed too long."

"Phee—" Kit stood too. He needed to go.

"Please send your sisters my condolences. Without a father to guide them, their lives will never be the same." She spoke of herself. He could see the sorrow in her eyes and approached to embrace her, to offer comfort, his body responding before his brain thought better of it.

"No."

He froze at her rejection, not just his body but some inner piece of himself. All the pleasure of seeing her again seeped out on a long sigh. Even as she stood before him, Ophelia was so far away.

"Please go, Mr. Ruthven." His family name fell from her lips with such disdain that bile rose in his throat.

Ophelia wasn't just angry with him. She loathed him.

Jaw clenched, gut roiling, Kit turned from her and headed for the door. Just past the threshold, he heard her voice and turned back.

"You'll be returning to London soon, I take it?" She sounded hopeful, relieved at the prospect of his departure.

Up to that moment, it had been his only desire. Suddenly, he wanted something else. Another glimpse of Ophelia Marsden. A chance to make her look at him with anything other than disdain.

"I'd planned to return immediately." Yes, that was definitely hope flashing in her lovely eyes and the breathless way she held her mouth. He'd seen the expression on her face before and, like the heartless rogue he was, he did exactly what he'd done then. He dashed it. "But perhaps I'll stay awhile."

CHAPTER FIVE

*"Gentlemen must control their passions. A man
who cannot control his passions will soon find
himself at their mercy."*
—THE RUTHVEN RULES FOR YOUNG MEN

Kit couldn't settle.

Stifled energy he'd normally expend on the stage, writing, or indulging in late-night pleasures bottled up until he had to move. Shoving the coverlet aside, he sat in his old bed and surveyed the space he'd once retreated to as boy to escape his father's anger. Its walls no longer offered any comfort or helped ease the knotted ache in the center of his chest.

From the moment he'd set foot in Briar Heath again, nothing had gone right.

He'd attended the funeral, thrown an obligatory handful of earth into the grave, and still failed to feel as he should about his father's death.

The initial thrill of seeing Ophelia had faded to a dull thrum in his veins and then a ceaseless thrashing in his head.

Sleep eluded him. Now, hours past dawn, setting to work in his father's study seemed a sensible distraction. Despite his impulsive, bull-headed reply to Ophelia the previous night, he needed to settle the man's business affairs and return to London. And he needed to start on his new play. A man like Dominic Fleet wouldn't wait. He'd simply find another playwright among the glut of aspiring dramatists living in the city.

As if trapped inside and grateful to escape, the scent of books and leather assailed him when Kit cracked the door of his father's study. Kit and his sisters had been forbidden entrance to his sanctuary. Unless punishment was in order. After giving a lashing for some misdeed, his father would order Kit to take a spot on the thick Aubusson rug marked by an enormous pink rose and deliver a lecture as dry as the rules in his etiquette books. He'd sharpen his chastisement until it cut deep, reminding Kit what a disappointment he was, expressing doubt that a child with his rebellious nature could truly be his son.

"You'll never amount to anything in life."

Ignoring the ugly echoes in his head, Kit sidestepped the pink rose and approached his father's leather throne. The chair had seemed much larger when he was a boy. Now it cowered at the sight of him.

"You've risen early." Sophia sounded far too cheery for such an ungodly hour. She glided across the rug with a tray in her hands. "I heard you moving around upstairs and then come down. Thought you might need a cup of tea."

"I'll require a whole pot. Couldn't sleep." The cup of tea she prepared for him felt fragile in Kit's hand, the girth of his thumb too large to fit through its gilded handle. He held the hot porcelain in his palm and wished the steaming brew inside was coffee. Preferably as dark and smoky as the London coffeehouses he favored.

"The solicitor arrives later this morning so that he can go over business matters with you."

"I've already seen the will." The document was an accurate reflection of their father—practical, free of sentiment, and far from generous. Each of Kit's sisters were allotted a modest dowry, but Kit hadn't received any funds outright. Instead, he'd been granted ownership of Ruthven Publishing, which seemed a good deal more burden than blessing.

"He can provide you with information about our agreements with suppliers and any investments Father made."

And, hopefully, how to sell the damn business so that they could all profit from the proceeds.

"Everything is hidden away." Kit swept his arm in the air above his father's spotlessly clean desk. Sophia or one of the maids must have tidied the space. When he was writing or working, his father had surrounded himself with clutter.

"I put his papers in order and stored them in the desk, organizing them as best I could." Tidying was Sophia's way. She had an abiding need to create order out of chaos.

"Shall I leave you to it?" As Ophelia had done, his sister glanced down at a watch pinned to the waist of her skirt. "I'll send a maid to warn you when the solicitor arrives. You can meet with him in here, if it's all right."

"Yes, of course." The oddness of Sophia asking anything of him, seeking his permission, struck Kit as so strange that he almost smiled. Then he remembered. Father was gone. Sophia, all of them, were in mourning. The frown marring her forehead, the shadows darkening the skin under her eyes, and the fact that they stood watching each other across their late father's private sanctum all reminded him. This was no time for levity.

"Join us, won't you?" he asked. "When the solicitor arrives?"

The lines between her pale brows deepened. "I rather thought you'd wish to handle it yourself."

"I'm out of my depth, Sophia. When I walked away from all of this"—Kit gestured around the dim room, but he referred to the entirety of his father's business—"I never expected to come back."

Her delicate features stiffened to match the hard edge in her gaze. "I suspect Papa didn't expect his heart to give out on him either." She spun so swiftly her black skirt flared behind her as she exited the room.

"Excellent way to start the day," Kit grumbled as he settled into his father's chair. Somewhere between Paddington Station and Briar Heath, he'd lost his ability to speak to women without incurring their wrath. He and Sophia had argued every day since his return from London, and he needed to stop thinking of Ophelia's reaction when she found him on her doorstep.

He'd been haunted all night by her expression of misery.

The sacred desk chair proved to be Lilliputian, so low Kit's knees nearly reached his chin. *Perhaps Father wasn't such a giant after all.*

Beginning with the top drawer, he flipped through billing documents and business correspondence, uncertain what he hoped to find. There would be no answers, no rule book for how to free himself from a business Leopold Ruthven spent years building up from a small concern to a publishing enterprise. This is where his father had always wished him. Stuck behind a desk. In charge of the family business.

Kit wanted none of it. None of the responsibility, nor any of the constraints that came with stepping into another man's shoes.

After slamming each drawer shut, he tapped the desktop, craving noise. The room was too quiet, the whole house too empty. His cramped flat off Seven Dials, constantly reverberating with London's clatter, suddenly held fresh appeal. Even the echo of his fingers hitting the desk's blotter sounded hollow. Skimming his hand along the edge of the desk, he found a narrow drawer receded into the woodwork. The lock held firm against his attempts to force it.

Kit scanned the desk and bookshelves. The key had to be nearby. His father was a practical man, above all else. Nothing under a paperweight or concealed beneath the lamp near the edge of the desk. Inside a polished wooden box, Kit found a fountain pen and dug under its velvet cushion. He spotted a key, tinier than his thumbnail, and tipped it out into his palm. As he examined the delicate thing, the bit of metal slipped through his fingers. Dropping to one knee, he studied the golds of the carpet design and spotted a brassy glint.

"Hello?" Phee's call was soft and uncertain. "Anyone in here?"

Kit raised his head and bashed it on the edge of the desk.

"Oh." Auburn eyebrows shot skyward when he popped up from behind the furniture. "You *are* here."

"Yes, I've entered the forbidden enclave. You should have come earlier. I actually dared to sit in his chair." Kit stood clutching the diminutive key in one hand and rubbing the walnut-sized bump on his head with the other. He tried to ignore how lovely Phee looked in the morning light and the damned brigade of bees that hummed in his chest whenever she was close. "You were in Father's study once before, weren't you?"

The moment was the only pleasant memory he had of the room.

"We were caught fishing in old Dunstan's pond." She nodded, her mouth tight and eyes hooded, giving nothing away.

"You tried to take the blame." Kit recalled being impressed with her bravery. He'd rarely seen anyone take on his father as Phee had with her twelve-year-old's share of courage.

"You wouldn't allow it. As soon as you confessed to instigating the expedition, he sent me home to my father. What did he do to you after I left?"

"Words mostly." He said it as flippantly as he could, trying to convince her—and himself—that his father's cutting verbal barrage hadn't struck as forcefully as his belt's lashes. "My father never tired of hearing himself speak."

A smile started to tip the edges of her mouth, then she ducked her head as if contrite. She glanced around the room before meeting his gaze. "I came to offer my condolences to your sisters, but I couldn't leave without offering you…" No more words came, but her mouth remained open. Kit didn't know whether she struggled to speak or simply refused to express the sentiment on the tip of her tongue.

"Offering me…?" he repeated encouragingly, but she wouldn't finish.

"Aunt Rose urged me to come," she finally choked out.

Ophelia's aunt had always been kind to him. Still, he was curious why she'd advise Phee to seek him out.

"She asked me to bring these." From a lumpy reticule, she extracted a square packet, neatly wrapped in wax paper and tied with twine. "Two of her lemon tarts. You used to love them." She frowned at *love*, swallowing hard, as if the word carried a bitter taste.

"Let's share them. I'll ring for more tea."

"No." Her brows winged up as if the suggestion shocked her. "No, I can't. I have pupils coming this afternoon."

"It's still morning."

"I need time to prepare."

Kit smiled. Convincing Ophelia Marsden to do anything she didn't wish to do had always been a losing proposition. "Hand over my tarts, then." He held out his palm and held his ground. He'd embraced this woman more times than he could count. Kissed her senseless until they both forgot their own names. Her timidity now was more out of character than if she'd suddenly become compliant.

She took two stiff strides forward and deposited the lemon confections at the front edge of his father's desk. "I'm sorry about your father. Truly. But I will wish you good day now and be off."

As soon as she turned and swept toward the door, the pounding in Kit's head built to a crescendo. He couldn't let another encounter with her end like this. However short-lived his stay in Briar Heath, he had no wish to be at odds with the woman who'd figured in all his happiest memories of the place.

"Wait." Calling her back was a dangerous proposition. He told himself he craved peace but nothing more. He couldn't allow himself to feel more. But making amends with Ophelia suddenly seemed essential, the only way he'd get through the next few weeks of playing Leopold Ruthven's dutiful son. "Will you help me with something?"

"With what?" Good start, that glance over her shoulder. Curiosity lit her gaze. Phee had always been every bit as inquisitive as stubborn.

"A very small key." Unfurling the fingers of his left hand, he tipped his palm toward her.

She lifted her chin and inspected the object. "A key to what?"

"Come over here, and I'll show you." He waved her over, but she didn't budge. "I won't bite, Ophelia."

A rush of pleasure trickled down his back like warm water when he said her name aloud. Or perhaps it was the way her skin bloomed in a ruddy blush. He loved sparking something in her besides ire.

"What must I do?" She lifted one hand and then the other, perching them on her lush hips. But she did approach, drawing up next to him behind his father's desk.

Her nearness electrified his senses. Everything else faded as he studied the freckles scattered across her nose and cheeks, the wisps of hair curling around her ears, the determination in her gaze.

"Your fingers are nimbler than mine. I've already dropped the thing once." Kit reached for her hand, and she flinched away from him. "Take the key."

She managed to retrieve it from his hand with minimal contact between them, though he felt the single stroke of her fingertips against his palm all the way to his groin.

"Now what?"

"Under my father's desk, there's a center drawer. If you just…" He bent to show her the drawer and its hidden lock, but she didn't join him. When he glanced up, he found her watching him with arms crossed.

"I can manage if you step aside."

He did, and she bent at the waist to inspect the drawer.

Casting a glance over her shoulder, she caught him studying her backside and scowled. "Why don't you wait over there?" She shooed him toward the bookshelves lining the far wall of the room.

"As you wish." A long view of her backside proved just as appealing.

"Is there a specific item you hope to find?" She fussed at the lock, her sighs of frustration paired with sounds of metal scratching wood.

"An amended will would be nice. Preferably one in which Father insists we sell the business and live happily ever after on the monies earned."

When she huffed out another sigh, Kit considered approaching, though he was enjoying the view far too much and doubted she'd allow him to get close enough to assist.

After wiggling and grumbling and trying again, Phee jerked back, pulling the narrow drawer free of its hiding place. Lifting the first item out, she shot him a guilty look and bit her lip.

"What is it?" Kit approached, and Ophelia pressed the rectangle to her chest. He held out his hand. "Let me see."

She chewed her bottom lip a moment, and Kit swallowed hard. Whatever she concealed, it caused her blush to spread, a rush of pink skimming down her neck. He wanted to trace the color with his fingers.

Finally, she thrust the object toward him.

Kit took what proved to be a photograph, faded and worn around the edges. Only the subject in the center remained perfectly clear. Not to mention scantily clad.

"Lily Verner." The lady's creamy shoulders, plump ankles, and a good portion of her ample décolletage were artfully displayed in a keepsake postcard photograph his father had apparently treasured.

"You know her?" Phee crossed her arms and narrowed her eyes.

"She's a well-known Gaiety Girl. Everyone in London knows her." But why had his father? Had he actually frequented the Gaiety Theater? Kit couldn't imagine his dour, upstanding father anywhere near the infamous music hall.

"Mmm." Ophelia made an odd sound, much more dubious than an acknowledgment. Was she jealous? Before Kit could read anything in her gaze, she turned back to the drawer.

"What else did he have hidden in there?" The interior was too shallow to hold much, but Ophelia lifted out a pile of what appeared to be newspaper clippings. "More beguiling ladies?" The Gaiety Girls often featured in the newspapers.

"No." Her hands trembled as she offered him the neatly cut bits of newsprint. "These are for you."

For him? What would his father save for him in a secret drawer?

Kit sifted the scraps. All of them mentioned his name— plays he'd performed in or written, his debut at Merrick

Theater, even a short essay he'd gotten published in a London theater journal. Before realizing he'd moved, the breath whooshed from his body, and he felt the uncomfortable seat of his father's chair hit his backside.

Ophelia stepped close, a sweet-scented presence at his elbow. "He cared, Kit. Despite how he criticized and condemned." She emphasized her words with a touch, offering the simple weight of her palm against his shoulder.

Kit flexed his arm to press into the heat of her hand, to soak up all the comfort she offered.

Feelings rushed in, a tangled jumble of guilt, anger, and sadness he usually kept at bay. The damned room, Ophelia's nearness, and his sleep-starved mind all conspired to intensify the emotion clawing its way up his throat, burning behind his eyes. It felt suspiciously like grief, and he wanted none of it.

Far easier was focusing on the woman at his side.

"And you, Ophelia? Do you still care?"

Chapter Six

*"Never allow anyone to convince you that
ladies are not as capable of reason and rational
judgements as men. Both sexes must strike a
balance between passion and prudence."*
—Miss Gilroy's Guidelines for Young Ladies

"*That* was a mistake," Ophelia muttered to herself as she stomped up the grassy path through the woods between Ruthven Hall and the Pembry estate. "Total folly."

Reaching into her reticule, she yanked out her daily task list. Duties to attend to and chores around the house were printed in neat, careful script above a hastily scrawled notation she'd added the night before.

Avoid Kit Ruthven.

She'd woken with every intention of steering clear of the man, vowing that if a social situation threw them together while he was in Briar Heath, she'd offer sympathy and nothing more. Kit came back to Briar Heath to bury his father. He and his sisters needed comfort, not her shallow worry that his first sight of her after so many years happened to be while she wore a soot-smeared gown.

Forgiveness seemed much simpler when he'd been off living his life in London, but seeing him, being so close she could feel the warmth of his body—nothing could have prepared her. Neither Ruthven's rule book nor her own *Guidelines* for ladies had a remedy for unexpectedly encountering the man one's heart had never quite forgotten.

Even after years of resolving to forgive him, past hurt welled up the moment she'd found him on her doorstep.

Getting her condolence call to the Ruthven sisters off her list immediately seemed the best approach. Chances were Kit would still be abed. London actors weren't known for rising with the sun.

The visit had gone well until she'd been foolish enough to inquire about him—only out of politeness, of course—on her way out. Sophia had very unhelpfully directed her to old Ruthven's study.

The moment she glimpsed Kit standing behind his father's desk, tall enough to dwarf the hideously ornate thing, all her intentions scattered like dust motes on the air. She'd only managed simple thoughts—Kit was near and bathed in sunlight. After missing him for years, she could speak to him, draw close enough to touch him. Despite every admonition, every rational argument, that was all she'd truly wished to do.

Nothing about pressing a hand to his shoulder had been intended to tempt her. But he'd been shockingly warm. His body was broad and firm, his muscles bunching and flexing in response to her touch.

And then that ridiculous question. It rang like a taunt in her mind. She clenched her fists as she recalled the low, purring quality of his voice. How dare he ask if she still cared? What did it matter? He would go back to London, and she would remain here.

She was on the cusp of accepting another man's marriage proposal. Wasn't she?

The prospect set off a wave of nausea. She swallowed against the queasiness and picked up her pace.

Kit's visit wouldn't alter the choices they'd made. Or the choice she still needed to make.

The path turned to gravel under her feet, and Ophelia shoved thoughts of Kit Ruthven aside as she drew in a lungful of cool air. She'd entered the grounds of Lady Pembry's estate and needed all her wits about her to face the group the countess summoned each year to plan the village's autumn fete. Someday she'd have to conquer her tendency to volunteer for everything. Not that participating in the festival was avoidable. Her mother, who'd been a childhood friend of the countess's, helped establish the event long before Phee was born. Over the years it had grown into an annual celebration that included games, displays, and activities beyond showing off the best bud or vegetable from village matrons' gardens.

After only one short rap on the door, a footman ushered her into the countess's favorite drawing room.

"Miss Marsden, don't you look fresh and lovely this morning." Lady Pembry didn't rise to greet her. Her clingy cluster of three miniature poodles vied for space on her lap and made movement difficult. Instead, she ushered Phee over with a sweeping gesture, her numerous glittering bracelets jangling out a merry tune as she indicated the other ladies in the room. "You know Mrs. Bickham, of course, and Mrs. Raybourn. The rest are on their way."

The silver-haired vicar's wife beamed a warm smile, and the elegant, dark-eyed Raybourn girls' mother offered a polite nod.

"And me, Mama. I'm here too." Lady Millicent, the countess's oldest and only unmarried daughter, called from the corner of the room. She stood, straightened the skirt of her pink frilled gown, and swept back a tawny lock of hair before snapping shut the book she'd been reading.

"I wasn't sure you'd find the power to drag yourself from the pages of your novel." The countess didn't favor her daughter's love of reading.

"That's the lovely thing about books, Mama." As she replied, Milly greeted Phee with the wink of one moss-green eye. "They wait for you precisely where you've left them."

Villagers referred to Lady Millicent as a bluestocking or, less generously, a spinster, but Phee knew her as the cleverest and most loyal of friends. The two had formed a bond as girls when they'd been sent to the same boarding school. Ophelia's parents had only been able to afford two years' tuition before Father resumed tutoring her at home, but Milly had endured five long years at the horrible place. She'd returned from the ordeal a more bookish and serious young lady, but neither the repressive headmistress nor bullying older girls had managed to crush her spirit.

"You look out of sorts." Milly spoke low as she sat on the settee next to Phee. They were distant enough from other guests to have a measure of privacy if they whispered. "Your cheeks have gone all pink and splotchy."

"I walked quickly. Your mother's glares are fearsome when I'm late." Phee wasn't sure why she concealed the real cause of her flustered state. If she trusted anyone with her secrets, it was Milly.

"Well, I'm glad you're well because I have news."

"Good news?" Phee could use a bit of her friend's pleasant tidings to distract from the tall, dark image of Kit freshly imprinted in her memory. His green pine scent still clung to her hand where she'd touched him.

"Let's just say it will please Mama. Have you heard who's arrived in the village?"

Milly knew. No point withholding any of it now. "I've seen him," Phee confessed.

"Already?"

"He called at Longacre yesterday. To torment me, I think." Whether he'd intended it or not, Kit's visit had consumed her thoughts.

"Why?" Milly turned a surprised glance Phee's way. "Did he press you about marriage?"

"Marriage?" Kit had never asked for her hand. He never would. Which was why she needed to stop thinking about him. Immediately.

She'd spoken too loudly. A maid dispensing tea and biscuits tipped her head in their direction.

"What are you two whispering about over there?" Lady Pembry wagged a bejeweled finger in their direction. "If it's at all intriguing, do come and sit next to me." When neither answered, the countess persisted. "Come, ladies, leave that comfortable settee for the others who'll be joining us."

As they obeyed and moved to chairs closer to Lady Pembry and her guests, Milly clutched Phee's arm and whispered, "Who are you talking about?"

"Kit Ruthven." Phee spoke out of the side of her mouth, fearing Lady Pembry's fame for being able to lip-read gossip from across a crowded room. "Who are *you* talking about?"

The moment they reached the two straight-back chairs Lady Pembry indicated, a footman announced a new visitor. "My lady, Lord Dunstan has arrived."

"Speak of the devil," Milly muttered before sitting down and busying herself arranging the ruffles of her gown.

Phee's queasiness returned with a vengeance. She took a warming sip the moment a maid handed her a steaming cup of mint tea.

"Dunstan, thank goodness you've returned safely from your adventures." The baron's entrance warranted Lady Pembry's effort to rise from the settee, despite the low-throated protest of her poodles. "I fretted the entire time you were gone."

"He was only in New York, Mama. Not the Serengeti." Milly injected the words so softly, Phee doubted anyone else heard.

"No need to fret, Lady Pembry. As you see, I've returned hale and hardy." The newly arrived traveler gripped the lapels of his jacket, puffed out his chest, and offered a self-satisfied grin that seemed to encompass each guest.

Lord Dunstan never failed to draw attention when he entered a room. Not because he possessed Kit's height or striking features but due to his wealth and title. He carried himself with an arrogant swagger, and while others deemed him attractive, his sandy hair, cold gray eyes, and symmetrical features had never appealed to Phee. Too many childhood memories of his cruel, high-handed treatment prevented her feeling more than what politeness demanded.

His trip to America had been a reprieve for her. Now he would expect her answer.

But seeing him again sparked only nervous agitation in her belly. No eagerness, not a sliver of affection or desire.

What if she refused him?

Falling out with influential aristocrats like the baron could mean the end of her tutoring services in the village. Briar Heath residents looked to their wealthiest landowners as touchstones. The Pembrys and Dunstans—and *The Ruthven Rules*, of course—had been dictating proper behavior for decades.

While the baron greeted those in attendance, two more guests arrived. The vicar joined his wife on the sofa, and Mrs. Hollingsworth, a longstanding and esteemed judge of the best-bloom competition, took a buttery damask chair next to the countess.

"How did Mr. Ruthven torment you?" Milly leaned close, but she spoke too loudly for her query to go unnoticed.

"Have you been troubled during my absence, Miss Marsden?" Lord Dunstan took a seat to Ophelia's right.

"Merely a figure of speech," Milly snapped. "I assure you Miss Marsden is no defenseless young maiden in need of saving."

Phee winced at the ire in her friend's tone. Milly and Lord Dunstan had a tendency to snipe rather than converse.

"Well, it's a comfort to know if she's ever in any danger, Lady Millicent, you can slay the enemy with your rapier-sharp tongue."

Observing the glare Milly and Dunstan exchanged, Phee mused again about the rancor between them. Milly acknowledged she did not like the man, though their families had known each other, intermarrying and making alliances, for centuries.

"Was it a fruitful journey, Lord Dunstan?" Phee considered his trip to America a safe topic, especially since the man enjoyed nothing so much as discussing his travels to acquire new objects to expand his collections. His eclectic taste led him to collect both antiquities and newfangled gadgets.

"Very fruitful, indeed." He leaned in close. "I've brought back a mechanism the likes of which England has never seen. All shall be revealed at Lady Pembry's fair, though I fear it will put the blooms and pies to shame."

Milly clenched her jaw and shot up from her chair, causing Lord Dunstan and Vicar Bickham to stand too. "Goodness, I just remembered. Would you join me in the conservatory, Ophelia? I left a book you loaned me there and must return it." She cast Phee an impatient look and jerked her chin in the direction of the conservatory before bolting toward the door.

Phee hurried after Milly, pretending not to see the countess's displeased glance. She found her near a wrought-iron bench in the glass-walled room, pacing in circles around a towering potted palm.

"Are you all right?" Phee counted on Milly's even temper, aside from occasional clashes with Lord Dunstan. When writing *Miss Gilroy's Guidelines*, she'd often considered Milly as a model of sensible female behavior.

"Yes, of course. Dunstan is beastly and completely self-absorbed, but that's to be expected. It was too much to hope that one transatlantic journey would transform the man." After perching on the bench, Milly patted the space beside her. "Forget about him. Come and tell me what happened when Christopher Ruthven visited you."

"Not my finest hour." Crumpling onto the bench, Phee let out a bone-deep sigh.

"That bad?"

"Worse than you can imagine."

"Nonsense." Milly patted Phee's arm. "I have a vivid imagination. Nothing could be as bad as what I'm thinking."

They both chuckled.

"I froze the minute I saw his face, Milly. All of it came back." Those honey-dark eyes were in her mind as if he stood before her again, staring down with that rakish grin tipping his broad mouth.

"You didn't swoon, did you?"

"No! Never." Almost.

"Then fear not. You were much more poised than memory allows. I'm sure of it. We always judge our own foibles harshly." Milly spoke with the certainty of a friend who assumed the best of those she loved. "Who could blame you for a lingering tenderness toward the man?"

"Not tenderness." Phee bit her lip as she remembered their exchange. "I was cross with myself for feeling anything. Irritated with him for looking so well. Pettiness. Anger. That's all I could manage for an old friend who's come back to mourn his father."

For a long moment, they sat side by side without speaking, breathing in the scents of greenery, damp earth, and the sweet aroma of hothouse roses.

"Well, he did leave abruptly all those years ago," Milly insisted. "He behaved abominably. He broke your heart. Didn't he? And he never bothered with a single visit."

"He left four years ago. I should have been prepared to see him again."

"Perhaps." Even Milly couldn't defend her on that point. "But he did look well when you saw him?"

"Better than well," Phee admitted. "Devastatingly handsome."

"So you *were* a bit pleased to see him?" Milly grinned and nudged her arm.

Phee bristled. Protest perched on the tip of her tongue. Then she closed her eyes and let out a shaky sigh. This was Milly. They told each other the truth. "I was never more relieved to see anyone in my life."

Milly scooted away, swiveled on the bench, and assessed Phee. "That sounds a good deal like affection."

"Irrelevant." Foolhardy too. Kit wasn't a man she could ever trust with her heart again. "He'll return to London soon." And she would return to tutoring, writing, and attempting to hold her household together for Juliet's sake.

Phee straightened her back, sitting up tall. "Next time I shall be better prepared."

"Certainly, my dear." Milly tapped her lip thoughtfully. "But a lady shouldn't throw away a perfectly good opportunity."

Count on Milly to offer sensible advice.

"You're right." Phee nodded with fresh resolve. "I should use Kit's visit to put bygones aside and look to the future." The words *sounded* magnificent. Now it was simply a matter of living up to them.

Milly slanted her an amused grin. "I meant the opportunity to be certain."

When Phee returned a quizzical look, Milly slid closer and asked quietly, "Why have you yet to give Dunstan an answer?"

Phee swallowed against a sudden knot in her throat and fiddled with the buttons of her high-necked gown. "Promising one's life to another is a difficult decision." She forced her hands into her lap, then noticed an ink stain on her middle finger and rubbed at it nervously.

Despite her open disdain for Dunstan, Milly rarely attempted to sway Phee's choice.

"Agreed, but would you wrestle so if Mr. Ruthven proposed?"

"Yes, of course." Dunstan might be unappealing, but Kit was unreliable. She needed stability. A house that didn't leak would be a fine start.

Milly stood and ran her finger along the blade of a potted palm. "Do you remember George Biddlethwaite?"

Grateful for the change of topic, Phee nodded eagerly. "The soldier. A friend of your brother's, wasn't he?" She recalled a lanky man with thick brown hair and kind eyes who'd been absent from the village for years.

"He never proposed." Milly turned back. "But when we kissed, I knew he was the only man I'd ever considered marrying."

"You favored him?" Phee couldn't recall Milly mentioning Biddlethwaite with any particular interest. Or any other man, for that matter. "Why didn't he propose?"

"A tale for another time." Milly settled on the bench again. Pink stained her cheeks to match the shade of her gown. "I only urge you to be sure of your feelings for Mr. Ruthven before making a decision you cannot alter."

A momentary silence followed Milly's gently spoken plea.

"If you're advising me to kiss Kit, I count it the single worst piece of advice you've ever given." Phee managed a nervous laugh, but her breath hitched at the thought. Her skin heated as if she'd stood too long in the sun.

"I admit to knowing little about matters of the heart." Milly abandoned their shared bench and approached a petite writing desk in the corner of the conservatory. After lifting a copy of *Miss Gilroy's Guidelines for Young Ladies* from the blotter, she hugged the volume to her chest. "But I wonder what Miss Gilroy would advise." She emphasized her jest with a wink.

Beyond her editor and Mr. Wellbeck, Lady Millicent was only other person who knew Miss Gilroy's true identity.

"She would advise me to choose wisely." Prudence. Practical decisions. Miss Gilroy's recommendations were clear, but if writing a book of advice had taught Phee anything, it was that offering guidance to others was much easier than avoiding pitfalls herself.

"Ah, wisdom," Milly mused. "My father used to say the only path to wisdom is to learn from our blunders."

Phee couldn't afford another blunder like allowing Kit Ruthven to shatter her heart. She wished she knew what counsel her own father would have given.

"You never told me about your visit to London." Milly's voice lifted to a cheery lilt with the change of topic. "I trust your publisher had encouraging news."

"Not entirely." Phew pinched the skin between her brows. A visit to the London offices of Ruthven Publishing loomed in the coming week. She didn't relish the prospect, though knowing Kit would be busy in Briar Heath gave her a bit of ease. "I must return to London."

"Your book is certainly drawing attention. Have you seen the letters published in the *Ladies' Journal?* Quite a stirring debate."

"I'm not going to kiss him." Phew vaguely heard mention of a newspaper and controversy regarding her book, but all her thoughts remained stuck on Kit. "I *will* find the strength to be unaffected the next time I see him."

"Wonderful." After depositing *Guidelines* on her desk, Milly approached, hooked her arm through Phee's, and led her back toward the drawing room. "You'll soon have a chance to put your resolve to the test."

"Will I?"

"Mmm, I'm afraid so. Mama has invited him for luncheon."

CHAPTER SEVEN

Asking Ophelia if she still cared for him had been unfair.
Barking at the solicitor because he could provide no details
about the recent financial transactions of Ruthven Publishing
had been rude. But agreeing to attend the countess's autumn
fete committee had been Kit's worst decision of all. And that
was saying something, considering that he'd behaved like a
complete dunderhead for most of the morning.

Now he was paying penance and experiencing a new
emotion. One he'd never imagined feeling. Empathy. For his
father.

Had the man truly endured day after day of fussy lun-
cheons and society chitchat? No wonder he'd been in a per-
petually foul mood.

Village leaders seemed to recall his father as an expert
on reason and decency. Kit wondered what the very proper
citizens of Briar Heath would think of the Gaiety Girl photo
hidden in his father's desk.

He craned his neck for a glimpse of Ophelia. Despite sunlight pouring through tall windows and gems glittering at the

necks, wrists, and fingers of Lady Pembry and her daughter, he considered Phee the only bright spot in the room.

Unfortunately, she'd claimed a chair at the other end of the table.

She spared him a single glance. Not a pleased-to-see-you look by any stretch but not an outright glare. Just a single tepid gaze, long enough for Kit to notice how the morning light brightened the blue of her eyes. Then she quickly turned away and tucked into her soup.

"What will you do now?" the vicar's wife asked in a treacle-sweet voice. The woman meant well, but she possessed an oddly fixed smile. Not to mention a knack for posing a question at the precise moment he'd taken a mouthful of vichyssoise. "Your father was such a clever man. He always knew just what to do."

"You will judge at the fete, won't you, Mr. Ruthven?" Lady Pembry cut in. She had a tendency to direct a fingery wave toward whomever she spoke, just in case they were too foolish to realize how conversations worked. "Your father could be relied upon to do so. Every year." She nodded solemnly, her lace collar snagging on the diamond choker at her throat.

"Will you take on Ruthven Publishing yourself and leave your other *pursuits* behind?" Vicar Bickham's grimace left no doubt as to his views on theater and Kit's departure from Briar Heath to become a playwright. The man had always been a gloomy, judgmental counterpoint to his wife's blithe personality.

Tugging at the tight noose of his necktie, Kit gritted his teeth before replying to the barrage of questions.

"There are many decisions to be made, Mrs. Bickham." He matched the lady's beaming smile before turning to the countess. "I fear I'm no expert when it comes to judging tarts and pies, my lady." Finally, he schooled his features into a serious mien for the vicar. "Selling my father's business seems the best course, but this delightful luncheon is the last place to discuss business concerns."

A hush fell over the table. Guests held their spoons aloft, stopping their jaws midswallow. A gurgling sound emerged from Lady Pembry as her eyes bulged and a flush stained her face. The vicar's eyebrows merged like bushy thunderclouds in the center of his forehead. Mrs. Raybourn sniffed scornfully while Mrs. Hollingsworth flailed herself with a lace handkerchief.

Even Ophelia stared wide-eyed at Kit.

"You cannot be serious, young man." The vicar's voice reeked of disdain and disappointment. Kit recognized the tone. It was the same his father had favored. "Ruthven devoted his life to the success of that enterprise. *The Ruthven Rules* has become a vital thread in the fabric of English life."

Kit quirked a grin. "I take it you were a devotee, Vicar."

"We all were." Poor Mrs. Hollingsworth sounded as if she might burst into tears.

Gripping the edge of the table, Kit took a steadying breath and fought the urge to bolt. He was an actor, dammit, at least when he needed to be. Playing the role of country gentleman for a few weeks was not beyond his abilities. Especially when an opportunity at the success he craved waited on the other side.

"We must arrange a meeting, Mr. Ruthven," Lord Dunstan, who Kit remembered as a conceited blusterer, called out from his spot next to Ophelia.

"Must we, Dunstan?" Kit was no more inclined to be bullied by the man now than he had been as a boy.

"I'm intrigued by your desire to sell. My father invested in Ruthven Publishing when it was no more than a single printing press in a dank London office. No Dunstan would wish to see the business fall into a stranger's hands."

The few bites of creamed soup soured in Kit's gut. He wanted nothing as much as a quick sale and to be done with Ruthven Publishing forever, but the thought of Dunstan lording ownership of the business over him and his sisters for the rest of their days turned his stomach.

"Your father would be so disappointed." If not for the stunned quiet still lingering in the room, none might have heard the vicar's wife's lament.

But Kit heard her. "I've no doubt you're correct, Mrs. Bickham. Disappointing my father is the one endeavor at which I've always excelled."

"Shall we discuss the harvest festival?" Ophelia's voice, soft and resonant, filled his body with a rush of warmth, soothing the irritation that had built from the moment he walked into Lady Pembry's drawing room.

"Yes, let us turn our conversation to the matter at hand." Lady Millicent lifted her spoon and clinked it against a crystal goblet. "I hereby call the annual harvest festival planning committee to order." She cast a scathing glance at Lord Dunstan. "All other matters shall be tabled and discussed at a more appropriate time."

Lady Millicent's intervention initially seemed a kindness, but two hours later the servants had cleared plates away, and they'd exhausted every possible aspect of organizing a village fete, from bunting to schedules to revising the rules for judging every plant and crafted item. Kit would have gladly handed Dunstan the keys to Ruthven Publishing for a pittance just to make it stop.

"Did you get all of that, Miss Marsden?" Lady Pembry waved at Phee, who nodded but kept her eyes down, still finishing off the notes she'd taken. Apparently she'd been designated as the gathering's scribe.

"Shall we adjourn?" Lady Millicent sounded as hopeful for an end to the discussion as Kit was.

"Yes," Dunstan replied, as if the question had been directed at him alone. "Having just returned from America, I have much to attend to at home."

"Then it's decided." Lady Millicent stood and clasped her hands together, slanting a glance at the baron. "Lord Dunstan is a busy man, so we will disperse."

After extracting himself from the countess's too-dainty chair, Kit beelined toward the door. Then he saw Ophelia and changed direction. She'd rushed off after his foolish question in his father's study. He didn't expect an answer, but he still craved a truce between them.

"How did I do?"

"Wonderfully." She yanked on one glove and cast him a skimming glance—somewhere in the region of his chin—before fumbling with the buttons at her wrist. "Assuming your goal was to shock or offend every person in the room."

"Come now. You must allow that I succeeded with Mrs. Bickham." He stepped closer to speak quietly. Their proximity afforded him a whiff of Phee's floral scent. "The lady smiled the whole afternoon."

His tease earned a sharp look, but at least it allowed him to gaze into her eyes.

"Mrs. B. always smiles," Phee insisted. "Don't you remember? You used to call her Beaming Bickham. Or have you forgotten?"

He hadn't, but he'd almost forgotten how much he loved Phee's auburn brows knitting together when he made her cross.

"Why come if you didn't intend to participate in the festival?"

"Because I was invited." And because he needed a reprieve from the memories haunting Ruthven Hall. After she'd left his father's study, he hadn't managed another useful thought all morning. "A visit to Lady Pembry seemed a bearable reintroduction to Briar Heath society."

"Well, if you can *bear* it, we do need assistance for the fete." She'd finally buttoned one glove and set to work on the other, tugging aggressively at the fabric until it tightened against her slim fingers. "The event expands every year."

"Then I'll help."

"You will?" Eyes wide, mouth agape, she seemed stunned to discover he possessed an ounce of generosity. Never mind that he'd regretted volunteering the moment the words were out. "Thank you."

But how could he regret the softening in her gaze or the breathy quality of her voice?

"Miss Marsden." Dunstan's unpleasant bark cut in as he approached to hover near Ophelia. "I'll escort you home."

"No, thank you, my lord." She moved toward the Pembry's entry hall. Lord Dunstan followed close behind.

"You needn't worry about inconveniencing me," the man insisted. "Longacre is on my way."

Kit's body tensed, fists balled at his sides. He hadn't struck a man in years, merely thrown a few false punches on stage, but Dunstan had him itching to land a clean blow. For years of tormenting both of them, lauding his title and wealth over all the less fortunate in the village, the aristocrat's comeuppance was long overdue.

"Walking is my preferred mode of transport, and I'm quite used to solitude." Phee pressed her lips together, a sure sign her decision was made, and nothing could dissuade her.

"Madness. A lady should not walk the woods alone." Clearly, the pompous lordling was too used to getting his way. "I'll dismiss my carriage and accompany you on foot."

"Dunstan." Kit took two long strides and wedged himself between the baron and Ophelia, blocking her from the man's view. "You wished to discuss the future of Ruthven Publishing. I can spare you a moment now."

"Another time, Ruthven." When Dunstan scowled, his moustache twitched above his lip like an angry caterpillar. "You're interrupting." Shorter than Kit, the baron straightened his back and stretched his neck as they stood face-to-face to compensate for the lack of inches between them.

"And you ignored Miss Marsden's refusal."

Ophelia scuttled toward the door. She paused only long enough to call over her shoulder, "I'll leave you to your bickering, gentlemen."

The baron jerked forward to follow her, but Kit stuck out an arm, blocking the aristocrat's way. "She does not require an escort. As she said. Repeatedly."

"Are you an expert on Miss Marsden's needs, Ruthven? You've been away so long. I'm surprised you remember her at all." The blue blood smirked, rolling back on his heels so that his chest protruded. Short he might be, but the years hadn't shaved an inch off the man's insufferable arrogance. "Why concern yourself with her now? Soon you'll sell your father's business and return to your bawdy theater."

Blood thrashed in Kit's ears, his heart rattling so fiercely he felt his pulse jitter through his body. He hadn't imagined himself capable of the self-control he summoned to resist attacking Dunstan in the middle of Lady Pembry's hallway. Theater life had blunted the rage his old childhood nemesis drew to the surface with a few snide words. Kit wrote of anger, even played it out on stage, but most often he stuffed it away. Raw, visceral, vibrating anger reminded him of one man, and he had no desire to emulate his father.

"Unless you've come home to get yourself a wife," Dunstan taunted.

At that moment, Kit felt certain he'd come to Briar Heath to give a certain blue blood a black eye and bloody nose.

"In here, Dunstan." Kit indicated the entrance to Lady Pembry's nearby conservatory with the tip of his head. Light poured from glass panels, filtering through leaves and the blooms of hundreds of plants. It seemed an odd setting for a round of fisticuffs, but Kit's blood was up, and he was ready to oblige, if that was the aristocrat's desire.

"Have you decided on a price for the whole concern?" Dunstan busied himself with straightening his cuffs, as if the answer did not concern him overmuch. "I understand there's a London office, and your father owned several presses."

"What do you want with her?" Kit rasped the question, his throat burning as if he'd already shouted all the epithets his playwright's mind was fashioning for the aristocrat.

"Miss Marsden?" The frown between Dunstan's brows indicated genuine confusion. The ridiculous man had no idea how close he was to being throttled. "She's spirited, quite pleasing to look at, intelligent, and practical. She possesses sufficient decorum to teach it to others, so I assume she'd make a fine baroness."

"You want to marry her." The realization didn't stun Kit, though it chilled him to the bone. He'd had his chance with Phee and lost. How could he blame any man for wooing her? Still, he loathed the notion of a peacock like Dunstan calling her his own.

"I asked. She has yet to give me her answer." They were the first words out of Dunstan's mouth that pleased Kit, and he worked hard to smother the grin twitching to break free.

The blue blood glared at him, bracing his arms across his chest. "I have reason to believe she'll accept."

"Why Ophelia?" Kit knew her worth, every quality that made her extraordinary, but Dunstan had been as cruel to her in childhood as he'd been to Kit. "There are other eligible young ladies in Briar Heath." Kit pointed in the direction of the drawing room. "Like a countess's unmarried daughter."

"Lady Millicent?" Dunstan sneered. "I seek a biddable wife, not a termagant. Lady Millicent has wealth enough to avoid marriage. The same cannot be said for Miss Marsden."

If the blue blood thought Phee was biddable, he didn't know her at all.

"Marry a woman because she has no other choice? Seems a hollow victory, Dunstan."

"I own half her land. Why not the rest?" The baron turned to look through the conservatory's glass walls. "Dunstan land stretches west of this estate as far as the eye can see. Go back in village history far enough, and you'll find Longacre belonged to my family, not hers."

The man had always been an insufferable prig, but now Kit realized he was also a fool. No one who cared for Phee could imagine her as a secondary prize to the acquisition of land. And he did care. Still. Far too much.

"You approached me to discuss your father's business, Ruthven. Name your price and tell me your man of business. I'll make inquiries and consider the purchase. Land provides a paltry income these days. Clever gentlemen recognize the need to choose diverse investments."

Kit ignored the implication that he was no gentleman and stared at the aristocrat's smug smirk, imagining different choices he could have made.

What if he'd stayed and taken over the publishing business as his father insisted? What if he'd offered Phee the life she deserved, a stable future with wealth enough to provide for all their needs?

"You're having second thoughts about selling?"

Apparently he wasn't a very good actor. "I meet with our London manager next week. I'll know more then."

"Very well. Come to Dunstan Park when you return." The baron offered the slightest of nods, all a commoner like Kit merited for leave-taking. "Good day, Ruthven."

A deep sigh fought its way up Kit's chest. Just before he exhaled, Dunstan turned back.

"Yes, do come to the house, Ruthven. You *did* know Miss Marsden once. Perhaps you can give me a bit of insight into how best to woo the lady."

Kit rallied all he knew about acting to summon a blank expression. Dunstan nodded again. Kit nodded too, only to get the man to leave.

Two words rang in his head, echoing through every fiber of his being. *Hell, no.*

CHAPTER EIGHT

---

*"Once you've reasoned through arguments,
consulted your common sense, and come to a
decision, trust in your own judgement, ladies."*
—MISS GILROY'S GUIDELINES FOR YOUNG LADIES

The morning after Lady Pembry's committee meeting, Phee headed out of doors for an early walk to sort her thoughts. At one point she veered toward Lord Dunstan's estate, stopped, turned back, retraced her path for several steps, and then pivoted to pace in the direction of his home once again.

Leaving matters unfinished wasn't her way. She hated loose threads, unchecked items on lists, and unanswered questions. Now that Dunstan was back in Briar Heath, she could no longer put off responding to his proposal.

Never mind who else had returned to the village. Kit had no part to play in her future.

There was just one rather important problem with approaching Lord Dunstan.

She hadn't decided. Or rather, she had and then changed her mind. She'd never been so muddled when making a decision in her life.

Lowering her gaze as she walked, Phee rolled her shoulders and tipped her head from side to side to ease the tension in her neck. Unfortunately, she had no cure for the tangle of unease in her chest.

She pulled a piece of folded foolscap from her skirt pocket. Two columns laid out the reasons for and arguments against accepting Dunstan's proposal. The list of reasons to marry was considerably longer than the other.

Phee shoved the list away. She wasn't even convinced by her own arguments.

Birdsong and the sound of water bubbling over rocks drew her to a side path running near Dunstan's stream. She'd loved the spot since childhood and spent many days in or near the water.

"Thinking of wading in?"

Phee inhaled sharply and jerked her gaze upward, following the sound of Kit's voice. He sat on the thick branch of an old tree, one long leg dangling, one booted foot braced against the oak's massive trunk.

"No, but that tree is ancient, so you're likely to fall in."

He chuckled until his laughter bloomed into a grin. "I suspect the only danger of injury would be if you decide to start skipping rocks."

"Nonsense. I'm quite proficient."

Kit lowered both legs and jumped from the oak tree, thudding to the ground in front of Phee.

"I beg to differ." He lifted a glossy black wave of hair from his forehead. "And I have the scar to prove it."

Phee longed to touch the spot where a fine line, only slightly darker than the rest of Kit's skin, slid into his hairline. He bent at the waist to give her a better view, tempting her to reach for him. He was so close. Near enough for her to press her fingertips to his skin.

She resisted.

"An accident on my first attempt." Despite her flippant reply, she remembered everything about the day he'd received the injury. Kit had been determined to teach her to skip rocks across the widest part of the stream. In her eagerness to impress him, she'd fumbled and let the smooth, heavy stone slip from her fingers too soon. "Perhaps your technique was to blame," she teased.

"Careful, Phee." He leaned an inch closer. Until she could see the threads of gold twined through the brown of his eyes. Feel his breath against her skin. "Men are quite sensitive about their technique." After arching one brow in challenge, he stared at her mouth, gazing so intently Phee thought he might claim her lips. "But I'm quite confident of mine."

Somehow they'd strayed from a discussion of rocks and streams.

In a frantic attempt to steer them back, Phee whispered, "*My* technique has improved since you've been gone."

Kit straightened to his full height, and Phee noted the rapid rise and fall of his chest. Her own breath was coming fast too, and she turned away from him.

"I should make my way back to Longacre." She had duties at home, and tutees due to arrive for lessons. Enough time had been squandered this morning.

"Show me."

Phee turned to find Kit squatting by the waterside, scanning the bank for prime skipping stones. She tried not to gape at the way his black trousers outlined his muscular thighs and firm backside. He collected as she watched, depositing two rocks in his waistcoat pocket and holding a third out to her.

"Come and display your prowess, Miss Marsden." He punctuated the words with a smile, dimples on each side of his mouth forming deep parentheses in his cheeks.

After casting a glance in the direction of Longacre, Phee reasoned that a single throw wouldn't take more than a moment. She stepped toward Kit and thrust out her hand. "Just once."

He stood and shot her a triumphant grin, dropping the rock into her palm. "If you're that good, one try is all you'll need."

Phee rubbed her fingers across the cool flat surface, recalling all his lessons and the times she'd come to this spot alone, tossing pebbles across the water to clear her thoughts.

Of course, a large, distracting, pine-scented man hadn't been hovering at her back during those visits.

"You mustn't stand so close," she grumbled over her shoulder. "I wouldn't wish to give you another scar."

In her periphery, she saw Kit lift both hands in the air and retreat several steps.

When she took a deep breath to steady her aim, Phee noticed something in her chest had loosened. The knotted ache she'd felt all morning had begun to ease.

Circling her thumb and forefinger around the outer edge of the stone, she pivoted left, then flung her arm out in front of her, releasing the rock parallel to the surface of the water.

Plink. Plunge. One solid skip and the pebble sank like a millstone into the stream.

Gritting her teeth, Phee glanced back to find Kit standing with arms crossed, one hand clamped over his mouth.

"Hmm," he mused, lowering his hands to his hips. "Want another go?"

"No," Phee ground out. "I don't have time for foolishness. As I said, I was just on my way home."

"Just once more?" Kit extracted a stone from his pocket and flipped it in his fingers.

Phee lifted her arm stiffly, hand open. Kit didn't drop the stone this time. He approached quickly—too quick for her to pull back—cupped her hand in his much larger palm, and curled her fingers around the little projectile.

Jerking away, Phee unfastened the buttons on the cuff of her throwing wrist, then swung her arm back and forth to ease the snug fit of her gown.

"Would you like assistance with your technique?" Kit queried in a playful tone.

"No," Phee growled.

"Carry on, then."

This time Phee took more care. Gripped the rock more gently, flicked her wrist more artfully, executed her toss on a long exhale. One plop, then another, and the bit of mineral sank along with any hope of besting Kit at skipping stones.

"You win," Phee conceded on a sigh, gazing out to where the stream's surface barely rippled. "I'm dreadful at this."

"Nonsense." Kit spoke behind her. Too close. He lowered his voice to a soothing timbre. "You just need a bit more practice."

What she needed was to leave, to forget about this silly interlude.

Then Kit touched her.

Phee jumped at the contact but didn't retreat. One hand lay heavy and warm against her waist. Kit held still, letting his heat seep under clothes. He held motionless, as if waiting for her to pull away.

"Or maybe," he whispered near her ear, "you need a reminder of technique."

Reaching around, he slid his fingers down her arm, deposited another stone in her palm, and clasped her hand far longer than necessary.

"Hold it gently," he instructed, still speaking in that low murmur that made her skin prickle with gooseflesh. "With confidence, but not too tight."

He pressed his body to hers. Phee could feel him at her back, his chest against her shoulders, his pelvis flush with her backside. He slid his hand across her belly, bracing her 'round the hips to twist her into position.

"Most important of all." His voice deepened, taking on a husky rasp that caused her toes to curl in her boots. "No matter how right the stone feels in your fingers." He curved his hand over hers. "You must be willing to let go." He spoke against her skin, his mouth skimming her cheek.

In one swift move, he eased her arm back and pushed forward. Phee let go. *Plink, plink, plink, plink.* A dozen lovely circles rippled out from each spot where the stone touched water.

She could feel the curve of Kit's grin against her face where he continued to nuzzle her cheek.

"Well done," he praised.

It was all too much. He overwhelmed her senses—his heat, his scent, his pleased tone.

When Phee stiffened in his embrace, he released her. "I must go. I have someplace I need to be." And it definitely wasn't here in his arms.

"May I walk with you?"

"No." She couldn't meet his gaze as she ran a hand over her hair to make sure her pins hadn't come loose. At every encounter, the man seemed to unravel her a bit more. "While you're visiting Briar Heath, we should keep our distance."

Kit froze as if he'd turned to stone. Feet braced, body stiff, he didn't move or speak or given any indication he'd heard her reply. Only his eyes revealed the maelstrom. Colors swirled like clouds in a storm and then darkened as he stared at her. A muscle jumped in his cheek. He clenched and unclenched his fists.

Phee knew she should go. Now. But she found herself as fixed to the spot where she stood as he seemed to be to his patch of ground.

"Why?" Despite his harsh tone, his face remained expressionless.

"Why?" she echoed, knitting her brows. Because he breached her defenses too easily. Because she enjoyed his nearness too much. "Because you've made your choices, and I must make mine."

He raised his arm as if he'd reach for her. Instead, he lifted his hand and raked it through his hair. As he started past her, Phee sidestepped to prevent his arm from brushing hers.

Kit stopped abruptly. Stepped toward her. Encircled her upper arm gently in his hand. He dipped his head until he could stare into her eyes.

He searched her face as if he'd locked something away, and she held the key. When he licked his lips, Phee's gaze snagged on a mouth she knew too well—full, sensual, tender when he wished to tease; firm when he wished to plunder.

Heaven help her, she wanted his kiss. Just one more time.

But he didn't kiss her. Not even close. He lowered his head, closed his eyes a moment, and sucked in a deep lungful of air.

Then he let her go.

"Thank you for coming, Mr. Croft." Kit settled into the miserable chair behind his father's desk as he welcomed the paper manufacturer and his wife. "And Mrs. Croft."

The lady lifted her eyes from a copy of his father's etiquette book only long enough to acknowledge his welcome.

Croft had been the first to respond to a round of notes Kit sent out to his father's associates, hoping to find a buyer for Ruthven Publishing who wasn't Lord Dunstan. Kit knew next to nothing about conducting business meetings, but Croft surprised him by arriving at Ruthven Hall with his wife. Though Mrs. C. appeared more content to listen than participate. She'd plucked a copy of *The Ruthven Rules for Young Ladies* from a shelf before taking a chair beside her husband.

"Appreciate the invitation, Mr. Ruthven," Mr. Croft said in his deep, rumbling voice. "We offer our condolences."

Kit nodded and considered all he knew about the man and his business. Sophia insisted Croft was one of Ruthven Publishing's key associates, and she'd heard their father mention Croft's interest in starting his own publishing business. If it was true, Kit hoped to make the man an offer he couldn't refuse.

"Oh," Mrs. Croft interjected, keeping her eyes glued to the pages of his father's book. Her silver brows furrowed as she continued to read. "Ridiculous."

"Have you found an exciting bit?" Kit teased.

Mrs. Croft cast him an unamused glance. Kit couldn't blame her. His father's books made him grumpy too.

"Let me not parse words or waste your time," he began. Drawing in a breath to voice his proposal, Kit caught scents wafting up from his clothes. Jasmine and fresh air and the water of Dunstan's stream.

He swallowed hard. His thoughts scattered. Scattered and reassembled in the shape of Ophelia.

He wanted to be back on that stream bank, holding her body against his, not sitting behind a desk.

Disturbing questions besieged him. Had her skin always been so soft? Had she always fit so perfectly in his arms?

A drumbeat began thudding in his head.

Had she walked away after he'd let her go and given Dunstan the answer he craved?

"Mr. Ruthven?" Croft cleared his throat, ending on a hum like the low note of a tuba.

"Would you like to buy my father's business, Mr. Croft?" Kit wanted the burden gone. Needed to shake off the memories and lures of Briar Heath and return to London. Preferably before he had to stomach the news of Ophelia's engagement.

Croft and his wife convened a discussion, both frowning as they leaned together and whispered in each other's ears.

"Forgive me, Mr. Ruthven, but we assumed we'd been invited here to settle accounts."

"Settle accounts? By all means." If the man was willing to buy his father's business, Kit would throw in a jig for free.

Mrs. Croft laid his father's book on her lap and bent to retrieve an item from her travel satchel. "All the details are there, sir."

The document listed amounts owed, sums that had gone unpaid for months, judging by the dates.

"Your father was ill," Mrs. Croft said softly. "The arrearage is understandable, but we rather hoped you'd square the matter now."

Kit had yet to see the balances of Ruthven Publishing's accounts. Sophia's assistance with their father's correspondence offered no insight into the ledger books. Kit hoped to learn more when he visited the London office. Whatever the balance, repaying the Crofts would make a sizable dent. They'd been more than generous to allow his father to carry such a debt.

Another thought struck, and he gripped the sheet of paper until his knuckles cracked. What if there were other such documents, other bills unpaid?

"I'll see that this taken care of." He would make it his first priority when he met with Ruthven's office manager.

The couple exchanged a glance, then nodded at Kit in unison, apparently satisfied.

"You're determined to sell the concern, then?" Mr. Croft leaned forward. Was that a glint of interest in the older man's eyes?

"Immediately." Kit tamped down his eagerness and cast Croft a rueful grin. "After all accounts are settled, nothing will alter my intention to sell."

Mrs. Croft edged forward in her chair and laid *The Ruthven Rules for Young Ladies* on the desk. "Forgive me saying so, Mr. Ruthven, but that book is ghastly."

Kit chuckled and crossed his hands over the volume. "I cannot disagree."

"Have you read it?" The lady narrowed an eye at him. Her interrogation style reminded him of Sophia's.

"I admit I have not." He'd been forced to read the original *Ruthven Rules* that spawned all the others but never the additional volumes for ladies, young men, brides, and every other group his father thought required rules. One book full of his father's strictures was enough to last him a lifetime.

Mrs. Croft pointed a finger at the offending volume. "Ladies must not engage in commerce, according to this book. I suppose women are too delicate, too weak, to manage more than the household menu."

"I didn't write the book," Kit protested. God forbid anyone think him a champion of his father's outdated notions.

"His father wrote them, Nessa," Mr. Croft pleaded with his wife on Kit's behalf.

The lady scrutinized, gazing at Kit without blinking. Finally, her mouth twitched into a toothy smile. "Fair enough, Mr. Ruthven, but might I offer a spot of advice?"

"Please." Any business advice was welcome, though he hoped to have no need for it much longer.

Croft looked on indulgently as his wife bent to dig in her satchel once again. When she sat up, the lady offered Kit a slim cloth-bound book.

"You might consider something more like this," she suggested.

"Another etiquette book?" The drum is his head beat with renewed fervor.

"Oh no, sir. Much more. My ladies' book club has chosen Miss Gilroy's guide this month, and it is causing quite a stir in the London papers. The notions are modern but sensible. All Englishwomen know what they mustn't do. Etiquette has been drilled in for generations. Why not a book that inspires young ladies rather than restricts them?"

Mrs. Croft spoke so passionately, her cheeks flamed with color and little sparks flared in her eyes. Even her husband looked taken aback.

Caught up in the lady's oration, Kit hadn't glanced down at the book she fervently recommended. When he did, he found the title familiar. *Miss Gilroy's Guidelines for Young Ladies.* The same volume he'd seen at Phee's.

"May I borrow this?" Suddenly he was curious what all the fuss was about.

Mrs. Croft bit her lower lip. "I wouldn't wish to part with my only copy, sir."

"I'll buy you another, Nessa," Mr. Croft reassured, "as soon as we're back in London."

"Very well." Even as she bobbed her head in agreement, the lady kept her gaze fixed on Miss Gilroy's book. "Does this mean you'd consider publishing something new and keeping your father's business?"

"No." Bills, suppliers, correspondence, ledger books—the sheer humdrum monotony of business nonsense made Kit shiver. But Mrs. Croft's question reminded him how he *should* be spending his time. Namely, working on a play for Fleet and selling Ruthven Publishing. "But if you and Mr. Croft bought the concern, you could publish whatever you liked."

The older man tugged thoughtfully at his beard. "Perhaps we can meet again once you've seen to the company's finances."

Mrs. Croft let out a little huff of protest, but she was gracious as they took their leave, even if she did cast one last longing glance back at Miss Gilroy's book.

Kit considered offering her one of his father's books to read on their train journey back to London, but the lady had done nothing to deserve that sort of torture.

He flipped *Miss Gilroy's Guidelines* in his hand after the Crofts departed. Whoever bought Ruthven's, would they publish anything people relished, rather than churning out tomes like his father's? *The Ruthven Rules* was the sort of book everyone was expected to own, but no one cared to read.

He shook his head. *Not my concern.*

Returning to his father's desk, he searched out a sheet of foolscap and began noting ideas for his play. Notions about characters and conflict fought through the thumping at his temples and the faint scent of flowers still clinging to his skin. His pen strayed to the paper's margin, and he found himself scribbling Phee's name.

Was she truly going to give herself to that blustering fool Dunstan?

Why did he bloody care?

I'm the fool. But he was right on one count. He'd been wise to keep away from Briar Heath. Absence had allowed him to forget the velvet softness of her skin; kept him ignorant about an odious aristocrat's proposal.

He glanced out the window and snorted in disgust.

Rolling green fields. Orderly hedgerows. A few fluffy sheep in a field across the way. Briar Heath looked so damned bucolic. Yet no place in England was so dangerous to his peace of mind.

CHAPTER NINE

TWO days after her confrontation with Kit at the stream, Phee stood on the Ruthven's doorstep. She patted the simple knot at the back of her head, tugged down her bodice, and smoothed the fabric of her skirt. One deep breath, two hard swallows, and she raised a hand to lift the door knocker. And held it aloft, biting her lip.

She was in no position to turn down an opportunity to earn tuition fees, but Sophia's note asking Phee to resume Clarissa's art lessons seemed a mixed blessing. Phee assumed the tutoring sessions would be postponed during the mourning period. Why start up again so quickly? And why here? She'd never been invited to tutor the girl at the Ruthven home. The prospect seemed sufficiently unappealing when Leopold Ruthven ruled his household like a tyrant, but now Kit lurked somewhere behind the house's tall oak doors.

The minute she dropped the brass lion's head knocker, she braced herself for another sight of him.

When would he return to London? Forgetting the man had been difficult when he was twenty miles away. Now, when she might encounter him around every corner—

"Are you here to see Mr. Ruthven, miss?" A housemaid interrupted her woolgathering.

"No." Definitely not. "Miss Sophia Ruthven, please."

"Right this way, miss." The mobcapped girl led her into the same drawing room where she'd met Sophia days before to offer condolences.

Phee took a chair by the window and looked out onto the leaf-strewn field beyond, trying not to think about where Kit might be in the large rambling house. Trying not to imagine she could smell his spice and forest scent in the air. She began tapping her heel against the carpet, then pressed a hand to her knee to force herself to stop.

"You came!" Clarissa rushed into the parlor, setting glass knickknacks rattling, and flounced onto the settee. "I'm so relieved. The house is nefariously quiet."

Phee pressed her lips together to stave off a grin. Clarissa's fondness for adverbs was almost as charming as the girl's tendency to add decorative flourishes to everything—her clothing, her artwork, even her sentences. Today she'd fashioned crepe paper violets and pinned them to the neckline of her black mourning dress. One had been stuffed into a blonde curl over her ear too.

"All my paints and brushes are upstairs in the nursery. Shall we go?"

As soon as Phee nodded, Clarissa took her by the hand and led her toward the house's main staircase.

"You might think a nursery sounds egregiously childish." Kit's sister turned back as she ascended the stairs. "But I assure you I've decorated it liberally with my paintings. Especially the ones you praised, Miss Marsden."

The young lady hadn't lied. The nursery, a room on the house's top floor, featured a vaulted ceiling festooned with papier-mâché birds and a garland she'd fashioned from buttons, bits of ribbon, and scraps of lace, stringing the whole from one gaslight sconce to the next around the room. Her art covered most of the simple striped wallpaper, as colorful and vibrant as Clarissa's personality.

"You were going to teach me how to draw hands next. It will prove exorbitantly helpful when I finish the piece I'm working on."

"What is it?" A largish canvas sat on an easel in the corner of the room, the whole of it draped in a paint-smeared cloth.

Clarissa chewed her thumbnail. "May I show you after our lesson?"

"Of course."

After taking seats at a long wooden table in the center of the room where pencils, brushes, and paints had been set out, it didn't take them long to set to work. What seemed a short time later, Phee checked her watch fob and found that nearly an hour had passed.

"We can ring for tea." Clarissa kept her blonde head bent over the table, busily shading her drawing of Phee's hand in various poses.

"I should get back home." Phee stood and placed her palms on the small of her back to stretch. Juliet had gone for her first Latin lesson with the vicar, and she wanted to hear how it had gone. No doubt her sister had asked to start by learning to pronounce the names of Latin numbers.

"I thought we'd invite my brother up first."

"Why?" Phee squeaked out the word and worked to temper the panicky flutter in her throat. An hour in the house and not a single sight of him. She'd convinced herself he might be away from home or otherwise occupied. "I'm sure that's not necessary."

"But I thought he could model for us."

Images of Kit in various modeling poses flitted through Phee's mind. Her breath caught in her throat, and she shook her head to push the notion away. "I don't think Mr. Ruthven..." Yes, call him by his father's name. Distance. That's what she needed. Unfortunately, she was standing inside the man's house.

"You could show me how to sketch a gentleman's hand," Clarissa continued. "They must be different from ladies' hands."

"Not at all. They are precisely the same." Now *she* was clinging to adverbs. "Exactly. Some gentlemen's hands might be larger than a lady's, but the basic shapes are the same. We needn't trouble your brother."

Though her excuse satisfied Clarissa, who went back to work on her drawing, Phee suddenly found it impossible to think of anything but the size and shape of Kit's hands.

She hadn't told Clarissa the entire truth. Some men's hands *were* different. Kit's weren't elegant and pale but large and broad-fingered. From the time he'd turned eighteen, growing inches taller seemingly overnight, everything about him had been fashioned on a grander scale. Kit's hands matched his long legs, broad chest, and shoulders as wide as a plank. The man was not made with the same mold as average men.

"Shall I come back on the same day next week?" To distract herself, Phee began tidying the pencils, smudging sticks, and rubber erasers they'd used during the lesson.

"Could you return tomorrow?" Clarissa set her drawing aside and leaned over the table, whispering, "Sophia says we can't go out, and I'm beginning to feel dreadfully trapped."

Phee sympathized. Mourning traditions were challenging for young ladies as spirited as Clarissa Ruthven.

"I'll return early next week. We can take a walk in the garden and start on landscape painting. Will that do?"

"Wonderfully." The girl beamed. Then her eyes bulged as her smile widened. "Kit! How did you know we wished for you to come up?"

A tickle began at the back of Phee's neck, and she felt as much as heard Kit approaching from behind as he entered the room.

"My ears were burning," he teased as he drew up next to Phee. "I didn't realize you'd come for a visit, Ophelia."

It wasn't entirely proper for him to use her first name. Neither of his sisters knew how close he and Phee had been to becoming lovers in those months before he left for London.

"Miss Ruthven invited me to come and give Clarissa her art lesson." She spared him one quick glance out of courtesy, focusing on his chin, the part of his body at her eye level. She tried not to notice that he was casually dressed, or that his shirt buttons were undone down to the hollow at the base of his throat.

"You did promise to show me your art, Clary." He pointed to the canvas on the easel. "What do you have under there?"

Clarissa sprang toward the easel, standing with her back to it as if fully prepared to defend it from marauders. "You can't see it. Either of you. Not yet."

"Fair enough." He skimmed his gaze around the room in a wide arc, pivoting on his heels, pausing to stare at Phee until the tickle at her nape spread down her back and arms and the length of her legs. Out of the corner of her eye, she caught him flashing a smile, apparently pleased with how thoroughly he unsettled her.

"Perhaps you can guide me, Miss Marsden."

"Me?"

"Show me what you've taught my sister." He shifted his gaze from the drawings and paintings lining the walls to Phee. "If you're such a good teacher, perhaps I should take some lessons."

She'd never glared at the brother of a student before, but none had ever deserved it as much as Kit Ruthven.

After taking a deep breath, Phee approached the wall at the back of the room. "We started with basic shapes." She pointed to a few of the first drawings Clarissa had produced under her tutelage. "Then moved on to still life. Objects one might find around the home."

Kit stepped toward a particular sketch and swept his finger against the paper's surface. He cast Phee a questioning glance. "Is that…?"

"It's a dinner knife. Cook let us borrow one from the kitchen for our composition."

"But the color. The red." He stared at a line of red water-color his sister had swiped across the blade of the knife. The wet pigment had run, adding a morbid subtext to the painting of a kitchen utensil.

"Yes, well." Phee turned so that Clarissa couldn't see her and whispered, "You'll note a definite theme."

"Good grief." He moved to the next series of sketches and watercolors. Several depicted items they'd found during an expedition around the village. One series Clarissa executed particularly well featured headstones in Briar Heath's church graveyard. Unfortunately, the young lady chose to add a few ghouls in the background, making sure to stream trails of red watercolor from their fingertips. As a dissonant counterpoint, each square or rectangle of watercolor paper had been decorated around the edges with hastily sketched flowers or stars or a smiling bunny.

Kit shot her a look of genuine concern.

"There's no need to worry," she whispered. "She has a colorful imagination."

"The main hue being blood red." He braced his arms across his chest and tilted his head, assessing the drawings again, and a little smirk began tipping the edges of his mouth. "A bit bloodthirsty, isn't she?"

"You didn't hear it from me," Phee replied quietly, "but I've occasionally spotted a penny dreadful in your sister's possession."

Kit cleared his throat. "You didn't hear it from me, but I sent them to her." After an indulgent glance at his sister, Kit squared his gaze on Phee. "I feared our father might do his best to snuff her spirit. Perhaps I should have been here to encourage her." The pain in his eyes made Phee's throat burn. Muscles in her arms twitched. Every instinct told her to reach for him.

"Your guilt benefits no one." She drew in a deep breath, wishing she'd spoken less harshly.

He didn't seem to take offense. In fact, he offered one of his appealing grins. "You can't scold away my regrets, Ophelia."

"Do you harbor regrets?" Phee wondered if he counted his feelings for her among his mistakes.

He laughed but with a mirthless rasping sound. "Regrets are my constant companions. They've been at my back for years. Now I must face them."

Kit looked straight at her as he spoke, studying her in a way that once made her believe he could see behind skin and bones to the thoughts in her head and the feelings in her heart. "Phee." He lifted a hand as if he'd touch her, then lowered a curled fist to his side.

"All right. If you're going to stand over there whispering about me, I'll show you," Clarissa announced from the corner of the room. She'd uncovered her painting and had taken up a tube of paint and a brush to add a few daubs of color.

Kit and Phee walked side by side toward the canvas. Clarissa stepped back to let them gaze at her creation, bouncing on her toes as she scanned their faces for reactions.

"Mercy," Kit breathed. "Definitely bloodthirsty."

"It's extraordinary," Phee added. "So full of movement." *And violence.* In the center of the ornately painted Gothic border, an angry young woman thrust a sword toward a miserable-looking young man. Judging by the fierce look on the lady's face, the gentleman didn't stand a chance. "Who does it depict?" Clarissa often chose characters from literature to appear in her recent paintings, though this piece was grander than anything she'd attempted before.

"It's Ophelia." Clarissa clasped her hands behind her back and smiled.

Kit sucked in a breath and stared at Phee, glancing down at her hands as if to ensure she hadn't tucked a sword under her skirt.

"Ophelia from the play," Clarissa added in an exaggerated tone of frustration. "Surely you know Shakespeare's play, Kit. Have you ever performed *Hamlet*?"

"I haven't, but I do know the play." He swiped one hand across his mouth and gently placed the other on his sister's slim shoulder. "Clary, sweet, Ophelia *dies* in the play."

"I do know that." Clarissa rolled her eyes and began shaking her head, setting a few golden ringlets bobbing against her neck. "But I don't think she should. She ought to be the one to uncover the plot, and Hamlet should be the villain. I like the notion of Ophelia avenging everyone."

After casting a bemused glance Phee's way, Kit fixed a smile on his face and patted his sister's shoulder. "In that case, it's splendid. What do you think, Clary? Should we invite Miss Marsden to join us for lunch?"

"No," Phee answered before they could offer. "Perhaps another time. Today I'm taking lunch with my sister."

Kit frowned, tension tightening the fullness of his lips.

"I'll be off, then." Despite declaring her intention to leave, an invisible string held Phee in place. Kit stood watching her as if he wished to speak but couldn't find the words. He swallowed hard, and she trailed her gaze down the length of his neck to that fascinating shadow at the base of his throat.

"I have work to get on with too," he said in the brusque but civil tone his sister Sophia usually employed. "Good day,

Miss Marsden." He strode out of the room, the weight of his footsteps thudding against the floorboards, without sparing her another look.

Her skin chilled. No, not her skin. Her chest, somewhere deep in the center. She longed for the cloak she'd left with the footman downstairs.

All the anger of their first encounters had gone, but it left her feeling empty. Except for regret. Every time she saw the man, she turned into a fool. Distracted by his scent and the desire to touch him. Sniping at him. Averting her eyes like a skittish miss. She had never been that.

And all of it was a facade, barriers erected to protect her heart. She was a terrible actress, apparently.

Somehow, she needed to face Kit and be unaffected. To show him, and prove to herself, that she could accept the here and now and not cling to whatever they'd been to each other in the past. He wouldn't be part of her future, but she did not wish to be his enemy.

"Are you all right, Miss Marsden? Suddenly you're a bit flushed."

"I am well, and I'll see you next week." Without letting herself think, Phee did what she hadn't allowed herself to do in many years. She gave into impulse and darted toward the stairwell.

The housemaid who'd admitted her called out in the downstairs hallway. "Can I help, miss?"

"Mr. Ruthven?"

"He's set himself up on the rear terrace. Shall I take you?"

"Just point the way, if you would."

The young lady indicated an area toward the back of the house. Phee walked quickly to keep from losing her nerve. Sunlight blinded her as she approached a set of glass-fronted French doors. She pushed through and found Kit lounging at a large wrought-iron table, piles of books and crumpled papers strewn around him. He'd perched his boot heels on the tabletop as he read from a piece of paper, leaning back in a chair that tipped precariously under his bulk.

When he noticed Phee approaching, he lowered the chair and swung his legs down. Bracing his feet on the ground, he rose to face her.

Phee kept striding toward him. *One kiss and I'll be done with it. One kiss and I'll get the man out of my head.*

"Ophe—"

Before he could finish speaking, she stepped toe to toe with him, reached up to place a hand on each side of his face, and pulled his mouth to hers for a kiss. A shallow, awkward joining of lips at first. But then more. She noticed the warmth of his mouth, the shallow wisp of his breath, how his body tensed at her touch. He let her kiss him rather than returning the gesture.

She went up on her toes for one more brush against his mouth, and it was over. Phee opened her eyes and took a backward step. Triumph zinged through her. She'd done it! And perhaps, after catching her breath, she would find the spell broken.

Then, as quick as the thrashing beat of her pulse, her world spun off kilter.

Kit flattened his hand against her belly. The length of his heated palm spanned the width of her waist. Gripping a handful of her blouse, he tugged her near. Not toe to toe but chest to chest. Thigh to thigh.

How had she forgotten this? How firm he was against every soft part of her. That the muscled, unyielding plane of his chest made her want to lean, to stop holding herself quite so upright. To press her cheek against his body and hear the reassuring rhythm of his impulsive heart. His arms were broad, as muscled as his shoulders, as if they'd been made to shelter her, strong enough to shield her.

Sunlight brightened his eyes to verdigris, far more green than brown. Dark stubble accentuated the perfect peaks of his upper lip, and his lower lip trembled a moment before he lowered his head and ran his tongue along the seam of her lips.

A moan escaped. Not hers, but his. And then those long, thick fingers she'd imagined moments before were on her, skimming tenderly along the edge of her jaw, sinking into the hair at her nape. He stroked behind her ear with his thumb, and she closed her eyes against the spasm of pleasure that ricocheted from her neck down into her belly, and lower, where he'd touched her once before. Only once. A bliss-soaked memory, that night. She would have given him all, but he'd held back.

Perhaps even then he'd known he was going to leave her.

"Do you want me to kiss you?" He was tormenting her with his lips against her cheek, nuzzling her skin, offering hot damp brushes of his mouth at the edge of hers.

Her knees began trembling when he nipped her lower lip.

"Do you need this as I do?" He traced his fingertip along her lips, and she opened her mouth to taste his skin. "Tell me."

A frantic nod was all she could manage before he touched his lips to hers. Phee gasped when his tongue filled her mouth, and then she melted against him. Sinking her fingers into the thick wave of hair curling against his collar, she sifted the silky strands before wrapping her palm around his neck to pull him down, to get him closer.

In a desperate, heated dance, they pushed and pulled at each other. Quick consuming kisses followed slow, drugging exploration that left them both breathless.

"I've missed you." There was a ragged catch in his voice, tenderness in his eyes.

His words chilled her to the bone. Even as he held her wrapped in his arms, all the pleasure of his nearness seeped away.

Missing Kit had been her preoccupation for years. The ache of his absence had brought her so low; some days it had been difficult to rise from her bed. But there had been Father to care for, and Juliet. She wasn't that empty echo of herself anymore. Never again would she plunge into those doldrums.

"I can't do this." She tipped her chin up and pushed away from Kit.

He let her slip from his arms but clasped her wrist. "Can you truly deny what's between us?"

"Yes." When she retreated a step, he released her wrist. "I've had years of practice."

Kit flinched, then hunched his shoulders and planted his feet wide as if he was bolted to the spot where she'd left him.

Lifting the front edge of her skirt an inch so that she could stride away from him with as much confidence as she'd approached, Phee forced herself to move. The first step pinched at her heart, the second a little less so. By the time she passed through the French doors, she could breathe again.

She drew in huge gulps of air to fill her lungs. She cupped a hand over her lips, still swollen from his kisses.

Kissing Kit was meant to give her control, to allow her to close a door on the past. Instead, she was shaking, perspiring under her gown, struggling to hear beyond the blood thrashing in her ears.

What if instead of barricading her heart, she'd opened the floodgates?

Two facts were clear: Giving in to impulse was a disastrous mistake, and if she was ever going to be the poised, practical woman she aspired to be, she could never kiss Kit Ruthven again.

Chapter Ten

"Men may labor in the city, but a true English
gentleman lives for the countryside."
—THE RUTHVEN RULES FOR YOUNG MEN

London smelled divine. Smoke and soot and the muck of a thousand horses couldn't dim Kit's pleasure at breathing city air again. He relished the bustle of bodies rushing past him as he made his way toward Ruthven Publishing's offices on Somerset Row. London's ever-churning hum had always been part of its appeal, yet now something was amiss.

The city usually offered freedom, license to behave as he wished, to devote himself to his work in the theater and join Grey in exploring London's diversions. Now, beyond the matter of his father's business, he couldn't shake the nagging sense he'd forgotten something back in Briar Heath.

He swallowed hard at the memory of Ophelia's kiss.

Finding a way to stoke that passion in her again dominated his thoughts, even as he stopped on the pavement outside his father's London office.

He'd only visited Ruthven Publishing once as a child, when his youthful disinterest in the business and enthusiasm for seeing other sites in London had enraged his father. The old man's shouts had sent employees scattering, and he'd never brought Kit to the capital again. Based on that single visit, Kit expected to find his father's style of controlled chaos at the company's headquarters. What he found instead was perfect order, clerks bent over their work, and a broad-shouldered, officious young man approaching the minute he crossed the threshold.

"Good morning. How may I assist you, sir?" The businessman's suit was better tailored than anything Kit owned, and his dark hair fell in an impressive glossy wave over his forehead. Everything about the young man had been polished to a high sheen.

"Would you direct me to the managing editor or office manager?" Kit glanced around the room full of men clacking away at typewriters and hunched over desks to see if any perked up at his request.

"He's one and the same person," the carefully groomed gentleman informed him. "You don't have an appointment, I take it." This was a great affront, judging by the narrowing of the office clerk's steely gaze.

"I don't need one." Kit made calls as impulse dictated or a situation demanded. Planning ahead had never been his way. "I own all of this now."

"Mr. Ruthven?" The confident glint in the editor-manager's pale blue eyes dimmed as his broad shoulders sagged. "Please accept my sincere condolences, sir." He stuck out a beefy hand. "I am Gabriel Adamson. I manage the London office and oversee the one in Edinburgh."

Kit's eyebrows shot up before he could school his expression. Adamson didn't look old enough to manage his own shaving razor. "You manage editorial and financial matters yourself?"

"I do, Mr. Ruthven." Adamson bristled and squared his shoulders. "And I understand *you* are an actor."

"A playwright." Kit grinned. Adamson was definitely his father's apprentice if he thought calling someone an *actor* was akin to damning them as the worst sort of sinner. "Spare me a few minutes of your time, Mr. Adamson. I need details about the company's finances and suspect you're the man with answers."

"This way, Mr. Ruthven." Adamson hesitated just long enough to let Kit know he didn't take kindly to impromptu meetings. Then he started off at an impressively precise stride for a man of his bulk, leading Kit into a sterile room.

"Was this my father's office?" The familiar scent of books and leather permeated the space.

"No." Adamson frowned. "He conducted business from home and rarely visited the city in the last few months."

The man knew more about his father than he did, and it unnerved Kit more than he expected it to.

"We hadn't spoken in many years," Kit offered by way of explanation, though he didn't owe Adamson one. He managed to stop short of attempting to justify why he'd avoided his father for years.

After taking a seat in front of Adamson's desk, Kit leaned forward, elbows on his knees. "I know very little about the business's finances, but I must if I am going to find a buyer."

"A buyer?" Adamson's clean-shaven jaw tightened, his voice turned sharp and clipped. "You mean to sell Ruthven Publishing?"

"As soon as I am able. Mr. Croft, my father's paper-manufacturer crony, may be interested. Do you know anyone who'd wish to buy?" Ten minutes in the tidy, efficiently run publishing office and Kit was ready to bolt. He spared a fond thought for the cramped confines of his London flat and the cluttered little desk in the corner where he'd written most of his plays.

"No prospects spring readily to mind." Adamson considered him a moment, fingers steepled under his chin, and then reached for a ledger on the shelf behind his desk. He slid the large account book toward Kit. "The current balance sheet marks the pages for this month's transactions."

Scanning the columns of numbers, Kit realized this was when a methodical nature like Adamson's came in handy. Though he'd never had occasion to study a financial ledger, he suspected few were as clear and systematized as the one in his hands. He flipped pages to glance back at the balances for the previous months and furrowed his brow.

"We're losing money." He flicked back to the totals from the previous year. "Quite a lot of it." Suddenly the exceeding confidence of the young man and the busyness of the office seemed pointless.

"The causes are manifold, Mr. Ruthven, but we shall persevere. As your father would have wished." The man sounded like a true believer, as convinced of his father's brilliance as was Vicar Bickham.

"Tell me those causes. All of them, and what we can do to reverse the situation. Specifically." The headache he'd been suffering for days began a pounding march along the back of his head. He needed to remind Adamson about paying the Crofts too.

"Costs rise each year. New publishing ventures spring up monthly, and our list of competitors grows. But it's sales, sir. Diminishing sales are at the heart of our losses."

Kit stared at the shelves behind the man's perfectly trimmed black hair and spied the entire series of *The Ruthven Rules*. Every edition, every version, from the original tome to all the variations for young ladies, gentlemen, etc. His father had been determined to leech every penny out of the success of his damned etiquette books.

"So no one's buying them anymore? I thought even our monarch kept a copy."

"I take it you don't read the newspapers, Mr. Ruthven." Adamson attempted something approximating a grin, but there was nothing like pleasure in the slash across his face. Turning to a tidy pile in a wire basket on his desk, he lifted a newspaper off the top and laid it on his desktop in front of Kit.

"The Etiquette Wars." Kit read a circled front page headline aloud and skimmed the rest of the piece. *The Ruthven Rules* had serious competition, it seemed, and currently from *Miss Gilroy's Guidelines for Young Ladies*. After reading a bit of the book, Kit understood why. Miss Gilroy's ideas were fresh, and his father's were stale.

"So everyone is writing etiquette books, and Ruthven's are too dry and outdated to compete." He could never understand the books' popularity. Why seek rules to dictate one's actions? Kit had spent his life wishing to make his own choices.

"We've updated all the volumes in recent years, but competitors continue to ride our coattails. Some even parody *The Ruthven Rules*. Novelty is appealing for a while, but I trust our etiquette books will stand the test of time."

"I see now why my father hired you. You sound just like him."

Adamson cast him an icy glare. "Books should carry meaning beyond the stringing together of pretty words. They should teach us lessons. Show us how we might aspire to a fate greater than the circumstances of our birth allow."

He suspected Adamson's loyalty to his father had less to do with etiquette than with being given a chance to succeed at a young age. The irony of the situation wasn't lost on Kit.

"We're losing money, Mr. Adamson. That is the relevant fact."

"Your father was a fine writer, but a—"

"Terrible manager?"

"Mr. Ruthven wished to reverse our failing fortunes." Adamson sat up taller in his chair and folded his hands in front of him. "But some of his choices were—"

"Ridiculous?"

"Speculative." The managing editor leaned forward and braced clenched fists on his desk. "You didn't respect your father, Mr. Ruthven?"

"We didn't know each other very well." *Or perhaps we knew each other too well.*

"May I resettle you in a spare office where you can peruse the ledgers?" Adamson slid a pocket watch from his vest, glancing down at its face. "We're considering a suit against Wellbeck Publishers. Their author satirized *The Rules for*

Young Ladies, and it's creating quite a stir. I'm meeting with an editor from Wellbeck's at the top of the hour."

The upstart meant to dismiss him, but Kit was having none of it. "I'll join your meeting."

"There's no need, Mr. Ruthven."

"I insist." A suit against another publishing house sounded like a drain of funds Ruthven Publishing couldn't afford, and Adamson seemed the zealous sort who'd turn a molehill into a crusade.

"Very well." The young managing editor sighed and stood, pausing to straighten his perfectly arranged jacket. "Do you care for coffee?"

"Deeply, and as dark as possible."

O phelia peeked at her editor as they walked, attempting to decide which of them was most nervous about the meeting. He was. Definitely. The giddy thrill of being in the city again kept her spirits buoyed, but Mr. Talbot appeared peaked and supremely miserable as they made their way toward the Ruthven Publishing offices.

For such an excitable man, he moved at a plodding pace, and Phee found it difficult to slow her gait to match. She wanted this meeting over as quickly as possible. With any luck, she'd have time for a wander through Hyde Park before catching her train back home. She'd canceled all of her lessons and appointments for the day. Even the folded task list in her pocket was blessedly short. Perhaps she'd take a later train and spend time at the British Museum.

She wasn't avoiding her return. Not precisely. But what harm was there in delaying her departure for a couple of hours? A tall, dark, impossibly broad-shouldered man was back in Briar Heath, no doubt waiting for her to explain why she'd kissed him.

She refused to dwell on the warmth of Kit's breath against her face, the familiar taste of him, and the sound of pleasure he made when she pressed her mouth to his. Nor to consider how he'd cradled her cheek the way he used to...*No. Not thinking about the kiss.*

Relishing this visit to the city was her main objective, just as soon as she got the meeting at Ruthven's out of the way.

"I prepared notes as you requested, Mr. Talbot, addressing every issue Ruthven's raised regarding similarities between my book and theirs."

Her editor glanced at her, a tremulous smile twitching under his mustache. "I'm sure you did, Miss Marsden. I have every confidence in your diligence and honesty." The way his Adam's apple bobbled as he swallowed convulsively blunted his reassuring words.

"But you're still concerned?"

"Not about the meeting." He swallowed again, then reached up to tug at his collar. "There is another bit of news I must convey, and I am searching for the best way to go about it."

"It's always better to express that which causes you pain to withhold." Phee turned her head and smiled, but Mr. Talbot didn't recognize the line from her book. In fact, he seemed so lost in thought he strode straight past the Ruthven office door.

"Mr. Talbot?" Phee pointed to the sign above her head. "This is it."

"Yes, yes, of course." The tall man ambled back toward her, his brow crinkled, eyes glossy. He took a deep breath and said, "I'm sorry, Miss Marsden, but Mr. Wellbeck has decided to release you from our contract. You may keep the sum already paid to you and any earnings due, of course, but Wellbeck's will no longer publish *Miss Gilroy's Guidelines*."

Phee's stomach dropped as all the air whooshed from her chest. She stared at the pavement, struggling to make sense of Talbot's rushed confession.

"Forgive me for telling you in this way. And at this moment. He only informed me minutes before you arrived. I should have told you immediately." Mr. Talbot laid his hand tentatively on her shoulder, withdrawing it a moment later. "I am sorry, Miss Marsden."

Phee nodded and tried to remember how to breathe.

"We're here to see Mr. Adamson," her soon-to-be-former editor said to a young man who opened the door of Ruthven Publishing to them.

"Yes, of course. Right this way." The clerk gestured to a room off a large main office that hummed with activity.

Why were they here? The entire meeting was pointless now. She'd barely earned enough to justify the hours she'd spent writing *Guidelines*. If the first print run was selling well, more funds would be coming. That was a relief. Telling herself that she'd no longer need to worry about others learning she'd written the book eased her mind too. Yet it all still dropped down on her like failure.

Miss Gilroy's Guidelines was more than a collection of controversial advice to young ladies. The work represented her heartfelt beliefs, and more, her independence. An attempt to strike out and earn by doing something she loved.

Talbot exchanged greetings with Mr. Adamson, who immediately stepped toward Phee.

"You must be Miss Marsden." The man looked like a pugilist stuffed into a gentleman's suit, broad and muscled, with striking blue eyes and hair blacker than Kit's.

As soon as he turned to lead them into his office, the air shifted, and Phee sniffed an appealing scent. Coffee, rich and smoky, and another aroma. *Kit.* His scent—sandalwood and cinnamon and the green of the countryside—wafted out of the office behind Mr. Adamson.

Panic kicked her pulse into a canter. With Talbot behind her and Adamson ahead, there was no place to go. Not a single moment to catch her breath or stop her heart from trying to thrash its way out of her chest.

The Ruthven Publishing man stepped aside and gestured for them to enter his office.

Phee looked straight into the honey brown eyes of the man she'd spent the entire morning trying not to think about. Years trying to forget.

Kit stood near a desk, frozen at the sight of her. He gripped a cup suspended halfway to his mouth, his knuckles as white as the porcelain.

"May I present our proprietor, the younger Mr. Ruthven? Fortuitous timing has allowed him to join our meeting."

Adamson gestured them toward chairs, and Mr. Talbot moved to take his. Phee and Kit stood motionless, staring at each other, mouths agape. Phee snapped her jaw shut first and forced her legs to carry her to a chair near Talbot.

"Miss Marsden. Or do you prefer Miss Gilroy?" Adamson pulled a copy of her book from his desk. Numerous pages were marked with slips of paper.

"Miss Marsden writes under a pen name." Mr. Talbot jumped in before she could answer. "But she is anxious that her real name not be associated with *Miss Gilroy's Guidelines*. She teaches decorum to those more favorable to Mr. Ruthven's precepts. She knew the elder Mr. Ruthven, you see."

"She knew *me*." Kit's possessive tone made the claim sound like a brag. He reached for her book, lifting it off of Mr. Adamson's desk. "We grew up together."

Phee ground her teeth and glared at Kit. Aside from the irritation of being talked *about* rather than *to*—a common dilemma for ladies that she'd addressed in chapter of twelve of *Guidelines*—she prayed he'd refrain from revealing more of their past relationship.

As if he read her mind, Kit winked at her and added, "Your secrets are safe with me, Miss Marsden."

The two editors exchanged a raised-brow glance before Mr. Talbot cleared his throat and interjected, "I know you have specific questions you wish to address, Mr. Adamson, but I received some unexpected news this morning…" He cast a questioning look at Phee, as if seeking her approval to proceed.

Gratified to finally be acknowledged directly, she nodded. Her editor took a deep breath before continuing.

A burst of deep rumbling laughter stopped him short. Kit, standing rather than sitting as the all the rest of them were, smiled at Phee over the edge of her book. "You wrote this? It's extraordinary." He flipped pages and skimmed the printed words. "I think you challenged every rule my father wrote."

"Thus, our potential suit, Mr. Ruthven." Adamson tapped the bookmarked volume on his desk. "And the newspapers' references to 'Etiquette Wars.' More a battle of principles over profligacy, if you ask me."

Kit came around and planted himself at the front edge of Adamson's desk, directly in front of Phee. The long length of his thighs filled her view. His bulk nearly blocked out Adamson's own broad frame. For a moment, he stared at the inches of carpet between their feet. Then his gaze lifted, along with one corner of his mouth. "I knew the high-necked gowns were a disguise." He whispered the words as if the two editors weren't sitting near enough to hear. "You're not some dour governess. You're Athena, wise and fierce, underneath all of that propriety and starch."

"Stop talking nonsense." He'd always had a talent for fantasy, for allowing his imagination unfettered freedom. She suspected it made him an excellent playwright. But Phee couldn't afford fantasy. She could barely afford another one of the high-necked gowns he obviously disdained.

Mr. Talbot, eyes bulging and skin reddening from holding his breath, blurted, "I'm afraid this meeting is a waste of time. I regret to say that Wellbeck's will no longer publish *Miss Gilroy's Guidelines for Young Ladies.*"

Every gaze riveted on her, but Phee studied the whorls in the polished wood of Mr. Adamson's desk near Kit's muscular thigh. Heat flared in her cheeks like a freshly fed fire. She didn't care if Mr. Talbot told the truth of the matter, but it stung that the tall, dark man towering over all of them was privy to her failure.

"Excellent news." Kit lifted her book in the air and beamed one of his infectious smiles.

Phee pressed a fist to the aching knot tightening in her chest. Impulsive, Kit had always been. A fantasist, perhaps. But never cruel. Indeed, he'd spent their childhood protecting her, showing her kindness when other children offered taunts because of her red hair and Shakespearean name. Was he truly so happy to see the downfall of a *Ruthven Rules* competitor? Especially if she was the competitor?

"You are out of order, Mr. Ruthven," Mr. Talbot exclaimed in the loudest voice she'd ever heard him employ. "This is no time for mirth."

"Oh, but it is." Kit stepped forward, so close his spice and greenery cologne scented every breath Phee took. He tossed her book back and forth between his palms, smiling down at the slim red volume. "If you're not going to publish Miss Marsden's book, then Ruthven's will."

CHAPTER ELEVEN

*"In matters of fashion, meal planning, and
social diversions, a feminine opinion should
be consulted on all occasions. But for life's
momentous choices, good sense should lead
every young lady to lean on the wisdom of her
father, husband, or brothers—men who place her
happiness above their own."*
—THE RUTHVEN RULES FOR YOUNG LADIES

*"Never forfeit your choices, ladies. Devote
as much—no, more!—diligent thought and
honest soul-searching to the great decisions
of your life as you do to the selection of a fine
hat at the milliner's or a juicy novel at the
lending library."*
—MISS GILROY'S GUIDELINES FOR YOUNG LADIES

"**N**o!" Phee shot of out of her chair and stood before him,
her bosom grazing his chest.

Kit relished the patches of pink staining her cheeks and the fire sparking in her eyes. Finally, a glimpse of the Ophelia he remembered, the fiery young woman who'd held him completely in her thrall.

"I beg your pardon, Mr. Ruthven." Adamson cut in gruffly. "While I am still managing editor at Ruthven Publishing, I will decide which books we acquire."

"Then you may not be managing editor for long." Kit didn't intend to carry through with the threat. Not entirely, anyway. The man seemed competent enough and couldn't be held responsible for his father's poor decisions, but fitting in the same room with Adamson's overconfidence was going to be a challenge.

"This is highly unusual. Not at all appropriate," Talbot muttered.

"Wellbeck is our competitor," Adamson pointlessly announced, his polished accent slipping as a bit of East End cockney filtered into his speech. "Miss Marsden—or Miss Gilroy, as she styles 'erself—and that bloody book are outselling *The Ruthven Rules for Young Ladies*."

"All the more reason to publish it." Kit didn't look at him, didn't want to bother with anyone but Ophelia. He could feel her breath lashing his face, see her chest heaving. If he dared one completely improper step forward, he'd be pressed against her, able to feel the racing beat of her heart reverberating through his body.

"Let me publish your book," he whispered for her ears alone.

"No." She swallowed and breathed deep, closing her eyes so that he could study the fan of sable lashes on her flushed cheek. When those lashes fluttered up, she shot him a fearsome glare. "If I'd wanted your father to publish my book, I would have submitted it to him."

"And he would have rejected it," Adamson threw in.

Kit cast the young man a quelling look, intimidating enough to earn him blessed silence, followed by an irritated sniff.

In the moment it took to quiet Adamson, Ophelia stepped away. She planted herself in front of the office's single window and stared out on the busy thoroughfare beyond.

"You cannot be serious, Mr. Ruthven." Talbot approached, mashing his hands together nervously. "Mr. Wellbeck won't be pleased with this turn of events."

"Then he shouldn't have decided to stop publishing Miss Marsden's book." Kit felt no ire toward Talbot or Wellbeck. They'd provided him with an opportunity. A chance to bolster sales. A perfect excuse to do something to redeem himself in Ophelia's eyes. That was what he craved most of all.

"Mr. Wellbeck made a practical decision." Adamson dared to interject but this time more quietly, his posh accent back in place. "*Miss Gilroy's Guidelines* has attracted a good deal of attention but not the sort any respectable publisher would covet."

"I thought you planned to sell your father's publishing business." Her voice. Finally. The only sound Kit wished to hear.

"Indeed, but I must make it successful first." Kit approached her, trying to leave her space, loath to box her in.

"Success is—" Adamson started, but Kit lifted a finger to stop him.

The room clouded with quiet tension. Kit heard Talbot drawing a breath to speak, and then Adamson, who never seemed to run out of words, but he only wanted to listen to Ophelia. One word.

"Let me do this for you," he said quietly to the soldier-straight line of her back.

"No." She whirled on him, setting red-gold strands ripping loose of their pins. The tight coiffure she wore settled in a wavy bundle at the base of her neck. She was too busy glaring at him to notice.

One by one, Ophelia cast a scathing glance at each man in the room. "I won't have any of you *gentlemen* deciding my fate. And you." She turned to Kit, poking a finger into the center of his chest. "I don't need you to save me."

When he reached up to grasp the long, slim finger digging into his waistcoat, she yanked her hand away and swept past him. "Good day to you, Mr. Adamson. Thank you for your faith in me, Mr. Talbot." She cast Kit a glance over her shoulder. "Good-bye, Mr. Ruthven."

"Sir."

"Mr. Ruthven."

Adamson and Talbot started a chorus of protest, but Kit couldn't be bothered with their concerns. "Not now, gentlemen. If you'll excuse me, I have a lady to pursue."

"How dare he?" Phee huffed and grumbled under her breath as she stomped away from Ruthven Publishing's offices.

She couldn't let him publish her book. *Miss Gilroy's Guidelines* represented her one taste of independence, an accomplishment she'd achieved on her own. Whatever she could earn from the book mattered less than keeping it out of the hands of Ruthven Publishing.

If Kit thought he could make amends by publishing her book, he was wrong. Did the infuriating man actually think he could undo all the years of missing him, aching to hear his voice, longing to touch him? No matter how many copies he printed, he could never give her back all those lonely years of wondering why he'd never returned.

For a while she'd decided he simply didn't care. That he was the selfish, depraved pleasure-seeker his father accused him of being. Except that she knew him better.

When he'd gone away to pursue his dream of being a playwright, she'd tried to love him enough with all the pieces of her broken heart to wish him well. Truly, she'd tried.

Follow your heart and flourish.

Through a blur of tears, she'd printed her mother's favorite saying on a square of paper in an attempt to close a chapter. She'd meant the saying as a reminder to herself as much as a wish for Kit. She would carry on with her life, and Kit with his.

It was none of her business if he found happiness in the arms of seductive actresses or a passel of stage-door admirers.

Scoundrel.

His brief return to Briar Heath changed nothing. Memories of a few breath-stealing kisses were all she'd have when he returned to the city. He'd asked to publish her book, but he wouldn't offer more. Even allowing him to publish wouldn't truly bind them together, since he'd expressed a desire to sell Ruthven Publishing as soon as he was able.

"Ophelia." Kit's deep voice rang out, and Phee jerked to a stop. Then she started walking again, quickening her pace. A few minutes of him gazing at her with those sultry eyes, beseeching her with sweet words, and she'd be tempted to agree to his ridiculous notion of publishing her book. Or worse, she'd let her gaze stray to his mouth and kiss him again.

She called back, "Please leave me alone." *As you did for four years.*

His footfalls stopped, and Phee slowed her pace. Another set of footsteps sounded from behind, but they weren't his. Even the rhythm of his gait was stuck in her head. A moment later a gentleman passed and tipped his bowler in her direction.

Maybe Kit had retreated and gone back to his father's office.

Spotting a bookshop window, Phee approached to gaze at blue leather-bound copies of Arthur Conan Doyle's *The Memoirs of Sherlock Holmes*. Tilting her head slightly, she cast a sideways glance down the lane.

Kit stood—no, reclined was a more accurate description—against a gate post. As soon as he noticed her looking his way, he latched his hands behind his back and turned, scanning the skyline, then a patch of neatly cut grass beyond a fence.

Phee huffed out a sigh, took a bolstering breath, and started toward him. "You're not going away, are you?"

He pivoted gracefully and ducked his head, causing a few silky strands of black hair to spill onto his forehead. When he drew near, her fingers itched to stroke them aside.

"I am, actually. Returning to the same village you are. Perhaps we could share a train car." He did that thing with his voice, pitched it into deep resonant bass notes that echoed in her chest.

"Nothing you say will convince me to let you publish my book."

"You do realize you've just issued a challenge?" He squinted one eye and tipped the corner of his mouth in a smirk.

"No, I didn't." Or at least she hadn't meant to, though she wasn't a bit surprised he'd take it as such. "If you'll excuse me, I'm afraid bickering with you isn't on my list today." To distract herself from staring into his green-flecked eyes, she dug in her skirt pocket for her task list. She needed to hold it in her hands, focus on what needed to be accomplished. Kit was ephemeral, his presence temporary. He belonged in his vibrant, bustling city. One glance at his languid ease as others rushed past proved how completely he'd embraced London's bustle.

"Let me see that." He offered his sizable palm. For some unfathomable reason, she laid her list down obligingly.

Flipping the paper upright with a flick of his fingers, he scanned her list and chuckled.

"Something amusing?"

"No." He furrowed his brow. "That's the problem. Don't you ever allow yourself a moment of enjoyment?"

After haphazardly folding her list and shoving it into his coat pocket, he reached out and took her hand, enfolding it completely in his.

"What do you think you're doing?" Her voice sounded appropriately indignant, but she didn't resist or pull away as she ought.

"I'm going to take you on an adventure." Kit drew her an inch closer, linking their arms at the elbow. "London is filled with amusements. Let's find some."

She should have refused, had intended to the moment he reached for her. But his body was enticingly warm, and he gazed at her with mirth dancing in his eyes. Phee missed that most of all. He'd always been the puckish one, encouraging her to set aside worries and pull her from duty into a bit of mischief.

"We have a train to catch," Phee reminded him. So much for lingering in London to avoid facing Kit again.

"Then you *will* share a train car with me?" A soft grin widened his mouth and a crescent dimple emerged on his left cheek. Clasping her arm, he started forward at a blistering pace, as if he feared she might change her mind about allowing him to lead her off on some unknown diversion.

"Where *are* you taking me?" As a rule, Phee loathed the unknown and unexpected. Misfortune came too often without warning. "To see a play?"

He slowed his stride so quickly she nearly stumbled. "Would you like to attend a play?"

"Only if it's one of yours." The truth came out before she could think of anything less enthusiastic to say.

"Be careful, Phee." He lifted a finger and swept it down her cheek, drawing close to whisper in her ear. "I'll kiss you again right here if you keep talking to me so sweetly."

She dodged away, slipping her arm from his. "No, you won't, and I don't have time for an adventure."

He grinned, as if he didn't believe a word of her denial. Which, of course, caused her gaze to fix on his mouth.

"You have just offered me a business proposal," she reminded him. "You can't combine kissing and commerce."

"Can you not?" Kit smirked, and Phee wondered if he often kept company with women who made kissing, and other intimacies, their business.

"You're a scoundrel."

Kit shrugged. "I know." No shame. No sign of those regrets he claimed to bear. He watched her with a flirtatious glint in his eyes, as if she was a confection he wished to savor.

Phee did her best not to scream in frustration.

"I fully acknowledge that I know much more about pleasure than business." He stepped toward her, bridging all the distance she'd created. "But you seem to forget one relevant fact."

"Which is?" She tapped her foot and crossed her arms. *She* was the one who recalled facts. He was the man who behaved as if their painful history was a distant memory.

"You refused my business proposal, Ophelia. Thus, there's nothing to keep us from"—he lifted his hand and gripped her chin, sweeping the pad of his thumb across her lower lip—"indulging any urge."

Phee jerked her head away from his fingers and snorted, then closed her eyes in horror. She never snorted. She taught her students not to snort. The man was so provoking, he made her forget every bit of decorum she touted to other young ladies.

Skirting past him, she began striding toward the train station.

Kit was on her heels a moment later. "Are you angry with me because I wish to publish your book or because I want to kiss you again?"

"Both." She kept marching toward the station. In a few pavement-eating strides Kit overtook her and planted himself in her path.

"Hyde Park is just there. Let me walk with you. We have to pass through to get to the station anyway." He offered her his arm, as any gentleman would when escorting his lady. Except that she wasn't his lady, and never would be.

A few blocks ahead, the park's close-clipped grass gave off a verdant scent in the midday sun, and the Serpentine glittered at its center. On each visit to London, the park beckoned to Phee more persistently than a siren. She often walked through to get to her destination but suspected there was much more to see.

Phee started walking again, but at a slower pace, and Kit fell in step beside her. Her silence seemed to unnerve him. He flicked his gaze toward her face a dozen times over the distance of a city block.

"You needn't look so grim, Phee. I promise not to kiss you again." When she glanced up to gauge his sincerity, he winked and added, "Unless you ask very nicely."

Total and absolute rogue.

He led her toward one of the quieter paths through the park, exactly the kind she preferred to traverse when visiting Wellbeck's. He seemed to know the area well and veered toward a spot where vendors sold food and wares from carts.

"Fortification for our journey?" He paid a man for a bag of roasted chestnuts and headed for a bench near the water. "Why don't we sit?"

She shook her head. Firmly. "I hadn't planned on stopping."

"Just for a moment while we eat." He softened his tone, tipped his head, and waited.

Apparently he remembered enough of their past to recall that nothing persuaded her as effectively as allowing her time to make her own decisions.

"Very well," she finally agreed, "but only for a moment."

After they were seated, Kit bounced a hot chestnut in his palm until it cooled, peeled back its shell, and offered her the first delicacy.

Slightly sweet, the texture was smooth, almost buttery, on her tongue. Kit watched her so hungrily she turned her gaze from his. Finally, he settled back against the bench and fixed his attention on boaters rowing across the Serpentine.

Phee took the opportunity to study him. His waistcoat had been fashioned in a lovely dark green fabric, but the garment was old, frayed at the edges. His outmoded suit did nothing to diminish the striking contrast of his trim waist and wide chest and shoulders. His black trousers were tight rather than tailored, revealing every muscular inch of his long legs. He wore his necktie looser than most and left his long hair to its own disheveled devices, except for his nervous habit of lifting a hand to push back the wave that continually hugged his forehead. She thought again how his looks hadn't changed, only improved.

"Surely staring at men isn't among the advice you offer in your book. If so, I'm definitely not allowing Clarissa to read it." Apparently nothing about his love for teasing her had changed.

Phee ignored his remark and reached into the bag for another chestnut. He seemed less interested in partaking than in watching her enjoy the treat.

"Your book truly is some of the cleverest writing I've read in a long while."

Phee pressed a fist to her mouth to keep from choking. The man would choose to shock her with a compliment when her mouth was full.

"Thank you," she finally managed. "As clever as your plays?"

Kit cast her a sideways grin. "My plays are popular. I'm not sure they're terribly ingenious." He looked out toward the Serpentine again. "Though I hope to change that."

"How?"

He leaned forward, bracing his elbows on his thighs. "I have an opportunity to write a play for the grandest theater in London." When he slumped back beside her, his weight caused the bench to vibrate. He let out a breathy chuckle. "Now I simply have to pull it off."

"You will."

He looked her way again, gifting her with a blinding smile. "I'm not sure I deserve such conviction."

Phee wasn't sure either, particularly in matters of the heart. But tenacity? The drive to achieve his goals? No one could doubt Kit on those counts.

They fell silent, and Phee noticed his scent, the rise and fall of his chest, his thigh and arm and elbow pressed against hers. Being with him was too easy.

"If I'd gone on an adventure with you, where did you plan to take me?" Phee disliked unknowns. Plans and looking ahead to the next task on her list made her days manageable.

"Telling you would ruin the surprise."

"I don't like surprises."

"You used to." His deep-set eyes were shockingly intense.

Phee glanced down and fussed with the cuffs of her coat, anything to avoid the snare of Kit's gaze. "Did you think I wouldn't change in four years?" She steeled herself and glanced up. "Perhaps you rarely spared a thought for me at all."

Kit's jaw tightened and his body jolted as if she'd struck him. He shot to his feet, and she expected him to walk away. Instead, he took two steps, turned, and approached until they were toe to toe. He leaned over her, bracing his palms on the back of the bench next to her shoulders. Arms caging her in, he hovered over her. Phee tipped her head back.

"I thought of you, Ophelia." His voice grew husky, barely above a whisper. "Too bloody often."

Phee clenched the wooden slats of the bench next to her thighs until her hands burned.

"Did I ever cross your mind?" He hunched his shoulders and lowered his head until they were nose to nose. "Kiss me, Ophelia," he rasped, more plea than command.

Tension wracked Phee's body. One inch forward and she could taste him again, drown in his intoxicating kisses, but she couldn't give him what he asked. Couldn't give in to what she wanted. One taste and she'd want more. Risk more.

He'd just told her his desire was to be here in London, writing a play for a grand playhouse. The city was where he longed to be. And the theater, where he thrived as he never had in Briar Heath.

She shook her head, never breaking their locked gaze.

Kit did. He closed his eyes and pressed his forehead to hers. "I always knew your stubbornness would be the death of me."

He lifted his hands from the bench, stood in front of her, and shoved a shaky hand through his hair.

Phee was shaking too, trembling from her forehead—where she still felt his heat—to the tips of her toes.

"We must have some fun before returning." Kit pointed to the stand of boats for hire along the east end of the lake. "Shall we?"

She'd often mused about renting one of the boats but had never had the gumption to do it alone. The breeze on the lake would be cool, the lap of the water soothing. Her legs still quivered like jelly, but eagerness to be on the water propelled her off the bench.

When she wobbled on her first step, Kit reached out and clasped her wrist. "So, to be clear, that's a *yes* to boating and a *no* to kissing?" he asked, his tone playful.

"Yes." Phee couldn't resist a fleeting grin. The man's persistence knew no bounds.

Stepping close, so near his legs tangled in her skirt, he stroked his finger along her wrist. Sensation flamed where he touched her and unfurled in ribbons of heat down the length of her body. "Do you have any idea how much I love hearing that word from your lips?"

"Miss Marsden?" Lord Dunstan's voice sounded in the distance. "You're in London."

Kit winced, and Phee stepped away from him, pressing the back of her hand to the fire in her cheeks. In the minutes it took the baron to reach their side, Phee willed her heartbeat to steady, and Kit let out a ragged sigh.

"Good afternoon, Ruthven. Back in your old stomping grounds, I see." As Dunstan spoke to Kit, Phee felt the baron's eyes on her. She prayed her cheeks weren't still ruddy. "Are you headed to the station, Miss Marsden? The two o'clock train?"

"Yes." The word burst out, and she couldn't take it back. Returning home made sense. Boating with Kit made none at all.

Kit blinked, his mouth open, shock and disappointment written in every line of his face, every muscle of his tensed stance. "I thought—"

"I should get back home. No matter how much London makes me wish to linger, time is always better spent seeing to duties at home." Phee spoke the words with such careful deliberation, both men frowned. She referred to Kit as much as to the city and wondered if he caught her meaning.

"We should be off," Lord Dunstan insisted. "The trains wait for no man or gentlewoman."

Kit said nothing when she offered him a polite "good day" and started off with the baron. Each step toward the station grew heavier, as if the pavement had turned to sand under her feet. Phee resisted the urge to look back.

"Miss Marsden?" A rush of warmth washed over her at the sound of his voice. Kit approached in quick thudding steps. "I believe you forgot something."

Phee closed her eyes, took a deep breath, and turned to face him. Lord Dunstan huffed a sigh and yanked out his pocket watch to emphasize the need for haste.

"Your list." Kit lifted the folded paper from his waistcoat pocket and reached for her hand, pressing the square into her palm. "I wouldn't want you to forget what you *should* do."

He strode west, his enormous gait allowing him to disappear around a corner before Phee and Dunstan resumed their walk toward the station.

The baron remained quiet until they'd taken seats opposite each other in the train car. "Quite a coincidence that your path should cross Mr. Ruthven's during your London outing." He examined her face, but Phee refused to be baited. Of all the man's traits she found irritating, Dunstan's attempts to manage her rankled most.

"Perhaps London isn't as large as it seems, my lord."

"London is the largest capital in the world," he snapped, as if offended on the metropolis's behalf. "The city's population exceeds four million."

"Then it's quite a coincidence our paths crossed too, my lord."

"Fortuitous, Miss Marsden. Since returning from my travels, I've hoped for a private word between us." He paused, inhaling sharply. "I wish to renew my proposal."

Phee clenched her jaw, and the rest of her body followed suit, muscles tensing one by one. The minute she'd stepped into the train car with Lord Dunstan, she feared he might broach the topic.

"I won't press you for an answer here and now," he reassured. "I merely wish you to know my intentions have not altered."

"Thank you, my lord." She was truly grateful for the reprieve, especially considering that her own intentions—about Kit, her book, and the baron's proposal—were more muddled than ever.

When she said nothing more, Lord Dunstan took up a copy of *The Sporting News* discarded by a previous passenger and began reading.

"Is that the *Times*, my lord?" The folded issued lay on the seat adjacent to the baron's thigh. Phee lifted her hand, and he passed her the newspaper.

She tried to read but found herself flipping pages, seeing none of the words. Questions filled her mind. Where had Kit rushed off to? To his theater or London lodgings? To visit a woman who awaited his return to the city?

A handful of encounters after four years, and the man could still steer her from all her practical intentions. She laid the newspaper aside and dug in her pocket for her list. What she should do, he'd called it. Easily said for a man who'd only ever done what he wished, who'd shirked every duty.

The paper in her pocket felt odd in her fingertips, a smoother texture than the type she used for her daily lists. She unfolded the scrap, noting its yellowed and tattered edges.

It wasn't her list at all but a slip of paper containing her own words. Words she'd written to Kit years before. *Follow your heart and flourish.*

CHAPTER TWELVE

_____

*"Marriage is the rightful pursuit of every young
lady, but wedlock should be entered into solemnly,
with full knowledge of its duties and obligations."*
—THE RUTHVEN RULES FOR YOUNG LADIES

Four days after parting from Phee in Hyde Park, Kit hadn't
called on her, written to her, or climbed the tree by the stream
hoping to find her rambling by. The lady asked that they keep
their distance. So be it.

But he hadn't been idle. Not entirely, anyway. He'd paced
his father's rug until his feet ached, discovered and downed
the old man's secret stash of whiskey, and even managed to
add a few pages to his play for Fleet.

But throughout all his days of fortitude, he'd ached—his
chest, his head, every inch of his body that he longed to mold
against Phee's.

How could the woman kiss him with such passion one
day and reject him the next?

He refused to pine. He was a rogue, and pining was out of the question. But he ached, and when he woke up on the morning of the long-touted village fete, he dressed and sped down the stairs with more haste than he had in four days.

After agreeing to Phee's request for help at the event, he'd received a note from Lady Millicent informing him of his essential role as a judge. As far as he could tell, it would involve sampling pies and tarts. Not, unfortunately, Phee's lips.

Now, sitting on the drawing room settee, his body buzzed with energy. He was eager to get to the festival grounds, but his sister insisted on having her say first.

"Clary must not accompany you." Sophia circled the drawing room, twisting mercilessly at a long strand of jet beads around her neck. She had turned fretting into a fine art. Even worked up as she was—color high, eyes shooting green fire—Sophia walked like a debutante who'd spent months balancing books on her head to improve her posture. "In a few months, perhaps exceptions could be endured, but we're not even a week past the funeral."

"Village fetes are meant to be enjoyed by the young." Kit adjusted his new tie and pulled down the edges of the waistcoat he'd found waiting for him in his bedchamber. The charcoal gray wasn't what he would have chosen for himself, but he recognized Sophia's exquisite taste in the fashionable cut of the garment and Clarissa's penchant for decoration in the intricate pattern of leaves and flourishes embroidered into the fabric.

"Did you drink too much absinthe while you were in London?" His sister cast him an expectant look, one blonde brow quirked high on her forehead.

"Never cared for the green fairy myself." Kit frowned. "Wait, how do you know about absinthe?"

"I do read, Christopher." Sophia sometimes employed an imperious tone to deflect questions she wished to avoid. The tactic worked a charm when he was young. Not anymore.

"I've no doubt you do, but now I find myself wondering exactly what kind of books you read." He quite liked the notion of Sophia rebelling against their father by reading books he'd denounce. She'd never been carefree, even as a child, but Kit found himself wishing for a means to ease her worries so that the curious young woman she'd once been could emerge again.

"I asked about drink because your memory continues to fail you. Have you forgotten everything about Briar Heath?"

If only he had. If only the place wasn't getting under his skin a bit more each day he remained. If only he didn't enjoy knowing Ophelia was close by, that the spot in England where he laid his head at night was a brisk walk away from where she lay hers.

"As children, we looked forward to the May fair all year," he reminded her. Three-legged races, the egg-and-spoon race, the steeplechase. Running out of doors seemed to figure a great deal in every childhood memory. And Ophelia. She was there too, whenever he looked back.

Sophia took a seat in the chair across him, folded her hands primly in her lap, and took a deep breath. "Lady Pembry's annual festival is nothing like the May fair. The countess and Miss Marsden's mother never intended their ladies' autumn flower show to spawn a village celebration."

"How frightful for them." Kit couldn't resist quoting their father. "Public celebration is such a nuisance."

"At least you haven't forgotten your skill for sarcasm." She heaved a sigh. "The fall festival has become a competition of sorts, not just flowers but baked goods, handicrafts, even technological marvels."

"Perfect. Something to feed Clarissa's curiosity and get her out in fresh air."

"Kit." Impressive how Sophia managed to infuse the single syllable with so much disapproval by simply making her voice rise at the end.

"Sophia."

His sister returned a stony grimace. For whatever reason, she'd decided that adhering to rules of mourning and bowing to expectation trumped giving their little sister a day out. *Well, damn and blast to the bloody rules.* "Clarissa wishes to accompany me. I'll take on the naysayers."

"Does that mean we can set off now?" Clary stepped into the room so quickly, she couldn't have been anywhere but outside the door, eavesdropping on every word of their conversation.

"And of course she's wearing a lavender dress instead of a black one." Sophia covered her mouth and closed her eyes.

Clarissa bit her lower lip and looked down at the flounces of her bodice. "I could find something extremely plain and colorless if I must."

"Nonsense. That shade matches your eyes." Kit stood and joined Clary in the doorway, but Sophia's slumped, defeated posture pulled him back. He drew up next to her and bent to kiss the top of his sister's head. "Fret less, won't you? Stop worrying so much about following the rules, Sophia." *We are free of him. Free of his stifling control.* "We can make our own rules now."

As he and Clarissa started toward the main entry hall, he heard Sophia's voice. A quiet murmur, as if she were speaking to herself. "That is not the way the world works and never will be."

Clary's enthusiasm as they walked toward the village green swept aside a bit of Kit's worry for Sophia.

"Do you think they'll have a knife-throwing booth?"

Kit quirked a brow at his sister. "If wearing a lavender dress gives Sophia the vapors, what do you think she'd say about you tossing knives?"

"Since you are the oldest, Sophia must do as you say." Clarissa seemed a little too pleased by the notion that he could overrule their sister, but she knew as well as he did that Sophia, as biddable as she seemed, had a streak of determination as long as the stream through Dunstan lands.

Kit forced his gaze away from the banks where he'd skipped rocks with Ophelia. Years ago he'd taught her to fish there too. Unfortunately, she insisted he release every captive, often naming each one as they set them free. After a while, he couldn't bring himself to cast his line in the water.

"You're woolgathering." Clary stared up at him and nearly tripped on a pebble in the path. Kit reached a hand out to steady her. "Is it because of Miss Marsden?"

"Ophelia?"

"I do like the way you say her name." Clary grinned as if she'd just successfully raided the biscuit jar.

"How?"

"As if you enjoy speaking it a great deal."

Kit started walking too quickly, as if he could escape the truth his little sister perceived so plainly. Clary rushed to catch up, and he forced himself to slow. She stopped him with a tug on the back of his jacket.

"Do you think anyone will ever say my name that way?"

He lifted a silky ringlet of her hair and gave it a playful tug. "Yes, sweet. I'm certain of it."

The moment Clary offered him a blinding smile, an object—a strange, enormous flying apparatus—soared into the sky above. They watched as it dove and weaved and rose again above an area about a mile ahead.

Clarissa clapped and jumped up and down. "It's Lord Dunstan!"

"Is it?" As much as the notion of Dunstan flying off into the clouds, far away from Phee, thrilled Kit, he couldn't make out anyone manning the airborne mechanism.

"He's an aeronaut, didn't you know?" Clary lifted the edge of her dress and sprinted ahead without waiting for his reply.

Minutes later, when he'd caught up to her at the edge of the village green, Kit thought for a moment he'd stumbled into a London street fair. A brass-playing trio had been elevated on a platform in the center of the crowd, buskers and barkers mingled with the villagers, and table after table of baked goods and floral displays scented the air. And at the edge of the grassy field, a group had gathered, mouths agape, watching as Lord Dunstan's strange contraption glided back to earth. The crowd clapped uproariously, and Clary led the crescendo. She'd found Phee's sister, Juliet, and the two were apparently competing to see who could clap loudest and bounce on their toes the highest.

Ophelia and Lady Millicent stood nearby, both garbed in matching gowns of a robin's egg hue. A ribbon worn over each of their shoulders and pinned at the opposite hip identified them as members of the Briar Heath Ladies' Society. The tall, straight figure of Ophelia drew him, and he caught her floral scent on the breeze as he approached the cluster around the flying machine.

"What's all the fuss?"

"Lord Dunstan is impressing us." Lady Millicent sounded anything but impressed as she turned to offer him an assessing glance.

Phee kept her eyes fixed on Dunstan, who stood in the center of a cluster of sycophants as he lectured them on the miracle of manned flight, steam power, and how clever he was for embracing both.

"The glider *is* remarkable." Phee sounded dazzled. Irritatingly so.

"Did he create it himself?" If he had, it made the man truly insufferable. More so than his looks, wealth, title, and unbearable arrogance already did.

"Not at all, Mr. Ruthven." Lady Millicent turned away from the Dunstan spectacle completely. "He's not creative like you and Miss Marsden. He's rich and possesses the funds to purchase others' creations or ancient artifacts some other man has dug up. He's a collector. That is all."

"Lord Dunstan is an aeronaut in his own right." Phee cast a teasing glance at her friend. "Give him that much credit at least. How many men could fly the Zephyr?"

"He named it?" From Kit's position, the contraption looked more like an enormous beige wide-winged bat than anything as lyrical as the god of the west wind.

Phee queried, "Don't you name your plays?" It seemed she wasn't only delighted with Dunstan's machine, but she was determined to defend the man himself.

"Every single one of them, but then, as Lady Millicent pointed out, they are my own creations."

"Are they?" Phee finally turned to face him. "I thought you often parodied other playwrights. Shakespeare, in particular."

Kit quirked a brow. "So you kept up with my work?"

"No."

Behind her, Lady Millicent offered one firm conspiratorial nod. Phee caught the gesture and narrowed her gaze at the noblewoman.

"Occasionally," Phee admitted. "If I bought a London periodical and you were mentioned, I didn't *avoid* reading your news."

"I'm touched." Kit pressed his palm over his heart. "You must come to London and attend a play."

"I rarely venture to the city." She glanced at her toes and then cast him a shuttered look.

He knew her too well. She couldn't hide the flare of heat behind those cool blue eyes. He'd bet his life her thoughts were right where his were. Back on that bench in Hyde Park, when he'd been an inch away from taking her mouth.

Nothing had changed. He wanted to kiss her now too. Hell, kissing was only the start of what he wanted to do with Ophelia. He was a wretch. A carnal beast, as one lady had once called him. Though, in fairness, she'd meant it as a compliment.

Perhaps Phee was right to deny the simmering desire between them. What could he offer her? A company he loathed that bled money by the day? A home in a Seven Dials hovel?

On the stream bank, she insisted they'd made their choices.

And now, because he'd chosen London and a specter of success he still hadn't grasped, he had to endure her clapping enthusiastically for another man. A man who'd already offered for her and intended to do so again. Marriage, a settled life in the countryside—perhaps an honorable man would want that for her. Would walk away and wish her well.

He'd never been honorable. He'd never even aspired to be.

"Milly?" Phee asked. "Shouldn't we send Mr. Ruthven off to the judging booths?"

Lady Millicent shook her head. "No, there's plenty of time until the baked goods competition." She rolled her eyes in the direction of Dunstan and his machine. "The innovation judging is first, so we must wait for Lord Dunstan to receive his ribbon."

"How do you know he'll win?" Kit had no idea what other technological marvels were entered, but he couldn't believe Dunstan was the most innovative man in Hertfordshire.

"He always wins," Lady Milly declared without an ounce of enthusiasm.

For Phee's sake. For the novelty of trying out honorableness for change, Kit clenched his teeth and did what went against his nature, but for which he'd been told he possessed a natural talent. He acted, grinning when he wished to grimace. He nodded appreciatively as Dunstan approached, when all he truly wished to do was pack the man back into his flying contraption and hurl him to the moon.

"Gob smacked, are you, Ruthven?" Dunstan, elaborate goggles perched on his head, removed leather gloves as he approached with his chest puffed out like a conquering hero. "Stunned into silence? I was rather hoping our resident playwright would wax rhapsodic after that display. Ever pen poetry, Ruthven? Perhaps you could devise an ode to the Zephyr."

The man tested every ounce of Kit's meager self-control. The baron wasn't just a braggart. He was an obstacle. Literally, as he planted himself between Kit and the spot where Ophelia stood with her sister and Clary as they examined the enormous wings of Dunstan's flying machine.

The baron stood too damned close to Phee, even lifted a hand as if he might touch her.

Kit braced himself, barely resisting the urge to lunge.

Dunstan gestured toward Ophelia's ear. "You have a strand of hair that's come loose, Miss Marsden. I know how ladies loathe being disheveled."

"Oh." Phee dutifully tucked the rebellious curl behind her ear. When had she become so damned biddable?

"Isn't she marvelous, Ruthven?" The fool was pointing at his flying machine, not at the woman beside him.

"Aeronautics don't interest me, Dunstan."

"Publishing never appealed to you either, but now you've taken on your father's business. Temporarily, at least." Dunstan reached up to remove his goggles and run a hand through his wind-twisted hair. "Speaking of which, you still haven't paid me a visit to discuss a purchase."

Kit ignored Dunstan and looked out across the crowd of villagers. Some had dispersed to sample the prize-winning delicacies on display. A few lingered around a stand that had been set up to disperse lemonade. The color and movement reminded him of London's bustle, but there was an appealing comfort to this gathering. He knew many of the faces. The woods that abutted the green had been his childhood romping grounds. The stream where he and Phee engaged in every sort of youthful mischief was babbling along just a few feet from where they stood. Why had escaping all of this seemed so essential?

London, for all its diversions, left him feeling rootless. Lodgings that only lasted for months. Acquaintances made and discarded in the course of a week. Sometimes an evening.

Suddenly, deeply, as completely as he wanted Phee, he craved roots. To plant himself in one spot.

With that craving came a certainty. He would never sell to Dunstan. He'd keep the damn business before seeing it in the blue blood's hands. Of course, if he kept Ruthven's, he'd have to sink his energy into dragging the whole bloody enterprise into the modern century. But wouldn't that be the ultimate coup against his father's outdated rule books?

When he looked back to address Dunstan, the baron had turned away, drawn by a pair of gentlemen inquiring about his Zephyr.

Kit gazed over everyone's heads—the one real benefit of his ungainly size—and looked for Clarissa. Dunstan approached Lady Millicent, and Kit heard him ask after

Phee. Dunstan's flying machine was no longer swooping overhead, but Kit sensed the aristocrat was always covetously circling around Phee. Like one of his artifacts or technological marvels, the man seemed determined to collect her.

The prospect stirred a terrifying primal urge in Kit to make Ophelia his own. To be worthy of her. To prove to her—to everyone—that he could be more than the man who'd abandoned duty to pursue fame in London.

Ophelia was nowhere to be seen. He started toward the edge of the fair, into the copse of trees bordering the stands and crowds. Lifting on the balls of his feet, he cast a look across the throng and didn't spy a single head covered with loose red curls.

"Are you looking for someone?" A few innocuous words, that resonant lilt in Ophelia's voice, and for the first time all day tension seeped out of his body.

"You. Always." He turned to discover her close but not nearly close enough. After narrowing the space between them in one long stride, Kit gripped her hand, stroking his thumb across the backs of her fingers.

Phee's body jolted in response. One touch and he affected her like no man ever had. But she'd vowed to be clear-headed, not to repeat her impulsive performance on the Ruthven's back terrace. But after finding that scrap of her note he'd apparently kept for years, didn't she owe him an explanation?

"I'm glad I found you." She slid her hand from his and looked back toward where Lady Millicent stood with the children. She could spare a few minutes to set out the boundaries between them. "I wish to explain my behavior in London. And before, on the terrace."

"If you're referring to our kiss—"

"A mistake that I vow not to repeat. We should make a rule about touching each other." Her cheeks began to heat. "Or rather, *not* touching each other. You stand far too close." Phee took an unsteady step back to emphasize her declaration. "And you touch me too freely."

"Correct me if I'm wrong, but you kissed me. Not that I'm complaining." Kit reclaimed the step she'd taken. "I wanted your mouth on mine again. I want your kiss now. Tomorrow. The next day too."

"That is impossible." Though with him so near, it seemed entirely possible. "I can explain." If he'd simply stop being so…close and enticing, and everything she should not desire. Phee swallowed hard, tried to look anywhere but at his lips, and fussed with the collar of her gown.

All the sounds of the fair carried on the breeze. She prayed no one could see them standing so close. Phee took a few steps to the left, and Kit followed until they stood near the trunk of a wide tree.

She watched him warily. Why was her resolve so flimsy? If he reached for her, she feared she'd go straight into his arms.

"I don't require an explanation, Phee."

"But I need to offer one. Perhaps I need to hear myself say it."

"Very well." He nodded and braced his arms across his chest. "I'm all ears."

His ears were the last part of his body she noticed. In fact, she couldn't see them at all past the waves of dark hair near his face. A breeze kicked up, slapping loose strands of hair against her cheek, but the same wind seemed to sift his hair gently, as her fingers itched to do.

"What I did on the terrace…" Phee flattened her palm on her chest. Kit stared intently at the spot, as if wanted his hand there too. "I did it to stem the urge."

"And did your plan succeed?" He drew one step closer. "Are you cured of me, Ophelia?"

She held up a hand. He approached until her palm pressed against his chest. She kept her gaze downcast, focusing on the swirling leaf design embroidered in the fabric of his waistcoat.

"I wrote a book advising young women to make practical choices. I must take my own advice."

"What does that mean?" Kit's body tensed. "Is Dunstan your practical choice?"

Phee's eyes widened. She couldn't conceal how much the prospect horrified her.

"So you're not in love with him." Kit's mouth tipped in a smile. He seemed to take satisfaction in their shared opinion of the man.

"I'm no longer interested in love." She lifted her chin, determined to convince him. And herself.

His eyes darkened and narrowed. A muscle ticked at the edge of his clenched jaw. "Is that my doing?" He lifted a hand to her cheek, his fingers trembling against her skin. "If another man hurt you, I'd have his head. I'm sorry, Ophelia."

"The past is done, Kit. We can't go back." Phee fought the burning in her throat and the tears threatening at the corners of her eyes. She'd come to explain herself. To set boundaries.

Not to speak of what came before or crumble into a teary mess.

"So you'll marry that arrogant fool?" He edged away from her, just a few steps.

"Isn't marriage the expectation for every young woman? And the snare most men wish to avoid for as long as they can?"

"As you know, I've never been keen on expectations. But Phee." He hunched his shoulders, ducking down to gaze at her eye to eye. "You mustn't marry him."

I know. Every feeling in her rebelled at the notion of exchanging vows with Dunstan. But there were at least ten logical reasons to do so, and the woman who'd been advising her for years saw the benefits of marrying Dunstan too. "Aunt Rose disagrees. She believes I should accept the baron's proposal." She lifted a hand to shade her eyes as she squinted up at him into the sunny sky overhead. "Do you have some rational argument to sway me?"

"Not a single one." Kit stepped closer. "Only this." Feather-gentle, he stroked the backs of his fingers down her cheek.

Phee knew what he intended, ached for it, despite all she'd said.

He pressed his lips to hers, coaxing her to open to him. When she did, he kissed her slowly, as if savoring the way her breath hitched. A breeze tangled a strand of her hair around his finger, and he grinned against her lips.

"You taste of lemony sweetness, as if you've spent the morning sampling Aunt Rose's tarts."

"I did." Mention of the fair and Aunt Rose reminded Phee where they were and that she had vowed not to do this. Again. "We should go back. Someone will see us."

"What if they do?" He gave her a chance to answer, but continued touching her, nuzzling her cheek, and tracing the line of her jaw with his lips.

"They would expect—" *Marriage. Commitment. Duty.* Everything Kit had sought to escape.

He stopped her with another kiss. Deeper, fiercer, as if he was starving and would never get his fill. She clutched at his waistcoat and slid a hand up to clasp the back of his neck. He cupped her breast in his palm, and she moaned against his lips.

She had to stop. They couldn't do this. Not here. Not ever.

"Kit." Phee back stepped to catch her breath, though they still stood scandalously close. "You shouldn't stand so near."

"I know." Bracing his palm on a patch of bark above her head, Kit frowned down at her. "In a moment I'll step away. Right now I'm trying desperately to concentrate on anything beyond how much I want pull you to the ground and pleasure you until you scream my name loud enough for everyone in the village to hear."

"You mustn't speak that way," she insisted. "Nor think it." Especially since their thoughts were frighteningly in accord.

"Forget what everyone else desires and what you should do. Tell me what *you* want." He tucked a finger under her chin and tilted her head up to look into her eyes.

What she wanted was impossible. Marriage and children and everything that men like Leopold Ruthven expected of women, but more. The passion Kit stoked in her matched with respect, the meeting of two minds, the opportunity to make her own choices and prove her own worth, even within the bonds of matrimony. "I want a great deal."

"And you deserve every bit of it." When Kit reached out to embrace her, Phee ducked under his arm.

"We should get back. Juliet will wonder where I've gone." She swiped two fingers across her lips—would she ever forget the heat of his mouth?—tucked her loosened hair behind her ears, and shook out the skirt of her gown. "We both know you'll return to London soon." She couldn't meet his eyes. Her voice had gone raw and scratchy. "Until then, let's agree to avoid this." She flicked a hand between them the way she'd swat at flies.

"Kissing, you mean?" He looked amused when she was trying so hard to focus on practicalities. "Can you not bring yourself to say the word?"

Huffing a sigh, she placed a hand on her hip. "I am quite capable of saying any word, but let's stop doing it."

"It?" Kit cocked an eyebrow and rolled a finger in the air, urging her on.

"Kissing," she drew out the word on a growl of frustration.

"Who's kissing?"

They both snapped their gazes toward the copse edge, where Clarissa stood with Juliet at her side.

"Yes, Phee, who's kissing?" Juliet scowled and examined them both from head to toe like a detective searching for clues.

"No one." Phee approached and put an arm around her sister. "We should get back. Lady Pembry has promised a puppet show at three."

"I still want to know about kissing," Clarissa insisted.

"Not at all an appropriate topic for a young lady." Phee lifted her empty arm to draw Clarissa toward her. "Let's stop talking about the subject for today, shall we?"

"Only for today?" Kit called after their retreating figures. "Does that mean we can talk about the subject tomorrow? And the next day?"

"No." *No.* She'd need to make a list of every reason to avoid Kit, every rational argument against ever finding herself in his arms again. Perhaps several sheets of *no*'s posted throughout Longacre would serve as reminder. He pulled her like a magnet, but she had to resist. The pain of their parting years ago—she could never endure that again.

She wrote of women being resilient and relying on their inner strength. Now it was time to find her own.

CHAPTER THIRTEEN

*"Decisiveness comes naturally to men but less so
to women. The key, ladies, is to aspire to reason
and to temper the emotional inclinations of your
unpredictable nature."*
—THE RUTHVEN RULES FOR YOUNG LADIES

He'd been in a black mood for days. Being in London's pea-soup fog and the mile walk between Hyde Park and St. James's Square should have cooled Kit's temper. Should have but, in fact, did not. He was striding so fiercely, gentlemen pulled their ladies out of his wake. Stomping mindlessly, all his thoughts were fixated on Phee and her damned stubborn insistence on denying the feelings between them.

Kit registered the street numbers as he passed and ground to a halt, studying the white-washed columns lining Pall Mall. Across the street, frock-coated gentlemen were being admitted at the address where he would find Grey. Apparently, his infamous scoundrel and self-professed miscreant of a friend was a member in good standing of one of the most exclusive gentleman's clubs in London.

After gaining entry with Grey's name, an attendant led Kit to the corner of a high-ceilinged room filled with chattering men and clouds of cigar smoke. The club's gaslight sconces were shaded in scarlet, casting everything in a warm glow. Grey reclined on a gilded settee, his boot heels perched on a red velvet cushion, hands folded over his chest, eyes closed.

Kit settled into a nearby chair, one actually wide and deep enough to contain his bulk, and considered whether to wake his friend.

"You found the club all right?" Grey opened one eye and sat up slowly, grimacing as if in pain. He held his head, which usually indicated he'd imbibed to excess.

"I managed well enough, considering that I've never had cause to set foot in Pall Mall." Kit swiped a hand across his mouth and tried to focus on his friend rather than the look in Phee's eyes before she'd walked away from him. "Who did you bribe to gain admission?"

"You have it the wrong way 'round, my friend. One of my ancestors founded this sumptuous pile." Grey signaled to a young man with a tray, dispensing brimming crystal tumblers to a pair of gray-haired gentlemen. "Drink? Food? They'll see to all of your basic needs here." Tipping back his own glass, Grey drained an amber liquid, handed the empty vessel to the attendant, and offered Kit a pained grin. "Not *all* of your basic needs, of course."

"I knew you had funds, but these surroundings suggest you're wealthy." Kit studied the crystal chandeliers above his head, the plush rug under his feet, the polished wood and leather covering every inch of the club. "Excessively so, apparently."

"Titled too." Grey stretched his back and then leaned forward, hunching his shoulders. "I've been avoiding all of this for years, hiding in the glow of the limelights. But now my father seems determined to do what I never dreamed he would."

Kit waited as his friend scrubbed a hand through his already disheveled hair.

"The man's dying." He offered the pronouncement accompanied by the least convincing smirk Kit had ever seen.

"I'm sorry." The pang of regret settling in Kit's chest was as much for Grey as for himself. Both of them had evaded their duties as sons, but his friend still had time to make amends.

Grey waved the sentiment away. "Aren't you the one due condolences? You have my deepest sympathies, Kit. I hope you know that."

"Of course I do." Kit glanced at the sumptuous club interior. "Though I'd prefer reimbursement for all the rounds you made me pay for at the pub."

A chuckle rumbled up from Grey's chest. "I was trying to be egalitarian."

"Tell me why we're here." Kit had been grateful to receive the note inviting him to meet, if only to distract from his ruminations, but Grey had been short on details.

"Tell me first why you look so grim."

"Must be the countryside." Kit attempted his own pasted-on grin.

"Ah, the rolling meadows of…Hertfordshire, wasn't it? You've been gone more than a few days. I thought perhaps you'd decided to stay."

"Not at all." He had considered staying, or perhaps he'd simply begun to dread leaving. Whichever it was, the vehemence of his denial caused Grey to narrow an eye. "Settling my father's business concerns will take longer than expected. You don't know anyone who'd wish to buy a publishing enterprise, by any chance?"

"I might." Grey sat forward and braced his elbows on his knees. "But come, you tend toward melancholia on occasion, but I've rarely seen you glower like this. What ails you?"

Kit rolled his shoulders and sighed. "How long do you have?"

"Look around, my friend. See any clocks? A club is meant to convince men we have nothing but time." Grey settled back against the settee, stretching his arms along the furniture's velvet frame. "Regale me."

Kit pinched the skin between his brows. "The villagers gape as if they expect me to ravage their daughters or transform into my father. I'm not sure which is worse. My younger sister is clever and pretty enough to snare any man, but she's become as rule-bound as our father. The youngest has a penchant for ghoulish drawings and blood."

"We should have hired her to design sets at Merrick's."

"Merrick should have hired my father. He was a fine actor. While convincing the entire village he was a saint, the man kept photographs of scantily clad women in his desk drawer."

"That's outrageous." Grey frowned. "Scantily clad women belong in a man's lap. Or in bed, if there's one at hand."

Kit rasped out a laugh on another long sigh. Some of it was seeping away, the frustration over Phee's stubbornness, the weight of expectation he felt at home, but the scent of

Phee still clung to his clothing. He fancied he could still taste her on his tongue.

"Fathers and sons disappoint each other. Little more hope for either of us there. But come, man, you've omitted the essential fact."

"Which is?"

"What's her name?"

Kit's mouth went dry. Not just dry. Barren. Like a desert. A large one. The sun-soaked Sahara, perhaps.

Grey, as he did so often, cut straight to the heart of the matter. Straight to the reason Kit's mind was muddled and his intentions wavering. He swallowed and opened his mouth, but no confession emerged. He didn't want to share any of what he felt for Phee.

"My God, it's worse than I feared." His titled scoundrel of a friend sat forward and scrubbed a hand over his face. "This explains everything. The phantom lady you always seek. The reason you look both invigorated by the country air and as miserable as I've ever seen you. Not to mention your disturbing bouts of abstinence."

Kit didn't know whether to be offended or amused by his friend's assessment. "No one has ever accused me of living a chaste life."

"Then it's her. Your country miss possesses that rusty organ that passes for your heart, and no other woman compares."

Grey had that bit right. Kit felt a little involuntary bob of his head and forced himself to still. The man was utterly and irritatingly correct, not that he'd ever admit as much. Women's adoration of Grey's face and men's approbation for his skill on the stage had already made the man an insufferable peacock.

Ophelia was incomparable.

Kit hadn't been avoiding entanglements for years because of an inability to curtail impulses or commit to one lady. Not even to preserve the freedom he'd won by escaping his father's control. He sometimes doubted the quality of his heart, but he could no longer deny that whatever its tattered, imperfect state, his heart had always belonged to Phee.

His chest throbbed as if someone landed a phantom blow. The realization knocked the air from his lungs. The truth was solid as bedrock. Irrefutable. He wanted Ophelia, had never stopped.

Yet what did acknowledging the fact change? With his father's company on the brink and an unfinished play that may or may not bring him the success he desired, his future was as uncertain as the day he'd arrived in London four years ago. He owned his father's house and possessed a healthier bank account, but both were irrevocably tied to Ruthven Publishing's fate.

"What has you so bound in knots, Ruthven? You've always struck me as a man who decides what he wants and pursues. If you desire this village girl, then have her. Surely you've inherited something from your publishing mogul father. Bring her to London. Settle her comfortably and within easy reach."

"She's no village girl." Kit shook with the effort not to strike out and wipe the knowing grin from his friend's face. "No one will *bring* her anywhere she does wish to go. And no man should *have* her unless he can offer everything she deserves and more."

"And you're not that man?"

Kit's gut clenched. "I don't know."

Grey turned solemn, reaching for his refilled glass and downing a long swig. "Perhaps you should allow the lady to decide."

"The lady has decided." Despite the delicious fervor of her kisses, Phee was determined to push him away. A drink had been left for Kit too. He reached for the sparkling crystal glass and swallowed a fiery mouthful of liquor.

"Another suitor?"

"Yes." An image of Dunstan's pompous face arose in Kit's mind, and he took another long draw of his drink. "But she'll refuse him too." Ophelia was far too sensible to marry the fop. Wasn't she?

"Well, now I want to meet her." Grey's short-lived solemnity ended as a mischievous smile curved his mouth.

A white hot flash of jealousy spasmed through Kit. He was used to Grey catching every lady's eye, but the notion of vying for Phee's attention turned Kit's blood to ice. He leaned forward on the settee, casting his friend a hard stare. "I'd prefer you didn't."

With both hands raised, palms out, Grey settled back and crossed his legs. "You know the solution as well as I do. If you're determined to keep the lady from every other man, you'll have to mar—" He coughed and pushed a fist to his chest. "Good God, there's a catch in my throat when I try to say the word."

The thought of marriage usually had a similar effect on Kit. A leg shackling, as Grey referred to wedlock. Constraint and the curtailing of liberty.

"Shall we talk about why we're here?" Grey emptied his glass and signaled for another.

"Seems a much safer topic." Kit settled into his chair and took another sip of whiskey.

"Your play for Fleet. How is it coming?"

"Quite well. Care to read a bit?" Kit retrieved a folded sheet from an inner coat pocket and handed it to Grey. He'd worked for days on the monologue he hoped to see his friend perform on stage at Fleet Theater.

After a moment's perusal, Grey chuckled. "You're bloody good, aren't you? Finish it, man. Send it to Fleet. He needs a triumph."

"How do you know? I thought you were loyal to Merrick."

"I've followed your lead and jumped ship, but Fleet's current play is dreadful. We need more of this." Grey's gaze turned beseeching. "However much I might wish to encourage your pursuit of this woman who's turned you into a glowering beast, we need you back in London. Or at the very least, a finished play."

"Soon."

"Excellent. If I must, I'll come and drag you back from Hertfordshire myself." Grey cocked his head. "Unless you've given yourself over to rusticating in the country. What of selling your father's business?"

"More complicated than I expected." As Kit learned about his father's dealings, he was beginning to understand the complexity of the enterprise.

"Why not keep the business?" Grey swept a hand lazily in the air. "You could publish whatever you wish. Your plays. My poetry."

"Grey, your poetry is lurid and obscene."

"Which is why you'd sell a thousand copies and make a fortune."

Kit chuckled and thought of Phee's book. He still wanted to publish *Miss Gilroy's Guidelines*, but any income or notice it might bring Ruthven Publishing paled in comparison with how much he wished to publish the book for her sake. He couldn't offer her a title or Dunstan's kind of wealth, but he could promote her literary efforts. And he loathed her need to hide behind a pen name to publish because of Briar Heath prudery and its narrow-minded residents who took their cues from his father.

Why must Ruthven Publishing go on as it had begun? The world was on the cusp of a new century. Change was in order. What he'd read of Ophelia's book spoke of young women shaping their own futures. Why not a similar guide for your young men? Why not a *Ruthven Rules* that looked forward rather than back?

"You're not here, are you, Ruthven?" Grey swiped a hand in front of Kit's face. "Ruminating on your country miss again?"

The phrase *country miss* set Kit's teeth on edge. Ophelia was much more. She managed her students, cared for her sister, and possessed a gift for writing. Yet beyond her accomplishments and beauty, she was the woman he wanted—to touch, to see, to talk with, to pleasure and protect.

"Tell Fleet he'll have the play within a week." Kit stood and retrieved the page of his play from Grey's fingers, stuffing it back in his coat pocket.

"You are coming back to London, then?"

"Not yet."

A scrap of paper fluttered to ground between Kit's boots, escaped from his pocket. He bent to snatch it up before Grey could inquire about the bit of letter he'd been carrying with him for years. But it wasn't the treasured piece of Ophelia's note, though the small square bore her handwriting.

Phee's list—neat lines of elegant script detailed the tasks she needed to accomplish that day—had fallen from the pocket of the same coat he'd worn that day with her in Hyde Park. Kit licked his lips, half amusement, half dread, imagining Phee's reaction when she realized he hadn't returned her list but the piece of her he'd been carrying around with him for years.

"Excellent shot." Lady Milly praised with full-throated enthusiasm. "I'll ignore the fact that you chose to land your arrow on my target rather than yours."

"Did I?" Heat infused Phee's cheeks. Her thoughts had wandered again, as they'd been doing for days. Since the day Kit Ruthven arrived in Briar Heath, to be exact. "Forgive me."

"Nothing to forgive. You're a marvelous archer. I should join the Raybourn twins and take lessons from you." Milly moved to the left of Phee, lifted her bow, drew in a deep breath, and let her arrow fly. The projectile thwacked into the hay-backed target near its outer edge. "You see. Dreadful."

"Dreadful is missing the target entirely, and you never do."

"That's because I imagine it's Dunstan when I aim."

Phee laughed and peered at the brightly painted target. "Then judging by your shot, you don't truly wish him any harm."

"Nonsense," Milly retorted. "I simply need to improve my aim." She reached into her quiver for another arrow. "But, more importantly, what are *your* wishes where Dunstan is concerned?"

Phee had already nocked her arrow and lined up her next shot, but she faltered at Milly's question.

"You must give the man an answer," Milly chided gently.

"I know."

"He came to visit Mama yesterday and spoke as if you'd already accepted him. Apparently silence equals acquiescence in his pompous mind."

"You truly loathe him."

Milly laughed, high-pitched with a brittle undertone. "I'm afraid I always have. From the time Mama took me to Dunstan Manor and they left us together in the nursery. As soon as Nanny turned her back, he yanked my hair." Reaching up, she twirled a gilded brown strand around her finger. "We've been battling each other ever since, and there is one skirmish I've yet to forgive."

Milly was kind, infallibly loyal, and forever willing to rush to a friend's defense. Phee couldn't imagine what Dunstan had done to earn her longstanding ire.

"He's petty, Ophelia. I'd never presume to make your choices for you, but I feel you should know what he's been saying, and what kind of man he is."

"Then tell me."

"I should have told you this from the start." Milly stared into the distance, toward a meadow strewn with golden oak leaves. "We were supposed to marry. But when I came of age, I rejected the union our parents had been orchestrating since our youth. Papa was frightfully angry. I'd offended his friend, old Lord Dunstan, you see. And Douglas too."

Phee rarely heard Milly refer to Lord Dunstan by his given name, and she'd never known the details of their shared history. She'd always suspected some hurt lingered between them. Every interaction she'd witnessed was tinged with bitterness.

"After a while, he spoke to me civilly," Milly continued. "I assumed he'd recovered from the slight, yet the moment I showed interest in another gentleman, Dunstan thwarted the match. Mama's always been fond of Douglas. After a few warning words to her and spreading a handful of spurious rumors in the village, Dunstan achieved his goal. Papa forbade a connection I hoped might flourish with time."

"Mr. Biddlethwaite?" Phee swallowed hard and pressed a fist to the lump of pain pinching above her corset.

"Yes," Milly said quietly.

Phee approached and placed a hand on Milly's arm. "I'm so sorry, Milly."

"Thank you, my friend, but that was many years ago."

Phee asked softly, "You're still in love with him?"

"No." Milly barely got the word out before pressing a hand to her middle. Her eyes had gone glassy, welling with emotion and unshed tears.

Phee laid down her bow and dislodged Milly's from her hands before settling them both on a bench near the Pembry's back terrace. She waited until her friend quieted and took a few deep breaths.

"You know how I detest weepy women," Milly said through sniffles. "Now I've become one."

"You haven't shed a single tear. I don't think we can call it a character flaw yet." In a quiet voice, almost a whisper, Phee said, "You never told me about Mr. Biddlethwaite."

"We kept our feelings secret, but Dunstan spies out everything. George was older, my brother's friend. I'm not sure he saw me as anything other than a nuisance for years." Milly offered Phee a tremulous grin. "Then our acquaintance blossomed into more, like you and Christopher Ruthven."

"There is no me and Kit."

"Oh Phee, you know my secret now, but I know yours too."

"Do you?"

"The man has your heart, and he brought you a great deal of happiness once." Milly clasped Phee's hand. "Four years' absence has not altered the way he looks at you either."

Milly was right. Her feelings for Kit had never waned, but she knew better than to trust his impulsive heart.

"Kit craves freedom above all else. He's made a life for himself in London, and hopes for more success with his plays. How could I ask him to remain in Briar Heath if he has no desire to do?"

Milly sighed wearily.

"Perhaps I'll never marry." The moment the words were out, Phee thought of London and imagined a life with Kit. She couldn't envision a place for herself in his theater world.

"Try harder," Milly teased. "That wasn't very convincing."

"I tried for years to forget him. Now he colors my every thought. Since father died, we've been making do, budgeting and curbing our wants down to needs. Now I find I want as I've never wanted anything before."

"I know a lady." Milly tapped a finger against her lips. "A Miss Gilroy. She advises young women to take their futures into their own hands."

Phee chuckled. "What are you suggesting?"

"I'm willing to embrace an unmarried future, but I won't accept a bleak existence." Milly stood to retrieve her bow and quiver. "If we're to settle on spinsterhood, shouldn't we seize every chance for a bit of passion?"

Phee glanced over one shoulder and then the other, looking for servants or a village spy. "You do realize what you're suggesting is scandalous?"

Milly grinned. "Mama would blame it on too much novel reading."

"Well, neither of us would ever concede that point." A shared love of novels had seen them through many a miserable homesick night at the boarding school.

Milly plucked at the string of her bow. "Mama's autumn ball is in a week. A perfect opportunity." She nocked an arrow and took aim. The shot landed near the first, and she emitted a growl of frustration.

"For?" Phee cocked a brow.

"A dance, or two, with Mr. Ruthven. A private moment in the maze garden." She tipped a grin at Phee.

"And if a bit of passion wreaks havoc with my heart?" Phee busied herself with taking up her bow. Private moments with Kit were precisely what she'd vowed to avoid. She'd even been successful for a few days, but distance hadn't kept him from her thoughts.

"You wrote a book of guidelines for young ladies, my dear." Milly turned to Phee with a hand perched on her hip.

"You oversee your home and students and have a list for each day of the week. Surely you can manage your feelings for one tempting playwright."

So Phee had been telling herself for two weeks. And failed at miserably every time she encountered Kit.

She took position in front of the targets next to Milly and caught her friend's eye. "You make it all sound so simple."

"There *is* one dilemma."

"Just one?" Phee could think of a dozen.

"Dunstan." Milly had an arrow ready but waited for Phee to take her shot. "You've made your decision, haven't you?"

"Many times." As often as she convinced herself with lists and reasons and Aunt Rose's logical arguments, her heart rebelled. "But I cannot marry him, and I mustn't keep him waiting any longer for my answer."

"Good." Milly lifted her bow and let her arrow go quickly, more instinct than steady aim. The shot pierced the ring just left of the target's center. She bounced on her toes and beamed at Phee triumphantly. "You should tell him before the ball. If you need me to, I'm willing to accompany you."

"No," Phee said grimly. "This task is long overdue, and I must go on my own."

CHAPTER FOURTEEN

"When conveying unpleasant tidings, do so swiftly and honestly. A difficult truth is always preferable to a happy lie."
—MISS GILROY'S GUIDELINES FOR YOUNG LADIES

The scent of coffee lured Kit out of his father's study toward the breakfast room like a smoky, seductive siren, and he was grateful for the reprieve. According to the paperwork Sophia stashed away, their father had been avoiding correspondence for months prior to his death. One ink supplier sent several exasperated letters before finally threatening to sever their contract altogether; another manufacturer sought a reply his father never sent, judging by the multiple missives from the company.

Getting Ruthven Publishing into any proper state to sell would take weeks, possibly months. During which he'd need to balance work on Fleet's play while mending business matters his father left unsettled. Managing Ruthven's from its

London office held no appeal, if it meant listening to Gabriel Adamson's self-important rambling.

Kit had come to the shocking realization that remaining in the home he'd been avoiding for years made sense. He'd moved out of his childhood bedroom into one of the guest suites and found countryside quiet conducive to creativity. His writing was flowing as never before.

In the breakfast room, his sisters sat eating in companionable silence. Sophia read from a newspaper by her elbow between bites, and Clary scribbled merrily on a slip of paper next to her teacup. Something about the familiarity of the sweetly domestic scene made Kit's chest ache.

After exchanging greetings, he filled a plate at the sideboard, joined them, and found a neatly folded copy of the *Times* next to his silverware. Unfortunately, he couldn't read a single headline because someone had placed an elegantly engraved invitation on top.

Sophia had taken to managing his social engagements like a fussy mama maneuvers a debutante through her first Season.

Kit skimmed the details and rolled his eyes. *So much for the bliss of country life.* "No one told me there would be a ball."

"There is always a ball, though it's truly more of a country dance." Sophia patted daintily at each edge of her mouth and laid down her napkin. "How could you have forgotten that Lady Pembry hosts a ball every year after the autumn festival?"

"How could you forget I spent my youth avoiding the social obligations our father was so fond of?" He hadn't forgotten the Pembry balls, of course. One in particular would always be seared in his memory.

"I'd be fond of them too if I was ever allowed to go," Clarissa groused. She hadn't finished chewing her bite of toast before speaking and gulped a bit of tea to keep from choking.

"Your day will come, Clary." Sophia smiled reassuringly before flattening her mouth in chastising moue. "And don't speak with your mouth full."

Clarissa nodded, waited until Sophia had gone back to sipping her tea, and rolled her eyes in Kit's direction.

He chuckled under his breath and lifted his cup in a toast. *Your day will come*, he mouthed.

After a bracing swig of coffee, he declared, "I won't attend." Not only did he have a play to write and business matters to attend to, but his dancing skills were rusty. The lessons his father insisted on seemed a distant memory. He'd last danced at a London music hall while too deep in his cups to recall any of it. Nowadays, he wouldn't know a proper quadrille from a country jig.

"You must." Sophia sat down the scone she'd raised to her mouth with irritated fervor. "Our family is respected in Briar Heath. Enough to receive an invitation from a countess. Father isn't here and mourning prevents me from accepting, so you must be our representative now."

"*Because* our family is in mourning, Lady Pembry will understand if I refuse." And he could avoid making a fool of himself in front of Briar Heath society, such as it was. And Ophelia, if she was there. He refrained from asking, loath to reveal to anyone how much their red-haired neighbor occupied his mind.

He had a dangerous ballroom history. At the only Pembry ball he'd ever attended, he'd fallen under Ophelia's spell. At twenty-two, he'd just returned from university in Oxfordshire. Phee had just turned eighteen. After seeing her infrequently during his years of study, that first glimpse had stolen his breath. He still wasn't certain he'd fully recovered.

"Brother." Sophia set down her teacup with enough force to scrape the delicate bone china bowl against its saucer. "It will embarrass all of us if you refuse Lady Pembry."

"Stop fretting." Kit laid his hand over his sister's. Sophia was the reasonable member of the family, sensible and strong-willed, but without their father's cruel edge. He didn't like seeing her unsettled. "If it means that much to you, I'll go to the damned ball."

After a shocked widening of her eyes, Sophia offered him the first genuine grin he'd seen since the funeral. "Thank you. You might enjoy yourself. Dancing can be invigorating. And now that you've inherited father's estate, you'll be considered quite a catch."

"Once they're sure I won't cause a scandal and they get over looking down their noses at me for how shabbily I'm dressed." He'd worn the only decent suit he had for their father's funeral.

"Perhaps we could have one of Papa's evening suits altered." Sophia tapped her bottom lip thoughtfully.

Clarissa giggled around a mouthful of eggs, clasping a hand over her mouth so she didn't splutter any of them out. "Kit is exceedingly tall. Much more so than Papa. The tailor will need miles more fabric."

"I've agreed to go to the bloody dance. They'll take me as I am." When Sophia's left eyebrow shot up, Kit clarified, "The polished society of Briar Heath, not the unmarried ladies. I have no interest in being *caught*." Even the word sounded unappealing, like a fish snagged in a net. "Don't expect more than my attendance."

"Lady Pembry will expect more. You must dance with a few of the young ladies," Sophia pressed. "There is often a lack of eligible men to partner them."

"Would you like to make a list? Pick the ones you wish me to squire around the dance floor." *Poor women.* "Choose those you don't particularly like, since they're apt to end the evening with crushed toes."

"Will you let me stowaway in your carriage?" Clarissa whispered out of the corner of her mouth.

"Not this time, love." Not that he could imagine ever attending a country dance again, even if he made it through this one unscathed. "But perhaps you could assist me with a dance lesson or two before the ball."

"Miss Marsden could teach you," Clary helpfully injected. "She gives lessons."

"Is there any subject she doesn't teach?" Kit coughed down a mouthful of coffee, immediately distracted by the notion of holding Ophelia in his arms, dancing with her as he had four years ago. They'd come so close to making love that night. He'd been a fool to ever let her go.

"She doesn't teach taxidermy, which is a shame." Clary slid an elbow onto the table and perched her dimpled chin on her hand, staring off wistfully. "I should very much like to learn."

Kit shot Sophia a worried glance, who mirrored the expression.

"Busy yourself with teaching our brother to dance, Clary, and I'll see if I can find him some suitable evening attire."

"**H**is lordship is in the annex, Miss Marsden. Follow me, please." Lord Dunstan's butler intoned the information with such gravitas, Phee wondered if she was dressed well enough to enter the "annex," whatever it might be.

Heaving a sigh, she glanced down at her dress. She'd come straight from archery with Milly and spotted a few grass stains on her hem. Her curls felt looser, no matter how many times she pressed at the pins in her hair. She shoved them in again as she followed the butler.

"Here we are, miss." The servant deposited Phee on the threshold of a room similar to Pembry Park's high-ceilinged conservatory, except there were no plants in sight. Cluttered shelves lined the walls and crates were stacked throughout. Some had been wrenched open with their straw stuffing escaping; others were seemingly untouched. She knew Dunstan was a collector, but she had no notion of the enormity of his collection.

Phee made her way toward the sound of male voices and found Lord Dunstan and another man near a camera in the center of the chaos. They stood in front of two long tables covered with artifacts, gadgets, sculptures, and art.

"Ah, Miss Marsden, I did not expect you today." Dunstan stared down his nose at her over a pair of spectacles she'd never seen him sport.

"Shall I return at a more convenient time?" Phee wasn't sure what he and the photographer were up to, but it looked as if might take a while.

"Not at all. In fact, your presence is quite useful." He nodded toward the man with the camera and pulled a wooden stool from below one of the tables. "Sit here."

Phee perched on the stool and tried to pull the clean part of her hem over to conceal the soiled area.

"Hodges, where are you, man?" Dunstan's shout echoed off the domed ceiling of the annex.

A moment later a young man emerged from the stacks carrying an object concealed under a cloth. Eyes wide, jaw clenched, he inched forward as if fearful he might cause the item harm.

"Careful, man. That artifact is worth more than you'll earn in a lifetime." Dunstan's bark only caused Hodges to jump and then proceed more slowly before laying his burden on the table.

Dunstan turned his back to Phee, busying himself with uncovering the object, then pivoted to face her. "Will you assist our cataloging efforts, Miss Marsden?"

"If I'm able, my lord." Phee was anxious to refuse Dunstan and be done with the matter of his proposal, but the man had been patient with her for months.

The baron and Hodges approached carrying a glittering gold object. Endless links of wafer thin gold leaves tinkled as the men lifted the artifact and placed it over Phee's hair. Another object, dozens of gold circlets, were placed across her neck. She held still, afraid to move, but each breath caused the gilded pendants to quiver.

"What is it?" she asked, trying to shift her gaze and study the strand of gold near her cheek.

Dunstan held up a finger. "Silence, Miss Marsden. Don't move."

The photographer ducked under a hood and directed his camera in her direction.

"I've never been photographed," she whispered. A strange panic set in. She was wearing an object that had likely been dug up from some ancient woman's tomb, and now she'd be captured in this moment forever. Neither man seemed bothered to ask her consent.

With a sizzling pop and burst of light, the flash blinded Phee. She could see nothing, but she felt Dunstan and his assistant remove the diadem and necklace, pulling her hair in the process.

"That one next, I think," Dunstan directed.

When her eyes adjusted to the light, Phee saw him approaching with another object. He reached out to drape the beaded pendant around her neck.

"No." Phee jumped off the stool and sidestepped away from him.

"Are you truly refusing to be useful?" Dunstan let out a sound halfway between a guffaw and a disgusted chuckle.

Pinching pain twisted in Phee's chest. Useful was what she'd tried to be her whole life, to her father after Mama's death, and now to Aunt Rose and Juliet as the household's breadwinner. Useful is what she hoped *Miss Gilroy's Guidelines* might be to young women like herself.

"I came to give you an answer, my lord."

Dunstan frowned in confusion before his eyes widened. "Leave us, gentlemen."

When they were alone, Phee's throat closed as if she'd swallowed one of those skipping stones from the stream.

"If you admire the diadem, Miss Marsden, I shall make it an engagement gift." He moved toward the table and stroked his finger along the gilded strands of hammered gold. "Unfortunately, it's too fragile to allow you to ever wear the jewels again, but we'll have the photograph."

"No." The word burst from Phee's lips like a breath she'd been holding too long. She shook her head and found her voice. "I cannot marry you."

"Of course you can." Facing Phee, Dunstan braced his arms across his chest. "If you need a bit longer to consider—"

"Please hear me, my lord. My answer is no." Saying the word a second time felt even better. Tension ebbed from her body, and she took a deep, steadying breath. "I was honored by your proposal and know every reason I should accept, but I cannot."

He stared at the tiled floor, then cast a gaze around his collection.

When it became clear he had nothing to say, Phee stepped forward to take her leave. "Good day to you, Lord Dunstan."

The moment she turned her back on him, Dunstan gripped her hard by the arm and spun Phee to face him.

"You're being a fool. I've admired your beauty and poise for years. I want you, Ophelia, despite your lack of title and breeding. You should be gratified by my interest." On a jagged inhale, he loosened his grip. "You're overwrought. Still mourning your father. I'll ask again, and you will accept."

Phee stared at the spot where he squeezed her but said nothing. There was no use arguing with the man. He did not truly see her, refused to hear her, but he'd convinced her on one point.

Refusing him was the best decision she'd ever made.

Twisting her arm, she slid from his hold and rushed from the room. At the threshold, she picked up her skirt and hurried past the dignified butler, straight out the front door.

Only when she was near the stream did she ease her pace, pressing a hand to her chest as she struggled to catch her breath. She glanced up at the old oak tree, wishing to find Kit there.

The weight of what she'd done rushed at her all at once. Relief came but worry too. There was still the leaky roof, the household bills, and Juliet's formal education to pay for.

More students? Another book? She'd find a way.

Phee rubbed at the pain in her arm as she walked toward Longacre.

Suddenly, spinsterhood didn't seem such a terrible prospect after all—no risk to her heart and no chance of ending up a voiceless artifact on a gentleman's shelf.

As she approached Longacre, clouds scattered overhead and waning afternoon light set its red brick façade aglow. Ivy hugging the arbor over the front door needed a trim, and the garden gate sagged on its hinges, but Phee still viewed the house as more haven than burden.

Inside, she found Juliet reading in a chair near the fireplace.

"Phee, what's happened?" Juliet chucked her book aside and rushed to Phee, reaching up to touch a few loose curls. "You look dreadful, and your hair is all mussed."

"I'm fine, but let's sit down." Phee clasped her sister's hand and led her back to their fireside chairs. "I have some news to share."

Juliet chewed at the nails of her right hand while she waited for her to begin. Phee couldn't bring herself to chastise her sister's nervous habit.

"You remember that Lord Dunstan asked me to marry him?"

Juliet nodded solemnly. "It's one of Aunt Rose's favorite topics. She says we could repair Longacre, and you'd go to live at the manor and everyone would have to call you Lady Dunstan."

"Well, none of that will come to pass because I've refused his offer." Phee kept her gaze glued on Juliet's, waiting for any sign of disappointment or the worry she was battling.

Dimples bloomed in Juliet's cheeks as she beamed. "That's wonderful."

"Is it?" Phee knitted her brows and relaxed against the back of her chair.

"You know my opinion of marriage," Juliet said with a sniff of disgust. For a twelve-year-old, she had surprisingly fixed opinions on numerous topics.

"I do indeed." Phee suspected time would alter Juliet's notions about men and matrimony, though her own experiences hadn't given Phee much cause to trust either.

"Don't you think it means something important," Juliet said, scooting to the edge of her chair, "that Papa named us after Shakespearian ladies who died for love?"

"Oh sweetheart." Phee leaned forward and swept a loose tress behind Juliet's ear. "Papa didn't choose our names." She swallowed against the burning in her throat and fought the tears threatening. For the thousandth time, Phee wished Juliet had known their sweet, optimistic mother. "Mama chose them. She adored those characters because they *believed* in love."

Juliet slumped back in her chair and chewed the nail of her index finger. She stared into the fire awhile and finally asked, "Do you believe in love, Phee?"

"Yes, sweet." Despite her claim to Kit and countless efforts to build walls around her heart, Phee did believe.

Before Phee or Juliet could say more, Aunt Rose bustled through the front door. "Ophelia, dear, I'm glad you've returned," she said as she entered the library. "I have a matter to discuss with you."

Phee closed her eyes and braced herself. She'd heard. Somehow, Aunt Rose already knew she'd refused Lord Dunstan. Rumors flew fast in Briar Heath.

"You cannot wear a day dress to a ball." Aunt Rose insisted.

A long exhale loosened the knot of anxiety in Phee's chest. The ball. Aunt Rose wanted to talk about the dress she planned to wear. Juliet must have told their aunt of her intention to wear a barely worn day dress.

"It's one evening, Aunt Rose. A few hours. My turquoise dress will do." With far too many frills to be any use as a work dress, Phee had relegated it to the rear of her wardrobe, but she liked the ruffles at the back and its bright blue color. "Might as well get some use out of the old thing."

"Why not buy a new dress?" Juliet had taken up her notebook and didn't bother lifting her gaze to inject a question.

"Not in our budget." *Not even if we doubled our budget.*

"Then make one." Juliet suggested. Problems never stirred her emotionally. She simply took each dilemma as a challenge for her logical mind. At times, however, she missed key details.

"Have you forgotten I'm a wretched seamstress?"

Aunt Rose cleared her throat loudly. "I've no wish to blow my own trumpet, but I've been putting needle to fabric since I was a child. Bring me the gown, Ophelia dear, and I'll see what I can do."

Phee feared what her aunt could do with her old dress. Aunt Rose had an alarming affinity for embellishment. Her lemon tarts were invariably plated with a garnish of mint leaves or a swirl of butter cream icing on top. Scones were accompanied by a sprig of lavender or a spiral of orange peel and sprinkled with raw sugar to catch the light.

What might she do with an already busy day dress to effect a ball gown transformation?

"Thank you, Aunt Rose. Whatever you can do will be much appreciated." Phee started toward her bedroom to fetch the dress, then turned back. "But remember, nothing too…" Phee waved a hand up and down her body. "Fancy."

As she shuffled toward her room, the prospect of the Pembry ball set Phee's teeth on edge. Now more than ever. Dunstan would be there, and probably Kit too.

How would she face him and think of anything but the last dance they'd shared?

Milly viewed the ball as an opportunity. Phee considered the event a potential disaster. One ball six years ago had been devastating to her heart.

That night filled with so much bliss still haunted her dreams. Memories of Kit were seared in her mind. He'd returned from university after two years' absence, and his raw masculine beauty had taken her breath away. They'd danced too close far too many times. She'd escaped with him into the Pembry estate's hedge maze, where they'd exchanged moonlit kisses and whispered promises and ended the evening in a smitten haze.

"Is Clary's brother the reason you dread the ball?" Juliet pushed past Phee's half-open bedroom door and plopped onto the edge of the bed. "It can't be because of a silly dress." She drew up her knees and folded her slippered feet underneath her, holding both hands out to warm them before the grate. "Or is it Lord Dunstan?"

Beyond being eminently practical, Juliet was also perceptive. She read Phee's mood as easily as Milly.

"It's not that I don't wish to go." Phee retrieved a knitted throw from the end of the bed and laid it over her sister's knees before sitting in the chair across from her. "I do enjoy dancing."

So many years had passed since that first ball. She'd changed. Kit had changed. The expectations born that night so many years ago had already been dashed. This time when he returned to London, it wouldn't break her heart.

"It seems an awful waste of time." Juliet scrunched up her nose as if she'd just smelled boiled brussels sprouts in the air.

"Awful, is it?" Phee reached out and patted her sister's knee. "Don't you ever dream of your first ball? You're a fine dancer."

"Precisely. I adore dancing, but at a ball you must wait on a gentleman to ask you. You can't dance how you wish, when you wish, or even with whomever you wish. I'd loathe that."

Phee couldn't contest any of her sister's complaints, but she couldn't imagine Juliet waiting on a gentleman to give her permission either. What a daring young lady she would be. Pride and eagerness to see her take on the world warred with worry for how others might treat her independent nature.

"One of them will ask you to dance, won't they? Probably both." Juliet pulled a blank sheet of paper from her notebook and began folding. "Which one will you choose?"

All her choices had been made. She'd refused Dunstan. For the most part, she'd resisted Kit and accepted that he'd soon return to London.

"Here. This will help you decide." Juliet slid forward and held out a device she'd fashioned from the paper. The object looked a bit like a four pointed flower. With her fingers tucked underneath, Juliet opened the folded flaps in one direction, then snapped them shut to open an opposite set of folds. On flaps inside, she scribbled KR and LD with the stub of pencil she always kept stowed in her pocket.

Phee tipped her head and studied Juliet's creation. "So I'm to leave choice to chance and the flick of a paper flap?" Her little sister wasn't usually given to anything as fanciful as chance.

"Not chance." Juliet pursed her lips in disdain. "Probability. Now pick a number. Your favorite one."

"Six." The day of her birthday and the number of years it'd been since that Pembry ball she'd never forget.

Juliet flipped the paper back and forth six times before allowing Phee to see. Her belly plummeted when she peaked inside. The paper fortune teller chose Dunstan, but Phee had made a choice too. A choice full of hope she had no right to feel. She'd wanted to see Kit's initials on the paper.

More than a new ball dress, additional pupils to swell the household budget, or a publisher for her book, Phee craved another dance with Kit.

But she was no longer that naïve girl she'd been years before, vulnerable and full of expectations. *Temper my feelings.* That's what Milly advised.

This time she'd be sensible. This time she wouldn't risk her heart. This time her dance with a rogue would require a few rules.

CHAPTER FIFTEEN

*"If a gentleman asks a young lady to dance,
she must accept. Only a prior agreement
to dance with another can excuse her.
Refusing an invitation to dance is an
incivility no proper young lady would
expect a reasonable man to bear."*
—THE RUTHVEN RULES FOR YOUNG LADIES

There were two types of coveted social invitations in Briar Heath—those to small dinner parties hosted by wealthy families like the Raybourns and those to elaborate extravaganzas organized by Lady Pembry. The countess prided herself on setting the standard for fashion and opulence in the county, which meant her events had to be memorable. She spared no expense for her annual autumn ball and insisted on a fresh theme every year.

After being announced with the pomp of royal presentation, Kit approached a colossal statue as gaudily painted as the theater boxes at Merrick Theater. The Egyptian-style figure stood with one foot forward and wore a breastplate glittering with unconvincing paste jewels. Other statues were positioned throughout the ballroom, along with lit torches set out at even intervals. Footmen monitored their smoking flames warily.

As Kit observed the decor, he noted a cluster of young ladies trailing him. The giggling gaggle took in his every move, then raised their fans to chatter excitedly. He caught words and phrases as they assessed him. *Actor. Scoundrel. So terribly tall.* They were either trying to be heard or doing a dreadful job of whispering.

"Not fond of Egypt, Mr. Ruthven?" Lady Millicent approached in a rustling cloud of yellow fabric dotted through with beading that made her glimmer in the gaslight.

"I've never had the opportunity to travel farther than London, my lady. Have you?" The wealthy and titled seemed mad for all things Egypt since the discoveries of Flinders Petrie became fascinating newspaper fodder.

"Only to France, though Miss Marsden and I often fantasize about an expedition to Egypt."

He tried to imagine Ophelia as a world traveler. As a child, she'd dreamed of places to visit one day, and, of course, being Ophelia, had created a list of lands to be explored. Now she seemed content with the uneventful quiet of Briar Heath.

"Have you seen Ophelia this evening?"

"No." Kit glanced around the room. A trickle of anticipation chased down his spine. Reluctance about attending the ball instantly ebbed away. He needed to see her. Dancing suddenly seemed appealing, if he could have Phee in his arms. "I wasn't aware she'd attend."

"Of course she's here. My mother is fond of Ophelia." Lady Millicent drew close. "I consider her my dearest friend. Her happiness is paramount to me. Treat her well, Mr. Ruthven, or there shall be consequences."

Kit looked down at the petite noblewoman at his elbow and would have chuckled at her scowl, but for the warning in her smoky green eyes, insisting he take her seriously. He admired her loyalty to Phee.

When she nudged his arm and narrowed her eyes, he promised, "We both want her happiness."

After flaring her aquiline nose at him, she offered a curt nod and retreated to a less threatening distance. "Your reassurance pleases me, but there is a significant difference between us." When she looked up, her features had softened. "I can only stand by and wish to see her settled and content. You have the power to offer her a happy future."

She didn't allow Kit to reply before turning and striding away, leaving him to contemplate whatever power he might have to make Phee happy. He felt someone watching him and turned his head, hoping to find his gaze tangling with turquoise eyes. Instead, he found one of the giggling young misses had made her way to his side.

"Mercy, you're so tall, my neck already aches from looking up at you." She grasped the fan tied to her wrist, attempted to flick it open, and fumbled with the clasp. "You are so handsome, Mr. Ruthven, it's worth the effort. Will you take me for a walk in the garden and kiss me? I've never kissed an actor before."

Apparently country misses had become very forthright while he'd been away. Impatient too, judging by how the young lady pursed her lips, preparing for his kiss. Her upturned eyes and dark hair put him in mind of a young man he'd known in the village years before. "I rarely kiss a woman to whom I haven't been introduced." He leaned down and she sucked in a huge breath. "I want to know what name to whisper before I take her mouth."

"Oh yes." She nodded vehemently, loosening the feather in her hair until it dangled over her left eye.

"George Booth isn't your brother, by any chance? Perhaps he could introduce us."

His question had the desired effect. The overeager debutante shivered as if he'd doused her with ice water. "You know my brother?" Apparently, Mr. Booth wouldn't be pleased to learn of her brazen flirtation.

"Many years ago."

"You won't tell him what I said?"

"Not a word."

She fled from him like a heroine in a melodrama escapes a monster, dress hiked above her ankles, feathers bobbing frantically in her hair, tiny ballroom slippers skidding on polished wood. But when she reached the harbor of her friends, Miss Booth glanced back with an expression of naked interest.

Chuckling at the young woman's silliness, Kit darted his gaze around the room, searching for Ophelia. The crowd of guests was relatively thin. If she was in attendance, where was she hiding?

Lady Millicent caught his eye and nudged her chin toward the far end of the ballroom. A dark wall of evening-suited gentlemen circled Lord Dunstan. The baron gesticulated wildly, no doubt regaling them with tales of his flying contraption.

Between the black-clad male bodies, Kit glimpsed a swath of sky blue.

He started toward her, striding too quickly, past the musicians still tuning their instruments, earning a few *tsks* from disgruntled guests forced to give way. A man near Dunstan sensed his approach and moved aside.

Kit's breath snagged in his throat.

Phee looked like a goddess caught in mortal men's snare. She glowed from head to toe in a blue gown embroidered with florets of gold thread that caught the gaslight, and her auburn hair had been swept up into a mass of loose curls that begged to be freed. A froth of gauzy fabric covered her décolletage, and Kit swallowed hard at how her gown emphasized her lush hips and bosom, all the delicious curves she usually tried to hide. He salivated like a starving man, eager to touch and taste and devote himself to loving every inch of her.

As if she sensed his perusal, Ophelia turned to face him. When she bit her lip and let her gaze trail down his body, he felt her glance like a touch that galvanized his senses.

Ignoring the men fawning over Dunstan, Kit claimed a spot in front of her.

"Mr. Ruthven," she greeted him with a polite nod. But Kit knew her too well. Knew those eyes, understood what the heated glow in them meant.

"Miss Marsden. Dance with me, and I'll do my best not to trod on your toes."

She cast a pained glance in Dunstan's direction.

The aristocrat immediately turned to Kit and insisted, "Miss Marsden has saved me the first two dances, Ruthven. Perhaps she'll allow you the third."

Kit willed Phee to look at him again. When she did, much of the fire in her gaze had gone out. She looked as he never wished to see her—tamed, cloistered, too damned in control. He wanted to reach for her, abscond with her, hide away where it was only he and she. He needed to remind her how easy it had been between them once. Show her how she affected him as no woman ever had. Ever would.

"The third dance, then, Mr. Ruthven?"

His jaw ached, his chest burned, and his knuckles cracked at how fiercely he'd balled his hands. He was dying to strike out, just when everyone expected him to behave like a gentleman.

"The third," he bit out. He'd wait for her, but he couldn't bear to stay and converse in the stiff, polite manner she was employing. Swiveling away from the group in front of Dunstan, Kit scanned the room for an exit. He spied terrace doors and beelined toward them. Once he'd pushed into the evening air, he could breathe again, but painfully, as if he'd swallowed broken glass and every jagged piece had lodged in his lungs.

The baron had not simply claimed the first two dances. The man was staking his claim on Phee, and she allowed it as if she was a woman without choices, a female who lacked the irritatingly stubborn will he knew to be her truest nature.

When the door creaked behind him, he breathed deep and prayed to smell her sweet jasmine scent in the air. Instead he felt a hand descend on his shoulder, too broad and heavy to belong to Phee.

"Ruthven, might we have a word?"

Kit faced Lord Dunstan, cocked a hip against the balustrade behind him, and crossed his arms. "Just one? Promise?"

"If we were to keep to a single word, I suspect you know which it would be."

Ophelia. Dunstan's gray eyes had turned to granite, his mouth set equally hard.

"If you're referring to Ophelia, we have nothing to say to each other." Kit pushed off the ledge and started back toward the ballroom.

"How much do you want for your father's publishing concern?"

Kit stopped but offered the aristocrat no answer. How had less than a month in the countryside tumbled his life on end? The urgency to sell Ruthven's had been replaced with wild notions of changing what his father had built, modernizing the enterprise, and printing books like Ophelia's, rather than promoting the outdated strictures in *The Ruthven Rules*. Of course, he had no experience managing a business, but he could learn.

"Wouldn't you rather be in London writing your plays and pleasuring actresses?" The blue blood pitched his voice low, attempting a bit of menace. "Leave Miss Marsden to the future you can't offer her. If you care for the lady, you'll go and stay away, Ruthven. I'm content to buy Ruthven Publishing if it ensures your departure from Briar Heath."

"Ruthven's is no longer for sale to you, Dunstan." Fury boiling in his veins, Kit turned and forced his mouth to curve into a grin. "Banishing me to London won't help. Ophelia will refuse you."

Pivoting on his heel, Kit started toward the ballroom, but the pleasure of turning his back on Dunstan was short-lived.

"I wouldn't expect a man who spent his life shirking duty to understand the impulse in others. When I ask Miss Marsden to marry me tonight, she won't refuse again."

Again? Now *that* was the best news he'd heard in weeks. Kit laughed and spun on his heel. "So she did refuse you." His pulse thrummed in his veins. He needed to find Phee and kiss the woman senseless. "You asked for my assistance with Ophelia once." He stepped closer, so swiftly the baron's eyes widened, and he stumbled back. "Heed this. Once the lady makes up her mind, she's 'more stubborn-hard than hammered iron.'"

From Dunstan's frown, he either didn't recognize the line from Shakespeare or wasn't pleased to hear that the lady he hoped to marry was as unbendable as metal.

However maddening, Kit adored Ophelia's single-mindedness.

Abandoning Dustan, Kit made his way into the ballroom. The dancing had just begun. His steps slowed as realization dawned.

If Phee's decisions were unwavering, perhaps he was the biggest fool of all.

Kit was causing a scene. Or, more accurately, inspiring one. The young ladies of Briar Heath flocked around him as if he were a succulent new treat to be sampled and savored, an unmarried man to add to their list of prospective grooms. If he had any plans to remain in the village and continue his father's business, perhaps their hopes would be well founded.

Phee knew differently.

She sympathized with the girls who couldn't take their eyes off of Kit. He dominated the room, towering over most men. His black evening suit accentuated the dark glossy waves of his hair, and the stark white of his shirt set off the strong angles of his jaw and sensual mouth. Whatever he'd experienced during his time in London, he'd acquired an irresistible confidence, a kind of disreputable swagger that set him apart.

She'd entered the ballroom hoping to find him. Unfortunately, Lord Dunstan had come at her like an onrushing train, requesting the first two dances within the hearing of Lady Pembry, whose encouraging nod made it impossible for Phee to refuse.

But when Kit appeared, he'd looked at her with such naked want that Dunstan and duty faded. Just for one night, she wanted a dance with Kit. Just for one night, she'd seize a bit of passion and put worries about the future aside.

"Forgive my delay, Miss Marsden." Dunstan appeared at her elbow, and Phee's heart sank. He'd been drawn off into a discussion with two gentlemen about a railroad venture, but apparently forgetting their dance was too much to hope for. He was being unusually genial for a man she'd rejected a week before.

Phee cast her gaze toward where Milly stood chatting with her mother.

Milly caught her eye and seemed to read Phee's desperation. A moment later, she began striding in their direction.

"Dunstan." Milly drew up between them, allowing Phee to step a few inches away from the baron. "Mama requires you to dance with Mrs. Belvedere. Her husband is indisposed this evening."

Dustan turned a glance Milly's way, a series of emotions playing across his features. "Later, Lady Millicent. I'm dancing this set with Miss Marsden." When he reached for Phee's arm, Milly tapped his hand with her folded fan.

"I'm afraid not. Mrs. Belvedere takes precedence, and you wouldn't want to disappoint our hostess." She cast a glance toward her mother, and Lady Pembry returned a fingery wave.

"I will seek you for the next set, Miss Marsden." Mouth set in a grim line, Dunstan nodded sharply at Milly and strode toward the elderly Mrs. Belvedere.

"He manages to make every promise sound like a threat." Milly said as she watched Dunstan's retreating back.

"Thank you. That was brilliantly done." Phee was already scanning the room for Kit.

"You're welcome." Milly grasped Phee's hand and beamed an encouraging smile. "I saw him heading out onto the terrace as soon as Dunstan approached you. Now go and make the most of this reprieve."

Phee didn't waste a moment before making her way toward the terrace doors, peeking over her shoulder to ensure Dunstan was well and truly occupied with Mrs. Belvedere.

The balcony was a swath of darkness, lit only by two Egyptian-style torches. A lady and gentleman lingered in one dark corner, but Kit had gone. Phee peered into the garden below, but clouds hid the moonlight, and she could make out nothing but the glimmer of lanterns set out among the greenery. She started down the steps and heard a chime of feminine laughter. Phee moved toward the sound, into a circle of tall bushes near the entrance of the hedge maze, and spied a tall man with a petite blonde.

"You'll regret this in the morning, Miss Booth," Kit whispered as he unlatched the lady's fingers from around his neck.

"Never," the girl insisted. "Oh Christopher, you can't frighten me off this time by saying you'll tell my brother. I long to do something worth regretting."

"I can assure you it won't be with me. Now let me escort you inside."

"I'll make my own way." In whirl of taffeta and cream satin, the girl stomped past Phee toward the terrace stairs. Phee watched until Miss Booth returned safely to the ballroom, then stepped into the shadows near Kit.

"That was very honorable of you."

Kit snapped his gaze toward her. In the darkness she could hear him move, the shift of his clothing, and then his warm hand encircled her wrist. "You know me better than to accuse me of being honorable."

He tugged gently, and Phee moved toward him until her chest grazed his. The sharp edge of his cheek, the shadow of his mouth, and the dark triangular slash of his eyebrow were all she could see. But she could feel more. His breath came fast and hot against her face, and her own heartbeat fluttered in her chest like a trapped bird.

"I used to know you, Mr. Ruthven."

The minute she said his name, his mouth crashed down on hers. Hard and yet impossibly soft, melting her bones, heating her blood. Just as quickly, he released her, but she held on, gripping his lapels as if she might fall.

"Don't call me Mr. Ruthven. You can't keep me away with that name."

"Will you kiss me every time I call you Mr. Ruthven?" The night air blew cold against her cheeks, but Kit was deliciously warm. The white of his waistcoat and shirt stood out in the dark, and Phee rested her palm on his chest, absorbing his heat, relishing the rioting beat of his heart.

"Will you regret each kiss?" He pulled her closer, snaking his hand up the middle of her back.

"Are you confusing me with Miss Booth?"

"Never." A flash of white told her he'd smiled in the darkness. He stroked a finger along her cheek, then lower, dipping into the hollow at the base of her throat. "I would never confuse you with any woman, but you do confuse me, Phee. Your kisses are full of fire, but then I see anguish in your eyes."

How could she maintain a wall around her heart when he was near? She'd struggled to keep her feelings in check from the moment Kit returned to Briar Heath.

Kit bent down, his breath stirring a loose curl near her ear. "The Miss Booths of the world are transparent, seeking ruination, assuming marriage will follow." He caught her cheek against his palm, and she leaned into his touch. "Tell me what *you* want."

"You." The truth freed something inside her, as if the fluttering bird in her chest finally escaped its cage. "I want you, Kit."

He stilled, his body tensing against hers. Phee braced one palm on his wide shoulder and reached her other hand up to touch the hard edge of his jaw. When she stroked the pad of her thumb across his bottom lip, he groaned.

Kit slid his hands down her back, gripped her backside, and pulled her flush against his body.

"Is this what you want?" His voice turned husky as he pressed into her, his hard thighs invading her skirts, a heated weight against the part of her that pulsed with need for him. Lowering his head, he skimmed his lips against her cheek. He placed a kiss near her ear and caught the delicate skin between his teeth.

"Yes." The word escaped on a moan because he was laving her neck, then tasting a spot behind her ear that made Phee's body quiver from her hips to her toes.

She wouldn't take it back, wouldn't deny what she wanted, and Kit didn't give her a chance. He eased his mouth onto hers, opened her as if she belonged to him, explored her with his tongue.

Phee lifted her arms, tightening them around Kit's neck.

He pulled back and whispered, "Come with me." Clasping her hand, he led her deeper into the hedge maze. Two turns, one right, and he stopped at a bench along the path. A candlelit lantern glinted at its side.

"I want to see you," he said, before reaching up to loosen the tulle gauze at the neck of her gown. He stroked a finger down the line of her cleavage. "Your skin is so soft, Ophelia. I need to touch and taste every inch." Gripping her 'round the waist, he dipped his head and pressed kisses to the swell of each breast, right to the edge where she spilled over the tight grip of her corset.

Phee never imagined feeling overdressed in a hedge maze, but suddenly she wanted her gown gone, to shed all the layers of clothing that kept Kit's warm mouth from her body. She reached up to tug her bodice down the only inch the tight fabric would allow.

"Are you reading my thoughts now?" Kit chuckled in the darkness, the damp heat of his breath tickling her too-sensitive skin. He slid long fingers inside her corset, past her chemise, and stroked her achingly taut nipple until she gasped.

Swallowing her gasp with a kiss, he leaned in until her back pressed against boxwood. Phee lost herself in the kiss, giving in to her aching need for him. She tugged at his waist-coat, pulling him closer. Cool air chased up her stockinged leg, and Phee felt Kit's fingers tugging the skirt of her gown, bunching the fabric in his fist, pulling her petticoats up too.

"Phee," he breathed against her lips when his hand brushed the bare flesh of her leg above her stocking. He bent and kissed her neck, nipping with his teeth, soothing with this tongue, as he reached for the waist of her drawers and slid two fingers inside. "I've needed to touch you for so long, love." His voice came in hot breath and a husky rumble against her neck, and Phee moaned when the tip of his finger slid into the damp curls at the apex of her thighs.

Too much. Quivering from head to toe, Phee couldn't catch her breath or remember a single rule she'd promised to abide by this evening. She pressed a palm to the firm heat of Kit's chest. "I think…" Except she couldn't think with the taste of him on her tongue and his wickedly clever fingers stroking her.

"Rules," she finally managed, and he stilled in her arms. "Please, Kit."

"What are you asking me, love?" He pulled back to gaze down at her, slid his hand from her drawers, and began lowering her skirt over her hips. "Anything you want. I'll give it to you."

She closed her eyes, planted a hand on her chest, and concentrated on the seemingly impossible task of steadying her galloping heartbeat.

"Ophelia." It wasn't his voice whispering her name in a frantic whisper but Milly's.

Kit released a frustrated growl and eased away from her, but he threaded his fingers through hers and held fast to her hand.

Milly entered the path a moment later. "Thank goodness I found you two." She nearly bumped into Kit before clutching at her belly as if she'd run all the way from the ballroom.

Kit squeezed Phee's hand as if he had no intention of letting go.

"Phee, you should return with me to the ballroom. A situation has arisen, and it's best if we nip it while it buds." She cast a glance toward Kit. "Will you wait several minutes before following us, Mr. Ruthven?"

Phee nodded and turned to follow Milly, but Kit held on tight.

"What's happened?" he asked. "What situation has arisen?"

"I'm afraid Miss Gilroy has been unmasked." Milly's tone was low and agitated. "But let's not make things worse by allowing someone to find Ophelia in the garden with you."

Tremors shook Phee's body, but not from the pleasure of Kit's touch.

"So everyone knows." All the bliss, all the warmth, all the joy of being cocooned in Kit's arms seeped away and Phee felt hollow. Shock caused her thoughts to rush but her heartbeat to stall to sluggish thuds. "My students' parents?"

"What does it matter?" Kit squeezed her hand. "You shouldn't be ashamed of what you've written."

"I'm concerned with consequences, not shame." Phee could sense his warmth through the skin of her fingers, despite how chilled and numb the rest of her body felt. "And not just for myself, but Juliet and Aunt Rose. Our home."

"We must go back inside," Milly urged, "and do what we can to stem the damage."

"Save me a dance, Phee." Kit held on as Milly began leading her away, only loosening his hold reluctantly.

But as Milly rushed her through the terrace doors, Phee knew she'd have no dances this evening.

"Come with me, my dear." Lady Pembry appeared, a worried frown marring her brow, and ushered both of them around the perimeter of the ballroom. Voices carried above the music, and Phee heard her name repeated along with another—*Miss Gilroy*. Mrs. Raybourn pointed at her; Phee heard her condemnation from across the crowded room.

"She wrote that awful book and gave it to my girls to read."

"The lady has an impressive ability to spread gossip at lightning speed," Milly whispered as they stepped out of the ballroom and into the main hall.

"Forgive me, Miss Marsden, but for your sake, perhaps it's best if you depart early." Lady Pembry waved toward a footman. "My carriage will deliver you home."

"I'm quite capable of walking, my lady."

"Now is not the time for stubbornness, Phee." Milly clasped her arm in a reassuring squeeze. "Mama and I will do our best to stem the rush of rumors." She glanced at her mother. "We should see that Mrs. Raybourn departs early too."

"But I wrote the book," Phee mumbled. From the start, she'd wished she could claim *Guidelines* as her own, but she'd feared what a man like Leopold Ruthven might do if her authorship became known in the village. Now it was clear the consequences had outlived him.

The Raybourns' tuition and those of however many other parents Mrs. Raybourn could turn against Phee would be lost tonight. Her livelihood, which provided for her aunt and sister and kept Longacre running, would dwindle away.

"Tomorrow, Miss Marsden." Lady Pembry signaled to a maid who approached with Phee's cloak and laid it gently on her shoulders. "All will look brighter tomorrow. Safe journey, my dear. I must get back."

"We'll do what we can to quiet Mrs. Raybourn." Milly embraced Phee. "And once Mama reads your book, I suspect she'll be as proud of you as I am."

Milly might have intended her words as balm, but Phee wondered if, now that the worst was done, she should return to the ballroom and face Mrs. Raybourn and every other naysayer of Briar Heath. Still, she couldn't ruin the ball for everyone else. Lady Pembry and her circle looked forward to her autumn dance all year.

Before stepping through the Pembrys' front door, Phee turned back to Milly. "If he looks for me, tell Kit I was sorry to depart early."

As she climbed into the Pembry carriage for the short journey home, Phee fought the sting of tears. For a fleeting moment, she'd allowed herself to indulge her desire for Kit, to forget rules and responsibilities. To behave as boldly as she advised other young ladies to do. Now her chest ached with a familiar pang of disappointment, the sting that always came when she allowed her heart to overrule her good sense.

Rules for Young...

were you, The Lady Pembry and her circle looked forward to
her attention there all year.

Before stepping through the Pembry front door, Phee
turned back to Millie. "If the hackster returns, tell Kit I'll be sorry
to be late and...

CHAPTER SIXTEEN

"Fortitude in misfortune. Courage in the face of
calamity. Bear up in times of trial, young men.
Adversity is the truest test of a man's worth."
—THE RUTHVEN RULES FOR YOUNG MEN

Notes began arriving the morning following the ball in a
trickle that gushed to a steady stream by late morning. While
most were delivered by servants, Phee wondered if some parents had been incensed enough to stomp a path straight to the
post box themselves. Most senders couched their rejection in
civil language. Others insisted on her unworthiness to tutor
young woman in the boldest terms. All cited her "terrible,"
"outrageous," and "disgraceful" book as the cause.

Juliet, who'd been tucked in bed when Phee returned
from the Pembry dance, rose with her usual cheerfulness,
but seemed to note Phee's attempts to hide her darkening
mood.

"Aunt Rose asked me to bring you chocolate." Juliet
entered the library with a brimming cup and set it carefully

on the edge of Phee's desk. "She says it cures everything that ails a body."

"Our aunt is a very wise woman."

"Are you ailing, then?" Juliet took up her notebook and settled into her favorite chair as if she might begin to write or draw, but instead she watched Phee warily. No family welcomed sickness, but Juliet knew their mother had died of fever two days after her birth, and they'd both tended to their father during months of the infection that finally shortened his life. She worried more than most children her age about the devastating effects of illness.

"Not at all. I'm perfectly healthy." Though their bank account wouldn't be after all of the pupils had gone. Phee's thoughts immediately turned to her writing, but she wasn't sure what putting pen to paper could earn. She would never write another etiquette book. Even out of print, *Miss Gilroy's Guidelines* was causing unimaginable turmoil.

"You're frowning as if something hurts, and you don't appear to have slept at all."

"I'm fine." Phee resisted the urge to jump up and examine herself in the hallway mirror.

"Are you mistaking me for some silly child?" Juliet's voice had taken on a resolute tone that reminded Phee of their mother. Setting the latest letter aside, she turned her full attention on her sister.

"I know you're not, better than anyone." Phee was forever impressed by Juliet's cleverness and maturity.

"Then tell me about those." She slid a pencil from behind her ear, loosening a single dark curl, and pointed at the letters. "You were happy when you left for the ball last night.

Now you're scowling, and there's a mountain of envelopes on your desk."

"I'm not scowling." Phee concentrated on trying to smooth her features and realized her head was pounding like a drum. Sleep had come in fits and starts, and she'd finally risen before sun-up with Kit on her heart and mind.

Juliet scrunched her lips, a sure sign of her displeasure. "Papa always said lies gnaw at the soul."

"I've never lied to you." At times, a simple fib would have been easier, but Phee had done her best to tell her sister the truth. She'd been honest about their father's worsening illness and their waning fortunes. There was only one secret she'd kept from Juliet, the same she'd kept from everyone but Milly.

"Then tell me what those letters say." Juliet set her notebook aside and sat up in her chair, hands folded in her lap.

Phee pressed two fingers to the throbbing between her eyes. "I wrote a book."

"I know that."

"You do?"

"I suspected as much." Lifting one hand, Juliet began ticking off facts, finger by finger. "First, you stayed up past my bedtime night after night. Second, we're always running out of paper and ink. And third, you've made more trips to London in the past month than you have in over a dozen years."

"You haven't been alive for over a dozen years."

"That's beside the point. Why haven't you allowed me to read your book? I love books." She looked truly offended.

"I was saving it until you got a bit older."

Her brown eyes went round as boiled sweets. "Is it scandalous?"

"No." Fingers clenching the fabric of her skirt, Phee fought past the lump that had suddenly formed in her throat and attempted to explain that every proper family in Briar Heath thought her the worst sort of a termagant. "It's a book of advice for young ladies."

Juliet reared her head back and squinted. "What sort of advice?"

Phee opened her desk drawer and retrieved the soiled copy Mrs. Raybourn had found in her daughters' possession and thrown on their grate. "This one's a bit mussed, but all the pages are clean."

"You'll let me read it, then?" Juliet bounced in her seat and snatched at the book as if she'd just been offered a Christmas gift.

"Only as much as you wish to."

"I intend to read every word." She'd already flipped to the first page, flattening it open with several gentle strokes and then turning to the dedication page. "Oh." Her lower lip began to quiver, and Phee approached to crouch next to her chair.

"Go on. Read it aloud."

After an enormous gulp, Juliet started reading in a breathy tone, just above a whisper. "To my dearest mother, who taught me what every young woman should aspire to be and gave me the best gift of all, my sister."

Juliet hurled herself into Phee's arms. She squeezed with surprising force, and Phee drew strength from her sister's affection. They would get through this downturn as they had all the others.

"What's all this, then?" Aunt Rose entered the room with a tea service balanced expertly on a small tray. "Don't tell me both of my young ladies are misty-eyed."

"I've never cried in my whole life." Juliet detached herself from Phee and swiped at each eye.

"Having swaddled you from the cradle and risen to feed you long before dawn, I beg to differ with you, Julie girl."

"Between tea and chocolate, you'll restore us in no time, Aunt Rose. Especially if you come and join us." Phee filled a cup and offered it to their beloved mother-aunt. As she reached for Juliet's cup, Phee noticed the tray contained more than refreshments. A letter lay tucked under the teapot's edge. Unlike the others she'd received, this note sported a wax seal marked with a large Dunstan insignia. She took the envelope and stuffed it into her skirt pocket.

"I'll stay with Juliet while you go." Aunt Rose watched from the corner rocking chair. After setting down her teacup, she took up a square of knitting. "Unless you wish me to accompany you as a chaperone." One silver eyebrow winged up in inquiry.

"Even if it is an invitation to call, I have no interest in visiting Lord Dunstan. There's too much to be done here." Phee cast a glance toward the pile of letters she'd yet to open. Aunt Rose knew she'd refused Dunstan's offer but still seemed to nurse hopes Phee would change her mind.

Catching Aunt Rose's notice, Phee tipped her head toward Juliet. She needed to reply to each and every letter, but she wouldn't get far with Juliet at her elbow quizzing her about their unpleasant content. Phee hoped she could salvage her reputation with at least a few parents until she came up with another way to earn funds.

Aunt Rose took her meaning instantly. Laying aside her knitting, she stood and lifted a hand toward Juliet.

"Come with me, lass. Bring your book if you like. I suspect our tea will go down much better with one of my fresh lavender scones."

With tea tray in hand, their aunt nudged her chin toward the kitchen, urging Juliet to precede her.

"You'll come and join us for lunch in a bit?" Juliet's cocoa eyes watched her trustingly, and Phee nodded quickly to reassure her sister.

"Are you unwell?" Sophia strode into the drawing room, planted a pale, slim hand on each black-clad hip, and cast Kit a scrutinizing gaze. "The housekeeper said you wished to see me. You look wretched. Did you imbibe too much at the Pembry ball?"

His head *was* spinning, and he'd slept like hell, but liquor wasn't the cause. Mostly, he'd been distracted with thoughts of Phee and felt drunk on the possibilities ahead. After a restless night of aching for her, he'd risen early, brimming with too much energy to remain abed another second.

After hours of pacing and thinking and planning, he'd finally sorted out a few ideas on paper and asked a maid to summon his sisters to the drawing room.

"None of the above." Kit waved her over to a round table he'd placed in the center of the drawing room. "Will you come and have a seat? I thought we'd take tea in here."

"Why?" Her sharp eyes widened bit by bit as she took in how furniture had been moved, chairs brought to circle the table, and the window coverings pulled aside to cast the room in midday light. "We take afternoon tea in the back parlor. Never the drawing room, unless we are entertaining guests."

"Do you know, Sophia?" Kit approached and laid an arm lightly across her shoulders, steering her toward the center table. "Every time you recite the rules, you only make me more determined to break them."

"Just put the papers and pens over there, Dolly, and the tea tray goes on the round table, Abigail." Clary led two housemaids into the drawing room. She carried a large flower arrangement herself and set it gingerly at the table's edge. Blooms of pink, yellow, and white ringed with greenery instantly sweetened air that was usually cloistered behind thick drapes.

Kit cast his younger sister a questioning glance.

"Flowers improve every space." Clary shrugged. "And this room needs cheering up." She leaned closer and whispered out of the corner of her mouth. "Honestly, every room does."

When the servants departed, they cast wary glances at Sophia. She stood vibrating like an agitated bird that might take flight at any moment, and she'd been in charge of the house long enough to garner their respect.

"One of you needs to explain this chaos to me." Sophia swept a hand around the sunlit room, her beaded jet bracelet and the rustle of inky lace on her bodice creating the only sound in the room. "Now."

"Kit has called a family meeting," Clary announced. "Tea is a necessity, I thought we should all have writing supplies, and you can't protest flowers."

Sophia stared at the cheerful bouquet, as if mustering an appropriate complaint.

"Why can't we speak in Father's study?" Sophia still refused to sit, though she eyed the cup of fragrant Oolong tea Clary was pouring with an impressive degree of poise. Apparently she'd learned some of her older sister's decorum after all. "That's where he used to conduct all of his meetings."

"This discussion has nothing to do with Father's preferences." Using the word to refer to a man who'd never treated him with warmth or offered a word of encouragement left a bitter taste in Kit's mouth. "We need to come together to determine Ruthven Publishing's future."

His father's study was drenched in the past, and the oppressive room still reeked of the man's cigar smoke. It was the last place Kit wished to discuss what lay ahead. Besides, Leopold Ruthven would haunt them all with a vengeance if he knew what Kit was about to suggest.

"No sugar and only a dash of milk." Clary lifted a teacup and added a fresh shortbread biscuit at the saucer's edge before offering both to Sophia.

Sophia took a sip of tea and turned her gaze on Kit. "I thought you were determined to sell to the highest bidder."

"Plans alter." His had undergone a sea change since his arrival in Briar Heath. Kit reached into his pocket and unfolded a page of hastily scribbled notes. "While I wish us to make decisions together, I've written down a few notions of my own."

Though he'd shared none of his ideas with Clary, she grinned at him encouragingly.

Kit opened his mouth to begin and found he needed to stand. Perhaps he'd chosen the wrong room. The quiet was as oppressive as the dark wood paneling and precise placement of every knickknack, every bloody portrait of Ruthven ancestors and dim oil paintings of men hunting foxes and fowls. His heart began thumping, and he cast his thoughts back to the hedge maze and the bliss of having Ophelia in his arms. He knew what he wanted. Now he simply had to pull it off.

"We need to modernize." Ignoring the little gasp of irritation from Sophia, he pressed on. "The twentieth century comes rushing on, and Ruthven's must change." He gazed long into Clary's round eyes and then into Sophia's narrowed ones, as clear and cutting as mirror glass. "The publishing house is ours to do with as we wish."

"Father left his business to you, Kit." No scorn or jealousy. Sophia simply stated the fact with a firm finality.

"On paper, yes, but if we are all in agreement, I wish to have Ruthven's ownership amended so that we're each allotted an equal share."

Clary fidgeted in her chair. A dimple near the corner of Sophia's mouth began quivering, as if a smile fought to break free. Instead, she took a long swig of tea and shot him a look Torquemada would have envied.

"That would only make sense if you were certain about maintaining Ruthven's. What's changed your mind about selling?"

"Circumstances." Now was not the time to mention Phee or any of the hope he'd tucked close to his rusty heart. "But you've hit on what must become our guiding precept, Sophia. Change. We must devote ourselves to transformation if Ruthven's is going to survive."

Fountain pen poised above a fresh piece of paper, Clary urged, "Tell us. What changes? What must we do?"

Kit flattened his scribbled sheet of notes between his hands. "The reading public is hungry, paper and ink are affordable, and we have connections with several suppliers. Ruthven's problem is our books. Father relied too heavily on the *Rules* and publishing awful poetry written by bored country squires. We must take another path."

"Penny dreadfuls?" Clary asked a bit too eagerly.

"No," Sophia insisted before lowering her eyes and fidgeting with the gilded handle of her teacup. "Though detective fiction is rather popular. I am quite fond of Mr. Conan Doyle's stories."

Kit and Clary cast surprised glances at their sister, who apparently had a secret taste for detective fiction.

"Both excellent suggestions," Kit praised, "and I'd like to add another. All of *The Ruthven Rules* must be updated. Truly updated. Not simply the addition of new rules, but the infusion of fresh thoughts. Modern notions of behavior, something more akin to this." He pulled Mrs. Croft's volume of *Miss Gilroy's Guidelines for Young Ladies* from his inner coat pocket and handed it to Sophia.

"This book is causing a stir in the village. Mrs. Raybourn railed against Miss Gilroy when paying her condolence call." Sophia examined the volume with interest, then opened to a random page. One brow shot up as she read.

"Not just here," Kit admitted. "The London papers have published a series of letters from the public, some celebrating the book. Other reviewers share Mrs. Raybourn's opinions. The initial print run was small. Wellbeck is cautious and committed to only two hundred volumes. Despite the attention it's drawn, he's bowed to pressure and released the author from her contract. I suggest we publish instead."

When Sophia laid the book down and frowned at him, Clary scooped it up. She smiled as she began reading, then laid a finger inside to hold her page and glanced at him. "And what does Miss Gilroy say to that?"

Kit cleared his throat. "Ophelia Marsden wrote the book." Rumors about her authorship spread like brush fire at the Pembry ball. He didn't fear exposing her with his admission. Mrs. Raybourn and others of her ilk had already done their worst. More, he saw no reason for Phee to hide. The book was delightful and thoroughly modern. After reading much of the volume, he felt nothing but pride.

"Well, that solves a bit of the mystery." Sophia sat her teacup down gently and curved one hand around the warm porcelain, assessing Kit so closely it made his skin itch. "She's the reason you want to do all of this."

"Miss Marsden?" Clary looked from Sophia to him and then back again, her brows drawing down into a confused frown. "I don't understand."

"After leaving her behind to become a famous London rogue, our brother is still in love with Ophelia Marsden."

Feeling exposed, Kit reached up to tighten his necktie, forgetting that he was at home and hadn't yet donned one.

He'd spent his four years in London insisting on shallow encounters. Entanglements and love were traps to be avoided. But not with Ophelia. With her, he sensed a rightness, that all he'd been avoiding, and whatever he'd escaped Briar Heath to find was fleeting. His moments with Phee mattered most. Those were what he craved more of, what he wished to gather up and hold onto.

"Wait—when did you fall in love with Miss Marsden?" Clary's grin belied the irritation in her tone. "And why am I the last to know everything?"

"I suspect he loved her from the first." Sophia took a sip of tea and offered a knowing grin of her own over the cup's rim.

"Nonsense." The first time he'd met Ophelia, she'd scared him half to death. He'd planted himself under an apple tree near Longacre to feast on a piece of fallen fruit, only to bolt out of the way when a fire-haired pixie climbed down from the branches. She'd scolded him for stealing the apple from her tree, and he'd stomped away, planning to avoid the tree and its screeching harpy.

Except that he couldn't stop thinking of the girl. Her wild leaf-tangled hair, the constellation of freckles dusting her nose and cheeks, and the way she glared at him with the clearest blue eyes he'd ever seen.

Kit glanced up from his woolgathering to find Clary smiling at him with her chin perched on her hand.

"And what happens when you tire of responsibilities?" Sophia asked pointedly. "How long before you wish to escape to London again?"

"It's true, then?" Clary asked. "You love her. Please tell me it's true. Other than you and Sophia, there's no one I like more than Miss Marsden."

Kit ignored Clary's enthusiasm and Sophia's doubt. "We're all agreed, then? *The Ruthven Rules* needs an overhaul, and we will acquire new authors? Publish *popular* fiction."

Clary nodded eagerly.

Sophia narrowed her eyes and dipped her head once in the affirmative, as if forcing herself to bear a decision she hadn't wholly embraced. "We must try to salvage Ruthven's," she said. "I would rather see the business altered than fall into the hands of a stranger."

A weight lifted off Kit's chest. If the three of them put their minds together, they could make Ruthven's into a business they could all be proud of. And a viable one, providing enough income to keep money worries at bay. He felt a bit breathless, as if he'd overcome an enormous hurdle.

More than anything, he wanted to see Ophelia. She'd fled the ball as if she had a reason for shame. In his opinion, the high and mighty of Briar Heath should be the ones experiencing remorse this morning.

He wasn't sure he could speak of love as freely as his sisters, but it was long past time to make his feelings clear.

CHAPTER SEVENTEEN

Kit spied two figures walking in the distance as he made his away across the field toward Longacre. Quickening his steps, he recognized the retreating figures of Phee's aunt and sister as they approached the main lane toward the village center. He lengthened his stride, eager for the chance to speak to Ophelia alone.

After knocking at the front door and getting no response, he twisted the knob and debated whether he should head inside. As a child, he'd come and gone from Longacre freely, but Phee had nearly refused him entrance a few weeks before.

"Ophelia," he called, for the umpteenth time and listened with his ear to the wood for any reply. None came, but he heard a thud, as if an object had fallen, and then an odd intermittent buzzing sound. Worried, he turned the latch and stepped inside. "Phee," he tried again, but heard only that awful sound. A bit like a sickly horn stuffed with cotton.

Following the noise, Kit pushed open the library door and found her slumped over her desk, one arm dangling off the side, the other tucked under her head.

"Phee." Rushing to her side, he placed a hand at her back and lifted the waterfall of hair that had slipped over her face. Her eyes were closed. "Are you all right?"

She mumbled incoherently, twitched her lashes, and then nuzzled into her arm again. A moment later that sound—the terrible sickly horn—gusted from her lips. A snore. Possibly the worst he'd ever heard.

Kit covered his mouth but couldn't stem a rumble of laughter.

Finally, Phee roused, pretty long lashes fluttering before she sat up with a start.

"Kit?" She rubbed one eye and pushed her hair aside. "What are you doing here? I fell asleep. Did Aunt Rose let you in?"

"Your aunt and sister are headed toward the village. I heard an odd sound and let myself in." He approached and examined her. With her hair down and cheeks flushed, she looked lovely, but the circles under her eyes were darker than his. "No sleep last night?"

"Not much," she admitted before cupping a hand across her mouth and letting out a huge yawn.

"You need some rest, Phee." He glanced behind her at stacks of envelopes on her desk, and she caught the direction his gaze.

"I can't. I have more letters to write before the last post." She turned back and shoved a stack of envelopes toward the corner of her desk, as if she wished to conceal them.

"Looks like quite a project." A few sheets of paper had been crumpled and discarded in a small pile near her bare feet. Her fingers were stained with ink, and she'd smudged a bit on her forehead. "Does it have anything to do with last night?"

The minute the question was out, Phee's gaze riveted on his. He knew she wasn't thinking of the rumors that had driven her from the ball, but the intoxicating moments they'd shared in the garden.

"I don't want to talk about last night." She sounded so weary. He hated the slump in her shoulders and the fatigue drawing down the corners of her mouth.

"Phee." He started toward her, and she pushed up from her chair.

"Aunt Rose and Juliet will be home soon. You should go." Pivoting as if she meant to lead him the few steps toward the door, she stumbled on a slipper by the fire. Kit reached out to steady her, and she let him take her arm, then let out another barely stifled yawn.

Bending down, he slipped a hand behind her knees and lifted Phee in his arms.

"What do you think you're doing?" She tried for outrage, but only managed to sound sleepy.

"Taking you up to bed." He closed his eyes a moment, willing his body to stop reacting as if he was doing so for any reason other than to insist she get some rest. As he started toward the stairs, she wriggled in his arms.

"I can manage on my own." She pushed a finger into his chest as she protested, then reached up to hook her arm around his neck. "You can't just come in here like some brute and..." She broke off midsentence and gazed up at him, eyelids droopy. "You're very warm."

So was she, warm and soft and sweetly scented. "You smell like jasmine," he whispered against her head, where she'd laid her cheek on his chest.

By the time he strode through the bedroom door, her eyes had drifted shut again. They flew open when he placed her on the bed.

"I'm sorry," she started. "I haven't had anything to eat and not nearly enough tea." She scooted to the edge of the bed. "I can't nap until I get those letters into the last post."

"Let me take care of them." He sat beside her on the bed and clasped her hand. "You need sleep."

"And you?" She cast him sideways gaze. "You have blue crescents under your eyes too. No sleep for you either?"

"My mind was too occupied for sleep."

"With?" She licked her lips, and Kit's gaze snagged on her mouth.

"Business, if you can believe it. And you, Phee. Always you." He wrapped a hand around her neck and pulled her close.

"I'm sorry you didn't get any rest." She reached up to feather a fingertip across the circle under his eye.

"Likewise."

She tipped her head back, and he took her lips gently. Forced himself to kiss her slowly, to savor the soft heat of her mouth, the way her breath caught as she leaned into him.

When he pulled back to gaze into her eyes, she turned her face aside and nuzzled his cheek. Kit slid his fingers through the long curling strands of her hair, pulling a few tresses over her shoulder so he could trace a path over her breast. God, she was beautiful.

And exhausted.

"Come on. Lie back, and I'll sit with you until you fall asleep." He suspected she'd drift off quickly.

Her shoulders stiffened, and he thought she might refuse. Instead, she scooted further back on the bed and stretched out on her side, facing him. Perching her cheek on her palm, she took on a siren's pose, if not for her drooping eyelids.

"Promise you'll post those letters?"

"Trust me." He craved her trust as much as he wanted her affection. He'd hurt her once, shattered her heart, but he hoped someday she might have a bit of faith in him again.

"They're letters to my students' parents," she admitted as she eased back onto her pillow. "Many of them sent notes after Mrs. Raybourn's rumormongering last night at the ball."

"Not good news, I take it." Kit reached for a throw at the foot of Phee's bed, settling it over her legs.

"Most of them relieved me of my tutoring services." She drew in a shaky breath. "All of them did."

"Truly?" Kit groaned and shook his head. "Over a book I wager most of them have never read?"

Phee pressed her lips together to repress another yawn. "None of them will read *Guidelines* now. Not only has Mrs. Raybourn painted me as the worst sort of influence on their daughters, but Mr. Wellbeck won't be selling any more copies of my book."

"Which is why you should allow Ruthven's to publish a new edition." He kept his tone light, offered her a grin, and tried not to reveal how much he wished to help her. Phee was far too self-reliant to ever love a man who would stifle her independence.

She shot him a quelling look, but an idea began to form in Kit's mind. He got lost in momentary woolgathering, but Phee's movements brought him back to the here and now. She lay on her back, stretched her arms above her head, and twisted her hips like a sinuous cat.

Kit sat still and quiet, watching her close her eyes and then force them open, fighting sleep. She reached for his hand and clasped his fingers.

"Don't forget the letters, Kit. I can't lose every bit of tuition."

"I promise."

When her eyes fluttered closed, she turned away from him but pulled his hand along with her. Arm curled around her, he leaned on the bed and listened to the steady rhythm of her breathing. His own eyelids grew heavy.

Why had he ever wanted to be anyplace but here by her side?

A soft mumble emerged, and he thought she spoke once more about the letters. He hoped she hadn't groveled. The Mrs. Raybourns of the world didn't merit an apology. If anything, she owed one to Phee.

"Stop worrying, love," he said quietly, desperate to reassure her. The woman devoted the same intense energy to worry as she did being stubborn.

Another murmur, and Kit hunched down to hear.

"Stay," she whispered. "Don't go."

"I'm right here, Phee." The words burned in his throat, and he choked on the guilt of what he'd done to thread her voice with that sad, pleading tone. She rarely showed an ounce of vulnerability to anyone.

Turning over to face him, she burrowed against his chest. Leaning back, he wrapped her in his arms. He'd never known such a fierce impulse to protect and love anyone in his life.

"Stay." Her plea came soft, barely a whisper, but he felt the heat of her breath through his shirt. Her fingers gripped the cloth, then loosened as she melted against him.

Just a few more minutes watching over her, and he vowed to go. She was sleeping soundly, and he had to mail those damned letters. Though he couldn't imagine why such small-minded fools deserved her efforts. If she ever allowed him to publish her book, he'd encourage her to do so under her own name, to claim her work as her own. London journalists already speculated about Miss Gilroy and why she'd yet to publicly weigh in on the debate about her book.

Perhaps Phee would be the one to end up a famous London writer after all.

Kit grinned, and his eyes slipped shut as he let his mind wander.

He jolted awake. Phee slept in his arms, mouth slightly ajar, snoring softly. What felt like a moment's slumber must have been much longer. The light filtering through the curtains had dimmed to dusk.

Carefully slipping out of Phee's arms, Kit settled her comfortably and pulled up the knitted throw. He tucked the blanket around her arms and legs to keep her warm.

As his hand crested her hip, his fingers snagged on a sharp edge. Lifting the blanket, he found an envelope protruding from her skirt. A broken wax seal bore an enormous "D," and Kit gritted his teeth as he tugged the note from Phee's pocket.

Only Dunstan would be pretentious enough to waste a wax seal for a note to travel half a mile.

As he laid the note on the bed beside her, another slip of paper fell from her pocket.

Ophelia's perfect handwriting and a list, of course. He immediately loathed the heading, which read *Rules for Kit*. His gut twisted in knots as he skimmed the rest. The first rule was to *Never speak of love or the future*. Rage flared, and disgust. More for himself than Ophelia.

He crumpled the list and tossed it aside, then tore Dunstan's missive from its envelope.

> *You will no doubt be relieved to hear that I wish to renew my proposal despite your foolhardy refusal and the revelations at Lady Pembry's ball. Your authorship of the scurrilous volume can easily be denied, and, yes, I remain willing to gift you the Trojan diadem as an engagement present.*
>
> *Call on me at your earliest convenience.*
> *—D.*

Kit slumped into the chair near Phee's bed. Sharp pain seared in his chest, as if the Ophelia of Clary's painting had taken up her sword and pierced him through the ribs. He scrubbed a hand across his face and lowered his gaze to the list she'd written to remind herself not to speak of love or a future with him.

And what of Dunstan's note? The blighter was disturbingly tenacious, and Kit couldn't deny the man's influence in the village. One word from the baron and Phee's standing could be restored. Would she reconsider the aristocrat's proposal now? Was it mere selfishness to stand in the way of a man who could offer her a settled future?

He stood and bent over Phee, pressing his lips to her forehead to place a kiss on the ink-smudged patch of skin above her brow.

He'd been a bloody fool to believe he could mend what he'd broken between them.

CHAPTER EIGHTEEN

---

*"Too often we conceal that which would give our
hearts ease to reveal. Ladies, consider your words
carefully but be forthright in your expression.
Speak your mind with grace and an open heart."*
—MISS GILROY'S GUIDELINES FOR YOUNG LADIES

In a tally of plans going spectacularly awry, even Juliet couldn't argue that the numbers were on Phee's side.

Her tutoring business had collapsed entirely. A publisher had contracted her book and then decried it completely. And Kit had come to the village for a few short weeks and returned to London, as she always knew he would.

Two days after his visit to Longacre, Aunt Rose passed on a bit of village gossip that the Ruthven prodigal had headed back to the city.

London was where he belonged, where he wished to be.

Phee bit her lip and cast her gaze out the train car window. Paddington Station was still miles off, but she imagined Kit in the city. Back in his theater world. Fawned over by actresses and seductresses far more skilled than Miss Booth of Briar Heath.

They hadn't made any promises. She wished he'd said good-bye, but her heart was intact, despite the persistent twinge behind her ribs. She rubbed two fingers over her sternum and focused on the list in her lap.

This was a new day. Sunbeams warmed her skin through the train car window, and she felt a—perhaps foolhardy— surge of anticipation. Despite the tattered schemes piled at her back, Phee had a fresh plan.

Never mind Kit's departure and the loss of nearly every single student on her roster. The note from Mr. Talbot had been too intriguing to ignore.

When she'd first spied the letter on her desk, she steeled herself to read another dismissal from a tutee's parents. Recognizing Mr. Talbot's slanted script piqued her curiosity. Rather than finding her null and void contract enclosed, the editor invited her to meet regarding a "change of heart" on Mr. Wellbeck's part, even offering to reimburse her travel expenses.

Whether or not Wellbeck intended to continue publishing her book, Phee had a list of a half dozen publishing houses she'd researched when initially submitting *Guidelines*. She would walk the streets of London all day if that's what it took to find a publisher willing to buy her book. Preferably one with more commitment to its contents than Mr. Wellbeck. New ideas for fictional stories had sparked in her mind, as far from etiquette and advice as she could get. Though she'd only managed to sketch out a few basic plot points, she'd present those too.

London came into view through the train window. St. Paul's Cathedral dome soared up like a beacon. Phee relished the prospect of a day in the city, despite the daunting task of finding a new publisher for her book. After Mrs. Raybourn's small-minded censure and neighbors treating her with chilly disdain, London held enormous appeal. She could understand why Kit escaped here. London was a city to get lost in, a place to leave expectation and duty behind and start anew.

Steam billowed up as the train rolled into Paddington Station, and a swarm of butterflies took flight in Phee's belly. The household coffers had dwindled to a pittance, and only two families had agreed to allow their daughters to resume her tutoring services. She had to find another means of earning. Currently, the only publisher she knew for certain wished to publish *Guidelines* was the one man she couldn't give her book to. She had no more wish to be beholden to Kit than to Lord Dunstan.

Surely others would be interested in publishing a book that had sold well, despite its critics. If nothing else, she suspected at least a few publishers would be will to take on Ruthven Publishing's longstanding stranglehold on the etiquette-book market.

"Is this your station too, miss?" A tall dark-haired young lady who'd shared her train car and kept her nose in a book for the entire journey stood at the carriage door.

"Yes. Thank you. I was lost in thought."

"I understand." The pretty traveler lifted the volume she'd been reading. "Books often intrigue me so completely I miss my stop."

Phee followed the young woman onto the platform. Phee's cheeks warmed when she peaked at the title of the lady's book. *Miss Gilroy's Guidelines for Young Ladies.* The well-dressed young woman must have purchased a copy before Wellbeck removed them from storefronts.

"Are you enjoying the book?" After the condemnations from countless students' parents, Phee was curious to hear a Londoner's opinion.

"Not enjoying it, no." The lady stopped and cast Phee a fervent gaze. "I'm adoring every word. Every Englishwoman should read Miss Gilroy's book." She cast a gaze around and leaned in. "Wellbeck's has stopped selling the volume, but there's a shop on Fawcett Lane that still has a few copies." After tipping her hat at Phee, the lady strode away.

Bolstered by her enthusiastic praise, Phee pivoted on her heel, took one bracing breath, and set off toward the offices of Wellbeck Publishing.

Finding the front desk clerk's chair empty, she waited only a moment before rapping on the frosted glass door of Mr. Talbot's office. After scurrying sounds within, the editor opened the door wide.

"What a pleasure to see you again, Miss Marsden. I'm so glad you've given us this opportunity." Rather than ushering Phee into his office, Talbot lifted an arm to direct her toward Wellbeck's more palatial domain.

"I haven't given anything yet, Mr. Talbot."

"Quite right." The older man blushed to his graying pate. "Hear us out, Miss Marsden." He gestured again toward his boss's office and waited for Phee to precede him.

She'd only met Wellbeck on one other occasion and found him intimidating and unpleasant. He tended to bark rather than speak, and he'd perfected the art of staring down his beakish nose over the rim of tiny metal pince-nez glasses.

Today, he was another man entirely. He welcomed her with open arms and a broad smile. "Come, come, Miss Marsden. Mr. Talbot, we've been remiss. See to tea for the young lady. Anything else you fancy, Miss Marsden?"

"Uh, no."

Wellbeck came around to assist her into a chair, though she'd been quite competent at seating herself for years, even taught other young ladies to sit in the most ladylike manner.

A moment later, Talbot returned bearing a small tray with a plain white teapot and three cups. She wasn't used to being fussed over, especially by gentlemen, but Mr. Talbot poured tea before offering her the first cup.

Wellbeck beamed at her. "Have you ever had a change of heart, Miss Marsden?"

Phee swallowed her hot tea too quickly and winced as the liquid burned a trail across her tongue. Wellbeck's comments caught her off guard. Change of heart? Kit came vibrantly to mind, but he was far too distracting to ponder.

When she didn't answer, Wellbeck waved apologetically. "Forgive my impertinence. I shall speak only of my own turn of the tide. Mr. Talbot conveyed this news previously, so allow me take my turn and say that we would very much like to publish your book."

Phee ignored the flutter of excitement in her belly, an echo of what she'd felt the first time. On this occasion, she wouldn't simply agree. As much Phee desperately needed income, she no longer trusted Wellbeck to keep his word or honor a contract.

Both men held their breath. Phee heard movement in the outer office and muffled ticking, as if somewhere a pocket watch insisted on being heard.

"I appreciate your interest, Mr. Wellbeck, but I must decline." The butterflies in her belly went wild as soon as the words were out. She didn't regret refusing Wellbeck's offer, but her body insisted that turning down income was utter folly.

Seated in the chair beside her, Mr. Talbot sagged in disappointment. Wellbeck shed his friendly mien, piercing her with a baleful scowl over the top of his glasses.

"So you're Ruthven's girl, are you?" The venom in his voice was as thick as the honey had been a moment earlier.

"I'm not anyone's girl, Mr. Wellbeck. I'm a spinster." The word scalded her tongue like the hot tea she'd swallowed. "I belong to no man and have both the burden and privilege of making choices for myself." Phee stood, vibrating with too much emotion to remain seated between two men who looked at her as if she'd lost her mind. "I choose to find a publisher who values the content of my book, and you do not." She spared her former editor a half-grin. "I wish you well, Mr. Talbot. Good day to you both."

Energy fizzed in her muscles like galvanic electricity. Each step away from Wellbeck's office made her feel stronger, more determined. Yet a question tickled at the back of her mind, one she hadn't taken the time to ask.

She heard Mr. Talbot's lanky shuffle behind her.

"Why, Mr. Talbot? What caused Mr. Wellbeck to change his mind about my book?"

"Rivalry, Miss Marsden." The upright man scrubbed a hand across his mouth, plucking at the edges of his grizzled beard. "Though I'm not privy to the details, Wellbeck and Ruthven loathed each other." After clasping his hands behind his back, the editor stared at the tips of his boots. "As soon as I told Mr. Wellbeck about the younger Ruthven's offer to publish your book, well—"

"He wants to best him."

"Indeed. I believe Mr. Wellbeck was glad to see the demise of Ruthven's. Everyone expected the man's son to quit the field."

She resisted a rush of temper to defend Kit. Though he was stubborn, he was something else. Having been the focus of his single-minded pursuit once, she knew the depth of his tenacity. While she invariably gave in to duty and necessity, no one could deter Kit when he set his mind on a goal.

The danger with Kit was that his goals could change on a whim.

"Will you allow him to publish your book?" Talbot grinned at her as if intrigued by the possibility.

"Perhaps I shall." Defiance brought a heady burst of confidence, but as she strode out of Wellbeck's, Phee immediately began to doubt. She'd spoken impulsively. Kit was the one who made breakneck decisions, not her.

Of course Ruthven's was just there, too close to allow her time to think. Her marching tread slowed as she approached. Pacing back and forth in front of the glass-fronted door, she argued the merits and risks in her head.

How could she let Kit publish her book? Everything between them was already tangled. The pleasure of foiling

Wellbeck wasn't an insubstantial consideration, but her book had been written in response to Ruthven's *Rules for Young Ladies*. No publisher in his right mind would publish both volumes. And what would happen when Kit sold his father's business? Would the new owner favor *Guidelines* or bow to the same outraged readers who'd plagued Wellbeck?

"Are you lost, Miss Marsden?" A gruff male voice emerged from the doorway of Ruthven Publishing, and Phee recognized the burly outline of Gabriel Adamson, lit from behind by bright gaslights. "Or is this some sort of one-woman protest?"

"Just contemplating my options, Mr. Adamson. Would you be so kind as to spare me a moment of your time?"

His black hair gleamed in cloud-filtered sunlight as Mr. Adamson stepped out onto the pavement, narrowed his eyes, and nodded curtly. "I'll spare you several moments if you'll cease perambulating in front of our place of business."

His office was as tidy as she remembered. More so, since most of the volumes of *The Ruthven Rules* had been removed from the shelves behind his desk. Curious, that.

After offering her a seat and taking his own behind the desk, the young man tented his fingers under his chin and stared at her expectantly.

"I'll not waste your time, Mr. Adamson. I've come to London to find a new publisher for my book."

He narrowed his clear blue eyes. "An ambitious objective."

"Who do you trust among the publishers of London?" Phee took Ruthven's young editor for a plain-speaking man and one with far more experience in the world of London publishing than she possessed.

"Not Wellbeck, of course. The man's an utter bounder." Apparently Adamson knew what she'd only just learned. Wellbeck's principles had all the permanence of soap bubbles.

"I have a list of prospects." Pulling her list out, she offered it to the broad-shouldered editor. "Would you have a look?"

He seemed to appreciate the fact that she sought his advice and scanned the paper with interest. "May I?" He lifted a fountain pen and scribbled for a moment. When he returned her slip of paper, he'd put a line through three publishers and added square tick boxes next to the remaining three. The man took lists seriously, and Phee couldn't help but grin.

"I notice Ruthven's isn't on your list, Miss Marsden."

"You said you did not wish to publish my book, Mr. Adamson." In fact, he'd added that Leopold Ruthven would have rejected it too.

"So I did." He looked as firmly decided against her as the first day she'd met him. "However—"

"Have you read *Miss Gilroy's Guidelines?*" Phee interrupted him, then sucked in a breath, attempting to temper frustration that had more to do with the past days' disappoints than Adamson's curt dismissal. "There are no outrages in its pages, sir. The book does not foment rebellion or advise women to behave in scandalous ways."

"No, but you do urge them to weigh duty against their desires."

"So you *have* read it." His paraphrase of her words left no doubt. Phee didn't try very hard to stifle a triumphant grin.

"My sister has. She's a voracious reader and, unfortunately, not terribly discerning." His mouth twitched. Phee thought the dour man might actually return her grin, but he merely cleared his throat and settled back in his chair. "She is also fourteen years of age. I'm afraid her recommendation does not sway me."

The heavy tread of footsteps drew Mr. Adamson's eyes to the threshold of his office. Whoever stood in the open doorway caused him to tense, his square jaw drawing hard and taut. A little muscle took to spasming in his cheek.

Before she had the chance to turn and see who'd entered, a prickle of awareness set Phee's nerves tingling. A familiar scent in the air made her pulse thrum in her veins.

"Ophelia?" There was a heart-wrenching thread of hopefulness in Kit's tone. When he stepped into the room, the same emotion lit his gaze.

"You're here," she whispered. Not in some actress's bed or planning his next success on the stage.

"I am."

"I'm here on business." Let there be no mistake about her intentions. Heaven forbid he think she'd followed him to London to hurl herself into his arms and beg him to return to Briar Heath. "Mr. Adamson was advising me."

"I see." Kit drew out the two syllables and cast Adamson a questioning glance. He seemed to be holding himself in place with adamantine effort. Then he drew in a deep breath and took one long stride in her direction.

"About my book."

"Your book?" A frown, then theater magic. He smoothed his face into an expressionless mask. "Have you changed your mind about allowing us to publish?"

"Do I get a vote?" Adamson rolled his chair back and stood, broad arms braced above his chest.

"No." Kit chuckled as if the man had said something amusing. "Did my father run this enterprise as a democracy?"

Adamson's shoulders stiffened. "I cannot say that he did, but he considered my recommendations."

"Perhaps next time, Mr. Adamson." Kit shot the young man a steely gaze. "Give us a moment."

The young editor held his ground, gritting his teeth long enough to make his displeasure known. As he strode from his office, he offered Kit a pointed glare as he passed.

"I'm sorry," Kit said as soon as Adamson departed. "I'll make an effort to hire more agreeable editors in future."

"The man wishes to act on his principles. Who can blame him?" It was more than she could say for Wellbeck. Phee swallowed against a lump in her throat. Kit looked striking in his new suit, and somehow, surprisingly, as if he belonged in a publishing office. "I'm sorry. Mr. Adamson saw me outside, and…I didn't know you'd be here."

"Don't. Please." He held up a hand. "You never have to apologize to me, Ophelia. Not ever. I'm pleased to see you."

When he stepped toward her, Phee knew he'd touch her. Heaven help how much she wanted him to. An aching heat flared in her body.

"More than pleased." The raw rumble of his voice made her shiver.

"Kit." Her sensible half—the woman who'd written *Guidelines*—knew perfectly well how to extract herself from temptation. So why did his name fall from her lips wantonly? More petition than refusal.

Her petition didn't work. Kit cast his gaze out the room's only window. "Are you planning to marry Dunstan?"

"No." The question was the last she expected. "I refused him."

"I'm glad you'll let us publish your book." He turned back to her, staring with such intensity Phee could almost feel the warmth of his lips against her cheek, the heat of his mouth on the column of her neck.

She hadn't agreed to anything yet, but he'd always been one to let his eagerness and enthusiasm propel him ahead of practical details.

When he stepped closer and dipped his head, Phee braced her free hand on the warm wall of his chest. "Remember? You can't mix kissing and commerce."

Stepping away, his mouth tipped in a halfhearted grin. "Says the woman who likes rules as much as my father did."

"Guidelines," Phee protested. How could he compare her to a man who'd treated him with such disdain?

"Ah yes." Kit raised a brow and crossed his arms. "Guidelines for young ladies. You only wrote rules for me."

He'd seen her list of rules, but they'd been more about guarding her heart than regulating his actions. After he'd carried her up to her bedroom and departed, she'd found them crumpled in her bedclothes.

"Ruthven's never agrees to an author's rules. We set our own terms." Adamson stood in the doorway with a sheaf of documents in his hands.

Phee stepped away from Kit, and he moved toward the window behind Adamson's desk. "Shall we all take a seat and discuss the contract?" Adamson arranged pens at the front edge of his desktop, fanning pages out for Phee's inspection.

Kit strode forward, took up a pen, and signed his name without looking at any of the typed terms. He lifted the same pen out to Phee.

It was all moving too fast, and she was buzzing for reasons that had nothing to do with contracting her book. Doubts assailed her. She'd signed Wellbeck's contract too quickly, flushed with excitement, humbled and gratified that anyone might care to read her book. This time she wanted to be certain. Striding forward, she skimmed the words on the first page, paragraph after paragraph of obscure legal language.

"Have you read it?" she asked Kit.

"The Ruthven contract? Yes. It's comparable to what you signed with Wellbeck, I suspect."

"My book. Have you read my book?"

"You know I have. I complimented you on its merits." Kit furrowed his brow as he scanned the shelf behind Adamson. "Even Adamson owns a copy."

"I do not *own* a copy," he declared as if testifying in court, loud enough for everyone to be certain of his innocence. "The one I brought for our meeting with Mr. Talbot belonged to my sister. I've since returned the volume to her."

"There, you see." Kit pointed at his managing editor. "Even Adamson's sister loves your book."

Perhaps Kit had read the book, but she still wondered if his commitment would be as flimsy as Wellbeck's. Wasn't a question of commitment at the heart of all that had passed between them?

Other publishers' offices dotted this street and the next. She'd intended to visit several before making this decision. As usual, her feelings for Kit obscured all her good sense.

"May I take these documents and consider them more thoroughly, Mr. Adamson?"

"By all means." The editor's striking slate-blue eyes ballooned and his full mouth split in a smile, apparently thrilled at the prospect of her refusing to sign at all. "Consider as long as you like."

"Thank you. I won't take up any more of your time today, gentlemen." She nodded to Adamson and then Kit before folding the contract and tucking it under her arm.

There was no question of Kit's letting her depart so easily. She sensed him moving behind her as she dashed into the main office. Before she could escape, his hand shot out above her head to push the front door open.

"You're having doubts." He followed her out of the building and stood gazing at her in that penetrating way of his.

"Constantly." Worry and doubt had become her constant companions since her mother's death. Kit's departure and her father's illness had only given her more practice. How could a man who avoided duty and flicked away obstacles as if they were lint on his coat sleeve understand? "You may mock my lists, but I've learned to plan and organize in order to prevent adversity. To remind myself what must be done and impose a bit of order."

"Even on me, apparently." One of his dark chocolate brows winged up, and Phee immediately saw parallels to how his father had attempted to control and stifle him.

"The rules I proposed weren't meant to control you but to free me." Passion without commitment. Freedom from worry about the future. How long had it been since she'd felt free? At the Pembry ball, she'd craved a taste of liberty from what should be done, if only for one night. Knowing full well that Kit would return to his life in the city and she would remain in the country, she'd wanted a moment of passion. And only with him.

He frowned as if he didn't understand.

"I'm not Miss Booth. I wasn't looking for a clumsy ruination, only to catch you in marriage afterward."

He pursed his lips, then dropped his gaze to the pavement and flicked the edges of his coat back to place a hand on each hip. Energy rippled off him as he clenched his jaw. A single step brought him so close his thighs brushed her skirt. One more and he eased her back into the alcove in front of Ruthven Publishing, pinning her between the office door and the heat of his body.

"All your planning, all your lists and rules leave no room for possibility. What of the unexpected?" The gruffness in his voice set off gooseflesh on her arms. He bowed his dark head, grazed his mouth across hers, then traced her tingling lips with the pad of his thumb. "Darling Phee, what if I've changed? What if I wish to be caught?"

CHAPTER NINETEEN

"A few words on the lure of scoundrels, rakes, and rogues. Ladies, we may acknowledge their attractions but must not fall. They will take all we have—body, heart, and peace of mind—and offer nothing more than transitory pleasure in return. As seductive as such men may be, avoid their inducements at all costs."

—MISS GILROY'S GUIDELINES FOR YOUNG LADIES

Timing determines whether a performance crashes or soars. It was the least of the lessons Kit had learned after four years in the theater. On the page and stage, he understood timing like the back of his hand. But when it came to matters of the heart, apparently he didn't know a blasted thing.

He'd chosen the wrong moment to confess his feelings to Phee. Or perhaps he'd been too oblique. The impulses she sparked in him were still a tumultuous jumble. Perhaps they always would be. He could live with that.

Long, awful minutes passed after his declaration, and she stood immobile, staring at him with a dumbstruck gaze.

"What I meant to say…" Was precisely what he'd bloody said. Good God, the woman had him aching day and night. Had she missed the hunger in his eyes? Or failed to taste his need for her in every kiss? "You must know how much I want you."

"Do you?" Ophelia had never been coy, never played the coquette. The wariness in her tone tore at his heart. Four years of absence had taught her to distrust, to doubt what they'd both known with fervent certainty before he'd gone. How could he blame her for losing whatever confidence she ever had in him?

"Let me show you how much." Reaching for her, he pressed her hand to his chest. Beyond her warmth and smooth, soft skin, he felt his heart thrashing between them. "Feel that? If I pressed my hand to your body, wouldn't I discover the same frantic beat?"

She caught the swell of her lower lip between her teeth, and he longed to soothe the spot with his tongue.

"I could provide other proof of my desire too, but not here with Adamson in view."

With a little shake of awareness, she looked toward the Ruthven offices and then scanned each end of Somerset Row. When she nudged his chest, Kit retreated and allowed her to step away, fighting the urge to haul her back against his body.

She strode away, as if she planned to escape without another word. Less than a block up the pavement, she turned back.

"May I have time to think?" Cheeks flushed, shoulders squared, Phee looked at his cheek, his nose, anywhere but his eyes. She waved a hand in his direction, sweeping up and down his body to encompass every inch from head to toe. "You make rational contemplation difficult."

So did she. Generally speaking, Kit was a proponent of thinking, but lately all his thoughts were jasmine-scented, wrapped 'round with strands of auburn hair, and ridiculously optimistic. That was all Ophelia's doing.

"Can you manage thinking and enjoying yourself at the same time?"

"Yes, of course." She puckered her brow as if reconsidering her hasty answer. After years of knowing Phee, Kit wondered if what she needed most was a holiday from worry. He'd been responsible for his sisters' future and his father's business for only a month. She'd been bearing the load of running a household, tutoring other people's children, and caring for Juliet years longer.

"Hyde Park," he said as the notion popped into his head.

"Pardon?"

"You promised me a boat ride on the Serpentine."

"I don't recall promising you anything." Despite her scolding governess tone, a flicker of interest lit her gaze.

"Come, Phee. Spare an hour—just you and me doing precisely as we please—and then we'll go back to dealing with duty and expectations." He lifted an arm to escort her.

She leaned forward a fraction. He thought surely she'd agree. Then it all came crashing down.

"No, I cannot." Her eyes shuttered at the same moment her mouth tightened into a determined line. "I came to

London with a purpose, and I mustn't get distracted. There are other publishers I wished to see."

"Let me guess. You have a list."

"If you're going to tease me—"

"I love your lists. I love…" *You.* Her glower and tapping foot indicated this was the wrong time to confess it. "I adore your desire to cram more usefulness into a day than I accomplish in a month. I admire your determination to do what must be done while the rest of us are busy giving in to rogue impulses."

"Not everyone. *You* are given to more impulses than any man I've ever known." She bit her lip, flooding the plump curve of flesh with color. The rush of pink to her cheeks darkened her freckles. He wondered which of his impulses was playing in her mind. "You're probably having some impulse now," she accused.

"Oh, I am." And her imperious school mistress tone and scathing glare only made his body respond in ways that would turn her heated blush into an inferno.

"Well?" She encouraged with the wave of her hand. "Tell me."

"No, I mustn't." Kit frowned. He wasn't in the habit of denial, and the words felt odd on his tongue. Like lines from a play he hadn't committed to memory. "I wouldn't wish to shock you." Keeping a smile from his lips after that line took utmost effort.

Phee's turquoise eyes rounded with curiosity. "I'm not some fragile miss, you know." She wagged a finger in the air. "Have you forgotten that I wrote a shocking book?" Without letting him answer, she seemed to recall another fact on her side and added, "My father once wrote an essay in support of Godwin's notions of free love."

"Did he indeed?" *Bollocks to that.* Kit had no interest whatsoever in free love. Once he made Ophelia his own, he planned to be greedy. There would be no sharing. And he would never give her a moment's doubt about his commitment. Ever.

"Go on," she pressed. "Shock me. Tell me your impulse."

Just one? He possessed none of her tutoring experience, but he wanted to teach her everything he knew. "Impulses come on like a starburst, love. One spark lights another until they all explode inside." The thought of touching her, pleasuring her, set off tremors of impatience in his belly. Kit licked his lips and tried to remember they were on a city street in broad daylight. He cared nothing for propriety, but for Ophelia's sake he had to find a way to refrain from ravishing her in front of London's publishing establishments. "I suppose there is a logic at play, for those who like order."

She narrowed an eye dubiously. "And what is the *logic* of your current impulse?"

"Pink." Now it was his turn to bite his lip and try to stem images of laying Ophelia out on her back, stripping her bare, licking—

"I don't understand." But she looked intrigued. He half expected her to pull out one of her bits of paper and take notes.

"The carnation flush of your mouth, the wet pink of your tongue." He was speaking nonsense. Kit wasn't even certain his brain was receiving any blood from his thrashing heart. He was all body now, a mountain of eager flesh. His want for her was years deep, a long desperate hunger. He moved closer, drinking in her scent. "Shall I continue?"

"Yes." The sharp nod of her head and slight parting of her lips told him she wanted more.

"When you bite your lip." He stared at her mouth. "Blood stains your flesh the sweetest pink. I want to kiss that color. My *impulse* is to follow that color, to watch it rush down your neck, under all those damnable buttons, to the tips of your breasts. To trace it with my lips. But that wouldn't be enough, love. I am determined to seek out every pink part of you, to kiss and taste and worship every spot."

Neither of them was prone to speechlessness. They were both writers, after all. Yet somehow he'd managed to stun her into silence twice in the span of twenty minutes.

That pink mouth he'd waxed rhapsodic about trembled before she lifted her chin and rasped out, "Let's take that boat ride."

He smiled in victory, though most of his body hadn't yet given up on imagining much more pleasurable ways to pass a Tuesday afternoon.

"Careful." Kit steadied her with a firm grip, and Phee took a seat in the boat's stern. A cool breeze chased across the Serpentine's surface, riffling her hair, but she was still burning inside. She hadn't stood near a raging fireplace, but she felt as if she had, and she was melting deep in the center of her need. In the place where impulses flourished. After so many years of denial, Kit stoked her longing to life with a few delicious words.

Could he feel her trembling?

He'd remained unusually silent during their ride to the park in a cramped hansom cab. Even when their cabman took a corner at breakneck speed, and she'd reached out to steady herself, pressing her palm against the taut, thick muscle of his thigh.

He had to seduce her, or she him. Her desire for the man was beginning to blot out every other thought.

As Kit balanced his tall frame on the bench in the center of the boat and took the oars, he offered a benign grin that made her doubt his acting abilities.

"When will you be returning to your work in the theater?" Because he would, and reminding herself of the fact was the best way forestall the twinge in her heart each time he looked at her, the way her body flared to life every time he touched her.

"Keen to be rid of me, are you?"

"No." Phee swallowed against the urge to say more, to confess that she'd always wished for him to stay. But that wasn't the way of things. People left. Loving someone didn't mean one ought to cling if he wished to soar.

"I've decided not to sell my father's publishing interests after all." He held his grin, but his gaze turned serious. "We have a mind to overthrow the old ways."

"We?" She couldn't imagine Mr. Adamson joining any sort of revolution, unless it was against Kit.

"My sisters and I. There will be legal knots to unravel, but I intend to give Sophia and Clary an equal share of Ruthven's."

"That's an excellent idea." Phee considered the benefits of Sophia's need for order and Clarissa's tendency toward ornamentation. Between the three of them, they could bring extraordinary talents to any enterprise.

Kit assessed her, tipping his head. "I thought you'd approve."

"More than approve. I think it's wonderful." Precisely the kind of opportunity she wished she could offer her own sister. Or at the very least a stable home and tuition to fund the university education their father had urged Juliet to seek. "But what of your theater work? Your plays?"

Rather than answer, he shrugged out of his coat, gripped the oars, and pushed toward her. Leaning back, he sliced the wooden blades into the water, pulling the small boat into motion with ease. Only his buttons struggled, straining to hold onto their stitched line of fabric as his muscles worked. Pushing toward her, pulling back, gaze fixed on hers, he cut through the water until they neared the center of the lake.

"You'll understand our intentions for Ruthven's better than anyone." The exertion of rowing added a breathless quality to his deep voice. "We wish to look forward to the new century, to adapt my father's books and publish fiction. Selling more is the chief goal."

"Will you publish your plays?"

He pursed his mouth as if contemplating the notion. "Perhaps." Water sluiced from the oars when he lifted them from the lake and leaned toward her, balancing his elbows on his knees. "You could assist our enterprise by allowing us to publish *Miss Gilroy's Guidelines*."

"Printing my book won't improve your fortunes. Have you forgotten that Wellbeck's was inundated with letters denouncing *Guidelines*?"

"I recall him parting with enough copies to outsell *The Ruthven Rules* for a while. A few letters won't deter me, Ophelia."

"You approve of young women taking charge of their fates, then?" At her teasing tone, his eyes lit in shades of gold and honey. Flecks of green too, rich emerald like the depths of Dunstan's pond. She needed to tease him more often.

"Come." Lifting a hand between them, he beckoned, "I'll demonstrate how much I approve."

Touching him was a mistake; moving closer was folly. The worst part was that being near Kit was the only place Phee wished to be.

"You'll need to stand." He tugged her up, but she gripped the edge of the boat.

"What if I tip us both out?"

"Trust me." Scooting to the edge of the boat's center bench, Kit made just enough room for her to sit beside him on the narrow slat. He tugged again and urged her over. "Turn your back to me. I've got you." With one hand on her waist and the other on her hip, he eased Phee down, sliding her body against his until they were hip to hip, thigh to thigh, shoulders brushing with every breath. He kept an arm around her waist, driving her mad with his scent and heat.

"Here, you take this one. I'll manage the other."

She took the oar in both hands and slapped it into the water.

"Wait, love." Kit turned to face her, his breath stirring loose hairs against her neck. "We have to work together. Build a rhythm. Like this."

Phee mimicked his movements, leaning forward and pulling back when he did, their bodies melded together, side by side. The water was surprisingly heavy, the effort greater than she anticipated. When she gasped on one hard pull, Kit turned his gaze to hers. This close she couldn't hide how he affected her. Whatever walls she'd constructed, they were dust now, and she only wanted his mouth on hers, his body this near but without the rustling layers of clothing between them.

"Do you think I'll succeed?" he asked on a husky whisper.

At seducing her? Oh yes. But the longer she drowned in his gaze, something beyond desire brightened his eyes. A vulnerability she hadn't seen since they were children. He spoke of filling his father's role, of making a choice he'd been avoiding for years.

"I do." Phee had no doubt Ruthven's old ways would yield to Kit's intelligence and tenacity.

"Despite my having no notion how to be a publisher?" Despite taking on a role his father had been attempting to force on him for years. She wondered what had caused his change of heart.

"You'll have your sisters to advise you. And Mr. Adamson, who I suspect has an opinion on every topic."

He chuckled at that. Pressed as close as they were, she felt the sound reverberating through his body.

"You could advise me too." He leaned in, his mouth one short dip of his head away from hers.

"Me?"

"You've managed your own tutoring endeavor." He gripped the oars, and Phee followed his lead. They pushed against the water and set the boat in motion toward the far edge of the lake.

"I instruct schoolgirls, most of whom only aspire to marry well."

"And you? Do you aspire to marry well?" Lightning swift, he slid an arm around her back, skimmed his lips across her cheek. Holding his breath, he waited for her answer.

"I vowed not to speak of marriage with you." Such a prudent, logical rule when she'd conceived her plan. But now, with the hard-muscled heat of him so near, she couldn't gather her wits enough to recall whether she'd intended to free him or protect her own heart.

"Yes." He released the word in a single breath against her cheek. "Seduction is what you want, isn't it?"

Phee marveled at how Kit's deep voice made a solution she'd thought so practical sound so brazen. But of course, he possessed years of practice being brazen.

She was the novice. He was a rogue with a scandalous reputation.

"How many women have you seduced?"

He blinked, then again. While he numbered his conquests, Phee counted the constellation of beauty marks on his face—one left of his nose, another higher on the right, a triangle cluster above his left brow. She noted twelve unique marks that decorated his slopes and angles, and still he remained silent.

"That many?" she teased, failing utterly to muster a smirk or lighthearted tone. She feared her voice quavered like her insides.

Finally, he turned to her. "Do you truly expect me to recall any of them when you consume every thought? When you're here, warm and soft and smelling so damn good." Reaching down, he clasped the top of her boot. He slid his fingers up, burrowing under her skirt and two layers of petticoats. "To be honest…" He claimed the flesh of her leg, just above the edge of her boot, cradling her in his heated grip. Sensation ribboned higher, pulsing low in her belly and at her core. Wickedly, brazenly, that's where she craved his touch. "I can think of nothing but freeing you from every stitch of clothing. Loving you as I should have done years ago."

"Yes." She wanted him more than plans and lists and a perfect, plotted future.

"We've reached the edge." Their boat bobbed in the lake, no longer drifting. Kit released her leg, and she hated the loss of his heat, but his hands were on her again quickly, a touch at her waist, another gripping her arm, assisting her to climb out of the little skiff. "Wait here."

While Kit dealt with returning their hired boat, Phee stood and absorbed the sounds of the park and the lively city beyond. She wanted to feel, only feel, but thoughts rushed in. Mama's decorum had got in too deep. Despite the rules she'd devised, she knew what her choice could mean. But while everything else seemed uncertain—the publication of her book, even the future of Longacre—her feelings for Kit were never in doubt.

He strode toward her, long powerful strides, with curled fists and lines creasing his forehead.

"Will you catch the next train back to Hertfordshire?" he asked when he'd reached her side. "Or do you truly wish to speak with other publishers today?"

"Neither." She clasped his hand, and he gripped her eagerly. "Do you still maintain lodgings here in London?"

"I do. Unfinished business, I suppose." Stepping close, he tipped his mouth in a sly grin. "I'll add it to my list."

"Take me there." No doubts. No regret. Just an eagerness to be alone with him.

Kit narrowed his gaze and stared above her head into the distance, as if he could glimpse his rented rooms from where they stood. "I fear you'll be mightily unimpressed. The neighborhood isn't at all the sort of place for a proper young lady."

The air rang with Phee's burst of laughter. Kit dipped his head and managed to look abashed.

She'd propositioned him for ruin, lost all of her tutoring students because of her audacious notions, and only a few days prior had almost given herself to him as she wished to do now.

"I shall worry about propriety later." Stepping into his arms, Phee reveled at how her curves melded with the hard length of him. "Right now, all I wish to be is yours."

CHAPTER TWENTY

Ophelia looked shockingly right in his Seven Dials bedroom. As if her color and curves were what the space had lacked all along. Their opposites made for an unexpected harmony—its dingy, dusty corners transformed into a cozy space when subjected to her intoxicating vitality and curious gaze. Every inch of the room fascinated her, judging by the close inspection she offered each surface. She flipped through the notes and scraps of unfinished plays on his desk, cracked open his battered wardrobe to stroke a hand down the arm of a threadbare coat, ran her finger over the mussed heap of clothing piled in the corner.

Then she stared at the bedstead a long while before drawing in a deep breath that lifted her breasts. The motion made his mouth water like the hungry creature he was.

One hand fidgeting with the buttons at the high neck of her gown, she finally turned to face him. "I have no notion how to do this." Phee knitted her auburn brows adorably. "Of course, I have *some* notion. Books and animals and... The physical components involved are clear to me." She glanced down at his groin, and then hastily up again.

His body responded as if she'd stroked him with that hot gaze, hardening eagerly until the anticipation of pleasuring her crested into a potent ache.

Kit started across the room slowly. That pink shade he adored glowed in her cheeks, and she ran her tongue over her lower lip, just as he intended to do again and again. When she opened her mouth to speak, no words emerged, just a sharp inhale. Then a soft mewl when he traced the swell of her lower lip with his thumb.

"Just feel, sweetheart." He cupped her cheek in his palm and found he was trembling. He'd wanted her, needed her, for so very long. "Know only this. I want you as I've never wanted anyone or anything in my life."

"That I know." She nodded, her gaze solemn. "For it's how I want you."

The smile that broke across his face was new, as if he was learning how to form the expression for the first time. His cheeks tightened and stretched, his heart thudding an irregular beat against his ribs.

Phee smiled up at him too, sweet and tremulous, and began unfastening the top buttons of her gown.

Kit caught her nimble fingers. "Those are mine to see to. God knows they've driven me mad long enough."

He should have let her carry on. Her lithe fingers would have made faster work of the endless line of buttons. His were thick and fumbling. But, for her sake, he couldn't rush this. He couldn't bear to disappoint her, or give her any cause to regret the gift she offered.

"Then I take it these are mine." Between his elbows, Ophelia lifted her arms and began unbuttoning his shirt and waistcoat, tugging at the loose knot of his neck cloth. The tangled slide of his limbs against a woman's had never felt so erotic, never ignited such a gnawing desperation to make her his own.

When the creamy swell of her breasts peeked out through the opening of her gown, his gut clenched, and the muscles in his legs began to spasm. He bent to place a kiss on the soft, plump flesh, wrapping an arm around her waist to pull her near.

Perhaps a bit of haste was in order after all. He needed to be rid of her dress, her corset and chemise, everything keeping her smooth pink skin from his gaze. She sensed his urgency and made fast work of the buttons across her belly. He peeled back her gown awkwardly, pulling and tugging until the bodice slid from her shoulders. He shaped his hands around the lush camber of her hips, still encased in the bondage of her corset.

"I want you free of this." He spun her in his arms and meant to start on the laces at her back. Instead he applied his mouth to the tantalizing slope of her nape. She tasted luscious and sweet, like ripe summer fruit.

"Hooks," she whispered breathily. "In the front."

Reaching around, he felt her working the fastenings expertly, pressing the edges of the garment together until her breasts swelled above the edge. He ran his fingers over her bare flesh until he found the knotted ribbon at the edge of her chemise and began working it loose. When she slid free of the corset, Kit filled his hands with her breasts, and Phee emitted a throaty sigh. Her nipples nudged insistently at the center of his palms. He licked his lips, eager to have them on his tongue.

Phee lifted her arms and began removing the pins in her hair. The position pushed her breasts further into his hands. On a husky groan, he kissed and laved the tender flesh of her neck, as soft, jasmine-scented curls tumbled across his cheek.

And that's when he knew. Even with Ophelia, he'd be a rogue. He wouldn't abide her list of rules. Already, he wanted more. One moment of loving her would never be enough.

There was a reason he'd sought her night after night in the theater. She was the only woman he craved.

"Help me with my skirt?"

The buttons were larger, but he still struggled to unfasten them with any degree of finesse. His nerves were too raw with need. The more of her he uncovered, the worse his thirst. She shimmied out of her skirts as he pushed her wide-necked chemise down her shoulders. As soon as her breasts were bare, she turned in his arms.

"Now you." Her eager hands worked the remainder of his buttons, pushed the fabric from his shoulders, and she exhaled a sharp gasp. "Goodness."

They'd never been this bare before each other, and never with so much longing stretching across the years between them.

"You're quite…extraordinary," she whispered. Offering his body the same hands-on inspection she afforded the furnishings in his room, she stroked her fingers across his chest up to the crest of his shoulder, shaping the muscles of his arm. Every stroke, each appreciative murmur, shot heat straight to his groin. Whether she knew it or not, the lady stoked want in him like a fire.

"Come, love." Clasping her hand, he led her toward the bed. When she perched nervously at the edge, Kit crouched and made fast work of removing her boots, rolling each stocking along the long shapely length of her legs. "Now, these"—he dragged his fingers down the backs of her calves—"are extraordinary."

"Except for the freckles. And the bramble scars."

"Darling Phee." Lowering to his knees, he kissed one freckle, licked its neighbor, nipped at another with the edge of his teeth. He ran a finger over the scar she'd earned when they'd both stumbled into a briar patch. "These speckles and marks are lovely because they're yours, as beautiful as every other part of you."

She'd clasped her arms over her breasts, and he prayed nerves and all the expectations she'd soaked in during a lifetime in Briar Heath weren't making her doubt. Only her drawers remained, virginally white cotton fabric decorated at the edge with delicate lace. He'd never wanted to shred an innocent piece of fabric so much in his life.

Go slow. Phee deserved to be loved with care. Especially this first time.

"Are you going to remove these?" Sliding one finger into the waist of her drawers, she arched her brow like a seasoned seductress. "And those?" Her eyes riveted on his trousers. When she swept her tongue across the seam of her lips, whatever measure of restraint he possessed snapped.

Closer. Phee needed Kit's skin against hers. In one swift move, he slid her drawers away and kneeled above her on the bed, hands braced on each side of her head. In the chill of the room, she'd covered her bosom, but now his deliciously warm chest caressed the aching tips of her breasts.

She needed to hold on to this moment, sear every sensation in memory, lock it away in her heart.

He nuzzled her cheek, ran a hand down her neck, his long fingers seeking out one taut pink nipple. When she gasped, he took her mouth in a searing kiss. Mercy, he was hot—the slide of his tongue, the heat of lips. Silky strands of ebony hair stroked her face as he kissed her. He tasted of cinnamon, this man she'd craved all her days.

With drugging caresses, he swept his fingers over her skin, sliding them down her body, across her stomach to the hollow of her navel.

More. A terrible trembling ache began between her thighs. She bucked against him, sensitive flesh rubbing the fabric of his trousers. "I want you free of these." She repeated his words between kisses, and he dipped his head and chuckled, a gust of steamy breath against her neck.

As much as she wanted him bare, she felt a moment of regret when Kit took all his heat away and stood beside the bed. Gaze locked on hers, he worked the fly of his trousers open and shucked the remainder of his clothing after toeing off his boots.

Phee gulped against the tickle in her throat. His *physical component* was as impressive as the rest of him, and she suddenly doubted whether pleasure could be accomplished between them without a good deal of pain. Nothing in her wished to turn back now, but she couldn't help a gulp of hesitation.

"Don't worry, love. We'll go slow." Even as he made the promise, his mouth trembled and fingers twitched eagerly beside his muscled thigh.

As he leaned over her again, Phee opened her knees, knowing just where he belonged. But he did not settle at her center. Instead, he bent his head and drew one tight nipple into his mouth. Sensation rioted through her, and Phee nearly bucked off the bed. The movement only seemed to encourage him. Kit worked his tongue around the tip of flesh that seemed connected to every nerve in her body. When he lifted his head, Phee let out a relieved sigh. Now he would take her, make her his. Whatever came of her future, this moment could never be taken away.

But he didn't press his heated length to where she ached for him. He was busy examining the flesh of her stomach, following circling strokes with open-mouthed kisses. When his finger dipped into the hollow of her navel, she bucked her hips again, and he grinned up at her. Gently, far too slowly, he slid his finger through her russet curls.

"Here, love? Is this where you need my touch?"

"Yes." Hissing out the word as he breached her slick center, Phee reached down to grasp his hand. Kit instantly stilled. "No." She didn't mean to stop him but to urge him on.

He cast a questioning glance, and she felt a blush firing her cheeks. "Please don't stop," she gasped before tightening her grip on his hand. "But tell me, won't you, if I do something wrong?"

"You won't. You can't. All your desires and impulses are right, and I'm happy to indulge them all." Removing his hand from her sex, he stroked damp fingers across her thigh and nudged her leg aside, opening her to his gaze. "There are no rules, Phee. This moment is ours."

He bent his glossy black head between her thighs and grinned up at her. "I'm going to shock you now." And he did, applying his mouth to the slick, swollen heart of her need. He licked at her hungrily, as if he was starving and she was his feast.

All the pleasure that had come before was nothing to this. Tighter, higher, she was spinning, and he was holding every thread. His fingers gripped her thighs as he stroked her with his tongue. One hand on his shoulder, another tangled in his hair, she pushed and bucked and writhed as every thought, every need centered on the ecstatic dance of his hot wet flesh on hers. Too much, too fast, he came at her relentlessly, laving her until she burst. Words came, bewildered cries, but not a bit of sense. And then Kit's long, glorious body was warming every inch of her. He took her mouth again and again. Between kisses, he whispered reassurances, sweet murmurs of praise and adoration, and Phee needed him to know.

"I missed you, Kit." She pushed her fingers into the wave of hair above his brow so that she could see his eyes. "I never stopped."

"I know." He was just where she wanted him, the hard hot length of him sliding against her. "Tell me again."

"I missed you—"

He eased in deeper, a minute thrust. But she was already so full. It wasn't the pain she anticipated, more of an unbearable stretching. "Is there more?"

One of his chuckles rumbled between them as he dipped his head to kiss her neck. "A bit more, I'm afraid."

He rocked into her another inch, and she hissed at the stretch, but she needed it too. Longed for more of him, even as she dreaded the pain. When he stroked his tongue across her lips, she bucked and drew him deeper. "Please." She needed him to move. And he did, taking her mouth as he thrust deep. She cried out against his lips.

"Only pleasure now, love." He began an exquisite rhythm, retreating until she moaned in protest and then filling her again. "This moment is ours." His breath came quickly, his voice a husky rasp. "I am yours." He shifted and began thrusting into her faster, deeper than before. "And you are mine."

"Yes." In her stubborn heart she'd always belonged to him.

"Tell me." His voice was a guttural growl.

"I'm yours." Her words seemed to stun him. A fierce expression broke over his face, and he lifted a hand to stroke her cheek as he moved against her. "You're mine," he said on a wonder-filled whisper. Then he closed his eyes, clenched his jaw, and let out a strangled groan as he called her name.

CHAPTER TWENTY-ONE

*"Don't dally once you've chosen a worthy
bride. Make your proposal in person and in
the clearest of language so the lady cannot
doubt your meaning."*
—THE RUTHVEN RULES FOR YOUNG MEN

Kit woke to the relentless brightness of sunlight peeking through parted curtains of his room in Ruthven Hall and emitted a frustrated growl. Despite the scent of jasmine clinging to his skin, Phee wasn't pressed against his body. He gripped the twisted bed sheet in his fist. She'd been tangled with him in fevered dreams, but now, in the harsh light or morning, he lay in a cold and decidedly empty bed.

After accompanying her back to Briar Heath, they'd parted after an all too brief kiss at the station. She'd been in such a hurry to get home to her sister, they'd gone their separate ways without making plans to see each other.

He'd always made it a practice with lovers not to remain overnight. To ensure he woke alone and unencumbered in the morning.

Now he never wished to wake alone again. He wanted Phee by his side. In his bed, and in his life.

The situation needed a remedy. Immediately. Forever.

Sitting up and shoving the bedding aside, Kit grinned ruefully, recalling the list Phee had prepared to keep him at bay. *No talk of the future. No mention of marriage.*

The rogue he'd been while in London would have considered them his guiding principles. Permanence had been a shackle to avoid, and forever seemed like a very long time.

Perhaps he didn't deserve Phee. Or forever. But he wanted them both, and he'd devote every impulse, every reckless bit of tenacity he possessed to loving her for the rest of his days. The time had come to move forward. He refused to be haunted by his father's damning words anymore. To hell with the accusation that he'd never succeed or achieve his goals. Phee made him believe in possibilities, and her love would always trounce his father's loathing.

After rushing through the mindless acts of washing and dressing, Kit stared at his bleary-eyed reflection in the mirror and pondered marriage. Despite avoiding the snare for years, the steps to achieving wedlock seemed clear enough. A license, a parson, and a willing bride seemed the minimum requirements. Two he felt more sure about than the third.

The question of matrimony had never been broached between him and Phee. He'd been too much of a selfish fool to ask four years ago. But surely she understood his intentions in those magic hours in his Seven Dials room. Failing to say the words couldn't change what they'd shared. He was hers, and she was his. They'd vowed that much. And wasn't that the heart of every marriage?

He rehearsed wording as he made his way downstairs. *Will you marry me?* Too wordy. Two words seemed better. Simpler. *Marry me.*

Shoving a hand through his hair, Kit cursed at himself under his breath. This wasn't a bloody play. Whatever his phrasing, the anxiety coiling in his belly had nothing to do with his delivery and everything to do with Phee's answer. Surely she wouldn't keep to her rule that they not speak of marriage or the future. Surely the fact she'd refused Dunstan wasn't a harbinger of how she'd respond to his proposal. A terrible possibility weighed on his mind. What if, in her forward-thinking way, Ophelia opposed marriage on principle?

He should have taken the time to memorize every word of *Miss Gilroy's Guidelines.*

Though the house was quiet, Kit entered the breakfast room, hoping to discover a fresh pot of tea or coffee set out. An odd sound echoed through wall. Laughter, distinctly male and oddly familiar, followed by a feminine trill. Following the sound, Kit pushed aside the half-open drawing room door to find Jasper Grey standing far too close to their housemaid.

"Grey? What the hell are you doing here?" As Kit stepped into the room, a perfumed purple blur hurtled toward him.

"Kitten! How I've missed you."

Kit turned in time to catch Tess before she plastered herself against his body. She wriggled in his arms, thrusting forward until her bosom crushed his chest.

"We've come to rescue you," Grey said as the housemaid scampered from the room. "I did promise I'd come and drag you back to London. Forgive the ungodly hour. Tess insisted we set out early."

"Speaking of which, where can I see to my morning ablutions, lovie?" She cast a knowing gaze at Grey and patted her hair. A few blonde locks had fallen from their pins. "I fear the train ride left me a bit mussed."

"Upstairs." Kit pointed her toward the drawing room door. "You'll no doubt find the maid lurking in the hall. She can direct you to a room where you can see to your hair."

After Tess sauntered out, Kit turned to Grey. "Why did you bring her here? Don't tell me you've fallen in love and can't bear to be parted." He couldn't blame Grey if that was the case. For the first time in his life, Kit understood how a woman could fill the void in a man's heart.

"Never." Grey snorted and let out a rumble of laughter. "As much as I'd like to say we've come on a social call, I have urgent business to discuss with you."

Which still didn't explain the petite actress's presence. "And Tess?"

"Didn't I tell you? She left Merrick's too. Tess is Fleet's new leading lady, on stage and off." When Grey noticed Kit's confused frown, he added, "They are lovers. The man takes her advice. Fulfills her every whim. If Tess wants your play, Fleet will grant her wish."

"He's already expressed interest in my next play." Though between his father's business affairs and relishing every moment he'd spent with Ophelia since returning to the countryside, the piece still wasn't finished.

"Apparently the man's fickle. He's considered and rejected two other playwrights since you left London." Grey grinned. "Though in all fairness, both were dreadful. Nothing to your talent. Please tell me you've finished the work for Fleet."

The play hadn't crossed Kit's mind in days. After all his years in London and months of envisioning success at Fleet's, a month in the countryside had changed everything. Just as he knew it would. Now, above all else, he craved a future with Phee. And, most unexpectedly, he wanted to manage Ruthven's. Not in his father's way but on his own terms. And Sophia's and Clary's.

"You haven't." Grey deflated and threw his lanky frame onto a settee. "What's happened to you, man? Are they keeping you captive?" He glanced around the room as if expecting to find manacles and chains attached to the walls.

"My father's publishing enterprise—"

"Which you intend to sell."

"May be worth keeping. Managing. Turning into a success."

"Bollocks." Grey narrowed his gaze. "This is about a woman."

Grey was right. Irritatingly and unerringly so. For Kit, keeping Ruthven's wasn't just about creating something for himself and his sisters. He craved success, even responsibility. A chance to prove to Ophelia that she could trust him to stay the course, to commit to an endeavor and triumph.

"She must be extraordinary. Only a goddess could make me embrace the tedium of countrified hell." Grey glanced out the window at the open field beyond. He shivered dramatically. "Perhaps not even then."

Kit looked out on the vista that had just caused Grey such horror. The open land appealed to him as much as London's crowded spaces. More so. That field led the way to Longacre.

"Come back to London, Kit. You're missed. Needed. If it's a beautiful woman you seek—"

"Oh, excuse me." Sophia stood in the shadow of the half-open drawing room door. "I didn't realize you were entertaining a guest."

No noise or happenstance at Ruthven Hall escaped his sister's notice. Kit knew the moment he heard Grey's laughter that Sophia would soon be seeking to solve the mystery of their early morning visitors.

She stepped fully into the room and assessed Grey with an intense head-to-toe appraisal.

The man shot to his feet, eyes wide, mouth slack. Out of the corner of his mouth, he whispered to Kit, "I understand."

Kit frowned at Grey's odd comment and took a breath to begin introductions when a clattering thud drew their attention upward.

"The new housemaid is forever dropping something," Sophia insisted. "I'll see to it." Without another word, she turned to depart, cast one last glance at Grey, and drew the door closed behind her.

"You have my apologies." Grey slumped onto the settee, sitting forward with his elbows braced on his knees.

"Do I? Why?"

"I underestimated the lady's inducements." He swiped two fingers across his mouth and swallowed hard. "But now that I've seen her, my God, man, that face." He waved his hand in the air, drawing down in a sinuous arc. "That figure. You are one lucky bastard."

"That is my sister, you lecher." In a ground-eating stride, Kit was on his friend, gripping Grey's lapels and hauling him from the settee. "She is not for you. And *you* are definitely not for her." Unclenching his fists, Kit released Grey's coat. "Don't look at her. Or speak to her for that matter."

Grey lifted his hands in the air and sidestepped away. Some remnant of rational thought snuck in, reminding Kit that his sister was a grown woman and a savvy one. Sophia would see through Grey's blatant brand of charm immediately.

"Forgive me," Kit managed through a clenched jaw. The much less rational part of him still wanted to throttle the man.

"Done." Grey pulled down his coat lapels, smoothing out the rumples. "I have sisters too, my friend."

Kit worked to steady his breathing while Grey smirked and lifted a triangular bronze brow.

"What?" Kit asked brusquely. He knew Grey well enough to recognize mirth in the man's eyes.

"I simply find it rather amazing." He flitted his gaze over a series of pastoral paintings that decorated the drawing room walls.

They were awful. Clary was right. The whole house needed new decor.

"Amazing?" If the man started going on about Sophia's allure again, Kit wasn't sure their friendship would survive the discussion.

"I mistook your sister for the young woman enticing you to remain in the countryside. If she's not the lady in question, there must be another goddess somewhere in this quiet little corner of England."

There was, and Kit needed to speak to her rather than waste another moment talking nonsense with his libertine friend.

"Grey, you'll need to excuse me. I was just on my way out when you arrived." Kit moved toward the door and hoped his friend would follow. If he and Tess hurried, they could catch the next train back to London.

"You can't go." Grey reached out as if he'd stop him, but then seemed to think better of it and lowered his hand to his side. "I haven't convinced you yet."

"Convinced me of what?"

"Returning to London. Fleet Theater needs your talent, and I promise the man can bring you greater rewards than you ever received at Merrick's. Don't allow some other upstart to grasp an opportunity that should be yours."

Kit shook his head, but Grey persisted.

"Success, man. It's what you've always craved. Far more than I do. Perhaps more than any man I've ever known. One play for Fleet could change your fortunes." Grey drew closer, lowering his voice. "Wouldn't that impress your country lady?"

Kit couldn't deny that the drive to achieve success still gnawed in him like a ferocious hunger.

Turning away from Grey, he strode to the window and stared across the field toward Longacre. Had Phee woken yet? Were her first thoughts of him as his had been of her? The pursuit of fame and fortune had pulled him away from her once.

"Mr. Ruthven? Pardon me, sir." The skittish young house-maid pushed into the drawing room, eyes huge, gaze drawn like a magnet to Grey. "Miss Ruthven says you must come upstairs."

"What is it?" What else would thwart his path to Ophelia this morning?

"The lady, sir. She's fallen."

Before Kit could question the maid further, Sophia strode into the room. Kit didn't miss the way Grey's gaze followed his sister's every move.

"The woman you left in your bedroom." Sophia raised her voice loud enough for half of Briar Heath to hear. Then, apparently contrite for her outburst, sucked in a deep breath and continued in a quieter tone. "She spilled water on the floor and managed, somehow, to sprain her ankle. I've sent for Dr. Weeks."

"I should go up to Tess." Grey started toward the door, passing far too close to Sophia.

"We should at least move her to a guest room." Sophia spoke to Kit but flitted glances at Grey, who lingered at her elbow.

"I can help." Grey spoke directly to Sophia. "Just tell me which room you'd like her moved to."

His friend had never been so eager to please anyone. Kit pinched the skin between his brows and exhaled a long sigh. Sophia was looking at him expectantly. She still hadn't been introduced to Grey and seemed to be waiting on Kit to conduct formalities.

"Sophia, this is—"

"Jasper Grey." The man stepped forward and sketched a ridiculous half bow. "Actor, reprobate, and irredeemable scoundrel." After gazing longingly at Sophia's hand, he shot her a wolfish grin. "I'd kiss your hand, Miss Ruthven, but I suspect your brother would have my head for it." Flicking back his carefully disheveled hair, he added, "I'm afraid I'm quite fond of my head."

"You were never in any danger, Mr. Grey. I have no intention of offering you my hand."

Grey let out a low chuckle. "Now I'm determined to kiss both of your hands."

"Shall we all go up and see to Tess?" Kit asked, interrupting an uncomfortably long stretch of silence in which Sophia and Grey stared at each other with a strange combination of wariness and intrigue.

As the three of them headed upstairs, Sophia led the way and Kit cast a glance at the clock in the hall. It seemed Tess and Grey wouldn't be departing quickly. Though Kit loathed the notion of leaving a scoundrel like Grey and his sister in the house alone together, he needed to visit Phee.

They'd lost enough time. He didn't want to wait another day to ask her to be his wife.

Six pounds four pence multiplied by three..."Isn't enough." Phee didn't need Juliet's talent for mathematics to understand the woeful state of their household finances. The lines in the account ledger were empty where they should have been full, and the current balance was several digits thin.

Kit. Lifting a finger to her mouth, Phee stroked the flesh of her lower lip, still sensitive from his kisses. Even when she worried, Kit burst in, coloring every thought.

From the moment she awoke, he'd been on her heart and mind. Memories of their lovemaking caused her body to respond as if they were alone in his London room again. As if his warm hands and hard body were pressed against her, loving her.

But despite a head full of fresh, blissful memories, old familiar worries wormed their way in too. They'd driven her out of bed to her desk, where she could review the household accounts. Subtracting the income they relied on from her tutoring made the balances even more dismal. Worse still, on a Wednesday morning she had no prospect of a single pupil coming for the remainder of the week. She worried the two who remained on her roster would eventually go too.

The pile of paper she used to make her lists and her favorite pen lay on the desk blotter in front of her. Phee pushed them aside.

What good had her lists done? They were flimsy attempts to control what refused to be tamed. The source of all her trouble and bad fortune. Her own wayward heart. Perhaps she was an "unnatural woman," as Mrs. Raybourn called in a letter denouncing Phee's book, her ideas, and her skills as a tutor.

She'd grown up torn between her mother's lessons in decorum and propriety, and her father's tendency to encourage both his daughters to follow their hearts' desires. He'd urged them to dream on a grand scale. Phee feared she'd inherited his stubborn nature too.

Rather than pursue new employment or find a more reliable publisher for her book, following her heart had been Phee's chief occupation for weeks. The previous afternoon had been its culmination. No lists or rules or guidelines kept her from choosing those moments with Kit. Despite Mama's lessons in propriety, knowing precisely what she should do, and having no doubt what others would think of her if they knew, she didn't regret a single moment.

Kit had thoroughly ruined her but not only in the way polite society meant the word.

The lovemaking in his London lodgings had been a revelation. More passion than she'd ever expected to experience in a lifetime. Precious hours she would never forget. Memories she would carry with her all of her days. And she never wanted to taste that kind of passion with any other man. *That* is how he'd ruined her.

They'd been so close, moved together in such exquisite harmony that Phee couldn't shake the sense he should be with her. Or that she should stride across the field toward Ruthven Hall and find him. Wherever Kit was seemed the place she should be.

He'd returned with her on an evening train to Briar Heath, but how long would he remain?

Her throat burned and tears began to fall in fat drops onto the desk blotter.

Why had she insisted on rules for seduction? *No talk of marriage. No planning for the future.* How could she have ever dreamed one moment with Kit would be enough? Maybe her need to control every aspect of her life, and quite unsuccessfully, would be her true ruination.

"Cup of tea, my dear?"

At the sound of her aunt's voice, Phee swiped away her tears.

"Or is this a predicament that requires chocolate?"

"Tea will do, Aunt Rose." Phee tried for an unaffected tone and lifted a handkerchief from her pocket to wipe her damp face and runny nose.

"Excellent. I have tea and scones at the ready." Her aunt entered a moment later with a small tea service, and Phee rushed to take the laden tray.

"I can pour." Filling their cups gave Phee something to do, and she prayed the signs of her tearful bout would wane before she had to face her aunt.

"Did your visit to the city go well, my dear?"

"Yes." Perhaps the best day of her life, though she could hardly divulge the details.

"Then something else has you out of sorts."

Phee drew in a deep breath and met her aunt's perceptive gaze. The time had come. Though Juliet knew about her writing, Phee had yet to speak to Aunt Rose about *Miss Gilroy's Guidelines*. She deserved the whole story. The dire state of their finances would affect them all.

"You may know I wrote a book."

"I do." Aunt Rose took a sip of tea and grinned at Phee before continuing. "Juliet is quite taken with your etiquette book."

"Not an etiquette book." That sounded too much like Ruthven's *Rules*. "I offer young women suggestions. Guidelines. The whole point is that young women should make up their own minds."

"Ah, of course." She sipped again at her tea and offered Phee another knowing grin. "And your suggestions have caused a bit of controversy, I understand."

"I've lost most of my tutoring pupils and gained the contempt of many in Briar Heath." Phee refrained from mentioning Lord

Dunstan. She had no wish to revive the debate with her aunt over the baron's desirability as a prospective groom.

"Young women's choices have consequences, then."

"Yes." Guilt swept down, heavy on Phee's shoulders. The warm tea soured in her belly. "I will find another way to keep us afloat, Aunt Rose. Some other occupation."

"Why not consider marriage?"

"Not every young woman chooses marriage." Phee breathed a heavy sigh. Only one man had ever proposed to her, and he wasn't the one her heart craved. *Stubborn, wayward heart.*

"I cannot recommend spinsterhood, my dear." Aunt Rose wasn't smiling anymore. Sadness welled in her gaze more than anything. "I do cherish my independence and every moment spent with you and your sister, but loneliness is a heavy toll to pay."

Phee frowned. Her first instinct was to deny her aunt's words. Since the day she'd come to live with them, Aunt Rose had never spent a day alone. Either their father, Phee, or Juliet were always with her. Yet Phee knew, understood today in a way she wouldn't have just a few days earlier, that Aunt Rose referred to the marriage of two minds, the loving companionship of another who is yours by choice, not out of necessity or family ties.

"If Lord Dunstan offers for you again—"

"He won't." He might be able to tolerate her authorship of a *scurrilous* book, but he and the whole village would denounce her entirely if they knew what she'd shared with Kit.

"Then he wasn't the cause of your tears?"

Phee shook her head, torn between confessing all and keeping her heartache to herself.

"Christopher Ruthven." Aunt Rose pronounced his name slowly, drawing out each syllable. "The young man who got you into so much trouble as a girl and haunted our doorstep like a stray cat."

Tipping her head, Phee scrutinized her aunt. "I never knew you disliked him." Aunt Rose had always been kind to Kit, as affectionate toward him as Father had been.

"I loved the boy." She sniffed and lowered her gaze. "But he broke your heart, didn't he? Jaunted off to London, never to return." Had Aunt Rose missed Kit too?

"But he did return." And nothing had been the same since.

"But does he mean to stay? Has he asked for your hand?"

"No." Phee shot out of her chair, rattling a table nearby. She steadied her cup and let out a tiny groan. This was the hardest part to admit. "I don't know."

Aunt Rose lifted a hand to her mouth and began to splutter on a bite of lavender scone. Phee moved to pat her back.

"You bewilder me, my dear." Aunt Rose reached for Phee's hand and tugged her around until they faced each other. "Young ladies making their own choices is well and good, but must you take away Mr. Ruthven's? What if the man wishes to marry you?"

"I'm not sure he does. He's never asked me." Etiquette and society's rules obligated a gentleman to propose to a young lady after they'd shared what Phee and Kit had in London, but Kit had never been terribly interested in rules.

Aunt Rose enfolded Phee's hands, gripping them with surprising strength. "Then perhaps, my dear, you should give him a chance to do so."

CHAPTER TWENTY-TWO

By late afternoon, Phee knew Kit wasn't coming. The disappointment bearing down on her wasn't rational. And telling herself so a hundred times hadn't eased the feeling at all. They'd made no plans to meet again after their return from London. For all she knew, he'd returned to the city on the first morning train.

Calling in at Ruthven Hall to spy out his whereabouts seemed foolish, especially if he'd already departed.

"We're off." Aunt Rose stepped into the parlor, wearing her traveling gown. Juliet stood in the hall behind her, grousing about putting on gloves.

"Off where?"

"It's Wednesday, Phee," Juliet reminded her without much enthusiasm. "We always go visiting on Wednesdays."

They did, and she was usually busy with students until the day's end. "I can go with you today, since my tutoring roster is clear." Phee stood and started toward her room. "Just give me a moment to get my cloak."

"I was hoping you'd take on an errand for me, my dear." Aunt Rose turned to Juliet, who lifted a neatly tied package from the hall table.

"Tarts," Juliet said with a toothy smile.

"After my lemon tarts won at the festival, the youngest Miss Ruthven made me promise to send a batch over." Aunt Rose offered Phee the beribboned box. "Take them while they're fresh, won't you, dear?"

Phee squinted one eye at her aunt, who beamed back with a beatifically innocent smile.

"Isn't a visit to the Ruthvens on your list for the day, Aunt Rose?"

Juliet glanced up at their aunt hopefully. Apparently the Ruthvens were a more appealing prospect than Mrs. Hollingsworth, who Aunt Rose enjoyed visiting, and Juliet did not.

"Not today." Aunt Rose fussed with the little bow on top when Phee took the package into her hands. "But you should go. Don't you think?"

Phee nodded, though she wasn't sure about the prospect at all. Even after she'd donned her coat and started across the field between Longacre and Ruthven Hall, she worried. Worried almost as much as she looked forward to seeing Kit again.

Even before she reached Ruthven Hall, Phee knew something was amiss. She recognized the village doctor's gig sitting in front of the house and picked up her skirts to run toward the door.

The frantic gaze of the housemaid who admitted her only ratcheted her fears. "I'm here to see Mr. Ruthven. Is someone ill?"

"Wait in there, please, miss." The girl pointed toward the drawing room. "I'll see if Mr. Ruthven is at home."

Phee paced the rug in the center of the room until she thought she'd go mad. She'd never been good at waiting. When she heard a woman's shriek overhead, she couldn't wait any longer. No maids or footmen were in sight to stop her when she peeked out of the drawing room, and she rushed up the stairs toward the sound of female moans.

Pushing through a door on her left, she reared back at the sight of Kit draped over a half-dressed woman reclining in bed.

"A kiss would lessen the pain," the woman said as she wrapped her arms around Kit's neck.

Kit grinned and placed a hand on her arm. "Grey would be more than happy to oblige, I'm sure."

"Jasper's a plaything, Kitten," she cooed. "You're the one who's won my heart."

Phee made a choked sound, and the lady snapped her gaze toward the door.

"Ophelia." Kit unlatched the woman's arms and stood.

"Thank goodness," whined the bedridden woman. "I rang for tea an hour ago." She squinted at Phee's hands. "But you don't have any tea."

Kit approached until Phee had to step back or have him pressed against her. He kept moving until they stood in the hall and closed the bedroom door behind them. The lady inside protested loudly, screeching his name.

"I can explain," he said over the woman's shouts.

"You needn't. I vowed to myself that I wouldn't entangle you." Though judging by the knots of pain in her chest, she'd done a terrible job of protecting her own heart.

"Too late." He reached for her, his hand warm, grip firm on her arm. "I am entangled, love. I want to be tangled up with you. Now and forever."

A saucy retort about the woman in his bed sprang to her lips, but another man's voice rang out before she could say a word.

"What have you done to her?" The stranger's voice was low, almost as deep as Kit's, and he carried himself like a man who expected others to take notice. "Hello," he said to Phee on a warm drawl. "It's her," he said to Kit. "The other goddess."

Kit crossed his arms and offered the man a sharp nod. "She's the one."

The handsome gentleman reached for Phee's hand, but Kit swiped his arm away. "I don't think so, Grey." Kit dipped his head toward the closed bedroom door. "Why don't you see to our mutual friend?"

The lady's calls had diminished, but every once in a while she let out a mournful high-pitched squeal.

"Thanks very much for getting her riled before sending me into the fray." Grey, as Kit had called the man, drew in a sharp breath through his nose. "What did you do to her anyhow?"

"I left the room and closed the door."

"Good God, man, that's the worst you could have done." Grey winked at Phee and then smirked at Kit. "You know Tess requires an audience."

After squaring his broad shoulders and running a hand through the reddish-brown waves of his hair, the man stepped into the bedroom with the lady Kit had been draped over moments before.

"Will you come with me, Phee?" He offered his hand, but she refused to take it.

"Where?"

"Someplace quiet where we can speak privately."

Phee nodded but didn't take his hand. He led her downstairs and into his father's study. Phee hesitated a moment on the threshold, but he urged her, beseeched her, really, with his dark gaze. When she stepped inside, he closed and latched the door.

"She's an actress," he started, answering the question she hadn't yet asked. "We worked together at Merrick Theater. She wished for more. I did not."

"You were never lovers?"

"Never."

Phee gnawed at her lower lip. She believed him but wasn't certain she should. "But she said you won her heart."

"She's mistaken. I never sought Tess's affection, and my heart was never on offer. It's taken. Has been, I suspect, since the day you jumped out of that tree and frightened me half to death." He smiled weakly, uncertainly.

"You didn't seem frightened."

"No. Fascinated. Intrigued. My interest in you was never in doubt."

"Except that you left." Phee realized she was still carrying Aunt Rose's box of tarts and had crumpled the ribbon while toting it under her arm.

"But now I'm here. With you." He started toward her, and Phee swallowed down a lump of anticipation in her throat. "Right where I want to be." He took the box of tarts from her hands and laid it on the desk behind her. "A culinary gift from Aunt Rose?"

"Tarts" was all she could manage. He was standing too near, smelling divine, warming the side of her body.

"Did you sample any?"

Phee shook her head and let out a little hiss when he cupped her cheek in his palm. She didn't pull back or shrink from his touch. She craved it too much.

"Pity. If you had, I'd get to taste their sweetness from your lips."

He dipped his head to kiss her, and her body flared as if they were bare and entwined in that rickety bed in London again. But she needed answers as much as she needed his kiss.

"Is this truly where you wish to be?" She pressed a hand to his chest and felt the galloping rhythm of his heart under her fingertips.

Kit frowned and pulled an inch away. "Yes, of course. I've thought of nothing but you since I opened my eyes this morning. I didn't invite Grey and Tess here, I assure you. They arrived unexpectedly, and then she twisted her ankle." Pausing his ramble, he stroked a finger down her cheek. "Where else would I wish to be?"

"London. Your theater. Your room in Seven Dials." It was hard to think, difficult to speak when his gaze kept riveting on her mouth, when his eyes were bright and warm as golden syrup. "Briar Heath has never felt like home to you. I can't remember when, but you told me that once."

Her words chilled all the heat between them. Kit stepped back. One step, then another, and he turned to slump down on the sofa arranged near the room's fireplace. He gazed at her hard, then buried his head in his hands.

Every impulse urged her to go to him, comfort him, but fear held her in place. She needed to hear his answer. To know whether he planned to leave Briar Heath. Leave her. Again.

"You're right, love." He sat up, hands slack between his knees. "I never belonged here, and this house never felt like home."

She couldn't hold back and went to him then. Lowering herself onto the sofa, she reached for his hand. He grasped hers eagerly, almost tight enough to hurt.

"So you'll go back to London." It wasn't a question. She knew the truth. As much as she wanted Kit by her side, she also wished for him to find the place where he belonged.

"Yes," he said.

Phee bit the inside of her cheek to stop the tears burning her eyes.

"But I'll always come home. The trains can take me there and back in a day, a few hours."

"What home? You said this has never been your home."

"You, love." Kit hooked a finger under her chin, drawing Phee's face toward his so that he could gaze into her eyes. "You're my home."

Phee braced a hand on his thigh so she didn't tip into his lap. She tried to make sense of what he was saying, but her heart seemed to know. A breath-stealing tickle swelled in her chest, like a cluster of butterflies taking wing.

"I'm your home?" She said the words as much for confirmation as to make herself believe.

"I was a fool to leave you." Little lines of worry formed between Kit's furrowed brow. "Regret will always color that decision and the hurt I caused. But I will never leave you again."

For a long moment, Phee soaked in his words. She'd forgiven him for going, but she struggled to believe he wanted to stay as much as she longed for him to do.

"Can you forgive me?" His voice broke as he squeezed her hand.

Phee wanted to show him. She leaned into Kit and pressed her mouth to his. Her kiss was tentative, a gentle brush against his lips. But one taste of him and she wanted more. Bracing her hands on his shoulders, she tipped toward him. Kit took her further, wrapping his hand around her waist and pulling her into his lap. He deepened the kiss, stole her breath. One hand stroked her back, gripped her hip; the other shaped her breast. His palm was pure heat and she arched against him. Gathering her skirts, he nudged her legs apart, one on each side of his. He tugged her hips until she was flush against him.

"There's far too much fabric between us." His lips tilted in a grin, carving long dimples on each side of his mouth.

"Yes," Phee whispered huskily. Layers and layers, but she could still feel the hard length of him between her legs.

He looped a finger in one of the curls pinned near her ear and slid it loose, pulling the tress down her neck. "I prefer you disheveled."

She preferred herself that way too. With her hair down, feet bare, corset off, she felt more alive. More herself. How many years had she resisted before Mama convinced her to pin up her hair? To concede at least that much to propriety.

"Wearing my hair unbound is a sign of wildness. Isn't that what your father said?" The man had loathed her on such a short acquaintance and never given her a chance to disprove his hasty judgements. *Fire-haired witch*, he'd christened her that day in his study. This very study. She looked around the wood-paneled walls, trying to recall the man. Her memory blurred. She could only feel this moment—Kit in her arms, his long, hard body snug against hers.

"Are you wild, my love?" Kit rocked his hips, stoking a pulsing need that made Phee gasp to catch her breath. The ache in her was a tightness, a taut tension waiting for release.

Wildness was in her. She'd always known as much. Mama's lessons and rules and guidelines were meant to tame her, to make her a proper young lady. Eager to please her mother, Phee sometimes worried her hungers and urges would burn her up inside if she set them free. Lists, duties, occupying herself with tutoring and writing held her impulses at bay. But only just. They were always there, banked but never extinguished. And no one but Kit knew how to spark them into flame.

Boldly, brazenly, she slid a hand between them, past the buttons of his trousers to the scalding ridge of his arousal. "I've spent so long trying not to be."

He cast his gaze down to where Phee moved her hand over him. When he hissed and caught her fingers, she feared she'd hurt him and stilled in his lap.

"You needn't curb your urges with me." Kit moved his hand lower as he spoke, and Phee squirmed against him. "I love your eagerness." He grinned when he found the opening of her drawers. Slipping past the ribboned closure, he stroked through her curls only a moment before sinking his finger inside her. "I love *you*, Ophelia."

"Kit." She fumbled over his buttons, desperate to feel his bare skin. When she pulled the final fastening free, he was such smooth, glorious heat in her hand. "Please, Kit."

He knew what she craved, knew how to sate her wild urges. With one hand on her hip, he guided her to take him inside. There was no pain this time, just a glorious fullness. One tilt of her hips and Kit let out a husky groan. She felt powerful and wanton. "You're mine."

He smiled at the echo of his words. "I'm yours." He tightened his fingers on her hip and pulled her hard against him. "I'm home."

Phee bent to take his mouth, to stroke his tongue with hers as he'd taught her to do. He moaned into her mouth, slid a hand into her hair to pull more tresses from their pins.

Gripping his shoulder with one hand, she pressed her other palm to his cheek. This was the man she wanted, not because she should. Not because she must. But because he understood her as no one ever had. He loved all the practical and wild parts of her.

As Phee rocked against Kit, he held her hips but let her build the rhythm. He watched her every move, breath gusting from his lips each time she took him deep.

"I love you," she managed on a breathy moan as her release rioted through her body.

Kit gripped her neck and pulled her in for a kiss, letting out his own muffled groan.

"Kit?" Sophia's resonant voice carried through the locked door. "The housemaids say you've barricaded yourself in the study."

Phee gasped and clapped a hand over her mouth. Kit closed his eyes, clenched his jaw. "Yes," he called toward the door, "I'll be out in a moment."

"Which I can understand," Sophia continued. "Your guests are atrocious. Especially Mr. Grey." A soft thud sounded against the door, as if Sophia had slumped against the wood. "They're leaving," she said quietly. "I thought you might wish to see them off."

All Kit wanted was the woman in his arms. Magnificent and full of passion, Phee was everything he'd ever craved. And he was a lucky bastard, as Grey so perceptively pointed out. But now she was shifting off him, and he wanted to haul her back in his arms.

But being a man who deserved Ophelia meant taking responsibility, even if it was for his bedraggled theater comrades. "Give me a bloody moment, Sophia."

Phee leaned against his shoulder as she got to her feet. Kit reached down to settle her skirt around her ankles, fighting the urge to flip the garment up, lay her down on the sofa, and make love to her again.

"Do you think Sophia knows I'm here with you?" Phee whispered the words as she shoved pins into loose strands of hair.

"Probably not." Even if she did, Kit intended to ask Phee to be his wife before the day's end. Worry over impropriety would soon be irrelevant. Kit buttoned his trousers and turned back to where Phee stood. She cast him a worried look as she bit the nail of her index finger.

"Don't fret. Just wait for me, love." He placed a kiss on her lush mouth and failed to keep it brief. Phee seemed to feel the same and reached up to stroke her fingers through the hair at his nape, sending sparks of pleasure down his back, his thighs, all the way to his toes. When they were both breathless, he smiled against her lips and whispered, "Wait for me. We have important matters to discuss."

Leaving Phee in his father's study was only possible because he told himself she'd be there when he returned.

The chaos he found in the front drawing room made him wish he'd never left the haven of his study. Sophia and Grey and Tess stood in the center of the room, bickering, while Clary sat cross-legged on the settee, watching the ruckus with wide eyes and swiping her pencil madly against the paper of her sketchbook.

"Would anyone like to tell me what's going on?"

"And there he is, the traitorous cad." Tess hobbled toward him, then reached for Grey, who lifted his arm to steady her. "Who was that red-haired strumpet who lured you away from me?"

Sophia snapped her gaze toward Kit, arching one fair brow in that imperious way of hers.

"She was a goddess," Grey interjected unhelpfully. "One of two in this idyllic little hamlet." He fixed his gaze on Sophia. Far too long, and far too heatedly. "Almost makes one consider a long sojourn in the countryside."

"Too bad your train is leaving in half an hour, Mr. Grey."

Kit grinned at Sophia's tart reply. Apparently Grey's charms hadn't worked their magic on her yet.

"There are other trains, Miss Ruthven." The scoundrel abandoned Tess and stepped closer to Sophia. His sister held her ground, but Kit noticed her eyes had gone a deeper shade of blue and the Cupid's bow of her upper lip trembled. "Goddesses, on the other hand…" Grey spoke in the low theatrical voice that made women swoon. "Are few and far between."

"And Tess's ankle will swell the longer she's on her feet." Kit pointed to the petite actress who glared at him as she leaned on an obliging wingback chair. "You should get her back to London."

"Yes, Mr. Grey. Surely your gaggle of female admirers back in London are longing for your next performance." Sophia nervously twirled her jet necklace around her finger, belying her caustic tone.

"I'm not leaving without him." Grey pointed at Kit.

"You'll have to, my friend. I have matters to attend to here." The most pressing of which was making Ophelia his wife. He could still taste her on his lips and most of his thoughts were still locked in that study with her.

"Then give me your play at least."

"The play's not finished." The piece was close. A few more days and he'd have something worthy of Fleet Theater. He hoped. "I'll send it as soon as I'm able."

"Good God, man, haste. Don't you want the success you've been working toward for years?"

"You know that I do."

"Then bring it yourself." Grey stepped close and leaned in to whisper. "You've stirred the hornet's nest with Tess. Fleet will take some convincing now."

"I'll see what I can do." Kit peeked over Grey's shoulder at Tess, who frowned back at him. "Though as I recall, you were quite adept at offering the lady solace for her broken heart."

Grey lifted his lips in a smirk. "Broken hearts are my specialty."

As Kit herded his friend and Tess toward the front door, Grey stopped short and turned back for a last glance at Sophia, who'd taken a seat on the settee with Clary. "Take care of your ladies, Kit. All of them."

"I'll do my best." Kit placed a hand on Grey's back and pushed him toward the door.

"And when you come to London," Grey added on the threshold, giving in to an actor's need for the last word, "bring Sophia so she can take in one of my performances and join my gaggle of admirers."

"Did you miss the fact that my sister is in mourning?"

"Is she?" Grey lifted onto his toes and leaned back for another glimpse into the drawing room. "Mercy. No woman should look that delicious in mourning clothes."

"Enough. Go now, or it's pistols at dawn. Your choice."

"This is me, going." Grey lifted one hand in the air, and offered the other to Tess to aid her down the steps. A footman rushed forward to help her into the Ruthven gig that would deliver them to the train station. Grey turned once Tess was tucked inside and waved at Kit. "This is me, waving good-bye." He cupped his hand around his mouth and whispered. Loudly. "Come to London soon."

Kit closed the door.

Two steps into the drawing room, Clary asked, "What red-haired woman?"

"Miss Marsden, I presume." Sophia looked far too smug.

"Miss Marsden came to visit, and no one told me?" Clary sprang from the sofa, dropping her sketchbook on the cushions. "Is she still here?"

I bloody well hope so.

"It's almost time for dinner. I'm sure she's returned home." Sophia stood and placed a hand on Clary's shoulder. "Speaking of which, we should ready ourselves for our dinner."

"We should have invited your friends to stay, Kit," Clary suggested.

"No." Kit and Sophia answered in unison and with equal vehemence.

"Upstairs." Sophia patted Clary's back and urged her toward the stairs. "I'll come up in a moment and help with your hair."

Once Clary was out of the room, Sophia crossed her arms and assessed him.

"Is Ophelia still locked in your study?"

"I am not holding her captive. But, yes, I very much hope she's waiting for me there."

"Do I need to remind you this is entirely inappropriate?" She heaved a weary sigh, like someone who'd been scolding wayward children all her life. "Apparently, I do."

"I'm going to ask her to marry me. Right now. As soon as I get back in that room."

His sister clasped a hand over her mouth, and Kit wasn't sure if she was appalled, horrified, or simply shocked that he'd finally bowed to more of their father's expectations.

"You're very rarely silent, Sophia."

In two quick strides, she stood before him. His sister stunned him by reaching out and taking him in a fierce embrace. When she pulled away, her blue-green eyes had gone glassy. "I'm rarely this happy. I wish you both nothing but joy."

"Thank you." There was more in Sophia's gaze than mere happiness for his good fortune. Kit sensed his sister longed for her own happy ending, and he sincerely wished her to find it. But not with Jasper Grey. Or any rogue of his ilk.

After she'd followed Clary upstairs, Kit started toward his study. *His* study. This rambling house his father built had never felt like home, but he intended to change that. Making love with Ophelia in each room seemed a good start, but he'd take Clary's advice and redecorate too.

At the threshold of *his* study, he took a deep bracing breath. *Marry me.* He only intended to speak the words once in his life.

As the door swung open, he choked on an exhale. She hadn't waited. The room was empty.

CHAPTER TWENTY-THREE

Choosing not to wait for Kit had proved an excruciating decision.

Phee paced the oddly floral carpet in his father's study until she couldn't wait any longer. Intending to duck out through the back terrace doors, she'd stopped near the main hall and overheard Kit offering good-byes to his theater friends.

Mr. Grey urged Kit to return to London. Asked him if he still craved the success he'd gone to the city seeking four years before. Kit admitted that he did. He'd told Phee as much on that bench in Hyde Park too.

How could she love him and wish to keep him here if London was where he truly wished to be? He'd assured her of the short train journey between the city and the village, but what if he tired of being torn between the two? Kit's impulses had always been for adventure, pleasure, enjoyment. He might bear Briar Heath society for a month but for years?

As Phee made her way back toward Longacre, she reasoned in her head against the urge to reverse course and return to Kit's arms. Juliet and Aunt Rose would return from their social calls soon and wonder where she'd gone. Aunt Rose, in particular, would wish to know the results of her tart delivery errand. What could she admit? That Kit encouraged her to release her wild nature, and they'd nearly made love in his father's study?

I'm home he'd said, and Phee saw the truth in his eyes. He'd always been seeking a belonging his father never allowed him to feel at home. But London, with all its enticements, was the one place he'd *chosen* to make a home. He spoke of ridding himself of his Seven Dials room without a hint of feeling, but she could easily imagine him there. She'd always have fond memories of that cozy little space.

The colors of dusk washed over Longacre as Phee approached through the vegetable garden. The house's loveliness always struck her at this time of day. A wave of wistfulness sparked a sharp ache in her chest. Longacre was the only home she and Juliet had ever known, a piece of their family's long history left in their keeping. Even if Kit could force himself to reside in the country, could she let Longacre go in order to make Ruthven Hall their home?

Movement in the front parlor window caught Phee's eye, though none of the lights in the house were lit. Seeing the windows dark, she'd assumed Aunt Rose and Juliet had not yet returned.

She began chafing her hands as she entered the parlor. A fire was definitely in order. Kneeling at the fireplace, she prepared kindling, lit a steady flame, and bent to shovel coals onto the grate. A noise at her back made her jump.

She turned to see a man lurking in the dim room. He stood near the window, outlined from behind by the darkening sky.

"I did not mean to startle you."

Phee recognized Lord Dunstan's voice but gripped the fire poker as she stood.

"If you had no wish to frighten me, you shouldn't have entered my home uninvited." She'd never spoken to him so coldly, never failed to give him the courtesy and respect his title and position in the village demanded. Tenacity was one thing. Now the man's behavior had gone beyond the pale.

When he strode forward, a twisted grin curved his mouth. The same he'd worn as an arrogant, bullying boy so many years ago.

"I came out of concern for you, Miss Marsden."

He'd said the words once before. On the day he'd come to Longacre and asked for her hand in marriage shortly after her father's death.

"Your concern has always been appreciated, but—"

"Shouldn't you be mine, Ophelia?"

Phee let out a shaky breath and fought down a wave of nausea. The man's persistence exhausted her, but it also pricked straight to her stubborn heart. The more he pressed for some union between them that was never meant to be, the less she wished to attempt kindness or patience.

"Please go, my lord, if you plan to renew that topic. My refusal must be sufficient."

"Your father thought you should be mine." Lord Dunstan moved toward her as he spoke. Phee tightened her grip on the metal poker. When he leaned in, she drew a deep breath and prepared to strike. But he wasn't reaching for her. He crouched down and began seeing to the unlit fire. "Did you know that, Ophelia?"

Her name sounded wrong on his lips. Too much emphasis on the O. None of the warmth and tenderness Kit infused into each syllable.

"Your father believed you would encourage my pursuit." He lifted his hand toward the metal implement in her hand. "May I have that?"

Phee looked at Dunstan, the fire poker, and decided to relent. Bashing a local aristocrat over the head didn't seem the best course of action. Though considering how he ignored her rejection, she wondered if it might finally get his attention.

After a moment of agitating the fire and heaping on coals, Lord Dunstan stood and swiped at the dirt on his fingers. "He said you were lonely. Broken-hearted."

"My father shouldn't have spoken so freely." Papa had been a talker. Eager to share his opinions, especially the most radical among them. But it pained Phee to know he'd spoken of her to Lord Dunstan. Two men plotting her fate. Papa had to know she'd never bend to such manipulation.

"He was concerned about you as well." Dunstan gestured to the two closely arranged chairs in front of the fire. "Shall we sit?"

"Only for a moment." Phee sat, but her body remained tense, ready to flee. Something about Dunstan's tone, his intense stare, put every nerve in her body on alert.

"You confound me, Miss Marsden."

"Do I, my lord? I'm not a terribly confusing woman." Kit had claimed she confused him, but she'd never considered herself mysterious. She'd never dabbled in secrets until she'd chosen a pen name for her book. And spent one glorious afternoon in a rented room with Kit in London.

"Oh, but you are." He leaned forward, much as Kit had done on that first day he'd visited her after returning to Briar Heath. Dunstan wasn't nearly as tall or long-legged as Kit. Even bending forward, there was no danger of their bodies brushing against each other. Phee tucked her knees in, just in case. "I am not a man given to strong emotion. Competitive? Yes. Determined on a course once I've fixed on a goal? Absolutely. But I so often win because I do not allow myself to be distracted by sentiment."

Phee stared at her folded hands. In many ways, he was describing the sort of resolve she'd often wished to possess. Not being competitive, perhaps, but devoting herself to a purpose without being waylaid by passion and emotion. She'd never quite achieved his brand of willpower.

"But you," Dunstan said on a choked whisper, as if some obstruction blocked his throat, "have completely upset the orderly progress of my life."

"No, my lord." Phee shook her head. She was not fond of the man's high-handed manner, but she'd never meant him any harm. And she'd never been coy or given him cause to hope. In her own mind, she may have wavered, but he never knew of her misgivings.

He braced his hands on the arms of the chair, gripping so tightly his knuckles went white against his skin. "I believe I may love you, Ophelia. I certainly want you."

"This is entirely inappropriate, my lord." Phee bolted from her chair and started toward the parlor door. "My aunt and sister will return soon."

"Are you concerned about a chaperone, Miss Marsden?" Dunstan stood too, braced his arms across his chest, and showed no indication he was interested in leaving. "You weren't concerned when you were with Mr. Ruthven."

Phee's cheeks flushed with heat. "Why are you here, my lord?" Her desire to see the back of him was almost as acute as her regret at not waiting for Kit as he'd asked her to.

"My solicitor's offices are quite near Hyde Park. You'll recall the day I met you not far from the park. We returned together on the train."

"I remember." Kit had asked to publish her book that day. She should have agreed to that too. "Were you following me?"

"I saw you again yesterday, walking with the same man, toward the same park. I observed a very *friendly* interlude between you and Mr. Ruthven on the Serpentine. Then your joint departure via cab to a wretched building in Seven Dials." Dunstan emitted a dry rasping sound. From the tilt of his mouth, Phee guessed he'd intended to chuckle. "What I did not observe was a chaperone."

"Are you attempting to shame me, Lord Dunstan? Threaten me? If your opinion of my behavior is so low, you must concede that I'm not the woman who should become your baroness."

"I concede nothing."

"You must. How dare you invade my home and privacy?" A shiver chased down her spine at the thought of him watching her, following her about London.

"I consider it protection, not invasion. I've been looking on for weeks as you gallivant to London and make a fool of yourself with Christopher Ruthven." He shook his head and offered her a pitying grin. "But you've been doing that since we were children, haven't you? Why do you think I told Mrs. Raybourn you'd authored that terrible book?"

"You?"

"What else was I to do when you disappeared into the garden like a wanton with Ruthven? You needed to be brought to heel, Ophelia."

He started toward her, and Phee flinched back. The look of hurt in his eyes shocked her, but not as much as watching him lower to one knee.

"Marry me, Ophelia. I suspect you're not a maid, and the book you've written will cause us no end of disgrace. But I can forgive you in time."

At the creak of the front door and thud of footsteps Phee's chest swelled with relief. She rushed toward the hall to greet her aunt and sister and slammed straight into a wall of forest-scented man.

"I'm glad to see you too, love." Kit bowed his head for a kiss, but Phee retreated from his arms.

"Lord Dunstan is here."

He seemed to take the warning in her tone and stormed past. By the time she reached the parlor, Kit had hauled Dunstan up by his lapels. The baron swiped a hand across his chest to dislodge Kit's hands.

"Tell me you aren't proposing to her again." Kit's voice was half growl. Phee had never seen him so enraged. "My God, man, is one refusal not sufficient?"

"This has nothing to do with you, Ruthven." Dunstan crossed his arms again, spread his feet into a wide stance, as if he had every intention of holding his ground, come what may. "My feelings for Miss Ruthven cannot be repressed. Believe me, I've attempted to quit them." Dunstan cast Phee a disturbingly heated gaze. "She will be mine. Longacre will be mine."

Phee was beginning to think single-minded determination wasn't a terribly appealing character quality after all.

"Longacre?" Kit knitted his brow, glancing back at Phee and then Dunstan.

"Her father owed a debt against the house," Dunstan proclaimed. "My father loaned Marsden funds that were never repaid."

"My father never mentioned any such thing." Phee knew they'd been struggling for years, but she believed Longacre was clear of any debt.

Dunstan snorted. "I can provide all the proof you might require, Phee."

"Don't call her that." Kit pointed a finger at Dunstan. "What does Longacre have to do with anything? Take the bloody house, Dunstan. Ophelia is mine."

"My God, you *have* had her." Dunstan shifted his gaze to Phee. "How could you offer yourself like a common strumpet?"

Kit stuck his arm out in a flash of movement, and Dunstan reeled back too slowly. Kit's fist grazed the baron's cheek, and the shorter man flailed his arms to regain balance. Unsuccessfully. He went down on one knee, much as he had a moment before, but now more winded and with a fresh abrasion.

"Ophelia is mine," Kit repeated as he loomed over the aristocrat.

Phee's head ached. All the blood rushed up, and a horrible din thrashed in her ears.

I'm yours. You're mine. Spoken in those delicious moments with Kit the words had been perfection. A binding, the invisible thread she'd always sensed connecting them to each other, a passion-born vow.

Now Kit's words sounded too much like Dunstan's. Both men wanted to claim her. Both had already decided her fate.

"I can offer you wealth and a title, Miss Marsden. All else can be overcome." Dunstan wobbled to his feet and shuffled toward her, but Kit took one long stride to block him.

"Ophelia is going to be my wife." Kit's voice had gone quiet. Frighteningly calm. "Nothing you say will persuade her otherwise."

"Is it true, Ophelia?" Dunstan let out a deep sigh and tipped his head to gaze around Kit's shoulder. "You've accepted Mr. Ruthven's proposal?"

A hush fell over the cramped parlor, and every sound there was to hear came loud and amplified. Fire spit and sparked in the grate. Coals fell, rearranging themselves. Phee focused on her own breath, coming in short pinching gasps, and listened for Kit's. Nothing. He held his breath, held his body tense and still. Waited for her answer.

"No, Lord Dunstan. He hasn't asked me."

Kit whirled on her, and the disappointment she'd seen in Dunstan's gaze was nothing to the agony in Kit's whiskey-brown eyes. "Phee, you must know I planned to ask you. If you'd waited for me—"

"I have been waiting for you for four years." Every word hurt, cutting deep into the pain she thought she'd put aside. The past hurt was altered now, tangled with all they'd shared. She had no wish to hurt anymore, but she didn't want her choices taken from her either. Didn't want two men—three if she counted her father's machinations with Dunstan—deciding her future. "I need to think."

"Marry me." Kit gripped both her arms, his touch both firm and tender. "Don't think. Just feel. You know that I love you."

Dunstan retreated toward the door. On the threshold he turned back. "Go on, Miss Marsden. Melt in his arms. Faint into a heap at his feet. Females are all the same. They cry for their independence but are swayed by a few pretty words. Women adore sentiment and charm." Dunstan sneered at both of them. "Remember that he is an actor. Sweet words are the man's stock-in-trade."

"Get out, you arrogant bastard," Kit roared. "Go, and stay away."

Lord Dunstan sniffed in haughty disdain and slammed the door as he departed.

"Phee?" The voice she loved, the man she loved, her name a petition on his lips.

Dunstan's words echoed in her mind. She loathed the sort of overemotional decision making he described. She advocated for young woman to make rational choices. Practical choices.

"Ophelia, will you marry me?" Kit's voice took on a reedy quality she'd never heard from him. Desperation.

"No. I don't know. I need to think. May I have time to think?"

Kit lifted his hands from her arms as if she'd burned him. His deep-set gaze glowed in the firelight but without emotion. He'd lowed the mask. Put on his actor's face. He wouldn't let her in.

Kit squared his shoulders and started for the door.

"Kit?"

"Think, Phee. Take the time you need, but don't forget to take your mother's advice." He closed the door behind him quietly.

Phee could still smell his scent in the air and drew in a deep breath. She lowered herself into a chair and tucked her knees under her chin. She stared at her mother's embroidery hanging on the wall. *Follow your heart and flourish.*

Her mother hadn't counted on the stubbornness of Phee's heart. Or how, once her heart had broken, she'd be determined to protect it. Phee wished she could love with her mother's open, trusting nature. Wished she knew how to follow her heart to Kit. To trust that he'd always come back to her.

Would Kit ever want her as much as he craved success? She couldn't help but yearn for him to desire her above all else. To be first on his list, more important than any goal or achievement.

When she'd stared at the saying her mother had stitched for so long that her head began to ache, she closed her eyes and a tear escaped. Then another. She didn't try to stifle them or wipe them away.

Even when her throat choked with sobs and her heart broke again.

CHAPTER TWENTY-FOUR

> *"A lady may speak more softly than a gentleman,*
> *but her tone does not lessen the value of her*
> *words. Speak softly, ladies, or at any reasonable*
> *volume you prefer, but never doubt that your*
> *voice should be heard."*
> —MISS GILROY'S GUIDELINES FOR YOUNG LADIES

One week later Phee received a letter that did not contain a dismissal from her tutoring duties, an offer from a publisher, or an attempt by Lord Dunstan to convince her to accept him. Again. Nor was the missive from Kit. After years of ignoring his letters, he'd given up on writing to her.

This note's lovely cream paper smelled faintly of roses. Before she read a word, Phee smiled at the loopy feminine script. "Milly."

Milly was rarely demanding, never bossy, but this letter cut to the point, directing Phee to appear at Pembry Park for luncheon at two. Nothing more.

She wanted to see Milly. Despite her sometimes questionable advice, no one had a better heart. Phee's own heart still ached, and after days of thinking and pondering, turning every possibility over in her mind, only her love for Kit rang true and clear. Trusting him—that was where she struggled. He'd offered her marriage, but what if he found matrimony to be as confining as his father's control? He'd spent four long years in London. Could he turn his back on that life so easily?

An hour later, as she set out for Pembry Park, Phee cast a glance back toward Ruthven Hall. She missed Kit as much after a week apart as she had all those lonely years.

Milly rushed out the front door before Phee had reached the steps. "I'm so glad you've come. We have a brilliant plan."

"We?" Phee had imagined a quiet luncheon with her friend, perhaps in the green oasis of the conservatory. *We* sounded utterly unappealing. Lady Pembry had always been generous and kind, but Phee couldn't divulge any of her heartache to her.

"Come inside and all of your questions will be answered." She sounded like a circus barker, urging Phee into a fortune teller's tent.

Phee gulped down her dread and followed Milly inside. *We* seemed to encompass half a dozen ladies of Briar Heath polished society. In the bright, spacious drawing room, Lady Pembry sat surrounded by Mrs. Hollingsworth, the vicar's wife, Milly older sister Olivia, and, most surprising of all, Sophia and Clarissa Ruthven.

"Come in, my dear." Lady Pembry's jewelry jangled like chimes as she waved Phee over. "Sit next to me. Don't mind the pups."

Each lady offered her a friendly greeting or pleasant smile, but Phee's stomach twisted and tumbled in her belly. What had she done to warrant an invitation to such a gathering?

Then she saw the answer. Her book. Many copies, in fact, were stacked on a low tea table in front of Lady Pembry's settee. Another pile lay on a desk in the corner of the room.

"We've all read it," Mrs. Hollingsworth said. Shockingly, she wore a grin. Phee recalled the lady's vehement defense of *The Ruthven Rules* last time she'd been at Pembry Park and now couldn't square her appropriation of *Guidelines*. How could anyone appreciate both books?

"My brother was right to offer to publish your book, Miss Marsden." Sophia Ruthven's warm tone drew Phee's attention to the opposite end of the room. Clarissa sat next to her, nodding vigorously. "We hope you'll reconsider allowing Ruthven's to do so."

"*Miss Gilroy's Guidelines* is thoroughly wonderful," Clarissa enthused. "Even if you and Kit…I hope you will, but if you don't, please do let us publish your book."

"I will." Phee had misgivings about accepting Kit's offer, but his sisters were thoroughly persuasive.

"Wonderful." Milly clapped her hands and beamed. "Now let's move on to the rest."

"I understand Mrs. Raybourn's gossip has damaged your tutoring endeavors, my dear." Lady Pembry sounded nearly as mournful as Phee felt. "Though I will continue to do my best to curb her influence, we think another course will prove useful."

"Any woman who reads your book will see its merit," Milly insisted. "We've acquired every copy we can and plan to send a copy to every female in Briar Heath."

Goodness. Wouldn't Mrs. Raybourn love her then? "And if every lady of Briar Heath doesn't see its merits?"

"Many will," Sophia insisted. "And I suspect they'll be quite determined to engage you to teach their daughters. If you're still interested in tutoring, that is." Kit's sister's knowing grin made Phee wonder just how much he'd shared.

"And don't forget—" Lady Pembry started.

"Yes, of course, Mama," Milly cut in. "We'd like to prepare letters of support before Ruthven's puts out the new edition. Not just reviews, but letters we'll send to the newspapers, including our names and endorsements of your ideas. There will always be cynics, but we can do our best to overcome them with enthusiasm. Mama knows the owner of a London lady's journal, and I know a journalist who writes for the *Times*."

Each lady watched Phee with a warmth she hadn't expected and wasn't sure how to absorb. The room had fallen quiet, barring the occasional sip of tea and the clink of silver spoons against porcelain.

"Thank you." The words didn't seem sufficient.

"You approve of our plans then, Miss Marsden?" Mrs. Bickham's soft voice matched her smile.

"I'm surprised." Phee cast her gaze across each lady's face. "Stunned, to be honest, but most of all I'm appreciative. Truly. From the bottom of my heart." She stared again at the pile of books. "Where did you get them? I thought Mr. Wellbeck removed them from all store fronts."

"Ruthven's acquired them," Sophia said, meeting Phee's gaze with an inscrutable grin teasing at the corners of her mouth. "My brother made Mr. Wellbeck an offer he couldn't refuse"

Kit had bought her books? Somehow overcome the loathing Wellbeck felt for her father and schemed to get the copies to Lady Pembry? So much for wondering if she'd crossed his mind in the last week.

Phee swallowed hard and pressed the back of her hand against the heat in her cheeks.

She couldn't stop meeting Sophia's gaze. Kit's sister so often withheld emotion and spoke with cool civility. Today she seemed different, offering Phee encouraging grins. Phee wanted to ask about Kit and hoped for a moment to speak to his sister alone.

"Shall we head to the table for luncheon?" Milly stood and ushered the group toward the dining room. As Phee passed, Milly caught hold of her elbow and whispered, "I have another matter I don't wish to share with the other ladies."

"I'm not sure I can bear more good news." Phee smiled for the first time in days.

"I have no news, but I did overhear a conversation between Mama and Lord Dunstan."

Phee cringed to imagine how he related her *second* refusal. She would have much preferred to convey the details to Milly herself.

"He said Kit Ruthven proposed to you."

"He did."

"And you refused him?" Milly's shocked tone set Phee's teeth on edge. She'd wrestled with the same question. Asked herself the same a dozen times. Telling him *yes* would be so easy. She only had to quiet the far-too-noisy warning voices of fear and uncertainty in her head.

"I couldn't help but overhear mention of my brother's name." Sophia Ruthven moved with catlike stealth. Milly and Phee both jumped at the sound of her voice. The tall, lovely blonde had positioned herself at Phee's side.

"Is he well, Miss Ruthven?"

"I couldn't say, Miss Marsden." She waited a beat and added, "Kit departed for London five days ago."

"London." A fist clamped around Phee's chest. Shallow little breaths were suddenly all she could manage. He'd gone back. Had been gone since her refusal. "Does he plan to return to Briar Heath?" Perhaps he'd decided the city truly was where he belonged. Not with her. Not the place he'd been trying to escape for years.

"An excellent question, Miss Marsden. Perhaps you should go and ask him."

Kit never truly appreciated the phrase *den of iniquity* until agreeing to share Grey's London lodgings. After five days, he was beginning to suspect the man's opulent Belgrave Square townhouse may have been the original inspiration for the term.

Individuals paraded in and out of the house, day and night. Not just women, though a female seemed forever at hand. Gentlemen friends of Jasper's treated the space as a smaller, intimate gentleman's club of sorts. In the week Kit had spent in London, he'd seen his friend rarely.

Amid the chaos of laughter, inebriated shouts, and pleasured screams and moans, Kit completed his play and had finally presented the whole to Dominic Fleet this morning. Tess still hadn't forgiven him. Not a single purr of *Kitten* fell from her lips during the entire meeting, but Fleet promised to read the play and send word about beginning production within a few days.

Waiting wore on his resolve. Each tick of the clock offered another opportunity to take a train back to Hertfordshire, find Ophelia, and convince her to be his wife. She'd asked for time to think. He didn't wish to wait one more second to begin their lives together.

Good job the rug in the room Grey provided looked expensive and hardy. He'd burn a hole through it, pacing, before he left this riotous den.

A lady's chortle, then a squeal, drifted through the walls of another upstairs room. Footsteps clattered down the hall outside his bedroom door, as if someone had given chase.

"Come back here, you wench," Grey called in a ridiculously melodramatic voice that would have caused all of London to doubt his acting skills.

Kit rolled his eyes, donned his coat, and decided a breath of fresh air was most definitely in order. The fumes of liquor and various perfumes were giving him a ripping headache.

He cast a glance both ways before entering the hall.

"Fanny, come out now." Grey stood, clothed only in trousers, on the landing above the stairwell, shouting down into the townhouse's main hall. "I've no patience for hide-and-seek this early in the morning."

Some bit of female protest drifted up from downstairs, but Kit couldn't make out the words.

"Busy morning?" Kit asked as he drew next to his friend.

Grey side-eyed him with a bleary gaze. "The lady likes to be chased. As predilections go, it's not the worst I've ever encountered. Just dashed exhausting at…" He squinted down at a long case clock in the hall. "How can it nearly be noon?"

"Time flies when you're chasing women." Didn't Kit know that to be true? Three weeks in Briar Heath had tipped his life on end, and he wouldn't change a single moment. Except the part when the woman he'd loved for years refused his offer of marriage.

An insistent knock sounded at the front door, and Grey scowled as if knocking on doors was far more offensive than the debauchery he got up to every day of the week. They stood like fools at the top of the stairs, staring at the painted wooden door and listening to the persistent thud of a door knocker, rather than taking a single move to rectify the situation.

"Is no one going to answer the door?" Grey shouted toward the ceiling.

"You fired the footman," Kit reminded his friend. "He was tupping two of the maids, and I believe they left with him. I hope they'll be happy."

"There must be others," Grey said incredulously, swiping a hand across his face.

"In London? I'm certain there are. Here, now, prepared to open your door? It doesn't appear so."

Grey heaved a weary sigh and stomped down the stairs. All the while, his caller offered additional knocks at even intervals. By the time he reached the door, Grey clamped two hands over his ears and offered a less-than-friendly welcome through the thick panel of wood. "Knock on that damned door again and I'll put my fist straight through."

One final much-less-vehement knock sounded against the wood. Grey nearly wrenched the door from its hinges.

"Hello, Mr. Grey."

Kit darted down the stairs. He couldn't see her beyond Grey's body, but Ophelia's voice was unmistakable. A few words in her resonant lilt, and his body fizzed with joy.

"I'm looking for—"

"Ophelia." Kit pushed past Grey as his friend stepped back, turned, and began searching for his lady companion in the drawing room. Smudges of fatigue shadowed the freckled skin under her eyes, and there wasn't a hint of pink in her cheeks, but Kit had never been more relieved to see anyone in his life.

"Kit, you *are* here." She remained on the doorstep, jaw set, blue eyes glowing in the morning light. "Sophia told me I'd find you here."

"I'm glad she did." His voice had gone raspy and raw. His tattered, rusty heart was in his throat, and every piece belonged to Ophelia. "Come in, or"—he cast a gaze toward the drawing room where Grey was on his hands and knees, looking under the settee—"I'll come out."

In answer, she swept past him, and he drew in a sweetened breath of her floral scent.

"Not in there," he warned when she started toward the drawing room. "There's a library this way." A book-filled room seemed a fitting place to plead his case with her again.

Bottles spilled in a clattering pile, some rolling across the floor, when Kit pushed the library door open. The frivolity had spread here too, apparently.

"What goes on in here?" Phee eyed a lacy piece of lady's lingerie dangling from a bookshelf just inside the door.

"More than either of us needs to know, I suspect." Kit pressed a fist to the center of his chest, fought to steady his breathing. He hadn't experienced this kind of gut-twisting fear since he'd faced his father as child. This moment mattered. Perhaps more than any ever had.

"Did you often join the festivities at Mr. Grey's townhouse?"

"No." Kit swallowed down the impulse to diminish his past. "But I was no saint during my years in London." Now was the time for the truth. She deserved as much, and she'd never let him get away with anything less.

"Then why give it up?" She'd positioned herself near the center of the room, clasped her hands before her, and squared her shoulders.

He still hadn't touched her, kissed her, and he fought the urge to think of anything else. *Think.* Phee was the thinker. He needed to learn her contemplative ways.

"You've returned to London," she continued. "Why not resume this life?"

"Will you be here?" He gestured around the book-lined room and noted more discarded clothing near a velvet settee.

"No." Phee's brows puckered as she followed his gaze and took in the rumpled lump of what appeared to be men's trousers. "Not here."

"Then I've no wish to be here either." Kit started toward her. She was too far away, and he was too tired of missing her. "Wherever you are, love, that is where I belong."

She leaned into him, planting two warm palms on his chest when he clasped an arm around her waist, and he closed his eyes against the exquisite relief of having her in his arms.

"Even if that belonging is in Briar Heath?" She was still frowning, not with displeasure or confusion but an earnestness that pinched at his heart.

"Briar Heath, Buckinghamshire, preferably not Belgravia." He tugged her closer until he could feel her breath against his face, feel her soft curves against the length of his body. "You are my home, Phee. I've been homesick for four years, but it wasn't for the village or that house my father built. I missed you. I always looked for you."

"Looked for me? You knew where I was."

"In the theater…" He'd never admitted his foolish, endless searching. "I looked for you every night. Imagined you sitting in a theater box watching every performance. Even then, all those years apart, you were my polestar, love."

"I love you, Kit." She rose onto her toes.

Kit took her the rest of the way, lifting her in his arms, tasting her mouth, pouring his heart into a kiss he hoped would mark the start of their future as man and wife. When he lowered her, he continued stroking her lips with his, greedy for more. "I love you, Phee. Marry me."

"Yes," she said on a breathless whisper.

He stilled against her. He'd wanted the word. Dreamed of hearing it from her lips. But he needed to hear it again. "Tell me."

"Yes, I will marry you." She chuckled and that delicious pink hue flooded her cheeks.

Kit kissed the color, stroked her cheek. "I will never leave you."

"You will follow your heart and flourish?" she teased, fingers plucking at the buttons of his shirt.

"Following my heart will always lead me back to you."

Her smile swept away all the fear he'd felt moments before, any doubt that she was his, and he was hers. The future wasn't colored anymore with a clawing hunger for success but an eagerness to savor every single day with Ophelia.

He swept his thumb across her mouth and lowered his head to taste her again.

A woman's sniffles drew both their gazes to the library doorway.

"You two may convince me marriage isn't a shackling prison after all." Grey slapped his palms together and began applauding as if he'd just watched himself perform on stage.

"So romantic." The scantily garbed young lady at his side lifted the edge of her sheer chemise and dabbed at her eyes.

Kit turned back to Phee, his soon-to-be wife. "I hope this doesn't mean we have to invite them to the wedding."

Phee peeked around his shoulder at Grey and his lady friend. "Oh, I think we should. If Mr. Grey is finally marriage-minded, it would be a disservice to the unwed ladies of Briar Heath not to do."

That sent Grey chasing his companion up the stairs, leaving them alone.

After only a moment of laughter, Kit kissed Ophelia again. And again. Until they were both breathless, until there was no doubt that together was precisely where they belonged.

Deafening applause greeted the actors when they stepped to the edge of the stage to take their final bows. Fleet Theater's floorboards shook as patrons near the pit began stomping their feet.

Grey, at center stage, turned his gaze toward the wings and reached out to urge Kit forward. "Come, man. Soak in this success."

Kit shook his head. He had a better view from the wings. But Grey was not to be deterred. He stormed toward Kit, gripped his arm, and dragged him to center stage.

Drawing in a deep lungful of stale playhouse air, Kit strode forward and joined the line of actors.

"Our talented playwright," Grey shouted.

Kit bowed with the rest of the troupe, then lifted a hand to block the glare of the arc lamps along the front of the stage as he searched faces in the boxes lining the west wall of the theater.

Ophelia lifted a hand and waved at him. He could make out the white of her glove, the flash of a smile, and the auburn curls of her glorious hair. Then she pressed a hand to her chest. When she placed her palm over her heart, Kit knew hers was as full as his. For a long moment, he fixed his gaze on her, drinking in the sight he'd sought so long. He smiled back and joy welled up, filling him whole.

When the curtains fell, Kit rushed past the rest of the troupe. Drunk on the success of his play's opening night, they laughed as they planned celebrations for the evening. Kit could think of only one way to commemorate the night's triumph.

As he made his way down the narrow passage toward Ophelia's theater box, the door slammed open, and Clary rushed toward him, nearly tripping on the lavender ruffles of her gown.

He caught her in his arms and swung her around, as he'd done since she was a child, before setting her down where she'd started.

"Properly spectacular," she said, her voice vibrating with excitement. "Utterly amazing."

"You liked it, then?"

She clutched at her throat, waved a hand, as if she couldn't catch her breath. Eyes huge, she finally managed, "It's perfect."

As he patted his sister on the back, Phee emerged from the theater box and swept toward him in a stunning blue gown that perfectly matched the cerulean shade of her eyes. Juliet followed close behind and beamed one of her rare smiles.

Phee laid her hand on his chest. "I'm so proud of you." Her words, her soft earnest smile, the warmth of her hand over his heart—Phee loosened something inside of Kit. A knot somewhere deep inside. The place where he'd buried years of pain and a secret yearning for his father's love and approbation.

Ophelia's approval mattered more. Her love was all he needed.

He bent to brush a kiss on her lips, resisting the temptation to take a deeper taste. Clary watched them far too closely, as if she planned to sketch the scene the moment she got home. Juliet tipped her head to study the theater's décor, as if kissing didn't interest her at all.

"Shall we head back home?" Kit asked. After months of work, layers of paint, and yards of wallpaper, Ruthven Hall was beginning to feel like home. Longacre remained a bone of contention with Lord Dunstan, but Kit had begun paying down Phee's father's debt. Most importantly, the man had finally given up his pursuit of Ophelia. Aunt Rose remained at Longacre, and Phee still pondered transforming the Marsden home into a progressive school for girls.

"You don't wish to join any of the others to celebrate?" Phee asked.

Kit arched a brow in his wife's direction. "I can think of far better ways to celebrate. Can't you?" He let his gaze drop to the swell of her bosom and licked his lips, counting the various ways.

"We have one errand before leaving the city," Clary cut in.

"Do we?" Though the evening was still young by London standards, Kit could imagine nothing more urgent than returning home to Briar Heath and spending the remainder of the night pleasuring his wife.

"We promised Sophia we'd stop by Ruthven's and pick up fresh copies of *The New Ruthven Rules for Young Ladies*," Clary announced. She, Ophelia, and Sophia had worked together on a new edition, and he knew the three were on tenterhooks waiting to see the first printing.

He'd hoped Sophia would attend the first performance of his play, but she'd stubbornly insisted on clinging to etiquette and not attending the theater for her last few months of mourning.

"Very well." Kit sighed and led his wife, Clary, and Juliet toward the back of the house.

Rather than split into two hansom cabs, they secured a four-wheeled growler for the journey to Somerset Row. Between the three ladies' gowns, they still had to squeeze in tight to fit. Yet no matter how many times he whispered in Phee's ear, urging her to sit on his lap—to save on space, of course—she glanced at Juliet and Clarissa and firmly shook her head. *Bloody propriety.*

Kit was shocked to see a light on at the Ruthven office when the cab deposited them on the pavement outside.

"Who would be here at this hour?" Clary asked as she peeked out the carriage window.

"Mr. Adamson," Phee announced. "He assured me he'd wait for us."

Kit wasn't sure why his wife and Adamson were in such close communication, but it didn't surprise him that the overeager young upstart would willingly burn the midnight oil.

"I can't wait to meet him," Clary added. "Ophelia says he's brawny."

"Does she indeed?" Kit cast his wife an inquisitive gaze.

"I believe I said bulky." She curled a hand around Kit's upper arm, shaping her palm over his bicep. "Nothing to compare to your bulk, husband."

Kit twisted his mouth in a grin and considered how much he ached to entwine his bulk with her luscious curves.

After two taps on the front-door glass, Adamson strode forward to admit them. A day in the office hadn't diminished a jot of the energy that seemed to vibrate off the man.

He nodded sharply at Kit, offered Phee and her sister a half-smile, and raised both eyebrows at the sight of Clarissa, who scrutinized his brawn as if he was a bug under a microscope's lens.

"Mr. Adamson," Phee started the introductions before Kit could do the deed. "May I introduce my sister, Miss Juliet Marsden, and Miss Clarissa Ruthven, co-owner of Ruthven's?" Phee placed a reassuring hand on Clary's back as Kit's sister stepped forward to offer Adamson her hand.

He scowled a moment, then relented, taking Clary's hand for only a moment.

"Can I see the rest?" Clary asked, apparently finished with her assessment of the dark-haired managing editor. Phee led the girls on a tour of the office.

"She's a child." Adamson seemed completely ruffled by the fact. "A child who owns a publishing house."

"Clarissa is sixteen years old. Technically, her legal ownership begins when she comes of age." Kit felt a tickle of laughter rumbling in his chest. "But yes, Gabriel, my little sister will one day be your boss."

"Unbelievable" was all the man could manage.

Female laughter rang out from the direction of Adamson's office. The man pivoted on his heel and started toward the sound at a rapid clip.

"What in God's name?" Adamson swiped at a white ribbon Clarissa was using to tie back the plain green curtains at the room's single window. It was the same ribbon she'd been wearing in her upswept curls all evening.

"I was just trying to add a bit of beauty to the room." Clary didn't seem perturbed by Adamson's hunched shoulders or fierce glower. "It's a very dour space."

"This is a place of industry. An office to conduct business." He was waving his brawny arms as he seethed. His polished accent slipped into a sharper London cadence. "Beauty 'as no place 'ere, *Miss* Ruthven."

Clary held her ground. Kit and Phee joined arms and watched the stalemate like gawking bystanders. Juliet seemed thoroughly amused. Adamson towered over Clary's petite frame, but she appeared determined not to be the one to relent.

Finally, Adamson sighed through gritted teeth, gripped the edges of his coat, and stepped away from her. She cast Phee, Kit, and Juliet a triumphant grin.

Kit lifted the stack of books to be delivered to Sophia, and urged his wife and the girls toward the front door. On the threshold, Clarissa turned back and called to Adamson. "I sincerely hope you'll change your mind, Mr. Adamson. A life without beauty, even as simple as a ribbon to pull back a curtain and expose a lovely view, isn't much of a life at all."

"Come on, Clary." The last thing Kit wanted was another skirmish between the two.

Minutes later, as they settled onto the train for the return journey to Briar Heath, Clary reclined next to Juliet and stared out the window, mumbling to herself.

"What's that, dear?" Phee inquired.

"Gabriel Adamson," she said. "He's very pretty, but I think he's the saddest man I've ever met."

Sad was the last word Kit would have chosen to describe the insufferably arrogant man. But when Phee scooted her body next to his and rested her head on his shoulder, he forgot Adamson and the disturbing worry of his youngest sister noticing any man at all. He let himself settle against his wife's warm, jasmine-scented body.

This, he thought as he placed a kiss against her hair, was right where he belonged.

When an infamous rake who has vowed to never marry
becomes entranced by a thoroughly proper woman
who has a secret that would shock society, sparks fly,
hair will be mussed, and passion will overwhelm!

A STUDY IN SCOUNDRELS
BY CHRISTY CARLYLE

Available April 2017

Give in to your Impulses . . .
Continue reading for excerpts from
our newest Avon Impulse books.
Available now wherever e-books are sold.

ALONG CAME LOVE
by Tracey Livesay

WHEN A MARQUESS
LOVES A WOMAN
THE SEASON'S ORIGINAL SERIES
by Vivienne Lorret

An Excerpt from

ALONG CAME LOVE

By Tracey Livesay

When free-spirited India Shaw finds herself
in trouble, she must rely on the one man she
never planned to see again—her baby's father.

Michael Black's cellphone vibrated against his chest and he pulled it from his inner pocket. The caller ID showed an unfamiliar number with "San Francisco, CA" beneath it, but no other identifying information.

His brows converged in the middle of his forehead. It was probably a wrong number. And yet his finger hovered and then pressed the green button.

"Hello?"

"Mike."

He straightened. Her voice stroked his hedonistic hotspots. The tingle caused by every whispered declaration, every lingering caress, hit him all at once.

"Indi."

"Long time, no hear."

Her forced gaiety jarred him loose from her vocal web and allowed his brain to function. Why had she left? Where had she been? What did she want? Why was she calling?

"I know I'm probably the last person you want to talk to and I understand, considering how I ended things and I—"

He remembered this about her, the stream of talking on an endless loop. His favorite remedy? A cock-stirring, toe curling kiss.

"Indi, spit it out."

A thick silence, and then—

"Can you post bail for me? I've been arrested for burglary."

Well *that* happened.

The door to the precinct closed behind Indi. Exhaustion weighed her down, leaving her head throbbing and her sight unfocused. She shivered, her cable knit sweater offering inadequate insulation from the chill.

If she had a bucket list, she could confidently check off this experience: get yourself arrested in an unfamiliar city. It hadn't been anything like *Orange is the New Black*—Thank God!—but she had met some interesting women while she'd been booked and processed. Turns out, her unstable living situations and various relocations equipped her with the unique skill set needed to survive the city's holding cell.

But she didn't do bucket lists. They were created for people who scurried through life afraid to take chances, regretting their caution when faced with their mortality. Indi's life *was* a bucket list. Hence, her current predicament.

"Where's Ryan?"

The brusque voice wrapped itself around her heart and squeezed. She stilled and her breath went on strike.

Those words. That tone. This situation. It wasn't how she'd pictured their reunion.

Though their best friends were married to one another, careful planning on her part would've given her several years to let time and distance erode the memories and allow them to communicate without her recalling the way he'd made her body quake with ecstasy. She'd be cool, look polished, and possess the proper grace to put them both at ease.

That had been the fantasy BN—Before Nugget. Now she'd settle for an encounter where she didn't look and smell like a cat lady's ashtray, and she possessed something other than an unplanned pregnancy and a felony charge.

Despite his harsh tone, the man leaning against the metallic silver Porsche Panamera—new; the last time she'd seen him, he'd been driving a Jaguar—was as gorgeous, as powerful, and as autocratic as the luxury sedan he drove. He'd tamed his blond curls—what a shame—into a sleek mass that shone beneath the street lamps and his body looked trim and powerful in a dark tailored suit and crisp white collared shirt without a tie. He could've been waiting for his date to a society gala and not standing in the street in front of the sheriff's office after midnight, waiting for the state judicial system's newest enrollee.

Indi hefted her backpack onto her shoulder, ignored the dips, swerves, and inversions occurring in her belly, and slowly descended the concrete steps. "He's finishing up the paperwork."

She'd forgotten how big he was. She was a tad taller than average and she knew from experience her eyes would be level with his chin, a chin now covered in downy blond fuzz. Experience also taught her the stubble would be a delicious abrasion against her skin.

"Do you have anything to say to me?"

She blinked. She had much to say to him. But here? Now?

She'd hated calling him. Truthfully, she would've hated calling anyone in this situation. Would rather have stayed behind bars and figured a way out of this mess. But this wasn't about her personal preferences. She needed to make decisions in Nugget's best interests. And *that* meant doing what was necessary to ensure she spent as little time in jail as possible.

She hadn't seen Mike in three months, since she'd awakened to see his face softened in sleep. Terrified of the feelings budding to life within her, she'd stealthily gathered up her belongings and left without looking back. And despite her behavior, when she'd called, he'd shown up. He deserved many things from her, starting with gratitude.

But did he have to be an arrogant ass about it?

She balled a fist in the folds of her skirt. "What else would you like me to say?"

He pushed away from the sex-mobile. "How about 'Thank you for canceling your plans and coming to get me'?"

Crap. She'd pulled him away from something. Or someone.

It was none of her business. She'd given up any say in who he spent time with the night she'd walked away.

"How in the hell did you get arrested for burglary?"

She swiped at the allegation. "Those are trumped up charges."

"So you didn't do it?"

"Of course not. I mean, breaking and entering makes you think of a cat burglar or someone in a ski mask robbing the place. That's not how it happened."

Mike narrowed his eyes and subjected her to his self-righteous stare. "Then why don't you tell me what happened."

An Excerpt from

WHEN A MARQUESS LOVES A WOMAN
The Season's Original Series

By Vivienne Lorret

Five years have passed since the Max Harwick
shared a scandalous kiss with Lady Juliet, only to
have her marry someone else. He's never forgiven
her . . . but he's never stopped loving her either.

Some days Lady Juliet Granworth wanted to fling open the nearest window sash and scream.

And it was all the Marquess of Thayne's fault.

"*Good evening, Saunders.*" A familiar baritone called from the foyer and drifted in through the open parlor door. *Max.*

Drat it all! He was a veritable devil. Only she didn't have to *speak* his name but simply *think* it for him to appear. She should have known better than to allow her thoughts to roam without a leash to tug them back to heel.

"I did not realize Lord Thayne would be attending dinner this evening," Zinnia said, her spine rigid as she perched on the edge of her cushion and darted a quick, concerned glance toward Juliet.

Marjorie looked to the open door, her brows knitted. "I did not realize it either. He said that he was attending—"

"Lord Fernwold's," Max supplied as he strode into the room, his dark blue coat parting to reveal a gray waistcoat and fitted blue trousers. He paused long enough to bow his dark head in greeting—at least to his mother and Zinnia. To Juliet, he offered no more than perfunctory scrutiny before heading to the sideboard, where a collection of crystal decanters waited. "The guests were turned away at the door. His lordship's mother is suffering a fever."

Juliet felt the flesh of her eyelids pucker slightly, her lashes drawing together. It was as close as she could come to glaring at him while still leaving her countenance unmoved. The last thing she wanted was for him, or anyone, to know how much his slight bothered her.

Marjorie tutted. "Again? Agnes seemed quite hale this afternoon in the park. Suspiciously, this has happened thrice before on the evenings of her daughter-in-law's parties. I tell you, Max, I would never do such a thing to your bride."

Max turned and ambled toward them, the stems of three sherry glasses in one large hand and a whiskey in the other. He stopped at the settee first, offering one to his mother and another to Zinnia. "Nor would you need to, for I would never marry a woman who would tolerate the manipulation." Then he moved around the table and extended a glass to Juliet, lowering his voice as he made one final comment. "Nor one whose slippers trod only the easiest path."

She scoffed. If marriage to Lord Granworth had been easy, then she would hate to know the alternative.

"I should not care for sherry this evening," Juliet said. And in retaliation against Max's rudeness, she reached out and curled her fingers around his whiskey.

Their fingers collided before she slipped the glass free. If she hadn't taken him off guard, he might have held fast. As it was, he opened his hand instantly as if scalded by her touch. But she knew that wasn't true because the heat of his skin nearly blistered her. The shock of it left the underside of her fingers prickly and somewhat raw.

To soothe it, she swirled the cool, golden liquor in the glass. Then, before lifting it to her lips, she met his gaze. His irises were a mixture of earthy brown and cloud gray. Years ago, those eyes were friendly and welcoming but now had turned cold, like puddles reflecting a winter sky. And because it pleased her to think of his eyes as mud puddles, that was what she thought of when she took a sip. Unfortunately, she didn't particularly care for whiskey and fought to hide a shudder as the sour liquid coated her tongue.

Max mocked her with a salute of his dainty goblet and tossed back the sherry in one swallow. Then the corner of his mouth flicked up in a smirk.

She knew that mouth intimately—the firm warm pressure of those lips, the exciting scrape of his teeth, the mesmeric skill of his tongue . . .

Unbidden warmth simmered beneath her skin as she recalled the kiss that had ruined her life. And for five years, she'd paid a dire price for one single transgression—a regretful and demeaning marriage, the sudden deaths of her parents, and the loss of everyone she held dear.

By comparison, returning to London to reclaim her life as a respected widow should have been simple. And it would have been if Max hadn't interfered.

Why did he have to hinder her fresh start?

Of course, she knew the answer. She'd wounded his ego years ago, and her return only served as a reminder. He didn't want her living four doors down from his mother—or likely within forty miles of him.